About the Author

Debut author Samantha Scordato has been penning stories in her journals for many years. She fell in love with Jane Austen at an early age and kept up with her love through an undergraduate degree in Fashion Merchandising and an MBA from Philadelphia University. After graduating, Samantha turned her attention to her two loves: Running a surf and skate shop and writing. FOLLOWING JANE is Samantha's first novel, but she is already at hard at work on another. For more information, please visit www.lifemythlegend.com.

FOLLOWING JANE
A Novel
Samantha Scordato

Visit Samantha's website at www.lifemythlegend.com.
Cover design by Caridad Piñeiro Scordato
Manufactured in the United States of America

Thank you to my friends and family and all the people who have always supported me, especially my mom who gave me the writing bug in the first place.

Prologue

Adventure is just around the corner . . .

"'I wonder who first discovered the efficacy of poetry in driving away love!'" Lizzie's mother said in her humorous British accent.

"'I have been used to consider poetry as the *food* of love,' said Darcy.'" Her mother looked over the edge of the book at Lizzie who was snuggled up in her bed, listening to her mother's melodic voice.

They had read this book countless times that Lizzie could quote it and so before her mother could continue with the line she finished it. "'Of a fine, stout, healthy love it may be. Everything nourishes what is strong already. But if it be only a slight, thin sort of inclination, I am sure one good sonnet will starve it entirely away.'"

"Good job, my dear." Lizzie's mom bent and kissed her forehead. "You remind me so much of Lizzie and not because you share her name." Her mother chuckled.

Lizzie didn't understand what her mother meant and so her mother attempted to explain.

"You may not get the right first impression of a person, but you will learn to see the true person as you grow along with them. Remember Lizzie, adventure is just around the corner. You just need to be able to hear the call. Happy eighth birthday, my dear Lizzie."

#

Even after her explanation, Lizzie had never understood those words. Every birthday her mother would repeat them. "Adventure is just around the corner."

Lizzie had never had an adventure. Her entire life had been so plain so far. She had gone to high school, graduated, attended a nice college, graduated, and was now in the midst of looking for a job like everyone else at her age.

What adventure was she supposed to be seeing around the corner?

Then one night she had gotten home late from her crappy minimum wage job and walked into the kitchen to see her mother sitting at the table with her dad holding her hands. They had both looked up at her when she walked in and asked her to sit down.

And that's when her normal boring life was shattered into way too many pieces.

Cancer? Her mom?

It was spreading so quickly that the doctors said they did not have much time left to spend with her mother.

In the months that followed, Lizzie had been at the hospital every night reading to her mother. All their favorite books. Until one night Lizzie's mom had stopped her from reading and had spoken those words again.

"Lizzie. Adventure is just around the corner. You just need to be able to hear the call."

"I never know what you mean by that." Lizzie had tried to laugh at the same silly words her mother repeated, wanting to bring her comfort.

"You will soon."

Chapter 1

The Calling

Lizzie sat by her mother's side, her mother's frail hand in her own.

The cancer had spread at such an alarming rate that Lizzie had had no time to accept the fact her mother was going to be ripped away from her at any minute.

Her mother's eyes opened and looked at Lizzie. "Lizzie, dear," she whispered weakly.

"Yeah, mom?" She leaned on the hospital bed to hear her mother better.

"When you go home, I need you to lift my bedside table. There is something in there for you. I hid it from your father because of his lack of imagination. But you, my little jellybean, are amazingly imaginative, and can solve the mystery."

Lizzie narrowed her gaze, confused. "I don't understand."

"You will. All will be explained when you go to my table. Take it, all of it, and go on an adventure. I love you."

"Mom…" Lizzie watched the heart monitor flat line.

"Mom!" she yelled, but she knew it was hopeless. She leaned over to kiss her mom's forehead as her dad rushed into the hospital room and stood there, dazed as he faced the reality of death.

"'To die would be an awfully big adventure'," she whispered, quoting *Peter Pan*, another favorite bedtime story.

She wiped the tears off her face and walked up to her father. Gave him a big hug before rushing out of the room, out of the hospital, and to her car. As she pulled up to her house, it seemed emptier already now that her mother was gone.

She hurried up the stairs to her parents' room and rushed over to her mother's bedside table. She remembered what her mother had said about lifting the table, but when she moved it, there was nothing but some dust and loose change on the floor beneath.

She collapsed to her knees and wept until her body felt almost beaten. She grabbed onto the table top to help her stand and the top shifted.

Her sobs quickly stopped and she moved the top again to make sure she wasn't seeing things. It lifted once more.

She swiped everything off the table top and tried to pull it up, but the top only budged a little before slamming shut again. She scrabbled away in shock and said, "No. N-n-no. No way!"

She slowly inched back to the table, gripped the wood tightly, and forced the top up once again. This time it gave and stayed open. Inside the table were stacks of one hundred dollar bills. When she lifted the bills away, it revealed an envelope with her name on it.

She opened it and pulled out a long letter in her mother's hand writing.

Lizzie,

It is the standard cliché of any tale that if you are reading this I am no longer with you on this Earth. It is also standard to give you a quest that at first you do not accept. However, being my daughter, and having the same love of books as I, you already know this.

We have read stories of adventure, mystery, love, and heartbreak, but we never got to live that same type of life. This is your chance to live it. For several years now I have been slowly saving up for you to take this journey.

I believe you are ready, and grown enough, to take this trip. Now that you have found the money, you need to accept the journey.

Oh wait... Your mother thinks of everything!

If you go into my closet and open the black trunk sitting beneath our clothes hampers, there is a tan leather backpack that has the start of your quest.

Do you hear the adventure calling now?

I love you, Lizzie, and I will miss you deeply. But I am watching over you and I promise to keep you safe.

Good Luck,

Mama Bear.

She shot up quickly and ran to the walk-in closet her parents shared. She shoved the stuff off the top of the black trunk and yanked it open. As she dug through some of her mom's old clothes and photos, she found the leather knapsack her mom had mentioned in the letter. She jerked it out of the trunk and searched through all the pockets.

That's when she found a wrinkled and folded piece of paper in the front pocket. As she slowly pulled it out, she realized the note was very old and delicate. So she carefully opened it.

Another letter, but not from her mother.

Dearest person or persons who discover this, the clever ones.

I rejoice in the fact you have found this letter. This piece of parchment is but the start of some mild amusement for you and I. By the end of the journey you will be able to find the universal truth, as well as a handsome reward.

We shall begin.

Cassandra never could leave my side. My closest friend and confidante. Reading, writing, and drama would help us pass the hour filled days until our parents were no longer able to afford the lifestyle to which we were accustomed.

The best of luck,

Jane Austen

"No. No way," she whispered, reading the name over and over again.

"Yes, Jane Austen," she heard from behind her.

She spun around to see her father standing in the doorway. His sunken eyes were red and puffy and told how truly destroyed he felt.

"Dad." She stood and walked up to him.

"She thought I didn't know." He tried to crack a smile, but it just caused more tears to fall.

She slipped into his arms as they both just stood there and cried. When they had both run out of tears, he let go of her and said, "She solved the first clue."

He reached down to Lizzie's hand and grabbed the back pack. He opened the larger storage area and pulled out a leather bound notebook. He turned to the first page and handed it to Lizzie. There was a note on the first page.

Document your journey to tell your children one day.

Jane's first clue refers to her younger years. She studied at Oxford until her parents hit hard times and were not able to afford it and pulled the girls out of school.

Oxford, England is your first stop.

"You need to do this, Lizzie. For her. For yourself," he choked out.

"But what about you?"

"I'll be fine as long as you promise to call every so often."

They hugged one more time and he looked away. "I need to make preparations for Mom's funeral and you need to start packing."

He patted her shoulder and walked out of the closet.

She clutched the notebook to her chest and returned to the trunk. She grabbed a few of her favorite mom t-shirts and then went to her room to begin packing. But as she did so, a thought suddenly came to her.

I can hear the call, Mom. Here goes nothing.

Chapter 2

Lizzie

Lizzie laughed with delight at the sight of the hotel her father had suggested as the taxicab pulled up in front of it. It looked just like she imagined something from Austen's time would look.

"Austen House, ma'am," the cabbie announced as he parked the car and stepped out to unload the suitcases from the trunk. Or as the British called it, the boot.

She thanked and paid the cabbie and after, trudged up the stairs with her suitcases.

A little old lady sat at the front desk, reading a book. Her white permed hair and knitted shawl were like something out of one of her novels and made Lizzie wish she had a grandma like this woman. When the door closed with a thump, the woman finally looked up and greeted Lizzie with a smile .

"Hello, deary. How can I help you this afternoon?"

Lizzie grabbed all her paperwork and placed it on the counter. "I'm here to check in," she said nervously, anxious about the adventure and about meeting new people. She had never been good at that.

"Of course you are! Last name, dear?"

"Price," she quickly answered.

The woman thumbed through a ledger and placed her finger on a name scrawled on the page.

"Lizzie?" she asked.

Lizzie nodded briskly.

"Well, Lizzie. Welcome to London and welcome to the Austen House. It looks like you will be staying with us for an extended length of time. Did anything bring you here in particular?"

"No, not really. Just traveling around England," she said hesitantly. She wasn't sure she should be telling people what she was actually doing in the country. It wasn't something her mother had told anyone, so why should she be putting it on blast?

"Well, if you will follow me, I will take you to your room."

The older woman grabbed a big brass key, walked from behind the counter, and around the corner to a hallway. Lizzie grabbed her bags and followed her as she slowly climbed the stairs.

"My name is Fanny," the woman said. "If you need anything, I am here until eleven every night."

Fanny trudge up the three flights of stairs and stopped in front of one of the doors. "Here is your room. Number 3-0-2." With shaky hands, she slipped the big brass key into the lock, turned it and let Lizzie in to the room.

"Thank you, Fanny." She dropped her bags on the bed and the door closed behind her.

Examining the room, she was pleasantly surprised at how spacious it was. In all the reviews of the hotels in London, she had read that they were no bigger than a closet. This room had a full-sized bed and a small desk and chair. The desk also held a nice-sized TV, some maps of the subway, and guides to the London landmarks.

She could be comfortable here.

Unzipping her bags, she pulled out the mounds of research she had done on Jane Austen before she left home in case she could not access the Internet or a printer. Eager to get started, she plopped the papers down at the desk and as she read through them, she took notes in her mother's notebook about what she was going to have to find in Oxford. Determined not to let anyone know why she was there, she called the university and set up a student tour, saying she was interested in taking some continuing studies courses and wanted to see what the university had to offer.

The admissions administrator helpfully arranged for her to come over the next day to see the grounds and their facilities.

Smiling, Lizzie ended the call and thought, *Oxford here I come.*

Chapter 3

Graham

Graham was always ready to support his girlfriend Caterina, but standing in a dark corner of an Oxford library while cameramen and scantily clad co-eds ran around dancing as they shot Caterina's latest video was not how he thought his day was supposed to pan out. Especially since she hadn't done that for him when he'd asked her to do a shoot with him and his band to help them out.

Her bad since his "little boy band" had shot to the top of the charts with a bullet because of that first homemade video. It had caught the eye of British promoters eager to find another group after the success of another boy band. He and his mates were there at the right time and with the right look and sound.

As the director shouted "Cut", Caterina walked over to him, kissed his cheek, and chugged a small bit of water. "How did it look?"

He forced a smile so big and bright it almost squinted his eyes closed. "Perfect. As always."

"Aww. You are such a sweetheart," she said, her attention already back on the video people. She squeezed his arm and walked back in front of the cameras.

Alone, again, he grabbed his phone to see what time it was and was shocked to see he had missed twenty-six text messages from the boys. Group chats were always entertaining.

C: Mornin everyone.

N: Bugger Off Christian! It's 1 in the afternoon.

E: Nick read my mind.

J: You know people just don't understand your musings Christian.

N: Musings? When did you start using such advanced words, Jude?

J: When I started to read the dictionary last night.

E: You made it all the way to 'm'?

J: Skipped a few of the less important letters.

C: And I get shit for sayin Mornin.

N: Haha.

E: Hahahaha.

J: Why is Graham not weighing in on this?

J: Did he die?

J: GRAHAM.

C: Calm your tits. He's with Caterina today.

J: Oh...

N: Jealous much?

C: reading my mind again Nick.

E: They're in Oxford right? Filming something?

N: Yep.

C: Yeah he mentioned it a few days ago.

C: Should we make you a calendar of his schedule?

J: Not bloody funny Christian!

E: I thought it was funny.

N: As did I...

N: Kara agrees...it was funny.

Graham laughed as he texted back his friends and fellow band members.

G: Wow boys. You know how to make a boy feel special. And yeah you were right I'm in Oxford in a library. I'm surprised they let them film in here.

N: They probably paid an insane amount to allow it.

G: I feel weird. Like I should be at least reading one of these ancient books.

The boys launched into another exchange about his overall weirdness, lack of book reading, and of course, being at Oxford, something that would have been impossible for boys like them.

But no longer.

Funny thing, fame, he thought and let himself enjoy his group chat with his friends.

#

Lizzie purposely let herself stay toward the back of the group and a few paces behind, hoping to be able to search the Oxford libraries as the tour went from one college to the next.

Based on the research she had done, she had finally figured out that Jane had likely hidden the next clue in a book in the Drama section. In the first library they visited, she caught sight of a student on his computer, jamming out to music in his headphones rather than studying. Peeling away from the tour group, she walked over to him, put her sweet smile on, and he smiled back.

"Hi. I'm here with the tour and I know you have no clue who I am, but I'm thinking about coming to school here. I was wondering, do the libraries have a common database where you can look up all the books you need for class?"

He sat up a little straighter at her smile and replied, "It does, actually. You can type in a major and it will pull up a list of all the books affiliated with said major."

"How far back does it go?" She sat down next to him as if they were old friends.

His face turn red with her attention to him and he stuttered, "Uh. . .uh. . .I-I-I think only a few years back."

She looked over at his computer. He was working on some kind of paper and was also logged onto the library's Wi-Fi and database.

"Could you show me, please?" She brightened her smile and moved closer to him. She wasn't a good flirt, but she knew she had a nice smile and that boys thought she was attractive. This was important enough to use everything she had to help her get what she needed.

He nodded and quickly typed away on his computer. As the site's search function popped up, she took the computer away from him and typed her keywords into the search fields. Over one thousand entries came up. She harrumphed and glanced at him.

"Can you search by the year they were published?" she asked.

He pointed to a small 'advanced search' button she hadn't seen in her rush. She typed in the year Jane would have been studying at Oxford and only twenty books popped up.

She couldn't contain her squeal of excitement and all the students around them popped up and stared at her like Meer cats coming out of their dens. She pecked him on the cheek and asked if she could pay him to print a copy of the list. He willingly obliged, but didn't take her money.

She caught up with the tour and as it progressed to the one library that contained quite a number of the books on the list she had just printed. As they made their way toward the building, she realized they were not entering the library.

"Why aren't we going in?" she asked.

"There's a private function going on and only authorized guests are allowed," the tour guide explained.

She'd come too far to accept that road block. As the group slowly walked down the street, she lagged behind. When she thought she had a good break from the group, she ran for the library. Surprisingly, the doors were unlocked and she snuck in and was instantly assaulted by loud music and women who were close to naked. Glancing around, no one seemed to notice she had walked in except one of the crew members.

No, not a crew member she realized from his buzzed head of hair and well-built frame. He stood staring at the action going on in the center of the library, but shot her a quick glance as she rushed in.

She immediately ducked down and crawled into one of the rows of books to avoid him seeing her again. When she was sure she was clear of prying eyes, she pulled out her list of books and glanced at the row number for her location. Luckily a few of the books on her list were in this row.

Time to find the one with the next clue and get out before anyone came to look for her.

Chapter 4

The Universal Truth

Graham was still group chatting with the boys when the library door flew open and a girl raced in. She looked like she had been running. Her long black hair was swept up into a ponytail and her skin was as white as paper.

When their eyes met, hers went wide. He was able to see, even at a distance, the amazing ice blue color of them that nearly froze him. He was about to smile, but she ducked into one of the aisles and he lost sight of her.

He looked back at Caterina, who was practicing her moves with the rest of the crew, and he slowly took steps back from that group to go look for the girl who had caught his attention and who wasn't supposed to be there in any case. Making sure no one was paying any mind to him as he left, he quickly made his way to the aisle she had rushed into. He peeked around the corner to find her searching through the books, a small piece of paper in her hands. Her tiny elegant-looking hands. She was average height, but he couldn't help but notice her slender and curvaceous body.

He entered the aisle not far from her and cleared his throat.

She jumped up to face him, clutching the paper to her chest in a death grip.

He chuckled, but she didn't look amused. Finally he said, "You know this particular library is closed today, right?"

She said nothing in response so he took a step closer and she quickly took a step back. He put his hands up as if in surrender. "I'm not here to tell you to leave. I thought I could help you find what you're looking for a bit quicker. Before someone who does care that you're in here kicks you out."

She just stood there silently again, staring at him with her ice blue gaze. He narrowed his gaze, confused. "Do you speak English?" he asked and suddenly found himself trying to do sign language.

That caused her to smile, relax a bit, and nod. "Yes."

She spoke so softly he barely heard her.

"What was that?" he asked, just to make sure she would talk again.

"Yes. I speak English," she said, but her accent was definitely not British.

"American?" he asked.

She smiled and nodded again.

He took a step closer and this time she didn't shy away. "Now what can I help you with?" he asked.

She grinned and shook her head. "Thanks, but I am good."

She again turned to search through the books in front of her.

He stood there, a bit baffled. Why wouldn't she want his assistance?

"I promise I can help," he said as he walked up to her. That's when he smelled the fruity and floral scent she wore and that seemed to suit her somehow.

She glanced at him from the corner of her eye. "Boy band wonder can help me? Sorry if I find it hard to believe someone wearing a Batman belt buckle can help me find an old book."

Boy band wonder....

"So you know who I am?"

"Not really." She continued walking down the aisle, scanning every shelf. "But your face is kind of everywhere I look along with four other faces so I figured, boy band."

"For a girl who could barely say two words a minute ago, you seem to be very chatty all of a sudden." He put his hands in his pockets as he followed her up the aisle.

"Maybe I'm hoping that if I answer your questions, you will somehow disappear." She raised her eyebrows in challenge and he was pleasantly intrigued by her feistiness.

"Fine. I get it." He glimpsed the letter clutched in her hand again. All he could quickly see was 'find the universal truth'.

He knew that was a quote. Well, a differently worded quote. Jane Austen. He had been in an adaptation of a Jane Austen book in school.

Time to mention something that would impress this girl.

"'It is a truth universally acknowledged that a single man in possession of good fortune must be in want of a wife.'"

She stopped dead in her tracks.

Score.

"Excuse me?" she asked. Her face spoke of priceless appreciation for his knowledge.

"Jane Austen. The universal truth." He pointed to her paper. She pulled it farther away from him. "You know she studied here when she was young, don't you?"

"I know," she said with a nervous hiss.

"Are you looking for one of her books? You're very far off in the S section." He leaned forward, trying to read more of the note.

#

Lizzie jerked the piece of paper away to hide it from him and searched along the row.

Graham...Graham...Graham, she thought as she walked and he followed.

Damn him. She couldn't keep thoughts of him from running in circles in her head as she kept on examining the shelves, trying to find the first book on her list.

How was he able to quote Jane Austen? And Pride and Prejudice nonetheless? And how much of the letter had he seen?

As she continued to look through the stacks of S's, she finally found the book she was looking for. Richard Sheridan's "The Rivals".

She reached up on her tiptoes and caressed the leather bound spine. The gold flaking used in the imprinting of the name was barely legible.

She drew the book off the shelf. It was so fragile.

"How could they let it get in this condition?" she whispered to herself.

She gently pulled back the front cover. Nothing. She flipped through the pages as carefully as she could, but nothing caught her attention. When she reached the back of the book, she noticed that the binding was already breaking away from the leather cover. Considering how old the book was, she was not surprised, but something else caught her eye as she was closing it.

Writing on the inside of the binding?

She pulled the pages away from the binding and found an elegantly written number two on the interior part of binding.

She drew away some more pages and an envelope came loose and fell out onto the floor.

"Oh my god." She smiled so hard at how proud her mom would be that she had found this clue and tears soon welled in her eyes from the joy of it.

"Oh my god!" another voice hissed from beside her.

Graham again. She had been so intent on her search, she hadn't realized that he was still tagging along beside her. His gaze skipped from the book, to her hand, to her face, and back again repeatedly.

"What are you doing? Do you realize you're destroying university property?"

"Thanks, Dad, but it was coming apart even before I touched it." She shoved the letter into her bag, put the book back on the shelf relatively in the same shape, and walked passed him, bumping into him in the process.

At the end of the aisle, she peered out and seeing that no one was paying any attention, hurried out of the library and sprinted down the street, all the time hoping that Graham was not following her.

Again.

When she was sure he wasn't, she walked at a brisk pace to the train station and quickly hopped on a train back to Austen House.

As she sat on the train, the anticipation of opening the envelope was close to killing her. When she finally made it to her hotel, she walked in to see Fanny just as she had been the day before. Shawl covering her shoulders and her head buried in a book. With a quick greeting at the older woman, she ran up to her room.

Shutting the door, she climbed onto the bed and pulled the old envelope out of her backpack. She gently pried open the wax seal that alone was probably worth more than her house because it was a seal from *the* Jane Austen.

Carefully, hands shaking, she slowly drew the letter from the envelope.

As she was about to read the letter, the hotel phone rang. She leaned over the bed to grab the phone.

"Hi, Fanny," she said politely, but with barely contained frustration at the delay in reading the letter.

"Sorry to disturb you, but there is a young gentleman here for you. Very friendly and quite handsome."

"Sorry, Fanny. You must have the wrong room. I don't know anyone in the country," Lizzie explained.

"My dear, you are the only young American woman in the hotel," Fanny replied.

Knowing that to continue arguing was useless, Lizzie hung up the phone and shot up off the bed for the walk to the lobby. As she reached the main floor, she said, "All right, Fanny who--"

The sight of the stranger turning around shocked her into silence.

"Graham?"

Chapter 5

Banding together

Graham caught sight of her coming down the stairs and when she stopped dead, he knew she remembered him. Well, how could she not?

She'd only met him a few hours ago.

"Graham?" she said again.

"So you do know this boy, Ms. Price?" Fanny looked both worried and relieved at the same time.

"Not really." Lizzie crossed her arms across her chest as she continued toward him. Her curvy hips swayed from side to side. Seeing the actual curves of her body, not hidden by a jacket, he was even more pleasantly surprised by how beautiful she was.

"How did you know I was here? Crazy stalker much?"

He took an awkward step toward her and grabbed the card he had in his pocket. "You dropped this when you bumped into me."

He handed her the hotel's business card and said, "You realize you could have gotten into massive amounts of trouble today. You broke into a closed library, you ripped the binding off a novel that is over one hundred years old, and you took something from it."

"Lizzie!" Fanny scolded.

Lizzie tried to defend herself. "It is not how it sounds."

"It is *exactly* how it sounds." He stared at Lizzie as he made his demand. "Now, I want to know what is going on or I will take out my mobile and dial the police right now. Who knows what they'll do. Maybe throw you out of the country."

He didn't mean to frighten her, but he was very glad so that it seemed to worked.

"Fine. Come upstairs and I'll explain."

He stared her down again memorizing that her eyes were still those crazy pools of ice. She lowered her arms and started up the stairs.

He looked over at Fanny who was waving and mouthing "Go."

He raced up the stairs to catch up to Lizzie as she marched down the hall and to her room. She opened the door and walked in.

He snagged the door before it closed, entered her room, and looked around in horror.

"Jesus! How long have you been here?" he glanced around again and could not find one uncluttered area in the room.

She shrugged, "It will be a day in about," she looked at her phone, "two hours."

"And you were able to cause this nuclear disaster?" he started to jump from open floor space to open floor space to follow her to the desk.

"Again…thanks, dad."

At the desk, she grabbed some papers and pushed them into his chest. "Now if you would stop complaining about my room, I can explain why I took something from one of the oldest universities in the world."

His mouth dropped open in surprise since he wasn't used to being put in his place by anyone. He was usually the one putting them in their places. But wanting to know what she was about, he did as she asked, sealing his lips and taking the papers. He scanned them quickly and saw the name at the bottom of a letter. He looked back up at her, disbelieving, and she just nudged him with, "Go ahead. Read it."

With each line he read, he was more and more baffled. Who was this girl and how had she gotten her hands on this letter? Was it even from *the* Jane Austen?

"Is this real?" he looked at her and she gave a singular nod.

"How did you find this?"

"I didn't find it, my mother did. She left it to me so that I could discover what Jane Austen wanted someone to find."

"What do you mean she left it to you?" It was obvious what he had asked made her uncomfortable.

"She…uh…she…passed away a few weeks ago."

He put the letter down on her bed and said, "I am so sorry."

"Why? You didn't know her. Or have anything to do with her death." She was back to being defensive, her arms wrapped right around her.

"I didn't mean it like that." Awkwardness had settled into the room and he felt even more uncomfortable because of the pain visible on her face. He glanced back at the letters on the bed.

"So this letter is why you were in Oxford? At the library?"

She nodded slowly, sat on the bed to grab the letter and explained. "My research told me that where she studied was the location of the next note, but 'drama' was the clue. Why would she mention 'drama' out of all the subjects she had studied at Oxford? So when I got to the school, I looked for the books they had listed in the library database for their drama studies."

"And you were able to narrow it down to one book? One play?" he said, astounded at Lizzie's thoroughness. She had obviously done more than her share of research.

"Twenty. Only the ones that were published and at the library during the time that Jane Austen would have been here."

As she explained her face lit up with excitement. "You happened to catch me finding the right one. And I almost skipped over it until I accidentally pulled the pages too hard and the binding broke and I found this."

She handed him the letter that he had seen her shove into her bag.

"What does it say?" he asked, feeling like a little kid again. His parents has used to draw fake treasure maps for him to find the 'buried treasure' in their backyard that was always a small box filled with a new toy.

"I didn't open it yet. I was just about to when Fanny called to tell me some weirdo was here to see me," she joked.

"I believe she called me a 'young gentleman' and handsome as well. " He playfully stood straight and very proper, causing them to both laugh.

Then he looked back at the letter. "How about we open it together?"

"No way," she said and snatched it out of his hands.

Reflexes like a cat, he thought.

"This is my journey," she said. "My mom sent me on this. Alone."

He raised an eyebrow. "She stated you need to do this alone?"

When she didn't reply, he said, "I can help."

She looked him up and down as if there was something weird about him.

"You look like you were on your way to something. This wasn't your final stop for the night, was it?"

Her words forced him to remember that he was only supposed to have been there for five minutes since he had Caterina in the car for their dinner date.

"What time is it?" He glanced over at the clock on the wall. "Oh, shit. I have to go. But listen. I will be back tomorrow. I want to help."

He was about to walk out of the room when he heard her reply, "I really don't want your help."

Smiling, he said, "Well, Lizzie, I don't really care."

Before she could say another word, he ran down the stairs and out to his car.

Caterina was leaning against the bumper, talking to someone on her cell phone.

"Finally he shows up."

She rolled her eyes and said to the person on the line, "We will talk later."

She hung up the phone and looked at him. "What the heck were you doing in there for twenty minutes?"

He wasn't a fan of lying, but he knew he couldn't tell her who was up there since she was the jealous sort. So he altered the truth a bit. "An old friend who just arrived from the States."

"The States?" she questioned.

"Yeah. Family lived here when we were kids and then they moved there." Another lie. It was coming more easily to him than he liked.

After Caterina had decided she needed a break from their two-year relationship a few months ago, something had changed in him. She had called him 'too tame', basically saying that he was as boring as watching paint dry. After that day, he had strived to be different. He cut off all of his hair and had gone all bad boy with an artistic sleeve of tattoos.

When she came back, liking his new self, his guard was still up and it had not come down fully. No matter how much he said he forgave her, deep down he knew he never would.

"Are you ready to go?" she asked with a pout, obviously still annoyed with him over his delay.

"Sure," he said, although he would have much rather stayed with Lizzie and helped her out.

Hopping into the car, they were soon on their way to dinner and a nightclub.

He intended to drown out all negative thoughts about Caterina with music and booze.

Chapter 6

Boys will be boys

Who did that boy think he was? Lizzie fumed.

Did he think he could just join in on this journey? And help? Help! Lizzie scoffed as she finally sat to read the next clue.

Hands shaking, she sat the bed and slowly opened the letter.

Cassandra and I loved this play until we could speak the written word with no playbook in our hands. We were so sad to leave it in Oxford, however, our parents were the loving type who bought us our very own copy to enjoy.

Congratulations are in order for you having discovered the second clue. You must be knowledgeable which is an agreeable trait. Catherine knew this, more than most, that although it was admirable it was not a trait worth marrying. Money is much more agreeable. It is able to bring an air of mystery to a relationship that is predicated on not knowing each other.

While money is mysterious, it is knowledge that will solve these mysteries.

This particular mystery will require the knowledge of the darkness as well as scandal.

Best of Luck,

Jane Austen

"What the actual hell?" She just stared at the paper and re-read the letter about a hundred times without being any closer to understanding what this clue might mean.

Her eyelids began to feel heavy from the excitement and activity of the day, so she put the note on the bedside table, pushed all the books and papers off her bed, shut off the lights and climbed beneath the sheets.

Sleep came so quickly and deeply that when she heard a knock on the door she wondered who would be knocking so late. But when she opened her eyes to see the rays of sun pouring through the window, she realized that it was actually morning.

Never a morning person, she was about to yell for Fanny to go away when another voice came from the other side of the door.

"Lizzie? It's Graham." His deep and raspy voice weirdly soothed her, making her want to cuddled more deeply into her covers, until she replayed what he had said.

"Graham?"

She shot up out of bed and ran to the door, but didn't open it.

"What are you doing here?" she said through the thick wood of the door.

She leaned her ear to the door to hear his reply.

"I told you I would be back. So here I am…back. May I come in? I feel a bit odd talking to a door."

His words brought a smile and she couldn't resist his accent. She opened the door.

Graham stood there in a basic long-sleeved grey shirt, a pair of dark well-fitting denim jeans, and sparkling white Converse. A messenger bag was slung over his shoulder. She laughed at how well put together he was for nine a.m. on a Saturday.

He didn't wait for any further invitation before walking in and sitting down on her messy and unmade bed. He pulled his messenger bag over his head and then yanked out a stack of paper and a copy of *Pride and Prejudice*.

"Did I say you could come in?" she asked, but truly couldn't pull off annoyed.

"No, but then again, you didn't stop me." He opened his book, but then looked over at her as if waiting for her instructions.

"I told you I didn't want your help." She walked to her suitcase and grabbed an oversized hoodie from it.

"And I believe I told you I didn't care and would be helping you anyway." He waved the Austen book above his head to reinforce his point.

"Wow, you own a Jane Austen novel. Your fans must drop their panties at the sight," she mocked.

She walked into the bathroom and stopped dead at the sight of her hair.

Oh my God! Did bees decide to nest in this!

She scooped up her brush and with rapid strokes, tugged it through the knots. Once it was semi-straight, she threw it into a messy bun to keep it under control.

From inside the bedroom, Graham called out, "Most girls don't know or care that I can quote the novels. And even though I pointed that I can quote *Pride and Prejudice,* you somehow still don't think I am valuable."

When she walked out of the bathroom she found Graham on the floor picking up a bunch of the papers she had strewn about. "What are you doing?"

"Cleaning. You can't say you actually get work done in this mess, can you?"

"I can and my mess has meaning. You have a lot of nerve to just come in here and make yourself comfortable."

She sat on the one clear spot on her bed and grabbed some of her research from another spot on the bed. The bed shifted for a moment and she looked over to see that Graham had sat across from her cross legged.

With a raised eyebrow, she asked, "Can I help you?"

"Let's get to it. Open the letter." He almost was almost jumping up and down in his excitement.

"Pushy."

"You will soon come to enjoy my presence." He smirked and continued, "Now open the letter…please."

"I already opened it." She reached over to the bedside table, grabbed the letter, and handed it to him. "Enjoy."

He jerked it from her fingers and read, his gaze skimming over the words almost hungrily.

She sat there, and instead of keeping her attention on her research papers, she watched his lips move as he read. She smiled at how he bit his lip and his eyes squinted when he was deep in thought. She could almost see why girls swooned.

"Is Catherine a relative?" he asked, looking up.

She shook the thoughts of him out of her head and cleared her throat.

"That was what I thought. But there was nothing dark about all the Catherines that were associated with Jane and her family. Not a single thing came up on them. They were clean as a whistle and nothing sparked anything filled with 'mystery'."

He chuckled as he grabbed his phone and began typing away. "You do not know how to Google correctly or maybe you were just too focused on the smaller details. Catherine, Jane Austen, Mystery." There was a small pause before he turned the screen of the phone towards her and with an accomplished smile continued, "Would you look at that. *Northanger Abbey* by Jane Austen."

She rolled her eyes, defeated, and grabbed the phone to read the small print on the phone. "Of course. *Northanger Abbey*. Catherine loved mystery novels. Most famously *Mysteries of Udolfo*. How could I not have seen that?" She hopped off the bed and searched through the papers on the ground. She got to the pile Graham had chosen to clean up and finally found her copy of *Northanger*.

"You could get some folders for all of this paper work. Stay organized," he said as he knelt down beside her to look through the book as well.

"You are really starting to sound like my father," she scoffed and started to skim the book. "There it is! *Mysteries of Udolfo*. But this mystery was solved. It sounds like Jane Austen wanted us to solve a mystery that hadn't been previously solved."

She shot a look at him and there was an evil, but happy grin on his face. "Us?"

She pushed him. "Oh shut up."

He laughed and she sat more comfortably on the floor and continued. "But in all seriousness, how are we supposed to solve a mystery from the 1700 and 1800s?"

"With knowledge of 'darkness and scandal'." He wiggled his arms and hands in a horrible attempt at a ghost impression. "How about we brainstorm? Think over every word she chose to use. She was a smart cookie and like you said, with the last note she uses specific words to make a point."

"Right. Good idea. I would have thought of that sooner or later." She was embarrassed that it hadn't been her first guess.

After a minute of silence, Lizzie finally pointed out something. "So why mention Catherine? Jane could have just said 'solve a mystery.'"

"Maybe to make you point out Catherine's favorite book? Which is what you did. Maybe the book has the mystery we need to solve." He took the book out of Lizzie's hand to read it himself. His smooth hand grazed hers and the heat that emanated from it was astounding. . .and worrisome.

"But that mystery was solved…and how did you know it was Catherine's favorite?"

"Well you mentioned it, but also because I read the book. When Henry mentions he lives in Northanger she is instantly in love with the fact he lives in her favorite novel's home. It almost cost her their relationship when she thinks there is actually a mystery to be solved."

She just stared at him in surprise as he spit out the novel's entire plot line.

He smirked as he caught her gawking, "What? Shocked that I read?"

She said nothing and stole the book back from him to look for more hints as he continued to sort her papers.

"How do you have all this time?" she asked. "If you're some international pop star shouldn't you be like shopping? Doing interviews? Making girls cry?"

She was hoping if she could annoy him enough he would not want to help the 'rude American girl' any more.

"You know who I am, but you obviously don't follow the news. My band mates and I have the month off before our very first European and U.S. tour. So I have a month to help you out." His eyes nearly closed again as his smile grew broad and unrestrained.

"You know you can get really bad wrinkles if you smile like that?" She scrunched her nose, trying to be disgusted when she was really getting a little bothered at how much she wanted to touch his soft-looking cheeks and find out how those smiling lips might feel against hers.

"And do you know you will run out of air before you are able to convince me not to help you?"

Their eyes met and connected since the first time since she saw him in the library. Something weird happened. An odd sensation moved through her. With the way he stared at her, it made her whole body warm.

As something crept into his gaze as well, he coughed and said, "As a peace offering how about I go and buy you a folder or two?"

He stood up to grab his wallet when there was a knock on the door.

"Lizzie? I saw your friend arrive so I made you some tea and biscuits."

Lizzie opened the door to let Fanny in. She carried a gorgeous tray loaded with a fine bone china tea service and delicious looking biscuits. Lizzie was genuinely touched at the thought Fanny had taken in caring for her.

"Thank you, Fanny." Lizzie accepted the tray from the older woman and brought it over to the small desk.

"Yes. Thank you, Fanny," Graham chimed in politely.

"Not a problem, Mr. Harris," Fanny said, but hesitated by the door to the room, clearly uncomfortable. "Actually, I was wondering if you wouldn't mind signing this for my granddaughter. She's a big fan of you boys. Well, at least I think she is. I haven't seen her in years. I would have asked last night but I will admit to being a bit star struck myself." She laughed and handed him a poster of himself.

Lizzie laughed at the sight of the poster.

He gazed at her with a confused expression.

"Your hair!" She pointed to the photo. He looked very young with his hair needle straight and swept across his forehead. "I mean...I can see why you shaved it!"

She playfully rubbed his buzzed head. The same heat she had felt when his hand had gently grazed hers erupted through her hand and up her arm. She yanked her hand away in response.

"Oh, Lizzie! Stop being so rude to the boy. From what I can tell he is trying to help you. Now apologize." Fanny reminded Lizzie of her mother when she was being scolded.

She dipped her head and twiddled her finger as she mumbled, "Sorry, Graham."

"Speak up. You will get nowhere in life mumbling." Fanny grabbed the now autographed photo and looked between the two of them.

Graham grinned and crossed his arms, eyeballing Lizzie with amusement.

She straightened her spine and spoke louder and more clearly. "I am sorry, Graham."

The surprised look on his face was reward enough for having to apologize.

Chapter 7

Girls will be girls

Graham's jaw nearly hit the floor as he got the apology he assumed would never come from Lizzie. Too independent and stubborn Lizzie.

When her hands had touched his head and stroked the short hairs there, gooseflesh had erupted on his neck. Caterina had done the same thing all the time and had never had the same affect. Mostly because she mocked the new buzz cut instead of appreciating it.

Caterina just didn't get that it was a symbol that she no longer had control over him. Same with the tattoos. But he suspected Lizzie would understand.

He quickly shook off the feelings coursing through his blood as he stood there after signing the nice lady's photo.

"That's much better, Lizzie," Fanny said, nodded her head, and looked back at him, " Thank you for this, Mr. Harris."

She walked out of the room, leaving them alone again, but as she walked down the stairs, he shouted out to her, "It's Graham, ma'am."

"It's Fanny, Graham," she shouted back.

He smiled boyishly and returned his attention to Lizzie, who was back at work, a cup of tea in her hand. As he watched her, something clicked in his head.

"Ask Fanny about the mystery."

"What?" She slammed her papers onto the desk, frustrated he had interrupted her again.

"A woman named Fanny is working in a hotel named the Austen House? I feel like that is fate giving us a sign. She has to know something." He was about to run down the stairs when she laid a dainty hand on his arm and stopped him.

"Wait." He looked from the hand up to her face.

How could her touch cause such an odd feeling in his heart?

She continued. "Fannie may be old, but she wasn't born in the 1800s. She probably knows as much as we do."

"It never hurts to ask."

She huffed out a breath. "Fine. But I will ask the questions."

He smiled with satisfaction as they walked down to the front desk.

Fanny was in a chair in the parlor, knitting what looked to be a scarf. When she heard their footsteps, she looked up.

"Was the tea not good?" she asked, clearly worried and rose as if to rush to make things right.

"No. No. The tea was perfect, actually," Lizzie said cheerily to soothe her concern.

She glanced between Fanny and Graham and then took a deep breath before awkwardly asking, "We came to ask you a few questions, if that's okay?"

"Of course. I hope that I can be helpful." Fanny smiled and sat back down in the chair.

Lizzie smiled and asked, "What do you know about the *Mysteries of Udolfo*?"

Fanny appeared both confused and impressed at the same time. "What an odd question," she said with a laugh. "That is the story within the story in *Northanger Abbey* correct?"

Both Lizzie and Graham nodded in response.

"I cannot say that I know much. I never read the story. The author, Ann Radcliffe, was not very popular either. She was not social like Jane. What people did know was that she never had children and some say she died under mysterious circumstances."

Lizzie's body froze with shock.

Graham knew he would have to be the one to ask the next question. "What do you mean by 'mysterious'?"

Fanny leaned back in the chair, relaxing a bit as she told her tale. "Well, no one knows how she died. Some people say she killed herself. Others say she was sick. Some even hazard to guess that her husband did it since she did not produce an heir."

With a cluck of her tongue and shake of her head, she finished with, "This is all hearsay, children. No facts are really known so it's best not to gossip."

"Of course," Lizzie blurted out. "Thank you so much for your help, Fanny."

She shot him a look and then sped up the stairs, leaving Graham standing in front of Fanny.

"Curiouser and curiouser." Fanny said as Lizzie disappeared up the stairs.

"How do you mean?" Graham asked, puzzled at her reaction to Lizzie.

"That girl is so bewildering at times, although I find it rather enjoyable having her company. Any company for that matter. Not many guests come through here lately, although in the past…" She trailed off as she just smiled at the empty staircase.

"Lately? As in a few days? Months?"

She shook her head, amused. "We had one other guest just for a night right before Lizzie came, but really, none for at least a year. When Lizzie showed up, it brought life back to this place. Life I had missed."

Fanny glanced at him and gently nudged him. "Shouldn't you be up there?" she said with a wink.

The heat of a blush warmed his face and he cleared his throat to explain. "It's not…I have a girlfriend. Lizzie is just…well we aren't even friends at this point."

He rubbed the back of his head, feeling awkward in the situation he had just been placed in. He jammed his other hand in his front pocket as he slowly walked up the stairs. But was soon taking them two at a time in his haste to be with Lizzie again.

When he walked into the room, she was sprawled on the bed with her laptop and notebook out, writing at a speed he had never seen before. She looked up when he shut her door and whispered, "Thanks."

His back hit the door as he feigned shock. "First an apology and now you're thanking me? I'm shocked."

"Oh, shut up," she said, trying to hide the smile playing on her luscious red lips. He wondered how soft they would feel on his own and on his neck.

Real shock hit him with those thoughts and he shook his head, trying to rid those images from his mind once again.

He really had no clue who this girl was or what she was up to. Plus, he had a girlfriend. Which reminded him to check up on her.

He grabbed his phone and saw that he had missed a call from Caterina and a text asking him where he had gone. He quickly texted back that he had run out to do some errands and would be back soon. Another lie. He detested lying and it didn't make him feel good that he was doing it more and more often with Caterina. That's when he decided he would tell Caterina the whole truth about what he was doing as soon as he got home.

"...Holborn," Lizzie said, finishing a sentence he hadn't even realized she had started.

"I'm sorry, what?" he asked.

"You seriously heard none of that?" She rolled her eyes, teasing him.

He shrugged to hide his embarrassment. "I heard Holborn, didn't I?"

"Wow. Way to come in at the very end there, Graham." She laughed and climbed off the bed with her notebook.

"Ann Radcliffe was born, raised, and died in Holborn. She traveled the world with her husband, but was always returned home to Holborn. I'm assuming that is where our next clue is, so it's time to head out."

She tossed her notebook on the bed, snatched up a handful of clothes and rushed to the bathroom. When she exited, she was dressed in an actual outfit instead of the comfy sweats she had been wearing. She grabbed her backpack and walked over to him.

He stepped aside as she opened the door.

"Well?" she asked.

"Well what?" He said, unsure of just what she wanted.

"Are you coming?" She smiled at him. The first real big, bright, and welcoming smile that she had directed at him.

"What do you plan to do? Walk around Holborn? Don't you think you should do a bit more research? That is a large part of London."

"That's what I plan to do. I can head to the library and some local spots. Go and ask the people there what they may know about Ann. It can't hurt."

"You didn't want to ask Fanny a second ago, but now you're willing to ask total strangers?" he said, although in truth, he wanted to go with her. The suspense was killing him, but he knew he couldn't go. Not until he talked to Caterina.

"Point taken, but I am still going. Are you?"

"I'm sorry. I can't go." He tried to be nonchalant about it, but he was disappointed inside. Even if he knew it was the right thing to do for the moment.

"I understand," she said with a shrug, although her disappointment was obvious.

She walked passed him and for a moment he was tempted to go with her and forget about Caterina.

But he knew how wrong that was until he had hashed things out with his girlfriend. He shook his head at how stupid he was to have let himself get into this mess, left Austen House, and walked to his car.

As he drove away from the hotel, he kept on asking himself the same thing over and over again.

How the hell am I going to explain this to Caterina?

Chapter 8

Alone in Holborn

Lizzie trudged up the stairs from the tube station. Holborn Station.

She pulled her coat tight to her body against the slight chill in the air as she walked around the streets, trying to get a sense of the place. It was not as she had expected. Instead of being filled with shoppers, pub crawlers, and fancy restaurants, it was very residential and cozy area.

As she strolled around, she snapped a few photos to send to her father that night so she could share her adventure with him.

When she walked down one block, a sign on a nearby lamp post caught her eye.

She ran across the street to see if it was something that might help her get a clue as to the 'mystery' in the next clue.

The sign said "Haunted Holborn". She smiled as she continued to read.

Experience the dark side of Holborn. The 2.7 kilometer walk lasts two hours and takes you through alleyways, haunted pubs, homes, and much more. We meet every night at the Holborn Tube Station at 7pm. Hope to see you ghouls there!

She almost squealed with excitement. Surely there had to be some mystery connected to one of the stops on the tour, maybe even something to do with Ann Radcliff!

She glanced at her watch to check the time, but it was just after one in the afternoon.

Six hours to go until the tour. What should I do with all that time?

She decided to just to continue walking around, checking out the sights. Maybe even finding the local library. First though, it was time for a small bite at the local grocer. Fanny's tea and biscuits had been delicious, but not enough to fill her for the day.

A few blocks away, she found an upscale grocery store, but since she was watching her pennies, she skipped it and pushed on to a small local deli where she picked up a sandwich and a soda. The deli was across the street from a cute little park and she took her sandwich and soda there and sat on a bench to enjoy her meal. The day was growing warmer and the bench was in the sun, chasing away her earlier chill.

As she ate, she wrote in her journal about what she had discovered, making notes and trying out different possibilities about where to look. When she finished her meal, she packed away her journal and gathered up her trash. Pulling out one of the maps that had been left for her at Austen House, she headed off again, exploring the streets and homes in the area. Finding the library and that it had already closed for the day. When she looked at her watch, she realized she had been walking for some time and needed to get back to the tube station.

Hurrying back, she found a large announcement board with several pamphlets about the Haunted Holborn walk just a few feet from the door of the station. She grabbed one of the pamphlets to see what the stops were on the tour and how much it would cost.

"Are you interested in the tour?"

She turned to find an older man standing there, staring at her. He wore a very nice, but well-worn, trench coat and held a large clipboard.

"Yes, I am," she said, smiling and nodding excitedly.

"I'm the tour guide. My name is Carl." He looked at his watch and pointed to some by the tube station. "We gather right over there in about twenty minutes."

"Thank you, Carl." She smiled at him again and walked over to the group that had already started to form. It was mostly older tourists and she was the youngest by several decades. As she stood there, it was odd that one of her first thoughts was about how much she wished Graham could have been there with her and what Graham would have done in this situation.

He'd certainly made an impression on her. Much more than any of her other boyfriends had during high school and college.

But then she reminded herself that Graham wasn't a boyfriend. Not even a friend considering they had only just met each other and really knew little about each other.

As she battled with herself about Graham, Carl walked up to the group. He asked everyone to sign in and pay the tour fee, which everyone happily obliged. But when she went to hand him her money, Carl only took half. She looked at him, confused, and he gave a caring smile. "You're one of my youngest tourists and I'm just appreciative that you're interested in the hauntings of Holborn."

He smiled even wider and winked at her from beneath his bushy white eyebrows. His eyes gleamed with humor and she couldn't control a small giggle. He really was an adorable old man. Maybe she could hook him up with Fanny. If Fanny was single although it seemed like she was. She hadn't seen nor heard of any Mister Fanny while she'd been at Austen House.

As the tour went on, Lizzie learned more and more about the culture of Holborn, but not much that was helping her to solve the next clue. She was starting to lose hope of finding the next clue. She thought about leaving the tour and just going back to the hotel to do more research when they walked into a quaint pub.

It had the charming features of old London and she stood up tiptoe to peer at all the old photos and memorabilia hanging on the walls and one picture caught her eye. A small black-framed photo sat just above one of the wooden booths and when she walked over, she read the name scribbled under the photo itself. She couldn't stop from smiling as she murmured, "Ann Radcliffe."

"That's correct," Carl said from beside her. She spun around to find him and the rest of the group staring at her.

Carl continued. "Ann Radcliffe's husband worked across the street in the newspaper industry and would frequent this bar before returning home to Ann. But this pub's history has a dark past as well. It used to be a molly house." Some people nodded and whispered amongst themselves, but Lizzie looked around to see that most, like her, had no clue what that was.

"A molly house?" she asked.

"It's similar to a cross-dressing bar and gay brothel in today's standards." Carl blushed and Lizzie chuckled at how adorable he was when embarrassed. "Men could dress up as women and also go upstairs to do other dirty deeds." He cleared his throat as some of the other people giggled at his obvious discomfort with the topic.

"Could this have been around the same time Ann's husband came to this bar?" she said quickly since her blood was rushing and pumping adrenaline into every single part of her body as excitement filled her that this might be connected to her next clue.

Carl looked at her, puzzled, but then began to do the math. "I'm not sure it was. More like he liked a pint before heading home. Are you an Ann Radcliffe fan?" he asked with a smile.

She shook her head. "Jane Austen."

He nodded as realization set in. "Ah...*Northanger Abbey*." He laughed, "The tale within a tale." He began to lead them out of the pub and Lizzie kept her eye on the photo. She knew that had to be related to her search. The pub did not have many people in it, but just swiping it off the wall at that moment wouldn't work. She would have to come up with a plan as to how to be able to examine the photo more closely. Still, she couldn't wipe the smile off her face. Not even when she climbed onto the very cramped tube and made her way back to the hotel.

Fanny was sitting in her chair, knitting, when she entered. As she noticed Lizzie's smile, she said, "You look so happy. Did Graham sweep you off your feet?"

All her happiness evaporated in a heartbeat. She rolled her eyes, thinking of Graham, and quickly replied, "No. He didn't come with me. I just went on a fun educational tour."

"And you're smiling about learning? Not a normal reaction from so many young people today."

"What can I say? I'm definitely not normal." She laughed and was about to walk up the stairs when she turned back to Fanny. "You know Graham is kind of famous, right?"

Fanny nodded. "Of course, I do."

She recalled the billboards she had seen all over town, but for the life of her, could only remember Graham's name. "What's the band's name again? I want to look up their music."

"No need," Fanny said. She walked into the room behind her and came back with two albums.

Lizzie laughed and shook her head, prompting Fanny to likewise grin.

"What? You are never too old to enjoy new music. Take a listen. I am sure you will not be disappointed. If you are, well, you can return the CDs and we'll never discuss it again." She smiled her gentle smile and sat back down to resume her knitting.

Lizzie grabbed the discs and thanked Fanny as she walked up to her room. She threw her stuff on the bed and then popped one of the CDs into her laptop. The catchy up beat tempos got her in a 'do something' mood, so began to clean her room. When the disc ended, she popped it out to put in the second CD.

She was surprised at what a different sound had. More mellow and melodic songs gave her inspiration to write in the journal her mom had left her. She wrote for at least an hour, replaying the CD as it came to an end.

As her hand cramped up from writing and her eyes began to droop, she lay down on the bed and the tones of the music lulled her to sleep.

Chapter 9

Alone with himself

Graham sped away from the neighborhood pub where he had gone for some time away from his new life. Everyone there knew him from before his newfound fame and just treated him like another mate. He had needed that after leaving Lizzie, confused about what to do with her and Caterina.

Lizzie.

Graham slammed his palm onto the steering wheel. He should have gone with Lizzie. He should have kept her safe. Who knew who she would run into? It wasn't his job to protect her, but he felt such a desire to. He wanted to head to Holborn to make sure she was okay, but he knew that would be a horrible idea. For one, he had no clue where she was and two, he had decided that he had to come clean to Caterina.

He pulled in front of his house and parked the car. Checking to see that no paparazzi or eager fans were around, he rushed up the stairs and into the front parlor.

It was silent. Weirdly silent. Caterina always had either music or the TV on and since she was a normally night owl, he had expected her to be up. Especially since it wasn't all that late at night.

Not too late to go back to the hotel and wait for Lizzie, he thought, but drove that thought out of his mind.

"Caterina?" he called out, wondering if she was even home.

He heard movement in the living room and walked there to find Caterina sitting up on the couch. She must have been taking a nap. She stretched and he watched her slender body move back and forth and the lower part of her abdomen, tan, and well fit, peak passed the hem of her shirt.

"Where were you? I called the boys, your friends at the studio. None of them knew where you went. I was really worried."

She sashayed over to him and wrapped her arms around his neck. Moved her hands up to caress his buzzed head. She frowned. "I still have no clue why you decided to shave off *all* your hair."

She rubbed her hand across his head and he tried to ignore the fact that he had no reaction to her touch. He tried to enjoy it, but failed.

But then she pressed her body to his, covered his lips with hers, and he forgot why he had even come home.

He spun and pushed her hard up against the wall. Frames rattled against the wall and some fell to the ground, but it didn't stop him. He traced the sides of her torso with his hands, lifting her sweatshirt up and over her head.

She played with the hem of his shirt and soon she was pulling it off just as fast as he was carrying her up the stairs to his bedroom.

She made quick work of his belt buckle and as she pushed his pants down, he pushed his hips against her sweat pant covered ones. Quickly he yanked the sweats down and she stepped out of them.

He grabbed her thighs and pulled her up to wrap her legs around his body, and moved back until the edge of the bed hit his knees.

Moans escaped her lips as he rocked his hips up into her and he turned and tossed her onto the bed.

But at that moment, as he broke the connection with her, he remembered why he had come home.

"Caterina."

She glanced up at him, eyes wide and filled with desire, biting her lower lip sexily. That look usually was enough to seduce him and make him forget everything that was wrong between them, but not this time.

"We need to talk. I need to tell you something."

"Now? Can't it wait? We are kind of in the middle of something."

She reached for the waistband of his boxer briefs, but he grabbed her hands and then sat next to her on the bed.

"No. It really can't," he said, met her gaze directly and kept hold of her hands so she would not try to change his mind. He knew that if he didn't tell her now, he might never do it.

"I lied today when I told you I was running errands. And I lied to you in Oxford when I said I was on the phone with the boys…and when I told you I was visiting a friend last night at the hotel."

She sat up straight like a shot, surprised, and stared at him as if seeing a different person. "What do you mean? You never lie."

"On set yesterday, I saw a girl sneak into the library. I went to help her so she could skip from getting into massive amounts of trouble. I caught her on some weird scavenger hunt thing. Last night I went to see what it was all about and it sounded so interesting and well. . .I went back this morning to help her solve the next clue."

As he spoke, he worried the story he had just told her sounded more ridiculous than his lies.

"You're joking right?" She smirked and laughed. "A scavenger hunt? What is it for? A school project? Bachelorette party? What exactly, because girls do not just go on random hunts in odd places if there's no reason."

"I don't know how she got started on the hunt, but the clues she had were written by Jane Austen!" he said, excited to be sharing this information with someone. But he soon felt like the stupidest man alive as Caterina fell onto the bed, laughing hysterically. And immediately after that, guilt slammed into him that he was sharing Lizzie's secret, something she probably wouldn't like.

"Jane Austen? Come on Graham! You might as well tell me you were cheating on me. That might have been a bit more believable." She choked back tears of amusement.

Her attitude frustrated him, and he scrubbed his face with annoyance. "I am serious, Caterina."

He stood, walked over to a small chair in the corner of the room and sat, needing space so he could continue his explanation. "The young woman's name is Lizzie. Her mother died a few weeks ago and left her a note from Jane Austen. The clues in the note led her to the library in Oxford where she found the second clue."

He glanced at Caterina whose laughter was finally subsiding as she sat, half naked, on the bed.

She looked straight into his eyes. "You're serious?"

It now looked like things were finally starting to click in her head thankfully. He nodded and leaned his elbows on his thighs, staring at her.

"So what are you exactly doing with this girl?" she asked, raising a perfectly sculpted eyebrow.

"We are trying to solve the clue."

"That's all?" She moved to the end of the bed and sat there, long lean legs dangling over the edge.

"That's all," he repeated, surged to his feet and walked back over to her. He grabbed her hands once again and brought them to his lips. "You should meet her. She could use another friend."

"And I have to be that friend?" she asked rudely, surprising him a bit. He wasn't accustomed to that tone from her.

"I intend to help her. At least for this month. And, well, I plan on being with her for a lot of my free time before the tour. That is, if she lets me after ditching her this afternoon."

"I can't believe you want to help her? What about spending your free time with me?" she almost screeched.

"This is a once in a lifetime challenge and I'll still have plenty of time for you." He shrugged, confused as to how she could be mad.

"Your job is a 'once in a lifetime' thing. Do you really want to go and possibly ruin it by traipsing around the country with some little nobody who may or may not be using you?" She jumped off the bed and began to pace back and forth in front of him.

"She is not a nobody. And for your information I used to be a 'nobody' as well not all that long ago. She isn't using me, because she didn't even want me helping and had no idea who I was at first. I insisted on helping her. You may not believe her, but you should at least believe me and trust my judgment."

He stood to try and comfort her, even though he didn't understand why he needed to. Anger filled him to the point that he didn't even want to be in the same room as her.

How could she think so little of a woman she had never met as well as so little about him?

She rolled her eyes and wrapped her arms around his lower waist, giving him that look again along with her sexy little pout as she apparently sensed his upset and attempted to soothe it. "Fine. I'll try to be friends with her. But if she tries anything funny, I will walk out and you better be behind me." She poked his chest angrily.

"Would you like to meet her tomorrow? I do owe her an apology," he said as Caterina roamed her hands his chest.

"You're planning on going there tomorrow? Really?" She stepped away a bit, obviously annoyed by his insistence.

He drew her back to him gently. "Come on, Caterina. I told you I owed her an apology. Plus we're still trying to solve the second clue," he said as he trailed a line of kisses down her neck.

She sighed, lifted her arm, and snaked up around his neck. Pressed her body against his as she kissed him once again.

Graham let go of any reservations and upset with Caterina. Things were as they should be again.

Everything was back to normal…almost.

Chapter 10

A day of reckoning

He woke up the next morning to the soft chirp of his cell phone alarm and Caterina's arm wrapped around his naked body.

He nudged her to wake up, but instead she just cuddled closer. "Caterina, we need to get up. We need to get ready to go to Lizzie's."

Her face contorted into one of disgust and she sighed heavily, pushed away from him to stretch and get herself up and out of bed.

He rushed out of bed and hurried to the shower. As he finished, he suspected that he had probably set a world record for one of the fastest showers ever.

As he walked back into the bedroom, Caterina was busy fixing her hair and applying makeup. He hoped it wouldn't take her as long as it normally did, but by the time he was dressed, she was ready to go.

Not that she was happy about it. She clearly was unenthusiastic about what she was about to do, but resigned to go with him, slouching and unhappy, as they walked to his car and drove to the hotel.

Fanny greeted him with a warm smile and a wide-eyed glance at Caterina, obviously confused as to why he had brought another young lady with him.

"Let me run up and get Lizzie for you," she said, put down her book and headed up the stairs to check on Lizzie.

Graham looked over at Caterina who was picking at her nails, unamused at the fact they had to wait.

"Could you at least pretend to be happy to be here?" he asked.

"Why? I didn't want to be here. You asked me and since I love you, I chose to come." She met his gaze directly, almost in challenge. In her heels she was as tall as him, sometimes taller.

He wanted to have it out with her, but realized this was not the time or place. Holding his anger in, he grabbed her hand and weaved his fingers through hers, trying to remind himself that they were a couple.

But all the time they stood there, it was hard not to think about the fact that he was more interested in seeing Lizzie, than staying with Caterina.

#

The music had still been playing when she woke and the sun had drowned the room with bright morning yellow.

She had shut off the music and gone to take a shower, all the time thinking about returning to Holborn and examining the photo in the pub. As she came out of the steamed up room, she heard a knock on the door.

"Graham, Fanny really needs to not let you up here," she said playfully as she wrapped the towel around herself more securely, not that she planned on opening the door half-naked.

"Actually, it's Fanny, dear," she said and Lizzie opened the door just a crack.

"Graham is downstairs and he brought a girl with him," Fanny said and she was obviously nervous as her gaze darted back to downstairs.

"Oh?" Lizzie said, a little embarrassed and likewise nervous about what it could mean that Graham was here and with a girl.

"May I come in?" Fanny said and Lizzie stepped aside and let the older woman into the room.

"I believe it may be his girlfriend," Fanny continued and Lizzie pulled her towel closer to her body as Fanny glanced around her room.

"Wow. You cleaned." Fanny smiled indulgently.

Lizzie laughed and nodded. "Yeah, last night. The music was inspiring in a way."

"I told you that you would enjoy it! So about Graham…"

"Oh right. Umm…Give me about ten minutes to dress and then send them up," she said and walked over to her suitcase to grab some clothing.

Fanny dipped her head in a nod and waved as she shut the door.

With a sigh, Lizzie held her clothes to her chest, fell onto her bed, and stared at the ceiling.

Great. Graham was here with his girlfriend.

Not at all what she expected and if she were honest with herself, not at all what she had hoped for his next visit. Not that she had expected him to dump his girlfriend for someone he had just met, but she had thought they'd connected and well . . .

Yeah, she had kind of hoped for more time alone with him to see where that connection would take them.

Dressing, she prepared herself for what was sure to be an awkward meeting.

#

Graham stood there nervously, his hand still clasping Caterina's as Fanny came down the stairs.

"Lizzie just needs a few minutes. She just got out of the shower. You can go up in a little bit."

Graham's mind went straight to thinking of Lizzie in the shower. Her thick brown-black hair slick as water cascaded down and onto her slender, but curvaceous body.

No. No. No. Don't go there, Graham.

He squeezed Caterina's hand to remind him she was his and that he loved that fact. She was his, the girl he had told that he loved and who had told him that she loved him, too.

He glanced at her and smiled, trying to hide what his mind had just pictured, and she smiled back before kissing him on the cheek. Her earlier upset seemed to have vanished and so he said, "Thanks for being so patient."

"Not a problem, Graham. I get that this is important to you," she said, which only made him feel worse. He didn't like being torn between his feelings for the two women.

After waiting impatiently for nearly five minutes, they walked up to Lizzie's room and he gently knocked on the door.

It flung open and something inside of him warmed at the sight of Lizzie, fresh out of the shower. Her beautiful ice-blue eyes gleaming with happiness and the creamy skin of her face filling with color at the sight of him.

It nearly took his breath away and he again squeezed Caterina's hand to remind himself of who he was in love with.

This feeling will pass, he told himself, but a little voice inside his head chided him.

Liar.

Chapter 11

Dealing with it

When he looked at her the way he did when she opened the door, Lizzie felt the oddest thing inside her. His angelic smile that made his eyes almost squint closed had her heart pumping at an alarming rate and made her feel as if it would burst from her chest.

But that feeling also caused her to smile just as enthusiastically back at him.

"Thank goodness you're okay."

He wrapped his arms around her head and pulled her into his chest. His strong musky scent entranced her senses and her body became instantly alive at his touch.

She gently pushed him off her to feign no interest in the affection and peered at his girlfriend who looked ready to pounce.

The young woman twirled one of her large ringlets between her fingers and glared up and down at Lizzie. It made her feel very self-conscious.

Graham tried to get past the moment by wrapping his arm around her and introducing them.

"Lizzie, this is Caterina. Caterina, this is Lizzie. Lizzie I told her everything about what we've been doing together," he confessed.

"What!" she nearly yelled, upset that he had shared what was supposed to be a secret.

"I didn't want to lie to her anymore. She needed to know where I was going and what I was doing. She wants to help," he said, pleading for understanding.

"Graham…" Lizzie rolled her eyes, shook her head, and invited them into her room. "Please come in so we can discuss this in private."

After they had entered, she turned around to see that Graham was smiling. "What?" she asked.

"You cleaned." His smile mixed with a laugh that caused that funny feeling in her chest again.

"Yeah, well after someone ditched me yesterday, I had a lot of time on my hands," she said with a smile as Graham did a slow walk around the room to inspect.

As he did so, Caterina let out a small chuckle and they both looked over at her and realized she had pulled out her phone and was now texting someone and ignoring them.

Graham looked back to Lizzie. "I am sorry," although she didn't know if it was about revealing her secret or Caterina's obvious disinterest. Or maybe both.

"On a positive note, I think I found the location of the next clue." She climbed across her bed to grab a pile of papers and handed them to him.

"Haunted Holborn?" he said as pulled out the small pamphlet for the tour she had taken.

"It sounds cheesy, but it was what brought me to the next clue." She flipped to the map in the pamphlet and pointed directly at the small star that marked the bar. "There was a picture of Ann Radcliffe in there. Her husband apparently frequented the bar every night before he would go home after work. It was also used as a molly house."

His confused look quickly had Lizzie explaining. "It was like a drag bar and brothel at one point, but I don't think it was when Radcliff went there."

"So why is her photo there?" He shook his head handing her the papers back and walking over to some more of her research.

She followed after him pulling out more of the paper work with her notes. "It makes no sense that he would put a photo of his wife in the pub. Someone else has to have put the photo there for another reason."

"Maybe they were trying to guilt him into going home?" he said, obviously questioning her research which was getting to her.

"I asked the tour guide if he knew why the photo was there, but all he said was that Radcliff used to have a pint there each night. It has to have been someone else who put the photo there."

"It's a lot of circumstantial evidence." He sat down in the chair and Lizzie was confused as to why he had such a hard time believing her. Especially since there was no way Radcliff would put a picture of his wife at the pub.

"Circumstantial?" Caterina finally chimed in, having apparently lost interest in her phone.

"Big word there, Graham. I'm no sleuth, but it looks like the girl did her homework."

Lizzie's jaw dropped. She was surprised that Caterina had even heard a word that she had been saying since she had seemed more interested in texting.

Caterina walked over to Graham and to look at all her papers and notes.

"Your girlfriend is on my side. Why not you?" Lizzie questioned.

"It's not about whose side I'm on. It's about what could be the next clue. The pub has changed a lot since the 1800's. It's hard to believe that photo has been there all that time."

"And sometimes things don't change all that much," Caterina chimed in with show of support.

Lizzie's jaw dropped again and Caterina shot a look at her.

Lizzie quickly cleared her throat. "Exactly," she said, trying not to sound so surprised. She leaned over to whisper so only Caterina could hear. "Thank you."

"I am not doing this for you," Caterina hissed under her breath and then turned to fully face Graham.

"I may not understand why you want to do this, Graham, but I will help because it'll get this done a lot quicker."

Graham's face showed the same befuddlement she felt.

Caterina moved closer to him and whispered something into his ear. He visibly reacted to the whisper as he closed his eyes and took quick, deep breaths as if trying to control himself.

Graham finally whispered, "Okay. Okay. Let's go to this pub."

Chapter 12

Return to Holborn

Caterina had whispered in his ear, "If we get to the pub, and find the clue, we can go home and celebrate."

Graham was angry. She didn't care what he wanted to do. She just wanted him to focus on her, no matter what.

He had closed his eyes to take a few deep breaths, clenching and unclenching his fists to control the anger.

When he finally opened his eyes and Lizzie turned around to face him, her ice blue eyes were glimmering with excitement.

It subsided his anger faster than any deep breathing could have done.

Returning her smile, he waited for her to grab her jacket and backpack and they made their way to the lobby.

But when they reached the front desk, Fanny was talking to someone on the phone, her face panic stricken.

He took two large steps towards her and asked, "Are you okay?"

When she didn't respond, Lizzie walked around the counter and tried to talk to her. "Fanny, what's wrong?"

"Fanny?" Caterina laughed out the name. Mocking that lovely lady was the straw that broke the camel's back.

"Caterina, shut it. If you have nothing nice, or productive to say…I don't really need to finish that sentence do I?" he said, but her face was not one of remorse or apology, but one of annoyance and growing anger.

"Excuse me." She rolled her neck and stepped away from the group. Never a good sign. He knew she was about to try and make a scene.

"You're being rude, Caterina. And it's not nice." He tried to stay calm to keep her from blowing up.

Unfortunately, he was too late.

"You dragged me here to help this girl," she almost yelled and pointed at Lizzie, who not only looked concerned for Fanny, but also for him.

Caterina continued with barely a pause for a breath. "I did. You ask me to trust you. I did. And you repay me by being the biggest arse I know and lecturing me about being polite!"

"Caterina," he said, his voice shaking with anger. "This is not the time or the place--"

Her yelling cut him off. "Is this because we broke up? Is this some sort of sick punishment? I made a mistake, okay!" she said, her eyes watering as she stared at him.

He could never resist when she cried. "Don't cry, Caterina," he cooed.

He walked to her, wrapped his arms around her waist, and pulled her close. "This is not punishment. I just really want to do this and I want you to be a part of it."

Her tears hit his shirt and he looked back over at Lizzie, who was deep in conversation with Fanny. Even though he was angry with Caterina, he hated to see girls cry, so he cradled her tighter into his chest, and tried to calm her down.

"While you two were arguing, and what looks like making up now, Fanny told me what's wrong," Lizzie said.

She made her way past them and over to the window.

Caterina and Graham joined her as she pulled the curtains back. Hundreds of cameras flashed in their faces and a throng of girls screamed his name.

Lizzie quickly shut them and motioned to where Fanny stood, handling another call.

"Her phone has been ringing off the hook thanks to the press and crazed fans booking rooms. This place is going to be a mad house in the next couple of days."

He let go of Caterina, who stumbled back a bit, and walked over to Fanny. "I am so sorry. I don't know how press finds out everything! It's ludicrous."

"Why are you apologizing? This place will be fully booked for the year by the end of the day. I will finally be able to afford a trip over to the states," Fanny said and smiled so wide it was contagious.

As Lizzie came back to Fanny's side and hugged the old lady, she laughed as well.

"Oh dear, I didn't mean to hold you up. You seemed to be on your way out." Fanny broke away from Lizzie and looked over at Graham.

"We can't get out now." Caterina pointed to the window and the crowd of fans and paparazzi.

"You can't go out the front, but you can make it out the back." Fanny smiled, walked out from the front desk, and led them through the kitchen to the back door.

Graham pulled open the door and smiled as he realized it was all clear back there since it was a private alley. He let Lizzie and Caterina out before him and turned to Fanny. "Thank you."

"You're welcome and a small bit of advice?" she said.

He nodded for her to continue and she did. "Get that girlfriend of yours a Xanax or something." She winked, shooed him out, and shut the back door.

He peered at Caterina, who must have heard what Fanny had said, and looked ready to start a catfight with the old lady. He kept a straight face as he joined her, but he was laughing on the inside.

They followed behind Lizzie to the end of the private alley, where she peered around the corner.

"We're clear."

She bolted out the alley before he could stop her and with a quick peek at Caterina, they both raced out after her.

Lizzie stood on the opposite side of the car where the paparazzi couldn't see her. He smirked and quickly unlocked the doors and that's when a few of the news people noticed him.

"Graham!" one screamed and soon they all turned toward the car.

Luckily they got into the car and sped away before the rush of the crowd made it impossible.

He looked over at Caterina, who was used to the cameras, and he then looked in his rear view mirror to see that Lizzie's eyes were wide and she was biting her lip with an excited smile.

He must have been watching her for too long because Caterina suddenly shouted, "Graham!"

He whipped his gaze back to the road to find a man crossing the street.

He slammed on the brakes and they all flew forward. When they hit the dash and seats, Caterina glared at him.

"Jesus! What are you doing?" She adjusted her seatbelt and sat back.

He glanced into the rear view mirror, met Lizzie's wide-eyed gaze and apologized. Then he returned his attention to the road and began to move again.

"Where are we going exactly?" Graham asked.

"Here's the address," Lizzie said and handed Caterina a piece of paper.

Graham waited as she entered the address it into the car's GPS system and after, they all sat in silence as the voice of the GPS read out the directions.

As Graham drove, he mentally reviewed all the information Lizzie had thrown at him that morning and realized they had no idea as to how to get the next clue.

"What's the plan?" he asked.

"What do you mean?" Lizzie said.

"When we get to this pub, we can't just take walk in, take the photo off the wall, and walk out. We have no way to get it with no one noticing."

"You always need your plans," Caterina spat as she looked over at him. "Can we for once just wing it?"

"I think Graham is right, Caterina. We need a plan," Lizzie said.

Caterina's head whipped around as she glared at Lizzie.

Graham placed a hand on Caterina's lap and rubbed his hand up and down her thigh to calm her. She grabbed his hand and wove her fingers through his as she settled down.

"I think I have an idea," Lizzie said softly, obviously uneasy. He knew Caterina could be intimidating at times and how that could make a person feel.

"Go ahead." He nodded, urging her on, as he continued to drive.

"We use the paparazzi and your crazed fans. Tell them where you'll be and at what time. They'll swarm the bar and the staff will be in a frenzy."

"And I'm assuming you'll be in the pub near the photo and grab it?"

She smiled and nodded eagerly. "You guessed it, Graham. Does that sound like a plan?"

"It does, Lizzie. It does," he said and watched as she searched her pockets. He wondered what she was looking for.

"You ok back there?" he asked, glancing in the rear view mirror.

"Yeah. Just looking for my phone. I was supposed to call my dad this morning. He'll get worried if I don't do it soon."

He heard the snick of her iPhone unlocking and the soft tap of her fingers as she dialed numbers.

"Hey, Dad. Hope everything is ok at home." There was a pause and the low mumble of something from her phone before she continued. "Yes, Dad. I've been having an interesting time to say the least. Mom would have loved it here, but I can't really talk long right now."

He heard the deep breath she took and could tell she was trying to control her emotions and calm her nerves. "Yes, Dad, I'll call you again soon. I love you," she said and hung up with a sniff.

"Why didn't you bring your mom to come to help you?" Caterina said sarcastically.

"Caterina!" he hushed.

"What?" she said, faking an innocent face.

"It's ok, Graham. My mom couldn't come and help because she passed away about a week ago. Cancer," Lizzie said, totally cool, calm, and in control, although he heard the emotion in her voice.

He had to give Lizzie credit for being a bit stronger than most people in Caterina's path.

"Oh…bummer," was all Caterina could muster up as an apology.

Graham rolled his eyes at her callousness and was about to blast her when the GPS said, "Arriving at destination."

They glanced at the GPS screen and then looked around to try and find their destination as Graham continued driving.

"Stop!" Lizzie said and pointed across the street.

He eased into a parking spot, parked, and glanced at the building. "That's the pub?"

It was a dilapidated mess and the sign was barely legible beneath all the ivy and vines climbing up the brick walls.

"Yep!" Lizzie said, unbuckled, and climbed out of the car. She leaned in through his window and said, "I'll head in and position myself by the photo."

Graham nodded. "We'll park the car around the corner so that we can try and make a clean getaway."

He waited until Lizzie had entered the bar, then drove around the corner and parked. He got out of the car and waited for Caterina to do the same. As her door slammed, he peered at Caterina, needing to clear the air about her attitude and her lack of caring.

"We need to talk, Caterina."

She rolled her eyes and leaned against the bumper of the car. "What, Graham?"

Anger filled him again and he bit out the words. "I told you last night that Lizzie's mother had passed away. Why on earth would you bring that up?"

"I forgot. Sorry," she said, but with no remorse. "Can we get this over with?"

He shook his head and walked around the corner. Near the door of the pub, he grabbed his phone from his pocket, snapped off a photo, and sent a short tweet about where he'd be.

Caterina surprised him by weaving her fingers through his and offering up an apologetic smile.

With that, they walked into the pub. Lizzie was sitting in a small booth holding a pint of lager. Lizzie pointed up and he glanced at the wall where the photo she and Caterina believed held the next clue was located.

He strolled over to Lizzie. "I've tweeted where I am and there should be girls flocking in here anytime soon."

Lizzie nodded and Caterina and he sat down together on one side of the booth. The barmaid came over to take their order and Caterina quickly ordered her standard cranberry and vodka and he ordered his basic water.

"Such a pansy!" Lizzie joked, but he knew that she was only kidding.

He laughed and corrected her. "Actually I'm not a big drinker. I used to never drink, but now with the boys I will sometimes have a pint or two. But I need to be alert right now."

"One beer isn't going to damage your alertness. Just saying," Caterina said, grabbed her glass, and took a large swig. No sooner had she downed it, the door of the pub opened and a small group of girls walked in, looking around a bit anxiously and confused.

But when they saw Graham they began to squeal and jump up and down excitedly.

"Showtime," he said with a smirk and straightened his clothing as the girls b-lined for him.

"Ladies, so glad you found us!" He smiled and they seemed to not be able to form sentences as they realized he was really there and really talking to them.

"So what can I do for you?"

"Can we get a few pictures and maybe autographs?" one of the braver girls said.

He could tell they were trying really hard not to cry and scream and he had to chuckle at their restraint.

"Of course! Let's go over there so that these lovely ladies can enjoy their drinks and food."

He put an arm around one of the girls and could feel that the poor girl was trembling with excitement.

As he stood a few feet away from the booth, more and more people began to crowd the pub and the locals likewise started to move close, finally realizing that someone famous was in their midst. With every minute that passed, the pub became more crowded until it was almost wall to wall people.

He kept trying to look over at Caterina and Lizzie, but he wasn't able to see them over the throng of people.

He hoped he was creating enough of a distraction, but as the jostling of the girls started getting crazier and their squeals almost ear-piercing, he knew he had to get out of there before it got dangerous for him and for all the young ladies surrounding him.

Chapter 13

Snatch and run

All Lizzie could see was Graham's head above the crowd of young girls and locals surrounding him.

Not a bartender or barmaid was in sight.

It was the perfect time to snatch the photo. She took a final swig of her pint for a small amount of liquid courage and then hopped up on the bouncy leather booth seat.

On tiptoe, she did another little bounce that gave her the height she needed to lift the photo off the nail. She plopped back down onto the seat, adrenaline coursing through her body.

Caterina glanced over at her with what was an almost evil, but impressed grin.

"What are you waiting for? Open it!" Caterina demanded.

"Not here." Lizzie shoved the frame into her backpack and stood up. She pushed past the edge of the crowd by the booth to head out of the pub and walk back to Graham's car.

"Wait!" Caterina shouted.

Some of the fan girls turned to look, but Graham soon grabbed their attention again by giving a bunch of the girls hugs which prompted another round of shrieks and squeals.

"Wait, Lizzie!" Caterina shouted again and Lizzie was shocked she even heard her. Caterina must have a voice an octave higher than everyone else. Just the sound of it made Lizzie's blood boil. She had no clue why, especially since she had only known Caterina for about three hours. Maybe it was that everything about the other young woman had nastiness in it.

Lizzie stopped and found Caterina pushing through all the crazed fans and until she stood right in front of Lizzie. Caterina was very tall and towered over Lizzie, who was a fairly average height.

"Where do you think you're going?" Caterina hissed.

"Back to the car like we agreed. Aren't you coming with me?" Lizzie asked as she continued to the door, Caterina hot on her heels.

"You have the clue, so you can go back to the hotel now. I'll wait for Graham to get away from the girls."

Lizzie didn't understand why Caterina was being so mean. But Lizzie had realized during the past three hours that Caterina was annoying, shallow, and really not interested in doing this. It was also extremely obvious she did not want Graham to be a part of the hunt either.

"Graham said to meet him by his car," she said. Caterina didn't reply and struck a pose filled with her bitchy attitude. Her hands went to her hips as she dropped one hip and looked Lizzie up and down.

Lizzie let out an exhausted breath and said, "Listen, Caterina. I know you don't want to be here. I also know you have strong objections to Graham being here. I'm not here to cause drama between you. I'm here to solve a mystery my mom didn't get a chance to do. You can tell Graham thanks for the help, but I really just want to finish this alone."

She put out a hand for Caterina to shake, but Caterina looked at it like it had a flesh eating disease and was wrapped in old bandages. Lizzie lowered her hand and walked out of the pub.

#

With a quick glance toward the door, Graham saw Lizzie's upset face as she left with the clue and without him. Caterina was also by the door, staring at it with a sly smile. He didn't want to think she had something to do with Lizzie leaving like that, but deep down he knew.

"All right, guys. Caterina and I need to get a move on. Thanks for coming to chat."

Gently he parted the crowd of girls and made his way over to Caterina. He wrapped an arm around her waist to lead her out and around the corner to his car, the throng of girls following just behind them. When he shut the doors of his car, he blurted out, "Where's Lizzie?"

"She grabbed the photo and ran," Caterina said with a start.

"Great," he said, although he wasn't feeling great. He forced a smile, but when he looked at Caterina, he could tell there was something she was leaving out. "What else is there, Caterina?"

Caterina looked over at him, mouth agape, not knowing what to say. But she finally found the words. "Lizzie doesn't want our help anymore. She only needed us today for a distraction. She said thanks, but that she wanted to finish this alone."

She reached over to grab his hand, but he jerked it away from her grasp.

"You're lying." His pulse quickened with anger.

Caterina shook her head vigorously to deny his words, but he didn't want to look at her. He was annoyed and frustrated. Silently he started the car and drove them back to his house. He pulled up in front of it and parked. Caterina climbed out, but he didn't move.

"Graham?" she asked, concerned. For once, he didn't doubt that she was actually worried. He glanced at her through the open window on his door.

"Aren't you coming in?"

"I have to talk to Lizzie," he said.

"I told you she doesn't want to see us." She slapped her hands on her thighs with frustration and anger.

"I need to hear that from her," he said and pulled away.

Chapter 14

The adventure continues. . .

Hurrying, Lizzie almost ran to the closest tube station and luckily, it wasn't long until the train arrived and she jumped on.

Despite possibly finding the next clue, she felt odd. Not happy anymore. In fact, she was upset.

She had lost the one person she felt could share the information with. After only three days, she had grown attached to his company.

Graham was smart. Thoughtful of other people's feelings, over his own sometimes. With that in mind, she hoped that no matter what Caterina told him, he would still come after her.

She changed tube lines and sat to think of where the next clue could possibly take her and the sadness dissipated as excitement rose up again. As the train pulled into her final destination, the anticipation was soon all she could think about. She climbed out of the underground station and headed towards the hotel.

When she made her way down the block, she realized that the paparazzi with their cameras had not left the front stoop. She crossed the street to get around them and then ran as quick as she could to the alley that led to the back door and into the kitchen.

She walked through the door with a smile at her small success. That's when she hit a hard body and stumbled back, but his strong arms came around her waist and kept her from falling. She looked up, confused. It was like seeing a ghost since despite her wishes, she hadn't expected to see him.

"Graham?"

He smiled charmingly.

Damn he is cute.

He laughed, his smile brightening, nodded, and helped her into the upright position.

"Well, now she's here," Fanny said, obviously answering a question Graham had asked before Lizzie had arrived.

"You two have fun," Fanny said, spun one of her knitting needles in her hand, and walked back to the front desk.

"What are you doing here?" she asked, trying to contain her excitement that he was really there.

"Caterina told me what you said. I needed to hear it from you," he said slowly.

"Whatever she said is probably the truth." Lizzie nervously adjusted her bag on her shoulder and wrapped her arms across her chest. She tried to walk past him, but he turned and grabbed her arm, pulled her back to face him. But he pulled too hard and she again collided with him.

His arms went back around her waist as he also stumbled from the impact.

She met his gaze as his darted around his face. She tried hard not to look him in the eye, afraid he'd see the truth there. Afraid that he'd see how glad she was that he was there.

#

Graham's gaze skipped over her face. Her irises were so small that the pools of blue were barely visible, but that confirmed to him that she wasn't telling the truth about what had happened with Caterina. But as he held her, her gaze slid to his and her pupils slowly widened confirming that she liked that he was here. That she liked being close to him.

"Tell me what you said," he whispered with a demanding undertone.

"What does it matter what I said?" she whispered back.

His gaze dipped down to her lips as she spoke and warmth filled him. He had to step back to give himself space and control what he was feeling for her.

"It just does," he said, shoving his hands into his jean pockets to keep from reaching for her again.

"I just said you didn't need to help anymore. Your girlfriend doesn't want to be a part of it and it's very obvious she doesn't want you helping either. So I told her you don't need to help me anymore." The whole time she spoke, she avoided his gaze and played with the hem of her shirt.

He snapped his fingers, realizing Caterina had stretched the truth of Lizzie's words.

Lizzie's head jerked up and he noted her confusion. He explained. "Caterina told me what you said, but I had a feeling she wasn't being totally honest about why you'd said it."

"Oh, okay." She turned to head up the stairs and he followed her.

"Are you going to open the next clue? I want to see it, too," he said.

She stopped on the stairs and he did as well. She just looked at him and said, "No. No way. Then you would still want to help and Caterina--"

He cut her off. "Screw Caterina."

"I bet you already do," she said with a wink as she continued up the stairs.

"That's not what--" he began, but blushed brightly, knowing he couldn't finish that sentence as she was just kidding him.

They walked up to her room and when she opened the door, she threw her bag on the bed and headed over to the bathroom.

He felt odd just standing there, but he wanted to see the clue. Badly.

He marched over to the backpack, pulled open the flap, and was about to yank the drawstring open when Lizzie returned and said, "What do you think you're doing?"

"I want to see the clue. I promise I will walk away and you will never hear from me again. If that's what you really want." He felt like a kid with his hand caught in the cookie jar.

She slapped his hands away from her bag and sat down on the bed across from him, "Are you sure you can stay away once you see the clue?" She was serious and he knew it.

He nodded, although he suspected it would be harder to stay away from her than anything to do with the clue.

"Promise," he said and sat pretzel-style on the bed, jumping slightly on the bed, and biting his bottom lip with impatience.

"You go from dad to child in a matter of seconds. Impressive Benjamin Button," she teased and laughed. She undid the tassels of the backpack, reached in and then pulled out the small frame with the photo. She examined the frame to see how it opened, but Graham was too impatient to wait any longer.

"Oh, come on, Lizzie." He yanked the frame out of her hands and hit the glass against her bedside table.

"Graham! That frame was antique!" she hollered.

"Were you planning to return it to the pub?" he raised an eyebrow with a laugh.

"Actually, yes. Now I'll have to get a replacement glass for it," she replied and he realized she was totally serious and kind of admired her for her honesty.

She reached across the bed to grab a pair of latex gloves from a bag sitting on the bed.

"You really came prepared."

"I didn't know what kind of shape the letters would be in and didn't want to damage them anymore." She took the frame back from him, dumped the glass into a wastepaper basket, and gently peeled the photo from the frame.

"There's no note," she said, disappointed when she removed the back of the frame. She dropped the frame to the bed and stared hard at the picture, lifting it to her face to examine it.

That's when he saw the writing.

"Lizzie."

She moved the photo away from her face and he pointed to the back of the photo.

She flipped the photo around and her face lit up. She squealed and shot to her feet on the bed and began to jump and dance around.

He laughed at how spontaneously joyful she was. It quickly spread to him and warmed his heart. She jumped one last time before landing on her knees and reaching over to hug him. The force of her embrace caused him to lean back on his hands and bring her full against him. He choked out another laugh to hide his reaction and she let go and sat back onto the mattress.

"Read it so I can leave," he joked and disappointment filled her gaze.

Was she actually upset he would no longer be nagging her to help? Could it be that she actually enjoyed his company?

She sat up straight, like a proper young lady, and began to read.

"*You, sir or madam, are very much worthy of this challenge. This image was published in the obituary for my dear friend, Ann. I wanted people to remember her long after she was gone and I'm glad to see that you have recognized her photo. That means she still lives on as I wanted. It also means that you have accomplished this true test of your deductive skill set.*

My astonishment at making your way to this third location and clue is difficult to explain. For me to not have a word is simply unheard of.

No matter, onto your next location. For a place where I despised, repulsed, and lost all creative thought, after my family and I were finally rid of the place it became inspired. One quarter will not shame you or your family once you arrive. The walls of homes can speak more than a novel.

Best of luck,
Jane"

"Wow! Amazing. Absolutely amazing," he said with a pleased grin. It was not only about the letter, but also about the delicate and precise way in which Lizzie read every word, as rich as the pages of an actual Austen novel.

"She was an amazing woman." She smiled and continued to scan the note several times with a face filled with admiration. Then looked up at him, kind of confused and almost expectant.

He looked around, trying to find the reason for her attitude. "What?" he asked, finding nothing out of the ordinary in the room.

"Shouldn't you be leaving? You heard the clue," she said nervously.

"Right. Right. That's what I said." He climbed off her bed slowly. Reluctantly.

"Thanks, Lizzie. For what it's worth, the past three days were a thrill. I hope the journey turns out to be everything your mother and you want it to be."

He walked to the door, but stopped and turned back. "But if you do decide you need my help."

He reached over to grab the hotel pen and pad, and quickly scribbled his number down. "Give me a call."

"Thanks," she said and for a moment it seemed as if she was going to change her mind, but then she motioned to the photo. "I'm just going to study this for a little bit and then return it to the pub,"

He nodded, walked out and down the stairs to the lobby. Fanny came out of the hotel's small living room where she had been knitting to meet him.

"How did it go, Graham?" she asked, holding her latest project in her hands.

"How did what go?" he asked, not really wanting to share what was happening.

"You looked pretty eager to speak with Lizzie. I assumed it was something important." She smiled with a glint of amusement in her eyes.

"Oh, no. It was nothing dire. But…um…I probably won't be around much anymore. It was lovely meeting you. I'll recommend this place to all my friends and family who come to visit," he said with a warm smile. He really did like Fanny and hoped the hotel would soon be doing better.

"Oh," she said, the one word filled with disappointment. "Well, thank you, Graham. Your kindness is always appreciated."

She walked around the counter to sit back at the desk, set aside her knitting and grabbed a thick novel. She began reading, reminding him of the first time he had seen her.

He snuck out the back door again, ran to his car, and sped home.

He kept repeating what he could remember of the clue to himself over and over, trying to figure out what it could mean. No matter what he had told Lizzie, he did want to help and be a part of her adventure.

If she would let him, that was.

When he pulled up to his home, the bedroom light was on. *Caterina must be waiting for him.*

He climbed up the stairs to his door and once inside, he walked slowly to the bedroom, not as eager to see Caterina as he had been with Lizzie.

Caterina was in bed, looking at a magazine.

She hopped off the bed and ran up to him. "Oh, thank God! I was worried."

"Why? You knew where I was going." He hugged her and pecked her one cheek awkwardly.

"So are you done with all of that Lizzie-Jane nonsense?" She pouted and gave him her puppy dog eyes since she clearly sensed his upset.

"It was not nonsense, but yes. You were right that she didn't want my help anymore."

He jerked off his shirt, unbuckled his belt and shucked off his pants.

He climbed into bed and she followed suit, snuggling close to him. Her mountains of thick hair covered his chest and he tried to swat all the stray hairs from tickling his nose, but it was impossible. He tried to ignore them and focus on sleep, but even as he tried to rest, images of Lizzie reading the clue and what it meant swirled around in his mind.

Caterina's soft snore told him she was already asleep, but he was awake long after, thinking of Lizzie and the clue.

Thinking of the clue over and over.

Thinking of Lizzie.

Chapter 15

Going it alone?

A knock on her door early the next morning dragged her from sleep. She stumbled to the door and was surprised to see that it was not Fanny bringing her morning tea and biscuits, but Graham.
"Graham what--"
He cut her off. "I broke up with Caterina last night."
"What?" she asked, confused and half-asleep still.
He wrapped his arms around her waist and pulled her against his hard chest. She had memorized the feel of that chest the night before when she had tumbled against him in her excitement. It felt just as good this morning.
She smiled nervously and asked, "Why are you here?"
"To be with you of course," he said with his boyish smirk and before she could reply, his lips crashed onto hers.
She shot up in bed, breathing heavily, and warm with sweat.
It had just been a dream. Just a dream, she thought as she glanced around her empty room.
A knock came on the door and she let out a small scream of mixed surprise and excitement.
"Lizzie, are you ok?" Fanny asked from the other side of the door, her voice muffled by the thick wood.
"Oh, Jesus," Lizzie whispered. "Yeah, I'm fine. Just a bad dream."
"Just came to bring you some tea and biscuits. May I come in?"
"Yes, of course," she called out, climbed out of bed, and opened the door.

Fanny strolled in with the tea service and walked over to the windows to open the curtains. Light poured into the room, causing Lizzie to squint and throw up her hand to block the harsh rays.

"Well, now that you've kicked Graham out, what will you do with your day?"

"I didn't kick Graham out…wait. How do you know he isn't helping me anymore?" she asked and grabbed one of Fanny's delicious scones off the plate.

"He told me last night as he was leaving," she said.

She poured a cup of tea and handed it to Lizzie. "That boy was a true friend, Lizzie."

She said it the same way Lizzie's mother would have. It made her feel both uncomfortable and soothed at the same time.

"I know, Fanny. But his girlfriend has been against him hanging out with me from the very first. I'm not about to get in-between that," Lizzie said around a mouthful of blueberry scone.

"That girl," Fanny shook her head. "For such a smart boy, he certainly made a bad decision picking that one."

"Fanny!" Lizzie laughed and nudged Fanny's shoulder playfully.

"You cannot disagree," Fanny said with a smile. "But anyway, enjoy your day. I will be busy filling up every room left in this place with frenzied fans. Be careful, they don't know who you are yet."

Fanny walked to the door and shut it behind her.

Lizzie ambled to the bed with her tea and scone and grabbed the clue from the night before to examine it. Amazingly, she knew the location even before she finished re-reading the clue.

Jane Austen had lived for several years in Bath and had despised every waking moment of it. She had written letters to her sister about how much she wished she were away from the place. But Bath was a fairly big city. There was more to the clue she needed to figure out.

Bzz. Bzz. Bzz.

Her phone vibrated on the bedside table, demanding attention. She reached for it and saw that it was her father calling. She jumped up and answered happily, "Daddy!"

"Jellybean! I got your message. How goes the traveling?" He sounded just as happy to hear her voice as she was to hear his.

"Amazing. I've found two clues. Dad this journey is real!" she gushed to him, so excited to tell him everything.

"That is great honey. Mom would never kid about Jane Austen," he said with a laugh. "Have you seen any of the sights yet? I have always wanted to know if Big Ben was really as big as it looks in movies."

"No. Not yet."

"Jellybean…you're in a foreign country! Your first *ever* foreign country! You need to take a break from all the clue hunting and go enjoy what is right outside your door. See what the world has to offer."

"I know dad. You sound like Graham." She shook her head and chuckled.

"Who's Graham?" her father asked. "Do I have to come over there?" he teasingly added.

"No, Dad. He's just a friend. I bumped into him one day and he ended up being really helpful." Even though it had only been a few days since they'd met, she already felt reminiscent.

"Well ask him to take you out then. Not on a date – I mean – you know. . ." her father said, obviously flustered.

She laughed at his awkwardness when it came to Lizzie and the opposite sex. Even at her age, he never liked to bring up her dating life.

"Dad, it's a bit complicated. He is kind of a pretty famous pop star and his girlfriend really dislikes me and the fact he has been helping me." She tried to boil it down to the basics for him.

"A pop star? Well, look at you Lizzie Price! How did you fall into that?" he joked.

"He caught me sneaking into a library for the second clue and nagged me to help. But his girlfriend was instantly not fond of me so last night brought our very brief friendship to an end," she explained as quickly as possible. She really didn't feel like rehashing the story.

"She's just threatened by you, Lizzie. That's all. But it also gives you more reason to go out. You need to find a replacement for your brief friendship with Mr. Pop Star. Plus a clear mind, some fresh air, could really help you figure out the new clue. Not to mention that I want to see some cheesy tourist photos of you at the sights. Pushing the London Eye, pinching Big Ben…"

She laughed hard at how lame her father could be as he finished with, "And as your father you need to listen."

"Using the dad card. Nice." She rolled her eyes. "Fine, Dad. For you, I will be a tourist."

"Great! Bye Lizzie, I love you."

"I love you too, Daddy." She smiled, keeping a brave face and tone in her voice for her father. She hung up the phone and climbed into the shower before dressing to face the day.

A day without Graham.

#

Graham sat with the rest of the boys for their weekly breakfast at Nick's flat and munched on his fruit bowl and toast.

"Graham, mate, where have you been the past few days? Saw your tweet about being at some dive bar in Holborn?" Nick asked.

"We went to visit a friend and it got chaotic." He said past the chunks of fruit in his mouth.

"Oh? Someone we know?" Emmet asked with a nudge.

"No. She's just a new friend," he said with a small laugh.

"She? Caterina is ok with you having a friend who is a girl? She almost tore you apart for hugging Kara and her band mates," Nick said with surprise.

"She wasn't thrilled and she scared her away. So I'll not be seeing Lizzie anytime soon."

"Lizzie?" Emmet asked.

Graham nodded and Emmet continued with his questions. "As in the girl who has been staying at that hotel you and Caterina were at this weekend?"

Again Graham nodded and ate some more of his breakfast, his gaze focused on the bowl of fruit before he finally looked around the table to see all the boys looking between each other, but never looking at him. They smirked, nodded, and laughed as if sharing some private joke.

Graham was frustrated. "What? What are you boys going on about?"

"Nothing. It's just odd you were with both of them," Christian said with a smirk and continued. "In an unknown hotel." He winked.

Nausea filled his gut. "Oh no, mate!"

Graham tossed a piece a toast at Christian. "I am so not you!"

Graham pushed his food away thanks to how disgusted he was feeling. "We were meeting up with Lizzie to go to the pub and had to sneak out the hotel. Lizzie is just a nice girl we ran into," he said and smiled.

"You say that about every girl. Even our fans. There has to be something different about her. Or just more to her," Nick said, pointing out the obvious.

Nick was always the one who could read him like a book. He hoped, in this one instance, Nick was oblivious to what was actually going on with him. Graham sure as hell did not want them suspecting that he had dreamed of kissing Lizzie's luscious red lips and moving down Lizzie's collarbone to her ample bosom. Especially not that he had done so last night as he had laid in bed with Caterina.

"You like her don't you?" Nick spit out, his eyes wide with surprise.

Every single pair of eyes was now looking at Graham and the boys had all frozen in their positions, waiting for his answer.

"What?" he scoffed, trying to laugh it off.

"I saw your eyes. You were hoping I couldn't read what you were thinking. Because it's just not right. You have a girlfriend, but you have another girl on your mind."

Nick scooped up some more of his breakfast to shove into his mouth.

Graham studied all the boys' reactions. They all seemed to have come to the same conclusion. Unable to sit there any longer and give them even more to talk about, he tossed his napkin on his plate, and shot to his feet. "You boys are mental! I have a girlfriend, whom I love deeply, and I plan to spend the rest of my life with her. Lizzie *was* a friend. A friend, who after three days, is no longer part of my life."

He stomped to the door, grabbed his jacket, and left Nick's flat. Hurrying to his car, he climbed in and drove home. When he pulled up to his house, he looked at his phone and was disappointed to see no missed calls or new text messages. He didn't know what he had expected.

Lizzie had been against him helping her out from the get go.

When he got out of the car and started to walk up the steps, Caterina burst through the door and skipped down the steps toward him.

"Hey, honey," she said, smiling as the met him on the stairs.

"Where are you going? I thought we were spending the day together?"

"I know. I know. But the production company called and they set up extra rehearsals for the tour. I need to get down there right away."

She swung her exercise bag over her shoulder and pecked him on the cheek as she rushed past him and down the rest of the stairs. As she reached her car, she turned to look at him and called out, "I will see you tonight. Promise to make it up."

Her sexy smile told him just what she had in mind for making it up.

"Okay…" he said, his voice trailing off as she hopped into her car and drove off.

He walked into the house and threw his stuff on the small table next to the door. Strolling through his now empty house, he wondered what he could do with his suddenly free time.

Jane Austen's clue quickly came to mind.

He went into his large office, sat down on the executive leather swivel chair, and quickly typed in the main words from the clue into the search engine. Grabbing a pad of paper and pen, he started to write down some of the main search items that caught his eye, hoping that when he went back to the paper to review them, it would make sense.

As he worked, he wondered if Lizzie was also working on the clue. Whether she had already solved it or if she still needed help.

Hoping it was the latter, he kept working at it, telling himself that it was all about helping a friend.

Ignoring thoughts of kissing Lizzie and what his band mates would say if he admitted what he was really feeling for his newfound friend.

#

Lizzie hopped on a train into central London, backpack in hand and carrying her map while she roamed around, enjoying the sights and sounds. Parliament. Westminster Abbey. Big Ben. Buckingham Palace.

She visited as many touristy places as her legs were willing to walk her to.

She had to thank her father for making her do this. She loved everything she saw. She knew her father would love the photos she took and that they would make him laugh.

When she stepped onto the London Eye and it climbed higher and higher, the view stunned her with its beauty. She looked toward the heavens and whispered, "Thanks, Mom."

As she walked back to the hotel, she noticed that the crowd of paparazzi had gotten larger. She had assumed that with Graham not being there the crowd would have died down. She again snuck in through the back door and marched to the front desk to say hello to Fanny. That's when she saw a group of boys standing around the counter, talking to her.

They all turned as Lizzie entered the room and they looked familiar. When she took a few steps closer she realized exactly who they were. They looked almost exactly like their photos on the album cover. Standing in front of her were the rest of Graham's boy band – Greetings From Victoria.

Chapter 16

Meeting the Boys

"Lizzie, these boys came to see you." Fanny said and walked around the desk to stand next to Lizzie, obviously feeling as if Lizzie needed some moral support.

"Hi, Lizzie, I'm Nick." The quaff-haired, half-sleeve tattooed boy put out his hand for her to shake. She grabbed it and soon all the boys were also waiting for her to introduce themselves.

"Emmet."

"Christian."

"Jude."

She walked down the line to shake each of their hands. "It is nice meeting all of you," she said, but then shook her head as she looked at all of them. "What are you guys doing here exactly?" she said in almost a whisper, still shocked by their visit.

Nick leaned in to whisper back, "Is there some place we can talk in private?"

"Yeah, sure. We can go to my room." She pointed to the stairs and they boys all began to walk up. Lizzie turned to Fanny and said, "Thanks, Fanny."

"You are very welcome." Fanny winked and looked each boy up and down as they made their way up the stairs. She looked over at Lizzie and then nudged her to follow them.

Lizzie trudged up the stairs and soon was walking past the boys, realizing she had to lead the way. When she went down her hallway and entered her room, all of them stood awkwardly at her door.

"You can come in," she said with a laugh.

They all piled into her room and sprawled all along the edges of her bed.

She dropped her stuff by the desk, sat, and faced them. Leaning forward, she brought her hands to her lips in a prayer-like formation and asked, "Why am I being graced with your presence right now?"

When they remained silent, she eyeballed each of the boys, silently pressing for an answer. They all looked at each other uneasily until Nick spoke up, apparently the one who would be answering for the group.

"We need you to keep doing whatever it is you're doing with Graham," Nick spit out.

"Yeah," Christian said with a wink.

"Shut, it Christian," Jude said and elbowed him. Christian nudged him back and the two extremely attractive boys interacted and laughed like little kids.

Nick rolled his eyes at the two young men now causing a massive ruckus and explained his earlier statement. "It's only been three days since you met him and his attitude has changed. He's back to being the old Graham."

"Before Caterina dumped him, slept with half of London, and then came crawling back," Emmet said with contempt.

He had a different accent than the other boys.

Possibly Irish, she thought. His hair looked different then in the album covers. Shorter and darker, bringing out the pale color of his skin although he was still as good looking as the other young men.

Of course, she was more taken aback by the new information she had gained from him than by their combined attractiveness. Although it did make sense considering the ways she had seen Graham and Caterina react to each other over the last few days.

When one of them wanted to be close, the other moved away. Caterina always seemed to want be touching Graham, while Graham seemed to try to distance himself without making it too obvious. Even Lizzie was able to tell he didn't trust Caterina, but she hadn't known the reason why until Emmet's statements.

"Wow. Way to put me on the spot here, guys I just met two minutes ago," she said and sat.

"I know it sounds crazy, but please hear us out," Jude chimed in. "We go on tour in a little less than a month. Our first European tour and it's a big deal for us."

"I get that you're going on a big tour. Continue," she said, rolling her eyes and caught Nick hiding his smirk.

"We need him at his peak so fans can see the real Graham. The one everyone likes. Being with you is giving us back Graham in his prime. And we know it's none of our business, but what exactly are you doing with him?" Jude asked nervously.

"Is that all you two think about?" Nick scolded, any hint of playfulness gone from his voice.

Christian and Jude almost cowered and the room became deadly silent. Lizzie decided it would have to be her who broke the tension.

"It's hard to explain. It's kind of a secret," she said.

Christian and Jude perked up, which she quickly shut down with, "No. Not that like that."

She pointed at both of them and they both looked dutifully punished. She glanced at Emmet and Nick, who seemed to be the more mature ones, and explained. "Graham was helping me solve a mystery my mother left me. He's a lot smarter than I would have ever given him credit for being a boy band member and all," she said with a smirk.

"Please let him continue to help," Nick practically begged, putting his hands out pleadingly.

"While I appreciate what he's done, it's really not up to me whether he continues to help or not." She met their wide-eyed gazes and since it looked like they needed her to continue with her explanation, she rolled her eyes and did so.

"Caterina isn't fond of the idea of Graham helping. To appease her, I told her that he didn't have to help me anymore, although I was hoping he still would. She told him that and so now, he's not helping me anymore."

"We can change that," Emmet said, shot up, and grabbed Lizzie's hand. Soon the rest of the boys followed suit, coming to their feet and standing in front of her expectantly.

"What are you guys doing?" she said with a nervous glance at them.

"Just come with us." Emmet pulled her out of the room and they were all soon rushing her down the stairs as quickly as they could. They hurried her past Fanny, who waved and said her goodbyes, before they raced out the front door and were instantly bombarded by the press.

They waved and smiled and pushed through the mass of reporters, Emmet still gripping Lizzie's hand tightly as he urged her into the car and the rest of the boys crammed themselves into the back seat.

"I feel like I am being kidnapped," she said, sitting stiffly in the passenger seat.

"Nothing of the sort. Of course, you know some girls would die to be in your position," Nick said and shot her a smile as he drove.

It only took about fifteen minutes before they pulled up in front of a gorgeous light blue house. It looked like one of the postcards she had seen of Portobello Market in the souvenir shop earlier that day. The boys hopped out of the car, but Lizzie was slow to exit onto the quiet and very nice residential street.

As they walked up the stairs, she prayed that if it was Graham's house, he wouldn't be upset about their unexpected visit.

#

Graham had spent the latter part of the morning researching Lizzie's next clue. He'd taken a break for a workout in his home gym and then a nap before heading back to his office and the clue.

He had gotten so lost in the research, that hours passed before he heard the front door closing and Caterina's voice echoed through the house as she called his name.

He glanced out the windows of his office and realized the sun was already setting. He rubbed his eyes, closed his Internet browser, and went to greet Caterina in the hallway.

She had dropped her bag in the foyer of the house and stood there, looking movie star beautiful and yet inside, he felt nothing. Especially nothing like he felt when Lizzie was around.

Caterina made an annoyed face as he stopped a few feet away from her obviously not all that excited to see her.

She sashayed up to him and hungrily covered his lips with hers. She dropped her fingers to his belt buckle and yanked it open and he stumbled forward a bit. A second later, she slowly and leisurely traced the waistband of his jeans and then drifted her hands down to his pelvis. Her gentle touch threw him off. She was usually more aggressive.

He moaned lightly, but pulled away from her and met her gaze. She looked put off, maybe even uncertain, but then he said, "I love you."

He didn't know why he said it. Maybe it was to prove it to himself, but she didn't reply or return his admission. She just smiled and kissed him harder. A second later, she jumped up and wrapped her legs around his waist.

Graham was only human and couldn't resist the invitation. He walked them over to the couch, laid her down on it and a second later, his shirt was flying off and onto the floor.

Caterina was reaching for his belt buckle again when a loud pounding on the door stopped them. He was about to ignore it when his cell phone beeped with the ringtone he had assigned to Nick.

"Damn," Graham said and pushed off the couch to go answer the door.

#

A shirtless Graham flung open the door, clearly angry as he gazed at all of the boys standing on this front step and crushing her dream that he wouldn't be upset to see her.

At that moment, however, any girl would look his torso up and down in amazement and Lizzie was exactly like every other girl. He had the right lean cuts on his stomach, outlining his abdominals, and the sharp V's low on his hips that just enhanced everything on his well-shaped body.

Pleasantly shocked, she couldn't stop from looking at him, although she didn't know why she was so surprised about just how gorgeous he was without his shirt on and his pants half-off. Even with his clothes on she'd had a clue that he was well-built.

She glanced at him as his gaze skipped over each of the boys and then landed squarely on her. When their eyes met, his went wide and he turned back to the boys and angrily said, "What are you guys doing here? With her?"

"Great to see you too, Mate. We would love to come in," Jude said and pushed past Graham. The rest of the boys followed him in.

Lizzie walked up to Graham and apologized. "I'm really sorry. They didn't tell me where we were going," she said, although she had kind of suspected where it was. "They just showed up at the hotel--"

Graham raised his hand to silence her and smiled politely. "No need to apologize. I know what they're trying to do. I'm just sorry they're dragging you into it." He stepped aside and invited her in with a sweep of his hand. "Welcome to my home."

She stepped past him, trying very hard not to, once again, give his torso a look over. She heard all the boys making a lot of noise and followed the sounds, making her way through Graham's house. She was really impressed with the layout of his home and the office she walked into was gorgeous.

A large mahogany desk sat on one side by windows that looked out into a garden. Plush couches and chairs were on the other side. Above the couch was their first gold album, although given their growing popularity, she suspected there would soon be more gold or even platinum albums there. There were also photos of all the boys, some from when before they started to get famous and were just a bunch of local guys from the neighborhood.

Graham walked in behind her and shut the door. He pulled out a chair for Lizzie and then wheeled his own desk chair over to sit beside her.

"What can I do for you guys?" he asked, getting straight to the point.

She understood his concern because she had also been bombarded by the arrival of his four band mates and had not been expecting to be in this current situation. If anything, she had wanted to try and avoid creating any tension between Graham and Caterina.

"Where's Caterina?" Nick asked.

"Probably upstairs by now. You did kind of interrupt us," Graham bit out angrily.

"You need to help Lizzie," Nick said in quick response.

Lizzie suspected that Nick was worried that Caterina would come down at any moment and he clearly did not want her to hear this conversation.

Graham shot her a surprised look and she quickly explained. "They know nothing about the mystery other than the fact you were helping me with something."

Graham looked back at his friends. "Why? Why do I need to help her?"

All four of the young men burst into explanations all at the same time, urging Graham not only to help her, but to reconsider what he had been doing with himself lately and how that had been affecting them.

Lizzie decided it was best not to listen at that point since it was about personal things between the four in which she had no part. Trying to avoid the discussion between the young men, she glanced around his office and when she spun her chair towards his desk, a book caught her eye.

Jane Austen's *Persuasion*.

She walked over to the desk to see exactly what he had been doing with the book. As she stood there, she noted all the scribbled notes that Graham had taken and the way the pages on the book were dog-eared, as if to mark off spots in the book.

She was so involved with trying to figure out what Graham had been doing, that she had no clue at all that the boys had all ceased conversation until their shadows fell over the papers on the desk.

Her gaze shot up to see all of them staring at her. Except Graham who stood by, looking decidedly uncomfortable about her discovery.

"What is all this?" Emmet asked, grabbing the book.

"It's nothing," Graham finally chimed in and pushed through them to clear off his desk.

"Graham," she whispered as she tried to stop him from hiding all the hard work he had done.

"It's nothing, Lizzie," he shot back quickly and defensively. He grabbed all his notes and the book and shoved them into a drawer.

"Graham...Oh, hey boys," Caterina said with fake surprise as she walked into the room in what Lizzie could only assume was Graham's shirt.

When Caterina saw Lizzie, her attitude changed drastically. "Lizzie," she said, her tone as cold as ice.

"I wasn't planning on coming here, Caterina. The boys--"

Nick cut her off immediately. "You don't need to defend your presence here."

"Actually, she does, Nick. She said she was done with us and our helping her with her little scavenger hunt." Caterina looked away from Nick and directly at her. "Now you bring all the boys into this? Just so you can have all the attention?" Caterina spat with acid in her words.

"Caterina!" Graham warned. "Do not attack Lizzie. She had nothing to do with this."

Anger rushed through his face and he clenched and unclenched his fists. His chest rose and fell quickly, but then he got control and his anger dissipated as he said, "The boys brought her here to hang out. You know them and their jokes."

"She's our friend as well, Caterina. We have every right to bring her where we go," Christian said, wrapped an arm around her shoulder, and pulled her to him.

"And when did you even know she existed? This morning? Over your silly breakfast routine," Caterina said, fuming at their defense of her.

"And what if it was?" Nick asked. "It just means her personality is so appealing we became instant friends." He smiled at Lizzie and even though Caterina made her feel like the size of an ant when she talked to her, now she felt like an ant not worth squishing when Nick talked her up.

Caterina glanced at Graham as if he would back her cruelty.

He walked over to Caterina's side, looked at all the boys and then straight at Lizzie. Something in his gaze told her he was not happy with his own decision, but that he had no other choice.

Graham put an arm around Caterina as he spoke slowly and softly. "I think you should all leave."

Lizzie couldn't fail to see the snide smirk on Caterina's face. She ran out the room and all she could think about was how badly she wanted to wipe that smirk right off that pretty little face.

But she chose to be smart about her anger.

She simply hopped into Nick's car and waited until the boys slowly ambled out of the house, all looking as defeated as she had felt with the first glance Caterina ever gave her.

Chapter 17

Making amends

Graham woke to a mouthful of Caterina's red-gold hair. He tried to spit it out, but it only seemed to come right back since she lay plastered against him with her head tucked right up beneath his chin.

Deciding he probably should get up anyway, he tried to maneuver out of bed without waking her.

Success, he thought as he made his way down to his office where all the craziness had unfolded two nights ago.

He had not talked to the boys since that night and felt miserable every time he thought about it. And then he thought about the look on Lizzie's face as she dashed out of the room.

It made him angry to think about the way Caterina had manipulated him with a simple flick of the wrist. She had some power over him that he could never seem to break away from. He didn't understand why he had no control of himself whenever she was around and why he could never say no to her.   Not even when she was being downright mean.

He plopped into his leather chair and started up his computer, but suddenly remembered he had thrown all his research into a drawer.

Pulling out the information, he skipped over his notes and then began to read *Persuasion*. Page after page slipped by and he began to lose hope of finding out where in Bath this next clue could be found.

Maybe it wasn't Bath, he thought for a moment, although he was almost certain it was after finding some of Jane's letters online. She had talked about how much she had hated living there. It had to be the right location, but finding the exact spot now proved to be impossible. And he didn't even know if Lizzie had found the answer already which meant he was just wasting his time.

Footsteps sounded down the hall, but he was so involved in the book that he didn't stop reading.

"Graham? Where are. . .Oh," Caterina said and walked into his office.

"Did you want me to make something for breakfast?" She walked over, pushed her way onto his lap and began kissing his neck. He instantly became aroused. She always knew what spots to hit. The same spots that caused him to drop the book on the floor with a resounding thump.

The sound caused her to jump a little and rub even more against his turned on state.

She looked down at the book and frowned. "Jane Austen?"

She grabbed the book from the floor and shot off his lap. "Really, Graham? I thought you were done with this? You just can't let that little slag go and do her own thing!" she yelled as she threw the book at him and stormed out of the office.

He let out an annoyed huff. Going to talk to her while she was this riled up would only cause a scene that he didn't need. He slammed the book on his desk and walked over to an empty space in his office to do some pushups. They always helped him take his mind off of things.

Lizzie, Caterina, and the boys included.

As he counted his pushups, his phone buzzed several times, but he ignored it. When he finished, he grabbed his phone off his desk.

```
        J: Graham! Graham!
        E: You can say it once mate he will
see it.
        C: Graham! There Jude I helped you
out.
        N: You two are hopeless
        J: Graham look at your damn phone! We
want to talk to you!
```

He was relieved to see they weren't mad at him and quickly joined into the conversation.

```
        G: You boys are so childish! Why must
I reply to these messages?
        E: Hallelujah
        J: Yay! Hi Graham! We missed you
buddy.
        G: I saw you two days ago.
```

C: True. But we didn't leave on the best of terms. We wanted to make sure we are all good?

G: Of course we are. Caterina just seems to be really on edge lately. I apologize on her behalf.

E: Not to make matters worse, but we're not the ones who deserve the apology.

N: Agreed. Lizzie seemed right pissed after we dropped her off.

C: She nearly broke the door off its hinges getting back into her hotel.

Graham knew they were right, but he also knew Caterina would never apologize to Lizzie. Especially after this morning's little argument.

G: That is an impossibility mates. I just need to stay away from that situation.

C: Graham, you know you want to continue helping Lizzie. And we know as well. We also know Caterina is not the same girl you fell in love with three years ago.

J: Christian makes a valid point.

C: You sound surprised.

J: Because I am

C: Twat.

N: Boys…back to the matter at hand. Christian is shockingly right. After she left you and then came back she was different. And so are you. Think about it.

G: I know you boys are trying to help my relationship but they are my relationships to change.

E: We are just trying to help you mate. We want you to be happy.

G: I know Emmett. I just need to sort these kinds of things out on my own.

E: Well we are here for you.

G: I know. And I do appreciate it. From all of you.

He tossed his phone back on the desk and walked to the kitchen. Caterina was busy slamming cupboards, pots, and pans as she made breakfast. He watched her for a while, taking in her every move. She used to be elegant and seemed to float on air, but now her moves were more every day. Human-like. Just ordinary gestures instead of angelic motions.

He walked over to stop her from bashing another pot on the counter and turned her to face him. Her features showed an emotion he had not seen in a very long time: Vulnerability. She was truly upset and obviously worrying about something.

"I'm sorry," she said, shook her head and dipped it down to avoid his gaze.

He placed his finger under her chin and gently urged her face upward until their gazes met again.

"I'm not the one you should be apologizing to and you know it." He tilted his head and raised an eyebrow to make sure his point got across.

She said nothing, but nodded, kissed him softly, and walked out of the kitchen.

He took a deep relieved breath and began cleaning up the mess she had left.

Again.

#

Lizzie had been fuming when she had gotten back to the hotel.

Caterina certainly did not deserve the kindness Graham constantly gave her. He barely raised his voice, and by the end of an argument that was clearly Caterina's fault, he'd be comforting her.

Unable to understand or accept that kind of relationship, Lizzie had rushed to her room to immerse herself in the hunt for the next clue.

But no matter what she tried to focus on, her mind always went back to Graham and the research he had been doing.

Why had he chosen *Persuasion* over all the other Jane Austen novels based in Bath?

She had gone to her suitcase of books, pulled out her copy of *Persuasion* and begun to re-read the novel that very night.

After a day and a half of reading and researching, she was beginning to lose all hope of finding the next clue.

How could she have solved the first two so quickly, but have this third one seem to be so much more complicated?

As if on cue, the room phone rang, sparing her from more frustration. She grabbed and said, "Hi, Fanny."

"Hello, deary. Nick is here to see you. Shall I send him up?" Fanny whispered, probably so no one else in the hotel could hear her. The fans that had checked into the hotel in the past few days seemed to have ear like hawks and perked up whenever any of the boy's names were mentioned.

Lizzie had really come to appreciate Fanny in the last few trying days. Even though she was swamped with all the other rooms being full, she still came into the room every morning with scones and tea and she had made a point of guarding Lizzie's privacy and that of her guests.

"Thank you, Fanny. You can send him up."

Lizzie jumped off the bed to do a quick check in the mirror and make sure she looked presentable considering it was such an early morning call. As she finished combing her hair, a gentle knock came at the door.

She opened it and Nick rushed into the room to avoid being seen. She shut the door gently to avoid waking the other guests and asked, "Did anyone see you?"

"No. Luckily I think most of our fans don't wake up until noon," he said with a smirk and lifted up a small brown bag. "I got you some brain food although I have no clue what you're up to. I figured that with all the paperwork, books, and research looking stuff, you need to keep your mind sharp."

"That was so thoughtful, Nick. Thank you." She grabbed the bag and opened it. A banana and muffin greeted her eyes and a tempting aroma teased her nostrils. "This muffin smells amazing."

"It's from my favorite place," he said as he looked around the room and then out the window.

She assumed he was trying to see how many paparazzi had followed him, but then he walked back over to the stacks of papers on her desk. He grabbed a pile of her papers and held them up in the air. "Will you ever tell any of us what you are doing?"

"I'm searching for something that was left behind by someone special." She stayed vague while hopefully giving him a halfway decent answer.

"Something?" he said with another smirk.

"I literally have no idea what it is to tell you the truth. My mom sent me on this mission totally blindsided," she said with a laugh and peeled the banana as her stomach growled noisily. She hadn't eaten a thing since the night before.

"So is Graham like your assistant or something?" he asked, trying to crack a joke.

She laughed. "No, he's not. He just decided to tag along. I wasn't a fan of it from the beginning, but Graham didn't take no as an acceptable answer."

Nick continued to pace around the room, deep in thought.

"Nick?" she asked. As he faced her, she said, "Why are you here?"

"Yeah, I guess there was a reason for my being here, huh?" He sat on the edge of the bed.

She sat down next to him. "I may only have met you forty-eight hours ago, but I have to say I'm able to read you pretty easily."

They both laughed and then there was a comfortable silence until Nick said, "I wanted to apologize for throwing you into that mess at Graham's. I had a feeling Caterina would be there, but I was hoping she wasn't. I don't know why he stays with her."

"He loves her," Lizzie stated.

"He's a moron." Nick looked really upset by this realization.

"Umm…Nick," she laid an arm around his shoulders and hugged him playfully. "Do you love him?"

He shot off the bed. "Whoa, Lizzie. No. I'm happily in love with my girlfriend. I just care about him. He's like family. If he isn't happy, we're all not happy. You've made him the happiest we've seen him in months."

"*I* do not make him happy, the thrill of the hunt does," she corrected.

"Sorry. You're right."

"And we had this discussion last time you were here. Caterina doesn't want him doing this with me. I cannot convince them differently and I don't need to." She shoved a large piece of the muffin into her mouth.

"I understand. I don't agree, but I understand. I wish there was a way to change that." He stood and shoved his hands into the pockets of his distressed leather biker jacket.

She brushed the muffin crumbs off of her lap and stood as well. "I'm sorry I couldn't help more. I do hope your tour goes well."

She smiled, trying to lighten the mood. She was sorry that she couldn't help the boys, but she knew nothing would come of her feeling sorry.

"No need to apologize. And thank you for what you've done already. I should probably leave now before people start waking up." He took a step closer and pulled a piece of paper out of his pocket.

"What is this? A phone directory?" She laughed as she saw the list of phone numbers on the paper.

He smiled. "In a way. It's all our numbers. Just in case you need some help or you just need a friend to talk to. I wasn't lying when I said our first impression was that you were extremely friendly. We do like you and hope you'll keep in touch. Hope to maybe see you soon."

He wrapped his arms around her head and pulled her into a strong bear hug.

She instantly reacted, feeling amazed to have found another friend in a foreign country. When he stepped back, she smiled and grabbed her phone from the bedside table.

"I am putting them in as soon as you leave," she said and waved her phone in the air.

Nick went to the door, turned, and smiled weakly. She tried to give him her brightest smile to make him feel better, but he simply turned and snuck out of the room. She glanced at the list of numbers and went over to her bedside to place the numbers with Graham's. She would eventually put them in her phone as she had said, but now it was back to solving the next clue.

She sat back down on her bed and started reading where she had left off in *Persuasion*. A few more hours passed and she was growing tired. Her eyes had dropped closed for all of two seconds when her room phone rang again.

"Yeah, Fanny--"

"I couldn't stop her," Fanny said sharply.

"What?" A second later a loud knock came at her door.

She hung up the phone and since the room did not have a peep hole, she placed her ear to the door and asked, "Who is it?"

"Caterina."

Lizzie moved away and ripped the door open. Sure enough, there stood Caterina in all her fashion model glory.

"Can I come in?" she said abruptly.

Lizzie assumed it was because Caterina didn't want to spend any more time than she had to in the hotel, much less in the same room with Lizzie.

"What are you doing here?" Lizzie asked as she let Caterina into her room.

When the door shut, Lizzie realized how confining the space in the room was. Caterina paced around the room much like Nick had done only a few hours prior. She said nothing, just looked around at all the notes and paperwork.

Lizzie rubbed her arms uncomfortably and finally spoke. "Caterina. I don't know why you're here, but I guess I should apologize for the way I burst into your house two days ago. The boys never told me where they were taking me and I'm sorry they blindsided you."

She now knew how Graham could cave into her every whim. Caterina, without saying a single word, intimidated Lizzie to the point where she was apologizing for something she didn't really feel she needed to apologize for.

"The boys? They're your friends now?" Caterina sneered.

Lizzie shrugged and Caterina scoffed, "Don't flatter yourself, sweetie. They're using you to get rid of me. I know they're no longer my biggest fans, but I don't need their approval. I got what I want."

She walked towards Lizzie with angry determination to bring her down. Caterina gave Lizzie a once over and then said, "I don't know what Graham sees in you. You're so plain and boring."

"He sees nothing in me, Caterina. He's just interested in what I'm doing. If you came here to scare me or bring me down you should know it won't be easy."

"Really? You think? I didn't say more than two words when I walked in and already had you apologizing." Caterina posed like she had just won the fight and Lizzie realized she had a point.

"Is that why you came? To prove you could get me to apologize?"

Lizzie was now just as mad as she had been that night when she saw the evil grin plastered on Caterina's face. Lizzie was not about to let her win another battle.

"I actually came to apologize for my behavior. But you have one of those faces that just makes me hateful and angry."

Caterina took a step back as if finally realizing that Lizzie was a force to be reckoned with. She snatched the book off the bed and laughed, confusing Lizzie. When Caterina saw Lizzie's reaction, her smile disappeared and she said, "We're not okay with each other, but Graham seems to be drawn to your hunt. I mean he's such a nerd. Reading a book over having sex?"

She laughed bitterly and tossed the book close to Lizzie. "You two must be on the same page, because he has been reading that book secretly for the past few days."

"Caterina, I am really confused as to why you're here. You attack me, then say you came to apologize, and now you're talking about Graham. So if there really is no rhyme or reason as to why you're here, I would prefer you just leave."

"I came to ask that you let Graham help you. He's been so depressed the past two days and it really kills the mood. After he does this silly little hunt he's in a better mood. I know all the boys will find out about this soon," Caterina said and lifted the piece of paper with the phone numbers Nick had left.

"But I want to make ground rules for this hunt of yours. He's home every night by ten. We are celebrities after all and need to keep up appearances. You do not put him in any sort of danger, you will not be seen in public together if I'm not there, and when you finish this whole stupid scavenger hunt, you put this place and all of us behind you and never speak to the boys or us again. Deal?"

Without waiting for Lizzie's reply, she walked over to the door and turned to look at Lizzie.

Lizzie had no clue what to say, so she chose to just nod, and walked over to the door to open it for Caterina to leave.

"I will tell Graham that you'll be expecting him tomorrow morning."

Caterina rushed out of the room and Lizzie shut the door and slid down until her butt hit the floor, surprise in every bone of her body.

"What the hell just happened?"

Chapter 18

The hunt is on. . .again

When Caterina had left the house, Graham knew that he could get away with doing more Jane research. As he skimmed the book, one place in Bath seemed to be way more prevalent than the others and he quickly jotted down the location to make sure he looked it up later.

As he continued to read, he felt more and more guilty for continuing the hunt he promised he would stop helping with. He thought of what Caterina would say if she caught him, yet again, looking for answers. Her attitude had changed drastically and he had no clue why.

He didn't know what happened to her in the month they had separated, but the change was not something he was fond of.

Or maybe it was him that had changed.

In the past, he had never argued or disagreed with her. Now it seemed like it was all they ever did. Well, that and sex. And even that was not the same.

He thought about Lizzie and how she would react to him being able to find the new clue all by himself. Her smile stayed in his mind longer than he expected and when he shook off thoughts of her, he put down the book and decided to get some work done for the boys.

Hours passed as he wrote out new lyrics and tried out some quick melodies on his guitar. He was still at work when Caterina came back later that night.

Her arms were filled with dozens of shopping bags. Top Shop, Selfridges, Burberry, and UniGlo were among the largest. Shopping sprees were her way of dealing with stress and problems.

He followed her into the living room to see what the total damage was, but she quickly ran up to him, wrapping her arms around him and planting a harsh kiss on his lips. It was hungry and forceful. Her other stress reliever was now about to happen, but he stopped her and pulled away.

"Good day?" he asked.

She nodded and leaned closer to crash her lips against his again.

He stumbled from the weight change and pulled her arms from around him.

"That's good to hear," he said and took a step back.

She stared at him, surprised and he said, "Aren't you going to ask how my day went?"

She huffed in frustration, but answered. "I assume you continued your hopeless fascination with Jane Austen, and then tried to hide it from me."

She grabbed some of the bags off the couch and started towards the stairs, but tilted her head to her side in gesture of fake surprise. "Oh, which reminds me. Lizzie is expecting you tomorrow morning."

"No, I actually didn't spend the day," he began and then stopped, really shocked as her words finally sank in.

"Wait. What?" He grabbed a bunch of her bags and followed her up the stairs to his room.

When they walked into the bedroom, she tossed the bags onto the bed and began to unpack them as he rushed in after her.

"You told me I needed to apologize and I did. I knew that no matter what I did, you would still try and do the hunt yourself, so I decided to let you continue."

Let me continue! Was he a dog that she could control so easily?

Sure he stopped, sort of, because she had told him to, but that was because he could tell she felt threatened by Lizzie and he didn't want her upset. But she didn't have the final say in his decision-making, and the fact she thought she did, infuriated him.

"Way to make me feel like a man, Caterina," he said sarcastically and tossed the rest of her bags on the bed.

"What are you on about now?" She rolled her eyes as she grabbed hangers from the closet to hang her new purchases. He quickly stopped her, tossing the clothing back on the bed.

"You're letting me go? Letting me go! Why not give me a tracking collar in case I get lost?" he said and flung his hands up in the air in frustration.

"You're being ridiculous," she said with a laugh.

"You don't need a collar, you have a phone." She smirked and again reached for the hangers and her clothing. The smirk was so evil he couldn't control the anger that suddenly hit him.

He was almost scared of himself as he reached into his pocket and pulled out the phone. "This phone?"

She just watched him and said nothing.

He tossed the phone across the room and it hit the wall with a loud thud and shattered.

She let out a light scream as the phone dropped to the ground and broke into several more pieces.

He walked away from her and heat flooded his face as he yelled, "I don't even know who you are anymore! When did you become this person who I sometimes cannot even look at because of how callous you are! You used to be a girl whose smile lit up my whole world. I could never get enough of that girl."

Fear swept over her face and tears welled in her eyes. He knew what he was saying hurt, but he couldn't stop. "But now…now, when you smile, it's so fake I feel my heart break. You left me. For a month, you left me because, as you put it, I was 'too tame'. You somehow always make me feel like I was the one in the wrong."

Her eyes were wide as a tear fell to her cheek, but he wasn't moved by the sight anymore.

He walked back over to her and knew he had to keep some distance between them as he continued to talk. "I appreciate you going to talk to Lizzie and apologizing, but I think I need to continue this journey alone."

"What are you saying? Are you. . .are you breaking up with me?" Her voice escalated in volume and tone with every word she spoke.

"I think we need to learn about ourselves again. Maybe after all of this is done, we can meet up to try and give this a better start."

He tried to put his hands on her arms to comfort her, but she shrugged them off in disgust.

Her features were no longer filled with upset. Hatred twisted them as tears freely fell down her cheeks.

"Don't touch me," she hissed. "You're choosing her over me? That girl who doesn't love you and will never love you the way I do? You're going to be so sorry you left me."

She stalked to the bed, grabbed her shopping bags and mumbled something about coming back the next day to get the rest of her things.

She stormed out of the room and the front door slammed hard enough to shake the entire house.

He let loose a long breath and said to himself, "I cannot believe I just did that."

Shocked filled him as a smile crept onto his face.

He looked around the bedroom and realized how empty it looked without her, but it didn't feel empty. It felt normal. He was even more surprised about how much he enjoyed the emptiness and how much freer he felt.

Despite that, sadness filled him at the loss of something that had once been special to him.

He lay down on the bed, tired from the long day and the battle of emotions he had just experienced. Closing his eyes, he replayed the fight, but soon his thoughts turned to Lizzie and her hunt.

He couldn't believe that Caterina had gone to her. Had "let him" participate again.

Anger rose up in him again, but he quickly set it aside with one thought.

Tomorrow he'd see Lizzie again.

#

His alarm buzzed and with a heavy thwack he shut it off. He had fallen asleep in his clothing. As he rubbed the sleep from his eyes, it hit him once again what Caterina had said the night before.

Lizzie is expecting you tomorrow morning.

He shot up and grabbed his keys and a jacket. He raced past his office, but then it occurred to him he should bring his research with him. He shoved everything into his messenger bag and hurried out the door.

The Austen House awning hung happily from the front entry and he smiled at how good it felt to be back. The paparazzi went wild when he walked up the stairs, asking annoyingly probing questions. He pushed past them, but when he finally made it inside, he noticed the small sea of girls milling around the lobby and parlor.

Shit.

They all turned to see who had walked in and started screaming the moment they saw him. He walked straight up to them with a finger on his lips, trying to quiet her.

"Please, ladies," he said and motioned with his hands for quiet. "I'd prefer not to ruin the slumber of all the other guests."

Miraculously, they quickly hushed and nodded.

Fanny was at the counter as always, her kind gaze and loving smile directed at him and the sensation of being home rocketed through him. To say thanks, he hugged each of the girls in the lobby who had listened to his plea. They were half-crying, half-laughing quietly while asking for photos and autographs. As he finished, they scurried away with happy smiles and he looked over at Fanny in exhaustion.

"Graham, dear. You are so nice to all of your fans. How do you keep up with it all?"

"I can't, but I try my best. Is Lizzie in? I need to speak with her," he said with a kind smile.

Her eyes lit up with excitement as she grabbed the phone. "I can give her a ring. First your band mate, then your girlfriend, and now you in the flesh. You're finally back."

Her tone was delighted tone as she waited, but Lizzie didn't answer the phone. She hung it up and looked at him. "No answer. She must be out."

But as soon as Fanny finished, he heard quick footsteps and turned to look at who was coming down the stairs.

"Lizzie! I was trying to ring you," Fanny said as Graham stood there silently, unable to form words as he reacted to her presence.

Lizzie's long, dark brown hair cascaded in waves down to her loose fitting V-neck. That was covered by a red cardigan that fell to mid-thigh over her black leggings. With his full attention on her outfit, he noticed she wore tan knee high boots and when he trailed his gaze back up her body their gazes met. There was a shy smile on her face. The face he had only seen in dreams the past two nights.

He braved a small smile and walked over to meet her as she reached the foot of the stairs.

"Lizzie," he said, his voice cracking and rough.

"Graham." She smiled wider and looked around, as if searching for the boys or Caterina. Seeing that he was alone, she said, "I was just about to head to Bath."

He smiled and chuckled at how she tried to act as if they had never stopped talking. He rubbed his shaved head and said, "That's interesting. I was about to go there as well. Do you need a ride?"

"Thanks, that would be nice," she said with a nod and began to walk to the back of the hotel.

"Where are you going?" He pointed to the front door. "They already know you're friends with all of us."

She gave him a worried look and hesitated, but then spoke up. "Are you sure? Caterina laid down some ground rules last night and being seen without her is a huge no-no."

"Really?" He raised his chin, intrigued to find out what were some of the other rules Caterina had laid down. "What else did she tell you?"

Lizzie quickly rattled off some of the most ludicrous rules he had ever heard. "You have a curfew, I shouldn't put you in danger, and that once all of this is concluded my friendship with you and the rest of your gang is over."

"Sounds like Caterina." He shook his head. "Funny thing is, she doesn't run my life."

He walked over to her, grabbed her hand, and pulled her toward the front door.

"Let's go to Bath."

He jerked open the door and urged her toward his car, ignoring the paparazzi busily snapping photos and asking questions again. As he gently tugged on her hand, she wove her fingers with his and squeezed as if to reassure him she was really going with him. At his car, he opened the car door for her and then ran to the other side to climb into the driver's seat.

His gaze met his for the second time that day, but it felt comfortable and familiar. Peaceful, but exciting.

"To Bath?" he asked again just to confirm she hadn't changed her mind.

"To Bath," she replied as he pulled away from the curb and the frenzied paparazzi before they could give chase.

Chapter 19

A visit to Bath

His face showed determination as Graham drove them to their newest clue destination.

Lizzie couldn't keep from watching him as his jaw muscles tensed and relaxed the farther they got from London. The muscles in his arms bunched and loosened as he maneuvered the steering wheel. The same steering wheel his fingers were strumming away on in time to the music on the radio.

She was attracted to him. Maybe Caterina could sense it as well. After her dream, and seeing him shirtless, she couldn't deny the fact that she found him to be very attractive, but she also knew that the brain inside that gorgeous head was filled with knowledge. Knowledge that had helped her solve the clues.

Her mom would have liked him. She'd have called him a sweet boy and visually stimulating. Her mom would probably also tease her and say that if Lizzie didn't get in his pants soon, she would. Her mom had those moments.

"Where in Bath do you think we will find this next clue?" he asked, snapping her back to reality. She hoped he had not caught her staring and daydreaming.

She reached for her notebook from her bag and then turned her attention to the road. "I think our first stop should be the Jane Austen Experience. It's a replica house of how Jane would have lived in the area. It also could hold some more info about her day-to-day life in Bath."

"This house wouldn't happen to be on Gay St. would it?" he looked over at her for a quick second.

Shock hit her. "Yeah…how did you--"

A smirk played on his lips as she said, "You finished
Persuasion didn't you?"

He nodded enthusiastically and she couldn't help but laugh.

"What?" he said with a chuckle.

"Nothing. I'm just impressed. That's all." She smiled and then
asked the next most obvious question. "What are we going to do when
we get there? You're not exactly normal."

He smirked. "I think I'm exceedingly normal."

She laughed again and said, "You know what I mean. People
are bound to recognize you."

"We'll stay covered. Sunglasses, hat, jacket. You know, the
basic incognito wear. I should be fine." With a shrug, he added, "Fanny
told me one of the boys came to see you yesterday."

She could instantly tell that he was probing to find out which
one of the boys had visited and decided to have a little fun. "Yep. He
was super nice. Brought me a muffin and banana."

"What did you two talk about?" He shot a quick glance at her
before looking back at the road.

"Stuff. Nothing important. He wanted to know what I was
doing in the country and I wanted to know why he cared so much." She
finished the sentence by making fish lips and trying to find something
intriguing in the car. Anything to keep hiding her enjoyment at his
annoyance.

"And did he happen to know Caterina was going to make an
appearance?" he asked, gritting his teeth with obvious displeasure.

"No. He didn't seem to. Although you didn't seem to know
either, so she was not putting it on blast. She showed up several hours
after he had left."

"You know I want to know which one of the boys visited you,
right?" He did another quick glance her way.

"I do," she replied, struggling to keep a straight face.

"And are you ever going to tell me which of them came to visit?
Or are you going to make me guess?" He rolled his eyes through the
question.

"Why does it matter which one of them came? He didn't say
anything embarrassing about you, and he obviously didn't want you to
find out about it." She did have logic on her side, but at the end of the
day, as much as she enjoyed annoying him, she knew there was no
reason to keep it from him.

"Ok, you win. It was Nick."

He stared at her with shock and she warned him with, "Eyes on the road, Graham."

From the corner of her eye she saw his head snap back toward the road. But she also caught the way he smiled with pleasure.

Apparently satisfied everything was cool, they continued the rest of the way in silence.

She enjoyed the sights of the farmlands along the sides of the road. Herds of sheep, goats, even horses pranced around the open land and she knew she would have to write about the drive. The silence was both calming and inspiring as she quickly penned her thoughts in her notebook. As she raised her head for a quick look at the road, she finally saw a sign announcing that Bath was straight ahead.

"Do you know the exact address of that Jane Austen Experience place?" he asked.

"I believe I scribbled it down in here." She skimmed through her notes and found where she had written it. "Yes. I do."

"Would you mind putting it into the GPS?" he asked politely.

"Sure, as long as you say please and thank you," she said with a teasing grin.

"Please and thank you," he repeated.

"Perfect." She leaned forward, entered the address, and the GPS quickly read out directions.

Lizzie watched as the houses began to get closer and closer and soon they were in the city. When the shops and pubs flew by she knew they were almost in the right location. She looked out the window as they entered a large traffic circle. Amazingly, half of the circle was a large building that was constructed along the curve of the circle and she snapped a quick photo with her phone.

As they went around the circle she caught a glimpse of the sign for the Jane Austen Experience.

"There!" she shouted just as the GPS announced that they were arriving at their destination. She bumped against the front dashboard as he stopped short in the middle of the road. Impatient drivers immediately honked at them to move on.

"Maybe we should find a place to park that's not the middle of a busy road," he kidded and continued to drive. She paid attention to every turn he made so that she would knew how to get back to the location. When he finally parked, she climbed out just as he did. He grabbed a coat and a baseball cap from the back seat and tossed his sunglasses on.

She couldn't help but laugh at how ridiculous he looked since it was pretty warm out and overcast. "People will know you're trying to hide with that outfit. Lose the hat." She walked over to him and plucked the sleeve of his jacket. "Do you have any emotional attachment to this thing?"

He glanced at it before quickly shaking his head.

She grabbed her bag and shuffled through all the stuff in it. "Great."

She pulled out her pocket knife and he shot away from her. "Whoa! What are you doing?"

"Calm down, pretty boy," she teased. She took hold of the arm of the jacket and cut off one of the buttons. Then she frayed the elbows to give it an extremely worn look. Closing the pocketknife, she again went to her bag and found her tinted lip-gloss. She rubbed a layer of it on her index and middle finger before looking all around his torso and face to decide where to put the stain. She finally reached up to his neck to gently press the fingers along his pulse point. His heart was pumping fast. Almost as fast as her own. When she pulled her fingers away, a passable hickey print was left.

"Perfect." She smiled and rubbed her fingers on her leggings to get rid of the faint remnants of lip gloss. "No one will think *the* Graham Harris would step out in public with a hickey on his neck and a jacket that looks like it was stolen from a homeless man," she said, patting herself on the back and taking a small bow.

He glanced at his reflection in the car window and looked himself up and down, admiring her handiwork. "Thanks. I'll have to do this trick again."

"Don't thank me yet. We have to see if it works first," she said. Smiling, she hurried off along the route she had memorized to the Jane Austen Experience.

He jogged to catch up with her. "So do you think the clue is in this place?"

"No. She didn't live in this exact house, but she did live on the street. I'm hoping the people working there know exactly where she lived."

"You are bloody brilliant," he exclaimed.

It was so stereotypically perfect she couldn't help but let out a small laugh. "My first 'bloody' usage. I'm ecstatic."

"Make a list. I promise, by the time you leave, I will say every single word." He grinned playfully.

"Deal," she said, smiling back at him. She wanted to ask where Caterina was, but she had a feeling it would ruin the mood, and quickly decided against it. She kept her mouth shut as they made their way up to the front of the house.

Men and women dressed in 1800s apparel greeted Lizzie and Graham and welcomed them to enter. Inside, they were invited to sign up for the upcoming guided tour as well as check out the gift shop.

Lizzie bolted up the stairs to the gift shop and saw the mountains of books about Jane Austen piled all around. *History of Jane, Becoming Jane,* and so many more. Lizzie perused the stacks and quickly snatched up a few.

"What on earth are you doing?" he said and stopped her from grabbing another book off the shelf.

"These can help. Plus my Internet is spotty at best at the hotel. Do you know Fanny refuses to get Wi-Fi? I have to borrow someone's who lives next door." She placed the books on the counter and the cashier began to ring them up with shock and pleased surprise on her face.

"So *Pride and Prejudice and Zombies* is going to help us solve what exactly?" He pulled the book from the pile.

She grabbed it back from him and said, "This one's for enjoyment."

The total for the books climb steadily and way too quickly. She grabbed her wallet from her backpack to pay, Graham placed his card into the chip and pin machine.

"What are you doing?" she asked and tried to push him away from entering his pin.

"You say they'll help, so we can both use them. Plus I can write this off as an expense from the band. I promise I'll let you pay for the next immense amount of books purchased." He smiled as with one hip bump, he pushed her aside playfully. He entered his pin and the woman handed him the receipt and the two large bags of books.

He grabbed them and grinned at her and Lizzie was once again in la-la land, thinking about how generous and kind he was being to a girl he had met barely a week ago. He had a heart larger than his chiseled chest and it always showed. He was a curve ball of emotions to her. He made her happy, annoyed, frustrated, cared for, and most importantly, he made her feel like she had a friend.

And friendship would be the only emotion she would be able to feel for him.

She took one of the bags from his hands to help him carry them and thought about how lucky Caterina was to have him love her. But Caterina was so superficial that she could never understand and take his full amount of love for her into consideration.

"What's next?" he asked. His smile was so wide his face crinkled from it, but it didn't detract from his good looks at all and she tried to memorize all those little creases and dimples and beauty.

"The tour," she said, finally looking away. "Hopefully we'll be able to ask enough questions that we can get info as to where the next clue is." She walked over to the sign-in sheet and wrote in their names for the next available slot.

"Great. While we wait should we do something productive?" They walked out the door and looked around.

"What did you have in mind?" she asked.

He peered around again and his gaze focused on a small coffee shop across the circle. "How about coffee and we read a bit?" He hefted his bag of books high. "And maybe we can get to know each other better? I've been on this hunt with you for a bit I'd love to know more besides your name, that you're American and quiet messy," he said and laughed.

"How could you forget my sheer brilliance?" She played the mockingly insulted act very well.

"I'm terribly sorry. How could I forget such a beautiful mind?" He walked around the circle as she pondered the fact he had just called something of hers beautiful. A blush crept onto her face as she caught up with him and they entered the shop.

They put their bags on one of the large leather seats by the windows and she plopped down next to them. He asked if she wanted anything, but she quickly declined. He would not be purchasing anything else for her that day. He got on line by the counter and she glanced out toward the street.

Her mother and she had loved doing this. People watching. Couples holding hands, families playing in the park, dog walkers, a homeless man sleeping on a bench, and school children who seemed to be on a field trip.

"See, there's one new thing I've already learned about you. You like to stare and daydream," he said.

She snapped her head around and found him sitting across from her in the other plush leather chair.

Clearing her throat she explained. "Not just stare. Watch, people in particular. My mom and I would play this game where we would make up stories about their lives. She said watching human interaction was always better than having it described for you on paper. But she loved books and paper was definitely the best thing for what we couldn't interact with or watch."

"Your mum sounds like she was quite the woman." He slowly took a sip of his drink and she sensed his caution at talking about her mom.

"She was. Every birthday, until I entered high school, we would get together a stack of our favorite books and just read aloud our favorite parts. J.M. Barrie, the Bronte sisters, Shakespeare, Jane Austen, obviously," she said with a laugh.

"I loved it. I don't know why she stopped once I entered high school. I think that maybe she thought I was too old or something." She pictured all the amazing memories she had with her mom. She didn't realize how long she had been in her daydreaming trance until she felt a soft graze of his thumb across her cheek.

Graham pulled his hand back, wet from the touch.

She quickly put her hand to her face. Her cheeks were damp from her tears. She wiped away the tears and then dabbed her face with a napkin. "Sorry. I didn't mean to get all sappy."

"You never have to apologize. It has only been a few weeks since she has passed, correct?" He half-smiled to reassure her.

"Yes. It still doesn't seem real. Thanks for be so understanding, Graham."

His gaze searched all around her face and she felt uncomfortable with the way he was watching her. Not in a bad way. In more of a, he shouldn't be looking at her that way, uncomfortable. She grabbed one of the books from the bag and tossed it to him.

He quickly grabbed the book and opened it to the first page. "Besides your messiness, brilliance, and what sounds to be the coolest mum ever…what else should I know about Lizzie…"

"Price," she finished for him.

"Bam! Another Austen reference. Lizzie Price. Did your mum do that on purpose? Fanny Price in *Mansfield Park* mixed with some Elizabeth Bennett from *Pride and Prejudice*?" he joked, but Lizzie had never actually thought about it.

"That's a great question. I never really put two and two together. So much for that brilliance I bragged about," she joked as she began to read her book.

They alternated between reading alone and then out loud. Chatted to pass the time until the next group was scheduled to do the tour. As they made their way back to the house, they arrived just in time to hear a costumed guide reading out the names for the upcoming tour.

When Lizzie heard her name being called out, she grabbed Graham's arm and they joined the rest of the tourists milling by the door. With little delay, the tour started a few minutes later.

As the led them through the house, the guide reenacted scenes that would have taken place in every day society and explained how Jane and her family would have fallen into the same sort of social positions.

They arrived at a large room and the guide examined the group.

"Do we have a young couple with us today?" he asked.

Everyone glanced around, including Lizzie and Graham, and Lizzie noticed most of the group consisted of families and older couples.

"Here's one," an elderly woman said and pointed at her and Graham.

Lizzie glanced at him to find that he was likewise looking at her. They quickly stepped away from each other and Lizzie tried to explain, "No. . .No, we're not. . .he has a girlfriend...not me."

"Well, you're very cute friends then," the woman said as the costumed guide took hold of their arms and hauled them to the center of the floor.

"Don't worry. I only need you for a small demonstration," he said with an eloquent flourish to his speech.

She shot a worried look at Graham, who was keeping his head down to avoid being recognized. She shrugged and decided to get whatever the demonstration was over with as fast as possible. The group clapped with appreciation as the guide directed them to stand across from each other.

"Now both of you raise your hands to the sides of your face, then put them out, but do not touch."

They immediately followed the man's directions, eager to be out of the limelight.

"I am very serious about not touching. In high society, if gloves were not worn, you did not touch. The contact was seen as indecent if you were not married. In addition, one had to carefully school their emotions. Let's see if you can do that."

Their palms didn't touch, but she could feel the heat from Graham's palms and electricity arced between them in that small space.

She stared at Graham's face, terrified that he could read her like a book, but she stood strong and tried to act nonchalant.

Out of the corner of her eye, she saw the tour guide huff and place his hands on his hips. "Dear, Sir. We cannot gauge your emotions with your sunglasses on."

The man yanked them off and two young girls in the group instantly squealed.

Graham faced the crowd, but Lizzie froze in place. She couldn't help but notice the look in Graham's eyes. It was similar to hers, trying so hard not to be able to show his interest, but making it all the more obvious with his gaze.

The girl's continued screams snapped her back to reality.

"Oh my, god! It's Graham Harris. From Greetings From Victoria!"

The rest of the people in the group ooh'd and ah'd and began to whisper with excitement.

"I am so sorry, Mr. Harris," the guide apologized and handed Graham back his shades.

Graham shook his head and forced a smile, but his body was tense. "No apologies necessary."

Lizzie could tell he was trying to hide his frustration, but masked it with a smile. He dropped his hands and said to the group, "I would truly appreciate if you just waited to tweet and text that we're here. I'll gladly take photos and sign autographs after the tour is over."

Seemingly more excited about spending additional time with Graham rather than sharing their good fortune, the people in the group quieted and nodded.

The earlier tension in Graham's body relaxed and she told herself to keep her a respectable distance from him for the rest of the tour. She didn't want people to get the wrong idea and possibly ruin his image by making them think that he was cheating on his girlfriend.

He turned back to the guide and said, "Shall we continue?"

The guide nodded and walked to the front of the group to continue the tour. Every time that Graham asked a question, it was followed by the barely contained chatter and shrieks of the young girls in the group.

When the tour concluded, and as promised, Graham posed for photos and signed autographs. While he was busy with all of that, she went up to her tour guide.

"Excuse me," she said and tapped his shoulder.

He turned and with an apologetic face, begged for forgiveness.

She waved off his apology and said, "It's really ok, Sir. I just had a few questions."

With a dip of his head, he said, "The least I can do is answer everything and anything you throw my way."

She grabbed her notebook and started rattling off questions. "You said this isn't the actual house Jane lived in?" At his nod, she continued. "But she did live on this street?"

"She did. About five houses up from here. It was one of several houses in which she lived. The Austens moved around a bit due to their money situation at the time. Their longest stay, however, was in a home on this street."

"You said 'several houses.' How many exactly?" She hoped it would be the answer she was looking for.

"I believe it was four."

"Did you say four?" Graham came out of nowhere to ask the question that had been on the tip of her tongue.

The man nodded nervously, confirming his answer.

"Thank you, Sir," Lizzie said with a polite smile and pulled Graham over to a secluded corner of the house. She leaned close and whispered, "Graham…do you know what that means?"

"That the simple cost of this tour just helped us find the next clue?" he whispered back.

They both did a little jump, but tried not to scream and bring attention to themselves. When they finished celebrating, he asked, "But how are we supposed to get into a private residence?"

"You're Graham Harris," she said with a laugh at the obviousness of the statement.

"Using me for my fame again? I see how this relationship works," he teased.

"Hey, you wanted to help." She grinned and they walked out of the house. He placed a gentle hand on her back to direct her down the block and her heart raced with that simple touch. She needed to control these reactions. If he caught on, he might not be so eager to help her anymore.

And now that he was finally back in her life, that was the last thing she wanted to happen.

Chapter 20

New friends, new feelings

Graham had maintained his cool as he was outed by the tour group and when they realized they might have solved the next clue. But as they walked down the block, he thought about how he felt about not touching Lizzie. It surprised him that he was still feeling such overwhelming emotions about her. That he was almost begging to touch her and couldn't resist laying a guiding hand at her back just to have that connection with her.

He knew now why men and women had been cautioned not to touch. The lack of it made it all the more alluring. Made it become a want and a need, but also a taboo pleasure.

"We're here," she exclaimed as they reached their location. A small plaque by the door confirmed it was once the Austen residence. They walked up the stairs and she pressed the doorbell.

Suddenly anxious, he grabbed her arm and turned her to face him. "What the heck are we going to say to get them to let us in?"

She offered up a playful smirk. "Just be your charming and famous self. I'm sure something will come to you," she said and turned back to stare at the door.

He bounced on the balls of his feet, trying to work up some kind of explanation for why they were there when the door opened. He didn't see anyone at first, until he looked down and met the wide-eyed gaze of the young girl looking up at him. She hopped up and down excitedly, let out a silent little scream and started to cry.

He bent down to meet her gaze directly and gave the girl a hug as she continued to cry on his shoulder.

"Wow! That worked out perfectly," Lizzie said with a laugh.

A young woman ran over to the door. "Rose...Rose, darling are you--"

"What are you doing with my daughter?" she shrieked and beat at him with the dish rag she held in her hand. "No one touches my daughter!"

He shot to his feet and put up his hands to defend himself. "Ma'am, please stop," he said while trying to stop her slaps with the rag.

"Mum! Mum! Stop! He's Graham from Greetings From Victoria," the young girl shouted and grabbed her mom's hands to get her to stop.

The young mother quickly froze and looked from her daughter to him. "You know this young man, Rose?"

"Yes, mummy. He's the best person ever. Him and his band mates," Rose exclaimed. She looked over at Graham with a great big grin and he returned the smile.

He stuck out his hand for her mother to shake. "It is very nice to meet you both. This is my friend Lizzie. We're both big fans of Jane Austen and wanted to see one of the actual houses she lived in."

He was trying to be as polite as he could to make sure the woman would not phone the police.

"Oh," was all the mother replied, still obviously uncertain about the entire situation.

"Mum, manners," the young girl said, repeating something she must have heard dozens of times from her mother.

"Please come in, Graham. Lizzie," Rose said, grabbed his hand and pulled him into house.

The house looked much like the Austen House they had just left, with the original hardwood floors and furniture with a very classic look.

"You have a gorgeous home, Rose," he said.

"Come see my room," she said, but he hesitated and shot a glance at her mother.

"Do you mind, Ma'am?" he asked, conscious of how delicate a situation this was.

"Go ahead," her mother said, relenting, and Rose showed him the way up the stairs.

"Thank you, Mum," Rose said with a giggle.

They trudged up the stairs and he back to see if Lizzie following them, but she wasn't.

At the top of the stairs, Rose pushed open a large door to reveal a room covered with posters of his face and ones of the rest of the boys.

"Wow, you really are a big fan. I'll have to tell the boys all about you," he said and chuckled, but felt awkward at all the pictures of himself plastered all around the room.

"I think I know why you're here," she whispered as she knelt and reached under her bed.

"To see this historical house of course," he said nervously.

"I may be ten, but I follow everything you do. I know you've been to several Jane Austen sites this week with that Lizzie girl."

She pulled a wooden box out from beneath the bed. "I think you're looking for this. I found it in my bedroom wall when we started to redecorate."

She handed it to him. The box was oak, handmade, and stained a dark color. When he lifted the lid, inside he found an old yellowed envelope with a large number four in a calligraphy font.

"I knew someone would come one day for this box. I never thought it would be my idol," she said excitedly.

He bent slightly and pecked her on the cheek. "Thank you, Rose. Thank you very, very much."

"No problem," she said as her hand went to the cheek he had kissed, almost as if she didn't believe it. She grabbed his free hand and they all returned downstairs where Lizzie sat in the den with Rose's mother.

Her mother looked over and asked her daughter, "Did you enjoy this lovely surprise visit?

"Yes, Mum. Graham was the perfect gentleman." She hugged him and then walked over to Lizzie, sat beside her on the couch and hugged her as well.

Surprise erupted on Lizzie's face, but it instantly turned to affection for the young girl.

"Graham has what you need," Rose said.

"I'm sorry," Lizzie asked, confused, as she looked over at Graham. He raised the box to show her what Rose meant.

Lizzie walked over to Graham and touched the top of the box reverently. He gently nudged it forward and smiled. "Go ahead. Open it."

She glanced at him with childlike amusement as she slowly lifted the top of the box.

He knew instantly when she saw the letter because she covered her mouth and tears welled up in her eyes.

"Rose found it and saved it for whoever showed up to look for it. It was in the wall. If walls could talk, huh? Easiest clue wouldn't you say?" he said with a laugh.

She let out a small chuckle as the tears fell from her eyes. He went to try and wipe them away, but she quickly did it before he could touch her. He assumed it was because she hadn't liked when he had brushed her tears away at the coffee shop. But her skin was so soft that he didn't want to stop touching her.

Rose then came over and stood between them, alternating between a look at Lizzie and one at Graham. "I hope you guys solve this and fast. Everyone says Graham and Caterina are on the outs because of his new friend Lizzie."

Rose raised smartphone for them to check out the news.

Graham saw the cliché split of photos of him and Caterina.

Lizzie gave him a wide-eyed look. "Is this true? Are you guys--"

"We're on break," he cut her off, trying to explain.

Obviously upset, Lizzie took a quick step back. "Was it because of this? Did she break up with you because of this?" She pointed to the box.

"No. And it's just a break. Besides, why would you think *she* dumped *me*?" He pulled the box away from her and held it tightly against his chest.

"It's probably because Caterina was with all those other guys when you did your first break," Rose said.

"Rose! How do you know that?" She pulled Rose away from them.

"We better go before we over stay our welcome." He winked at Rose.

Lizzie nodded and pulled open her bag so he could place the box into it.

"Thank you so much for your hospitality. And Rose, thank you for the lovely gift," he said.

"Of course, Graham. Thank you for making such awesome music." She waved as Graham opened the door for Lizzie and they left.

They had barely taken a few steps when Lizzie started hopping up and down with excitement.

"I can't believe this," she shouted. "We're on the fourth clue! Sure we don't know how many there actually are, but four is good," she said and inhaled and exhaled deeply to try to contain herself.

She was positively glowing and he loved seeing her joy, but they couldn't stay for long.

"I am sure twitter is buzzing with my location at this point. Should we head back to the hotel to open this clue?"

"Are you really sure that you should? I know you want to help, but if Caterina is already pissed, what makes you think us being seen together will make it better? I don't need her showing up again," she said timidly.

"Why would you care?" he asked.

"Because she's scary as hell when she needs to be." Lizzie's eyes went wide with shock that he didn't realize that fact. Then she laughed at him, which was another contrary signal.

"What's so funny? You basically said she makes you piss yourself." He narrowed his eyes, confused.

"I never said anything like that. But you seem shocked by what I said. New News? No one has told you that before?" she asked and crooked her head to look up at him.

They reached his car and he quickly unlocked the doors for them to climb in. After they sat, he glanced at her. No one had ever told him anything like what Lizzie had just said. Caterina had always been decently mannered in front of him and his friends. Minus her small outbursts toward Lizzie, of course.

Was the problem just with Lizzie?

"Wait. No one has ever told you before?" she asked as he pulled away from the curb and started back to London.

He was silent as he drove, thinking about what Lizzie had said. Concerned about what people, especially his friends and his family, had been saying about his girlfriend. Well, ex-girlfriend at the moment.

Had he let Caterina blind him to her real self? The one that others seemed to see so easily?

Shaking his head, he reminded himself of all the times in the last week when Caterina had made him so angry. So why had he been shocked by Lizzie's statement?

The bigger question was, what did he plan to do about it?

Chapter 21

The road back to London

The silence in the car was killing her.

She knew she had struck a nerve with the whole 'your ex-girlfriend is a psycho bitch' thing. To be honest, she had thought he knew. How could he not?

As they drove along through the country, the sun was starting to lower on the horizon and she watched the shades of orange, purples, and blues as she toyed with the tassels of her bag.

They pulled up to the hotel to find that the crowd of press people had not died down. He shut off the car, and she unbuckled her belt and climbed out. The paparazzi immediately surged forward and Lizzie tried to run through the crowd, but it was impossible.

People tugged at her to look in different directions, screaming her name, and panic set in. She searched all around for what direction to go, but all she saw were more and more cameras being shoved in her face. She covered her face with her arm, tried to shove past, and wished that every single one of them would disappear.

Suddenly a strong arm wrapped around her waist and gently pulled her close. She looked to find Graham beside her, pushing his way through the crowd.

His chivalry provided her a bit more calm. His care for her helped her find the strength to push past all the reporters and get to the front door of the hotel. When they made it through the front door, he quickly pulled his hand off her waist.

For some reason, her earlier comfort fled and she felt as if he had just yanked his hand away from something diseased.

Graham slammed the door shut and she jumped at the sound. She turned to find Fanny running toward them. The older woman wrapped her arms around Lizzie and it was another pleasant surprise of the day. Lizzie quickly hugged her back and squeezed hard before finally letting her go.

"Lizzie, dear. I've been worried sick about you. Graham, oh Graham," she said and walked over. She hugged him like she had Lizzie and he smiled. It was the first one Lizzie had seen since they had found the clue.

"Don't worry, Fanny. We're fine. I'm used to all of these press people and paparazzi," he said with a shrug.

"But poor Lizzie isn't." She raised her soft elderly hand to cup Lizzie's cheek.

"I think you should find a new place to stay. The press never leave and the fans have literally camped out outside their rooms just to get a glimpse of the boys," Fanny said.

Lizzie's eyes bulged with disbelief. "Fanny! Where would I go?"

"There are hundreds of hotels in London. Thousands even."

"But what about you?" Lizzie said, panicking. She didn't want to leave Fanny alone in all this chaos, especially since she had been the cause of it.

"What about me, Dear? I'm fine. You can stay somewhere else for a while. Just until the press dies down and then you can come back," she said and smiled. It warmed Lizzie's heart, especially as she said, "Your room will still be here."

Lizzie knew Fanny was right. Leaving made the most sense. She quickly hugged Fanny once again, fighting the stinging in her eyes. Why was she so upset to leave a woman she had only known a week? she thought as she pulled away and ran up the stairs to her room.

"Lizzie," Graham shouted, but she didn't stop. She ripped open her door and began packing up all her clothing and papers. Her research, books, cameras, and computer were all shoved into her suitcase and backpack.

She wiped away the tears that were falling as she packed, feeling suddenly so alone.

Crying three times in one day? Why am I such a freaking pansy?

She was so upset. Maybe because she was about to lose another woman in her life.

"Lizzie, you know that's not true." She heard her mother's voice in her head. *"I'm still here in your heart and mind. Fanny is trying to protect you like any mother would."*

The door slammed and she spun to find Graham standing there with more than her fake lip gloss kiss all over his face. She laughed harder than she would have expected.

"Those girls will stop at nothing," he said, breathing heavily.

She grabbed a tissue and handed it to him. He took it, thanked her and scrubbed his face with the tissue.

She returned to packing, but felt his eyes on her back. "What is it Graham?"

"I was thinking about something." His voice trailed off and she turned to look at him, arms full of clothing.

"Fanny is right that you need a new place to stay," he said.

"Great, Graham. You followed me to tell me you agree with her? Was that supposed to be helpful or something?" She didn't mean to snap, but she was frustrated.

She tossed her pile of clothing into her suitcase.

"Stay with me," he blurted out.

She had to repeat it a few times in her head to make sure she had heard him correctly.

Her heart was pounding as she considered his suggestion. He wanted her to stay in his home? "I don't think that is the brightest idea. But as a last resort, I will take you up on the offer."

"Why only a last resort? The paparazzi aren't allowed anywhere near my home. We'll be able to work around the clock before I leave in three weeks and won't be able to help. By that point all the press will have hopefully died down. If we don't finish solving this, you can return to the Austen House."

He walked over to stand next to her and began to neatly fold her clothing to help her pack.

"Do I have to bring up the Caterina issue yet again?" She snatched the clothing he had folded and tossed it in with the rest.

"Why do you have to bring her into this?" he said with a huff and continued folding.

"Because you just broke up, I hazard to guess because of this whole situation. And now you want me to come and stay with you?"

"Not everything Caterina and me do, or I should say did, revolves around you and this hunt, Lizzie," he said in a pained whisper.

He folded one last blouse, tossed it into her suitcase and walked away from her and to the door.

She knew she had upset him, but she also knew she had a valid point. She refused to look at him, knowing that if she saw his upset, she would just want to kiss him and make it better.

"My offer will continue to stand," he said. "You're more than welcome to stay. The boys, I'm sure, would be thrilled," he said, trying to lighten the mood.

"Thanks, Graham. I'll be fine," she said, zipped up the one bag and tossed it on the ground to wait for the next suitcase. The click of the door made her pause and she looked to find Graham gone. She plopped on the tiny empty part of the bed and stared at the door.

Needing something to make her feel happy, she grabbed her phone to call her father. He was quick to answer.

"You're quite the popular girl over there," he teased even before greeting her. "I can't look at a single entertainment section without seeing your face. My daughter is apparently a home wrecker."

"I'm not dad! But way to say, 'hey jellybean. I love and miss you so much' in the unconventional way," she said sarcastically.

"Well, it's just a surprise. You've always been the apple of my eye, but now you are world known as being the apple of another man's wandering eye."

"It's not like that at all. Graham and I are just friends. And I don't want to be the girl who broke up one of the largest 'It' couples. There's no positive way to spin that in my favor."

One-handedly, she grabbed the last of the shirts Graham had folded and threw them into her suitcase. She glanced around at how bare the room was becoming as she finished packing.

"Why must you always be negative?" her father said. "We didn't raise you to be Debbie Downer, you should be Penny Positive, or something ridiculous like that. But moving along, how is everything going?"

"Great. I. . .well, we found the fourth clue. But when I got back to the hotel to open it, the lovely woman who owns the place told me I should find somewhere new to stay for a little while. Until the paparazzi cool down."

"She's watching out for you, Kiddo. And it seems as though your friendship with Graham was rekindled since last we spoke. Why not stay with him?"

It was almost as if her father knew what had just transpired. She cleared her throat to explain. "Well he did offer but--"

Her father cut her off. "But what? He offered. He sees nothing wrong in it. I know you think you're causing problems in his relationship, but from what I've read, most people are relieved by the break up. Stay with the boy, Lizzie. He could probably use a friend right now."

"My father, who threatened one of my ex-boyfriends by cleaning his gun while asking them questions, is telling me to stay at a boy's house? Am I missing something here?" She couldn't seriously believe what she was hearing.

"A free stay would be cost efficient. Plus you don't have feelings for the boy, so I have no fear that you'll become the next girl on one of those teenaged mom show."

"I'm not a teenager anymore, but I get where you're going." She sighed. She didn't think telling her father that she found Graham attractive and intellectually stimulating would put his mind at ease. So she resigned herself to doing as he asked. "Fine, Dad. I'll call Graham tomorrow and practically beg him to let me stay."

"Great. Now I can pay off some more of your student loans," he joked.

"Very funny, Dad, but mom left me enough money to live here for a year and still pay off my loans. Nice try, though. I need to finish packing to get out of here tomorrow."

"Ok, Honey. And you tell that Graham if he lays a hand on you inappropriately, I will get the closest fighter jet over there and blow his house and him to bits," he teased.

"I would also be in that house, Dad." She rolled her eyes at his ridiculous comments.

"I would call you and tell you to leave before I bombed it," he said, rationalizing his comment.

"Whatever you say, Dad. I love you."

"I love you, too, Jellybean." She heard his slight sniffle, but knew not to bring it up. She hung up the phone and placed it next to her on the bed. Grabbing her backpack, she filled it with whatever loose odds and ends were around the room.

As she shoved things in, she felt the box and decided to take it out, but save it for last. When the box lay on the bed, she was beyond tempted to open it. She lifted the lid gently and pulled out the letter. When she turned it and saw the wax seal, she picked at it, but stopped. Graham would want to be there to open it. Graham *should* be there.

She gently stowed it back into the box, sat on the ground, and brought her knees to her chin.

She glanced at her bedside table and saw the list of the phone numbers. She saw the first name, large and bolded. Nick. She snagged the list and then her phone.

There was a short ring before an extremely feminine voice answered.

"Nick's phone."

Lizzie sat straight up, feeling awkward that Nick hadn't answered. "Hi. I was wondering if I could speak with Nick. It's Lizzie. I'm a friend of--"

"Oh, I know who you are," the young woman said. "Let me get him for you."

The young woman called out for Nick.

There was some mumbled talking and then a quick, "Lizzie? Are you ok? What's wrong?"

She smiled at how concerned he sounded and replied, "I'm fine. I…umm…you said if I needed anything to give you a call?"

Silence on the line caused her to assume he meant for her to continue. "Did that include a place to stay for the night? Fanny told me it would be safer if I stay somewhere else."

"You don't need to explain. Kara and I will be there in twenty minutes. And Lizzie?"

"Yeah?"

"I'm glad you called."

She smiled so brightly that even after she hung up the phone, she continued to smile as she packed up the rest of the little things around the room.

About a half an hour later, her room phone rang, probably for the last time. She answered. "Hello?"

"Lizzie, Nick and Kara are here for you," Fanny said softly and with a hint of a sniffle.

"Thank you, Fanny. I'll be right down." She hung up the phone and gave a final glance at the room as she walked out of the door. She wheeled her suitcases along the hall where a few girls sate outside their rooms on their phones, tablets, laptop, and every other technological gadget she could ever think of. Some looked at her as she passed and sneered. Others snapped photos, but not one said a word to her.

She thump-thump-thumped down the stairs, but when she made it to the front desk, no one was there. She looked around and heard Fanny's voice in the small living room.

Lizzie walked in to find Nick, and a young woman who she assumed was Kara, sitting and chatting with Fanny.

"Hey, Nick," Lizzie said. He offered a concerned smile and stood to give her a large, warm, friendly hug. When he released her, he introduced the young woman.

"Lizzie, this is Kara. Kara, Lizzie." He voice was filled with such love when he said Kara's name. He then continued with a joke. "Lizzie is our new lost boy."

"Lost boy? I thought she was hunting Jane Austen not Peter Pan." Kara walked over to stand by Nick. Her pastel blue hair made her fair complexion look even more snowy white. She stuck out her hand for Lizzie to shake.

Lizzie quickly took hold of the soft dainty hand and gave it a gentle shake. She explained with a laugh, "Peter Pan is the character not the author. But you're super awesome for getting his poor reference."

Kara also gave a small chuckle and grabbed one of her bags. "How about we get you out of here?"

Lizzie nodded and glanced at Fanny, who just sat there stoically with a cup of tea in her hands. Lizzie peered at Nick, who seemed to know without her having to say anything that she wanted some time to say goodbye to Fanny.

He grabbed Lizzie's other suitcase and left the room with Kara. Lizzie walked over to crouch in front of Fanny, but Fanny spoke first. "This place will not be the same without you. You brought life back into this place. The Austen House will feel empty."

Tears pricked at her eyes. "Fanny, there are no other words or ways for me to say thank you for all you've done for me. And it was only a week and a half! I promise, no I *swear*, I'll be back."

"Do not swear, Lizzie. Has Romeo and Juliet taught you nothing about swearing?" Fanny placed a hand on Lizzie's cheek. "Go. Nick will be wanting to leave soon. I'll miss you, my dear Lizzie."

Lizzie grabbed the hand on her cheek, gave it a gentle squeeze, and stood to leave. Before she left, she turned back for a final farewell to Fanny. "Romeo swore on the moon which changes constantly. I swear on the land this building sits on, I'll be back."

"That's my girl," Fanny said and smiled, but with the smile, a tear fell. She quickly wiped it away and went back to sipping her tea, but her hands were shaky as she did so.

Lizzie knew at that moment that she loved Fanny like she was a family member. She was the grandmother she'd never had.

I will *be back, Fanny. I promise that.*

Chapter 22

A woman scorned

Lizzie definitely had a point.

It frustrated the hell out of Graham that she could never accept kindness, but this time she had a valid point. He walked up to his door and something seemed strange. When he examined the door, he realized the door was open. Just a bit, but enough for him to realize it wasn't locked.

He pushed the door open and saw straight through to the living. Only there was no living room left. The couch, TV, everything was gone.

"What the..." He rushed to the kitchen to find see the refrigerator door was wide open. The contents were strewn all over inside and on the floor. Everything else on the counters was either gone or trashed.

He suddenly knew. He knew and regretted the fact that he could have been so stupid.

"Caterina," he hissed under his breath as he grabbed the new phone that had replaced the one she had also trashed.

"Hello, Graham," she said calmly, obviously expecting his call.

"What the *actual* fuck Caterina?" He seethed as he looked all around and ran up to his bedroom to see what she had done there.

"Oh, Graham. I like when you get all worked up. However, I can assure you that I have no idea what you're talking about." Her voice was sultry and filled with feigned innocence.

"The couch? The TV?" he said and walked into his bedroom.

"My bedroom!" he said. Everything was on the floor and his bed sheets, pillows, and comforter were shredded to pieces.

"Oh. That. I was just taking what I paid for," she said.

"How is trashing my room taking what you paid for?" He couldn't be calm, no matter how hard he tried.

"That was just for fun, Sweetheart. Plus that was *our* room for quite some time, Graham. I was rounding up all of my clothing and thought, 'Why not make his day brighter by leaving him a mess? He just loves to clean up. Don't you, Graham?" she said, her voice sickly sweet. The kind of sweet that he knew came from evil.

Before his brain could stop his mouth, his anger spewed out. "You little bitch."

"Wow, Graham has a bit of a temper. Tsk, Tsk," she mocked.

"Who the hell have you become, Caterina? I have no clue who you are anymore. Stay away from this house, stay away from my friends, and stay the hell away from me."

He hung up the phone, tempted to throw it across the room again. As he held it up it vibrated and he quickly answered, "And I am getting a new number, you psycho!"

"Graham?" a male voice replied.

He glanced at his phone. A photo of Nick and his name appeared on the screen. He put the phone back to his ear and said, "Sorry, mate. I thought you were someone else."

"Caterina?" Nick laughed, not understanding just how seriously pissed off Graham was.

"Yeah." He sat down on the end of the bed and took a large calming breath.

"What's up, mate?" he asked, starting to feel slightly calmer.

"I'm with Lizzie," Nick said in a hushed tone.

"What? How? Why? Where?" Graham shot out questions with another rush of anger.

Why would she be with Nick and not him?

"We're at my house. She's with Kara right now. She called and told me Fanny had asked her to leave. I didn't get much more than that because I didn't want upset her more, but I have to ask you...Why isn't she at your house right now?"

"I offered," he bit out. "She said she didn't want to make matters worse with Caterina. I don't see how much worse they can get," he said as he fell back onto the bed. Feathers and stuffing flew up around him.

"What happened?" Nick asked.

"Caterina must have come back when I was out with Lizzie today. She trashed the entire house. Took the couch and the TV. Made a mess of all my food and the kitchen. Then she came up to my bedroom and ruined everything in here. I'm currently lying on a mound of stuffing and feather." He spit out a feather as it landed on his mouth.

"That bird is crazy. You shouldn't stay there tonight. Come here. Maybe you can convince Lizzie to come back to your house tomorrow, after you have the locks changed of course. Kara wouldn't mind another stowaway. She seems to be getting along with Lizzie swell. I can hear their girly giggles from my office."

That's when Graham sprung up off the bed. "My office!"

He ran down the stairs and whipped open the door to his office. His computer was gone and all of his hours of research were currently confetti tossed all across the floor.

"Bloody freakin' hell!" He slapped his hand on his forehead.

"Pack a bag and get over here before she comes back to make a scene," Nick warned.

"Right. I'll be there in about an hour. You should probably give Lizzie a bit of a warning."

He hung up and trudged back to his room to fill a duffle with some clothing for the night.

When he was done, he hurried out and locked the door. Not that it would keep out Caterina for the moment. With a quick look to make sure she wasn't around, he raced to his car, tossed the bag onto his passenger seat, and drove off. The drive gave him time to think of ways to convince Lizzie to stay with him, as well as think of all the things he needed to do. New locks, keys, and reset the passwords on the security system to make sure he'd be safe. A new computer, TV, and so many other things the list was never-ending.

He put the car in park, not even realizing he had made it to Nick's house.

Despite his earlier concerns, the sight of Nick's house, and what waited within, made him feel better. He grabbed his bag and almost skipped to the front door. There was laughter inside that stopped when he rang the doorbell. He leaned over to peer through one of the sidelight windows, but the entryway was dark. He was only able to make out a shadow coming towards the door. When the door opened, he was surprised to find it was Lizzie.

"Hey I--"

Lizzie cut him off by jumping up and latching her arms around his neck, nearly lifting herself off the ground with an incredibly strong hug. She caressed the top of his head with one hand. The comfort it created caused him to drop his duffle and wrap his arms around her waist, pulling her ever closer. He nuzzled his head into her neck where he inhaled her fruity perfume and felt her racing pulse.

She drew away and landed back fully on her feet. "Are you ok?" she asked, nearly flooring him with that most basic question.

He smiled, but not a single word came to his mind. She stepped away, took hold of his duffle, and walked into the house. She had grown comfortable with that house in the past couple of hours she had been there. He followed her into the living room where Nick and Kara sat at their coffee table with all of Lizzie's notes, Jane's letters, and a stacks of books spread across the entire length.

"What's this?" he asked, staring at all of them.

"I told Lizzie she needed to tell us what she was really doing here. Just in case we're about to take in a wanted fugitive," Nick said playfully. With a shrug he continued. "After a long five minutes of nagging, and poking, she broke down and spilled her secrets. Mostly because I told her you were coming for the night and she wanted to read the new clue without having to be secretive about it. Mate, this girl is a freaking genius."

His heart did a small flip with Nick's news. "You didn't open it yet?"

Lizzie shook her head, took a seat next to Kara, and placed the oak box on the table.

He walked over and joined the group by kneeling by the coffee table.

Lizzie pushed the box over to him, anticipation evident in her smile.

He lifted the lid and removed the letter. He carefully broke open the wax seal and drew out the letter. He handed the letter to Lizzie, but she put her palms up and pushed his hand back.

She shook her head. "I read the last one. This one is all yours."

She sat with her legs bent like a pretzel and bounced them the excitement that he was about to read the next clue.

He looked at Nick and Kara, who seemed to be sharing the same excitement. He read.

"Another congratulatory statement is in order. However I have grown accustomed to you now finding these letters and will not say such basic ironic statements." His friends all let out a small laugh. "First impressions are misleading in ways that people who choose to rapidly judge, without full knowledge of situations, will soon look like fools.

Lasting impressions are founded upon societal dances, where on the outskirts women gossip and men speak in hushed tones. The dancers are able to converse with their partners, even if their partner is barley tolerable.

The gossiping women will talk all night, but come Sunday morning, walking into church, between those sacred walls, their mouths close and are replaced with smiles. Once or twice gossip can still slip into the order of the day and ruin a small congregation.

Best of luck, Jane Austen," he finished and looked up to a most amusing sight.

All three of their faces were scrunched as they thought about the clue. He knew he couldn't let the opportunity pass to snap a photo. The flash took them all by surprise and he turned his phone to show them what they all looked like.

"I could not miss taking that photo," he joked.

They all laughed and Lizzie reached for the letter to reread it herself.

He was mesmerized by her lips as they moved when she whispered certain lines in her head and stared upward from the paper to absorb what she had read. She lay back onto the floor and her shirt lifted a bit. He followed her flat belly to the slight rise of her hip bones. He admired how shapely her body was lying down.

Someone cleared their throat and he glanced at Kara, who had caught him watching Lizzie. She said nothing and stood. She said to Nick, "I think I need to sleep on this clue a bit. Nick, wouldn't you agree?"

Nick's eyes went wide as his gaze shifted between all the papers, Lizzie, and Kara. He seemed to finally get the hint and peered between Graham and Lizzie.

Hopping up from the couch, he said, "Right. Yes. That sounds like a smart idea, Kara. Graham, you can show Lizzie the guest room?"

Graham nodded and Lizzie sat back up to say goodnight to the couple as they walked out of the room.

"Do you want me to show you the guest room?" he asked.

She shook her head. "No, thanks. I want to do a little more research, but you can go. After what you just went through, I imagine you're exhausted." She picked up some of her papers and skimmed through the information.

"Emotionally, yes, I'm exhausted. Physically, I'm wired from the adrenaline. I'd enjoy helping in any way I can." He scooted around the table to sit next to her. He could smell her perfume again and was tempted to take a deep inhale of the scent. He chose not to, warning himself that she might think he was insane and slightly creepy.

He lifted Jane's letter off the table and leaning forward, rested his forearm on the edge.

"Do you have any ideas?" he asked.

She put her handful of papers in her lap and stared hard at the clue in his hand. "Considering I loved her stories so much, I never took the time to learn about her life. This whole situation is a crazy and surreal blur to me. And as I learn more about Jane, I feel even more connected to her life, her characters, and oddly enough, myself."

"How so?" he asked.

"It's weird. Her life still seems so common now. Like the things she said and did. The relationships she had and didn't have are still happening to people now. Love and hate. Miscommunications and misunderstandings. Women empowerment and so many basics, ya know?" Lizzie glanced at him with unrestrained amusement making her eyes glitter. Her cheeks were flush, an almost crimson red he had never seen before.

He inched his body closer and asked, "How are you learning about yourself?"

"Well, this whole journey has taught me a lot. But Jane, in particular, has taught me to follow what I believe and enjoy the ride, and that sometimes things will simply come to you."

She scanned his features, trying hard to not meet his gaze, and he could see her pulse racing.

He liked the fact that he was making her nervous and it spurred him on.

"Like what?" He moved a strand of her hair that was blocking the side of her face from his.

"The fourth clue was literally handed to us, and well…I found friends just because I stumbled into a closed library and the annoying famous kid wanted to help," she joked, turning away from him.

He moved as well, losing the growing connection between them.

"And what is this twenty questions?" Lizzie asked. This is not about me. It is about the new clue."

She gathered up her papers once again and a spark flared to life in her gaze. She had found something. He didn't know how he knew it, but he was sure.

"What? Have you got something?" He peered over her shoulder at the paper she was reviewing.

"The part in the clue about a dance partner being barely tolerable. It's from *Pride and Prejudice*. Lizzie over hears Mr. Darcy talking with Mr. Bingley about how she is a barely tolerable dance partner." She shuffled a few papers around and grabbed the *Pride and Prejudice* book. She flipped through the pages until she found the one she wanted.

"See," she said and held out the book to him.

He quickly read the scene and handed her back the book. "So are we supposed to attend some public ball somewhere? I do have some new moves I have been dying to use."

He jumped up, took hold of Lizzie's hand and pulled her to her feet.

"Thanks, but no thanks, Graham. I do not dance."

She tried to sit back down, but he pulled harder and her body crashed against his.

"But we learned such great moves in Bath this afternoon," he joked and swayed back and forth with her. Hesitantly, he placed a hand on the small of her back and released her arm so he could hold her hand.

She laughed and tilted her head back to gaze up at him. "But I am not wearing gloves and we are touching! Did you learn nothing?"

Laughter bubbled up inside him as well and he licked his lips at how tempting her skin looked. He resisted the urge to touch her more and said, "You're so right. Where are my manners? How about I just sweep you off your feet with my skills?"

He swayed a bit deeper until he was able to dip her. He held her in his strong grip and then with a small pull, they were standing straight again, noses grazing. Her gaze widened and darkened with the contact. He spun her out quickly and then spun her back, bent to sweep one arm under her knees and the other squarely on her waist to hold her high against him.

She let out a light squeal and wrapped her arms around his neck. She buried her face into his neck and her gentle breaths caused the hairs on the back of his neck to stand up. Pulling her head away, she looked up at him and their gazes met.

This close he was able to see the flecks of gray in the ice blue of her eyes.

Emotion flooded through him. Too much emotion that he wasn't ready to handle right now.

He bent down to let her feet touch the ground and stepped away.

She gave him a confused look, but seemed to understand he needed space. She walked over to her suitcase and asked, "Where did you learn to dance?"

"Caterina was a waitress at a local club. It was how we met." He regretted mentioning her as soon as he did. Awkwardness rose up instantly.

"Cool," she replied hesitantly. She jerked the handle up on her rolling bag and glanced at him again. "It's getting late. We should probably--"

"Yeah, of course. I'll show you to your room," he said, the earlier moment of pleasure gone.

"Let me get the heavy one," he said and took the bigger bag from her. He rolled it past her and to stairs. Hefting it up, he walked up the stairs and down a large hall to a room at the far end. He opened the door and rolled her bag in.

"This room is bigger than my room and my parent's room combined. It's gorgeous," she gushed and fell onto an immense bed.

He was still feeling extremely awkward about bringing up Caterina and decided not to linger with her. "Goodnight, Lizzie."

"Wait. Where are you staying? I'll see you in the morning, right?"

"The couch we were just leaning on is my bed for the night. It's odd that a house this big only has one guest room. To be fair, the other spare room is filled with Kara's clothing and Nick's hair products," he joked.

"Well, it's not very fair that you'll be on the couch. That's not a good place to relax after the day you've had. Come on," she said and patted the extra space on the bed next to her.

He stared at her in disbelief. "Are you sure?"

She rolled her eyes. "It's just sleep, Graham. Plus if you try anything, my dad taught me how to castrate a man with my bare hands," she teased.

He couldn't contain his chuckle. "I'll be right back. Let me get my things from downstairs."

He headed out and went down to get his duffle bag. His heart was racing.

Why?

He didn't understand. She was just being kind, he told himself. The couch would have been a miserable time.

But he was just newly single. What does that matter? he asked himself.

Nick's voice answered in his head. "You like her don't you?"

Did he? Was that why he wasn't upset, but actually relieved, that Caterina was out of the picture?

Graham slowly walked back up the stairs, his mind reeling as he went over and around all the thoughts. When he returned to the bedroom, he peeked in the door.

Lizzie was already fast asleep. Her hand was tucked under her face, cupping her own cheek. Her lips were slightly parted and her breathing was steady and light. She looked so peaceful and pretty.

A smile crept onto his face.

He put down his duffle bag gently and found his pajama pants. He quietly undressed and slipped into them before he slowly and carefully climbed into bed.

He didn't disturb Lizzie as he climbed under the covers and shut the lights off.

He lay there, staring at the ceiling. Listening to Lizzie's soft regular breath. Occasionally staring at her and smiling as her peace spread to him.

It had been a good day, but the night had started off rough.

As he glanced at Lizzie again, it occurred to him that the night was ending way better than it had started.

Chapter 23

New beginnings

Lizzie covered her eyes as sunshine broke through the windows.

When she went to bury her face into her pillow she realized her head was not on a pillow, but on a chiseled and very bare chest.

My lips are on a naked torso right now. Don't look up...Don't look up.

She didn't listen to her own inner voice and looked up the torso to see the face that had been haunting her dreams the past few days.

Graham.

She jumped up and scurried to the other end of the bed. Unfortunately, as she scurried she hit the end of the bed, couldn't stop herself and fell off.

She landed with a loud thump.

"Lizzie?" he asked, his morning voice husky.

She shot up with wide doe eyes and bit her bottom lip, trying hard not to show how embarrassed she was.

"What happened?" he said and sat up.

She looked up and down his body and her eyes went to a certain lower extremity that was tenting the sheets. Her eyes nearly jumped out of their sockets as she spun on her heel so she didn't have to face him. "Umm...I'm just gonna go take a shower."

She heard him move and whisper, "Oh, God."

His voice louder so she was sure to hear him, he said, "It is morning. I had no control."

"It's okay," she replied, shut the bathroom door, and then leaned against it, trying to stifle a laugh. She covered her mouth and ran the water for her shower. Undressing, she jumped beneath the stream of hot water. As it hit her body, it relaxed her tension and freed her mind.

It also gave her time to question her feelings for Graham. Which caused the tension to come back and the free space in her mind was totally filled with thoughts of Graham.

She forced away those thoughts and the tension. Hurried to finish her shower.

As she climbed out, she wrapped herself up in a towel, looked around, and silently cursed herself. She had left her change of clothes out in the room.

With Graham.

She slowly opened the door and peeked around.

Graham wasn't in the room. Taking a deep breath, she ran to her suitcase to change as fast as she could.

As she pulled on her jeans, she heard the click of the door opening. She shot her gaze to the entryway to see Graham standing there, a piece of toast hanging out of his mouth and a plate in his hand. His gaze trailed up and down her body.

"Oh, Jesus." She grabbed her shirt to try and cover herself.

He took an awkward bite of the toast, put the plate with the toast down on a nearby dresser and took a few hurried steps toward her.

She gripped her shirt to her chest even harder as he placed his hand on her bare waist and turned her slightly.

He bent his head and said, "You have a tattoo."

"Wow! What? When did that get there?" She was trying to be sarcastic to hide the fact that her body was on fire with his touch, but she wasn't sure it played that way.

He half-smiled and with a small laugh said, "It's very gorgeous. What does it mean exactly?"

"It says, 'I'm youth, I'm joy, I'm a little bird that has broken out of the egg'."

She tossed her shirt over her head before he could ask any more questions.

"And the birds are part of the meaning?" he asked, taking a step back.

"They're not birds." She walked past him to grab her hair brush.

"What are they?"

"You and all your questions can get a bit frustrating, Graham," she rushed out, feigning annoyance to try to get him to stop asking questions.

"I'm just trying to learn more about you. At least one of us is trying to do that." He whispered the last sentence, but she heard it loud and clear.

"Really? That's rich, Graham," she said, now truly annoyed. "Maybe I don't need to ask a million questions to know who someone is. Ever think of that? I told you I watch people. I did it for years with my mother. You think I learned nothing from that?"

"Then tell me what you know about me?" He jammed his arms across his chest and waited to be proved correct.

She stood right in front of him, ready to prove him wrong.

"You're a neat freak who is obsessed with superheroes, one more so than any other. Batman. You're cautious, but can also let go. You've become more liberated in the last few months due to your first break with Caterina. You have some weird fear of sporks...I still haven't figured out why, but you never seem to use them. You are the most sensible, or one of the more sensible ones, in the band. Not going too crazy with tattoos, but a nicely designed one, a bit like you are trying to conform in a non-conformist sort of way. And last, but not least, you are still, somewhat, in love with your psychotic ex-girlfriend."

She stopped to finally draw a breath, watched his face, and knew that she had won.

His arms were no longer crossed, but hung at his sides. He no longer stood as tall as he had before. He seemed slightly upset by her revelations, so she held back a little as she said, "How'd I do?"

He said nothing.

She lowered her gaze and gave her head a small shake. She didn't wait for him to respond and headed downstairs to resume work on solving the next clue.

When she arrived in the living room, she found Kara there, surrounded by all their notes, a pen in her mouth and the papers covering face. The only way Lizzie was able to tell it was Kara was the blue hair sticking out.

She must have heard her since she put the papers down and looked over.

"Lizzie! I think I got part of the clue!" She hopped up and handed Lizzie the papers she had in her hands.

Lizzie scanned them, but found nothing that made any sense. "What am I looking at?"

"Jane first title for *Pride and Prejudice* was *First Impressions*. In the letter she states that first impressions are misleading."

Lizzie saw where Kara was going and started hopping excitedly, then stopped dead when she realized what she had mentioned last night. "She also used her own character's quote of being barely tolerable. A quote from *Pride and Prejudice!*"

"Exactly! I think your next clue will be found in *Pride and Prejudice*," Kara gushed.

"Oh my God, Kara. You're amazing." Lizzie wrapped her arms around the blue-haired pixie and jumped around in unison.

"Should I be worried?" Nick's said with a laugh.

As they slowed their jumping and released each other, Lizzie turned and realized Graham was standing next to Nick, an amused smile on his face.

"This gorgeous, gorgeous, girl just figured out where we can find the next clue!" Lizzie exclaimed.

Nick's eyes went wide and he walked over to Kara. He lifted her off her feet and spun her around with a big hug. "That's my girl."

Lizzie laughed and walked over to Graham. She stood next to him to take in the happy sight of Kara and Nick. She mischievously elbowed Graham in the ribs and looked up at him.

"Wanna know where it can be found?" she asked.

"That's why I'm here," he said and shrugged, trying to still act like the cool distant guy.

"*Pride and Prejudice*," she said with a smirk.

He clapped his hands and rubbed them together. "Shall we start reading?"

"No," she answered quickly. He shot a sharp confused glance at her.

She continued. "You need to go get your locks changed and put things in order at your house. I'm going to help you clean."

"You? Clean?" he teased, but as she smiled and looked up at him, it was obvious that he was genuinely touched by her offer. He wrapped an arm around her shoulders and pulled her into a half-hug.

"We want to help too, Mate. We can get all the boys there to help. I'm sure their lives were going to be dull today anyway," Nick said. He grabbed his phone and quickly texted out a long message.

"Sent," he said and continued. "You go and get new locks and keys, Graham. Kara, Lizzie, and I will start cleaning and unpacking Lizzie's stuff into your guest room."

"What?" Lizzie and Graham said in perfect unison.

Nick walked over to stand in front of Lizzie. "You asked to stay the night. Night over. Graham said he offered you a longer term stay so…"

Lizzie glanced at Graham and saw his dude-I'm-going-to-kill-you-in-a-loving-way look.

She then glanced back at Nick who licked his bottom lip and winked at Graham. After the weird interaction, he walked over to Kara, wrapped an arm around her waist, and led them out of the room.

"I am so sorry, Lizzie. I'll go and talk to him about the whole living situation." Graham turned to leave, but she stopped him by grabbing his arm.

"Wait. He had a point. I did only ask to stay the one night. But if your offer no longer stands, I can just look for another hotel to stay in," she said and met his gaze directly.

"Don't be ridiculous, of course my offer still stands. I just thought you would be against it," he said, slightly embarrassed.

She smiled, feeling wanted somewhere, which was a new feeling for her. Sure, her parents always gave her the kind of love and attention most parents would, but to have a non-family member want her was different and enjoyable.

"As long as I can get my own room, and you learn to knock before entering, I will gladly take you up on your offer. And like you said, now we can work around the clock until you leave in…" She looked at the date of her phone. "Two weeks and five days."

"I did say that didn't I?" He rubbed his head with a nervously happy smile.

It was a bit confusing at first, but then she was able to read the smile like it was in a novel. It told a story. He was anticipating her stay. Happy, but trying to conceal just how happy he was.

She soon found herself smiling with a similar happy-confused kind of smile.

"I better pack up all my gear," she said and walked past him to the staircase.

"Yeah, and I better go get a new lock and keys." He grabbed his keys from the table and dangled them next to his head. "See you soon," he said, smiled, and walked toward the front door.

She nodded and started up the stairs calmly. When she heard the front door close, she ran up to her room to throw everything into her suitcase as fast as she could.

#

Graham arranged for the locksmith to put in new locks and called the security company to reset the password Caterina was using.

As he walked up the stairs to his home, he heard loud yells and laughter from behind his door. He flung open the door to see the boys doing random chores around his home. As he walked around, he took in what they were all doing for him.

Jude and Christian were cleaning the kitchen. Josh, a tech on the tour, was working on the layout of the couch and chairs while Emmet was setting up the new TV and entertainment system.

They all waved and shouted out greetings as he skipped up his stairs to his bedroom.

When he walked in, Nick was hanging his clothes back up and another of their friends, Andy, was shoving all the ripped up sheets and blankets into rubbish bags.

"Graham! You're back! Great! You can help up finish up in here," Nick said and patted Graham's back rather hard.

"Yeah, sure. How did you lot get in here?" he asked, concerned after what had happened with Caterina.

"You gave us all emergency keys to your place, remember? And we thought we should probably get here before they don't work anymore. I put Lizzie's cases in the guest room across the way. Is that ok?" Nick nudged him toward the hall.

Graham glanced across to see the suitcases sitting on the large king-sized bed in the guest room. He then remembered walking around the house and not seeing her in any of the rooms. He looked at Nick and asked, "Where is she? I didn't see her downstairs."

"Her and Kara are working on something super important top secret mumbo jumbo in your office," Andy chimed as he tossed more stuff and sheets into the bag.

Graham dropped his bags on the ground and hurried down to his office. He was about to barge in, but remembered the agreement to knock when the door was closed. Better safe than sorry, he thought as knocked lightly on the door.

"Come in," Lizzie said, the sound of her voice angelic.

He flung open the door. Kara was sitting at his desk, typing away on a new computer, and Lizzie was on the floor surrounded by piles of shredded paper and his tape dispenser. She looked up at him with a bright white smile.

"You knocked," she joked.

"You asked me to," he replied. He went to her and looked at her as she taped things together.

"What on Earth are you doing?"

She smiled again and handed him a completely taped up batch of what was once shredded paper and explained. "I couldn't let all your hard work be wasted. You did a lot of research."

"This is so unnecessary," he said, smiled and bent down in front of her. "But I do appreciate it."

He met her gaze, but then they heard an immense crash from the kitchen followed by loud cries from Jude. All three of them looked toward the door and Lizzie huffed out a breath.

"You should probably check on them. Last time they were hitting each other with the spray faucet," she said with a laugh.

He nodded and stood back up to walk out of the room. As he was leaving, he couldn't help but overhear Kara say to Lizzie, "Jesus, girl. If you undressed him with your eyes any harder, his clothes would have *literally* come off!"

Graham felt the heat flood his face and his heart beat faster at the thought of Lizzie undressing him.

He made his way to the kitchen to find Christian throwing grapes at Jude, who was running around the kitchen with pots and pans, using them as shields to try and defend himself.

"Seriously guys?" Graham yelled. They stopped instantly and looked at him with some of the most guilty-puppy-faces he had ever seen.

It was hard to stay mad at them with those faces and with all the work they were doing on his behalf.

"Thank you, mates," he said and joined them in the food fight.

#

"Cheers, mates. Thank you so much for all your help. It's appreciated. Except Christian and Jude, who seemed to make more of a mess of the kitchen than it had previously been in," Graham teased as he funneled everyone out the front door.

When he shut the door, he made sure he turned the new lock, set the security system, and then made his way to his office to see how Lizzie was doing.

He knocked on the door again and heard a tired, "Come in."

He opened the door. There was a lot less confetti and many more full pages. He was very impressed.

"Wow. You're almost done," he said, showing just how impressed he was.

She smiled. "I was always a fan of puzzles."

He sat down across from her and the piles of carefully taped pages. "You've been working all day. It's nearly eleven. Time to go to sleep. We can finish this tomorrow."

"It's fine, really. I'm not that tired and I'm almost done." Although as she said that, she rubbed her eyes and stretched. He could tell she was lying. The bags under her eyes told him just how tired she really was.

He stood back up and put out his hand. "Come on, Lizzie."

"I'm fine, Graham," she argued.

"Fine. You leave me no other option." He bent down and swept her up into his arms.

"Graham! What are you doing?" She kicked her legs and tried to get him to release her.

He ignored her and walked out of the room and to the stairs. She continued to kick and shout and he put her down in front of the stairs.

She faced him with a satisfied smile. "Giving up?" she asked.

"No. I just need a better angle to carry you." He once again bent down, but this time he tossed her over his shoulder.

She again began kicking and screaming, but it was playful complaining.

When he got to the top of the stairs, he took a deep breath and walked over to her room. At the edge of the bed, he bent and flipped her body over him, but the weight change caused him to fall on top of her.

She was laughing under him and her body vibrated with the force of her laughter.

He couldn't stop watching her and the joy on her face.

When she opened her eyes and saw him gazing at her, her laughed stopped instantaneously.

He knew he should get up and walk away, but his mind and body were not on the same wavelength. He raised his hand to her cheek. The skin was as warm and soft as he remembered from his brief touch of it in Bath. He traced her ruby red lips with his thumb, stroking them gently. They were softer than he had imagined and much more plump.

Her hand covered his and gently pulled it off her cheek.

He was disappointed, but then she turned her head to glance at his wrist. She stroked his wrist tattoo with his thumb and grinned.

"I like this tattoo," she whispered and then looked back up at him. "What does it mean?"

He rolled over, off of her, and onto the empty part of the bed. He stared up at the ceiling and said, "Time will tell the story."

He peered at her and a mocking smile crept over her face.

"Touché." She sat up and leaned forward. "If you're going to force me to sleep, shouldn't you be going to bed as well?"

He pushed off the bed and hopped up by the edge of it.

"Fair enough," he said and walked to the door. "Sleep well, Lizzie."

"Sleep well, Graham," she said, a happy smile on her face.

He walked out and crossed the hallway to his own room. He sat on the edge of his bed and rubbed his temples.

What the hell was I doing?

You were going to kiss her, you idiot!

It was her damn eyes. And her skin. And her lips. They looked like two plump strawberries ripe for picking.

Oh come on, Graham. When did you become such a girl?

When you hang out with one who is obsessed with authors and their descriptiveness, that's when, his inner voice shot back.

"Shit," he cursed and fell back onto his bed.

Having Lizzie around wasn't going to be as easy as he had thought.

Chapter 24

Temptation

What the hell? Lizzie thought.

Had he just been about to...

No...no way! He is so off limits. He just broke up with his girlfriend!

Lizzie control your emotions...this sucks.

She climbed into bed, not even bothering to change.

Maybe I had something on my lip and he was just trying to rub it off.

Her mind continued to make up excuses as to what had happened.

It slowly put her into an unsettling sleep filled with thoughts of Graham and the memory of his touch.

#

She woke abruptly to very loud rumbles and flashes of light outside the window. Rain beat loudly against the glass.

She took a few deep breaths to calm herself, looked over at the alarm clock and groaned. It was late. She should have woken up already to finish the puzzle of papers.

She jumped out of the bed, not even bothering to change, threw on a hoodie and walked downstairs.

She smelled eggs, but as she walked into the kitchen, no one was there and there was no food anywhere. She shrugged and walked over to the office. Inside, her piles of paper were no more and Graham was laid out on the couch, reading.

"Morning," he said with a smile. "I left you some breakfast on the desk. I assumed you would want something to start the day."

She glanced over to the desk to see a plate with the eggs she had smelled earlier.

"Thank you," she said and grinned. "Where are all the shreds of paper?"

"I happen to like puzzles as well. The storm woke me up about an hour ago and I had to keep my mind busy." He smirked ruefully and nudged her toward the papers that sat next to the eggs on his desk.

She walked over and saw that all the shreds of paper had been put back together. *All* of his notes and research.

"This is impressive. Graham. So is the smell of those eggs. Thank you." She sat down in the big chair and was about to dive into the eggs when she saw her mother's copy of *Pride and Prejudice* sitting next to the food. She looked up Graham again with amazement in her gaze.

He had obviously been waiting for her reaction since he gave a satisfied smile.

"I unpacked all of your books and research. Like I said, I had to keep my mind busy." He pointed to his office window and the storm raging outside.

She nodded and took a bite of the eggs, which were cooked to perfection, grabbed her book and read as she ate. When she had finished the eggs, she took her empty plate back to the kitchen and aware of Graham's neat freakness, she rinsed it and put it in the dishwasher. Then she returned to the office where together they read and read, pointing out possible hints or clues within the book.

They read out scenes to each other and joked about the wording or the stupidity of the men or the families and wondered how young people such as themselves had survived in such restrictive times.

"I'm going to make some tea. Would you like a cup?" Graham asked as he rose from the couch and stretched.

She looked up from her book and likewise rose, since his desk chair was kind of uncomfortable. It was meant for man's bigger butt and not her small one.

"That would be great. Thank you," she said and as the door shut behind him, she quickly took the opportunity to jump out of the chair and run to the couch. She lay down to continue reading.

When he walked in minutes later, he laughed and shook his head, a smile on his face.

"Clever girl." He arched his eyebrows and walked to where her head lay on the couch. It was big enough for him to sit down next to her. He handed her the cup of tea and she sat up to take a sip.

"The desk chair was getting uncomfortable after all those hours of sitting in it," she said and heard a bit of whine in her voice. She cringed because it reminded her of how Caterina would act to get her way with Graham.

"Yeah, yeah," he said and rolled his eyes. He put his mug of tea down on the side table and grabbed his book to continue.

"Plus, you didn't call fives. I had every right to take the seat," she teased and took another sip of tea. Placed her mug on the coffee table beside his. She tried not to think how right it looked for their two mugs to be sitting there as they sat beside each other on the couch.

"Although I don't know what 'fives' is, I don't mind the fact my seat was taken." He smiled and looked away from his book and down at her as she lay on the couch.

She held the book above her face to read which also allowed her to sneak a peek at him every now and then. The rain still pelted against the window, but the thunder and lightning slowly subsided. Her arms grew tired, but she was compelled to keep reading even as she struggled to keep her eyes open.

Something else was lulling her to sleep.

Graham was humming as he played with her hair.

She tried to convince herself to move away from him and stop the way he was making her feel. But the feel of his fingers grazing her scalp, running through the rest of her hair, and his humming, were alluring enough to keep her exactly where she was.

Chapter 25

A new start and new feelings

Graham had no clue what he had been doing until he Lizzie stirred a bit next to him.

He looked at her. Her eyes were closed and the book rose and fell as it sat on her chest.

That was when he realized his finger was entangled in her lush black-brown hair. It was soft and smooth, making running his fingers through it a piece of cake.

With Caterina it had been impossible to even brush a strand of hair out of her face. Her bright red curls were a tangle like a rat's nest. When she had taken the time to get it straightened, there was so much styling product in it that his hands would feel sticky and wrong after he touched it.

He stopped himself short. He needed to stop comparing the two girls since he felt guilty every time he did so. Even though Lizzie came out the clear winner in every category that he compared, it was not fair to either party.

But it was tough not to compare them, he thought as he leaned his head back on the couch and stared at the ceiling as his fingers continued to play with her hair. It was peaceful being here with her. Touching her, he thought, and didn't stop.

#

He shot his head up as something moved on his lap. Rubbing his eyes with his hand, he realized what had moved in his lap.

Lizzie's head rested on his thigh and his arm lay across her chest.

She said nothing when he woke and simply tried to gently turn the page of her book.

He removed his arm from around her body and cleared his throat.

She quickly sat up and looked over at him.

"Sorry," he apologized, not sure as to why he did.

"Why?" she said with a shrug. She popped off the couch and walked over to his desk. She sat in front of his new computer and typed rapidly, as if she had found something while he napped. He rubbed his eyes again and went over to see what she was searching for.

He leaned an arm on the desk and his hand on the top of the desk chair as he watched her skim through pages and pages of Google searches.

"What exactly are you looking for?" he asked.

"In the clue Jane mentions 'church.' Why? It doesn't seem important to the rest of the clue. Why of all the possible places did she choose church?" she said, explaining her rationale.

Déjà vu hit him as she spoke.

It was like the first time she had explained a clue to him. He also knew if he didn't question her reasoning, she wouldn't explain much further. He wanted to hear her logic. "Well, they did frequent church a bit more than we do today, but how is that clue implied in *Pride and Prejudice?* Also, the locations in *Pride and Prejudice* aren't real locations. None of the locations in her books are real places."

She stopped typing and swiveled the chair to face him. He shifted a bit closer to her, but then quickly retreated.

Her face showed how annoyed she was when he questioned her. But he knew she loved explaining her reasoning even as she rolled her eyes at his request.

"In the story, a friend of Darcy sits with Lizzie in church and divulges the fact that Mr. Darcy was the one who split Mr. Bingley and Lizzie's sister Jane. Gossip…in a church…ringing any bells? And as for your issue with the locations, Austen had to base the locations on places she did know. All authors base locations, characters, and scenarios on actual people, places, and things."

She turned back to the computer to continue scanning the search results.

He skimmed through the searches as fast as he could and one thing immediately caught his eyes. He shouted, "Stop!"

She lifted her hands off the mouse and keyboard and he pointed to one of the sites. "Look."

It read "Jane Austen Tour Locations."

He reached over her, taking control of the mouse and keyboard, and clicked on the link. On the first page a slideshow of images was scrolling across the screen. An image of a small church popped up and he quickly clicked to see what information the web page would provide.

"Steventon Church, where Jane's father was rector, is nearly untouched since the time she spent there. Located in the sparsely populated Hampshire area, this Austen location boasts gorgeous open land visuals and an eerily captivating cemetery," she read aloud.

He watched as, with every word, the smile on her face grew wider. She glanced at him and said, "Do you know what this means?"

"You asked me that with the last clue. This whole scenario is full of déjà vu." He laughed, moved around the desk and stood in the open area in the office. He put his arms out and waved her over, "Come on."

"What?" she said, confused.

"Just come here," he said in a friendly, but demanding voice.

She stood up, walked over, and he dropped his arms to grab her hands. They were as soft and creamy as they had been days ago. He smiled at how perfectly they fit in his hands.

He slowly began to jump up and down and her laughter echoed in the room as she soon jumped up and down with him, celebrating the progress they'd made with the last clue. He wrapped his arms around her waist and spun her around. Her squeal of happiness brought him more joy than possibly solving the clue.

She nuzzled her head against his neck and he felt her smiling lips against his collarbone. It felt so good he didn't want to let her go.

When he finally put her down, her hands trailed down to his chest and then away from him completely. It was odd how empty he felt when she let go of him.

She strolled to the windows and looked back at him. "So, Steventon tomorrow?" she asked.

He said nothing, but smiled and nodded. She smiled as she looked at the window and he followed her gaze. Orange and purple streaks filled the sky as the sun started to set.

"Well the rain finally let up," she said. "I'm going to walk to the market to grab some food. I'm pretty sure you used the last of the eggs this morning and....," she coughed, covering up the name she said, before finishing. "Took or destroyed the rest."

She'd meant Caterina and didn't want to say her name aloud, but he knew. Whether it was to spare him awkwardness or just because she had an obvious dislike for the girl, he found himself grateful not to hear his ex's name.

"You don't want me to come with you?" he asked politely.

She shook her head. "We wouldn't want people seeing us together and making more assumptions yet again. No more wrong ideas."

She walked over to the door, but he instinctively reached out to grab her arm and gently urge her to face him once more.

"So what is the right idea about the two of us together?" He brushed the indent of her elbow with his thumb and her gaze dropped down where he touched her.

"I don't know what you mean by that. We're friends, aren't we?" She inhaled deeply and met his gaze again, making him question himself and how to answer. Did she want him to confirm the fact they were friends or did she want him to disagree and say they were something more?

He must have taken too long to respond.

She drew her arm away from his touch and walked out of the room.

He covered his face with his hands and rubbed them up and down in frustration. He finally flung them away and slapped his legs angrily.

Why were women so complicated?

Or maybe they weren't complicated and he just didn't understand what they wanted, the little voice in his head answered.

He rushed out of the office and up the stairs. When he looked into the open door of Lizzie's room, she was shoving money in the front pocket of her tan backpack. She tossed the bag over her shoulder and walked to the door where he stood there, staring at her like an idiot.

"I'm just gonna get some basics. Bread, eggs, milk, blah blah..." She smiled, darted past him and down the stairs.

"Wait! I should pay!" he shouted after her.

"You bought the books and offered me a free room. Least I can do is buy some food," she shouted back.

As he heard the front door close, he once again reminded himself.

Women are too complicated.

The little voice in his head said, "Idiot."

Chapter 26

A welcome guest

Lizzie pushed the headphones into her ears and walked down the street, bopping to the beat of Greetings from Victoria's latest release. She didn't have to walk long before she saw a grocery store. She rushed into a nearby TescoExpress and grabbed a shopping basket.

As she strolled up and down the aisles, she grabbed the few things they needed, but as she turned down one aisle, someone tapped her shoulder.

She whirled and dropped the basket in shock.

"Caterina?" she whispered as she felt something seeping from her basket and into her Freewaters shoes.

"You're not Graham, but I will definitely take it," she said with an evil smirk.

"What are you doing here?" Lizzie spit out nervously and looked around to see if CCTV cameras would be able to record the scene Caterina was about to make.

"Aw. Little Lizzie looks a little scared. What? Didn't think I would try to get Graham back so you couldn't have him all to yourself? I'm surprised he's already sending you to get stuff from the market. He used to ask me to do it all the time," Caterina said and took a menacing step closer to Lizzie.

Lizzie bent down to try and clean up the mess at her feet and salvage what she could. The eggs had broken along with a small bottle of juice.

Caterina chose to bend down and 'help' as well.

"Look at you, cleaning messes just like Graham. It's such a shame he'll never love you. Never the way you love him," she said in her usual sickly sweet voice.

It made Lizzie's blood boil.

"Caterina, you're insane. I don't lo-love Graham and I don't care what his feelings are toward me. You have it in your head I asked him to help. That I wanted to ruin your relationship. News flash. Graham *begged* to help me. He snuck around behind *your* back to continue helping *me*. Graham wanted something you couldn't give him…adventure."

Lizzie had no clue where any of that came from, but she wasn't proud that she had sunk to Caterina's level of venom. Even with that, she felt a rush of adrenaline as she proved her point to Graham's ex.

Caterina's face showed surprise only for a second and then immediately went back to her standard callous and bored look.

"My, my. Growing a backbone all of a sudden. Graham might not enjoy that. He likes his girls to be submissive, begging for him." Caterina's gaze filled with undisguised lust.

"Why does everything come back to Graham and sex with you? If you have an issue with me, be straight and man the hell up," Lizzie said and stood, slipping a bit on the slimy egg. Luckily she was able to stabilize herself.

Caterina also stood up slowly, arching her back to make her butt pop out sexily. "Because with Graham it is all about himself and sex. I'm trying to prepare you, lover girl. If you don't give him what he really wants soon, he'll toss you back to that old hag Fanny. Right now you're just wasting time and space for him. Once he's done with you, he'll toss you away just like he did me."

Caterina pivoted on one heel and sauntered off, but Lizzie wouldn't let that vile girl have the last word.

"You're wrong, Caterina. I will *never* be like you. I don't need a man to make me feel worthwhile."

Caterina stalled for a second as if she'd taken a direct hit, but didn't look back. The other woman brushed imaginary dirt off her thigh and walked out of the market.

Lizzie went back to the chore she had started, calling someone over to clean up the broken items, returning for more eggs and juice and the rest of the items they needed. Minutes later, she finally stood on line at the cash register to pay for the food.

The walk back to Graham's was a blur.

Caterina certainly knew how to make Lizzie question everything that was happening.

Graham had never seemed the type to just want women for sex, but Caterina had been with him for close to three years and so presumably knew him well.

But what about last night, Lizzie? she asked herself. He almost kissed you. You can't deny that anymore. What do you think would have happened? You're not ten anymore. A kiss is not just a kiss.

She trudged up the stairs to Graham's door, but it was locked and she had forgotten to grab a key. She rang the bell and after a few seconds, footsteps sounded in the hall. The door opened a crack and Graham peered out. His eyebrows rose as he flung open the door.

"I guess I should have had a key made for you as well," he said with a laugh.

She nodded and walked past him to the kitchen where she tossed the bags on the counter and began to unpack.

He followed her in and began putting the food away, being the helpful Graham she thought he was, but Caterina's ugly words lingered in her head.

He is probably doing it to get you to fall for it and you are, Lizzie, she said to herself.

"What did you buy?" he asked.

She said nothing as she continued to unpack and separate fridge items from pantry items.

"Lizzie?" he asked, obviously wondering about her silence.

She looked at him and he stood there staring, confused.

She marched over and stood right in front of him. Her gaze darted back and forth from his amazing blue eyes to his lips. Finally she raised her hand and wrapped it around the back of his neck. The short hairs of his buzz cut tickled her palm.

She rose on her tiptoes and gentle drew his head close to hers.

A second later, his lips crashed forcefully onto hers.

She closed her eyes and hoped he wouldn't pull away.

His hands slid across the sides of her hips and wrapped around her waist.

But then he seemed to reconsider what was happening, and he moved his hands back to her sides to try and push her away gently.

Even with that, he didn't break the kiss and seconds later, his push became a pull as he wrapped his arms around her body again. He lifted her gently off her tiptoes, holding her as close as he could. She didn't even realize that they had been moving until her lower back hit the counter.

They never disengaged from the kiss and as their tongues began a dance for dominance, he roamed his hands all over her body. He trailed one hand under her shirt and massaged her bra-clad breast.

She leaned her head back, finally shifting away to draw a shaky breath moan as he continued to caress her breast.

He took advantage of the break to latch his lips onto her neck and suck tenderly.

What am I doing? Am I really about to do this to prove a point? What would Jane do? What would Jane do? *Jane would not even be in this situation*! Lizzie, either focus on him, or end this right now, she scolded herself.

As if he was reading her mind, he pulled away and took a few steps back, breathing heavily.

"Lizzie, I--"

He couldn't seem to finish what he was trying to say. Shakily, he rubbed his lips as he obviously struggled with himself. His body language told her that he didn't know what to do.

She hesitantly approached him and took hold of the hand rubbing his lips. She placed it in the middle of her chest so he could feel how fast her heart was beating.

He had no clue what she had just been through at the market, but she was determined not to let the fear Caterina had created taint what was happening.

She whispered, "Don't question this, not now. Just let it happen."

She took another step toward him, crushing their hands between their bodies, and raised herself on tiptoes.

His nose grazed hers before he tenderly nuzzled his nose against her lips.

She kissed it lightly, but the kiss didn't stay gentle.

Graham didn't hold back this time. As she wrapped her free hand around his neck, he dropped his hand to her waist and under her shirt once more. With his free hand, made slow enticing circles on her hipbones with his thumbs.

She loved all the feelings coursing through her body. His touch was gentle, but had rushes of roughness that she was totally enjoying. With every touch, more and more desire ravaged her body.

He pulled back. "Is everything in the refrigerator that needs to be?"

She laughed. "Are you serious?"

"I just want to make sure your purchases don't go to waste," he said with a boyish grin and leaned down to kiss her neck again.

She looked around the kitchen. "The eggs need to go in."

"Nope. Eggs don't need to be refrigerated." He bit her collar bone and her knees liquefied into jelly. The arm he had wrapped around her waist was now the only thing supporting her.

"That's gross," she said through a moan. "Why did you even ask?"

"Just making sure we can leave the kitchen."

He grabbed her thighs which caused her to jump a bit, which seemed to be what he wanted because her feet came off the ground and she wrapped her legs around his waist as he walked out of the kitchen.

Her body rubbed against his in all the right places and her moans were more and more frequent as the heat built between them. Soon he was bending down with her and she reacted, loosening her legs until she was straddling him on his new couch.

"Glad they finished building this," she said and giggled, but when she looked at him, worry and concern filled his gaze.

Maybe Caterina was wrong. He seems to be questioning this more than I am, She thought.

She shifted her head down and kissed his neck. That's when a needy moan finally escaped his lips.

Now that she knew she found the right spot, she bit down gently, he grabbed her waist with his hands and pushed his pelvis up against her center. That's when she felt what she had seen tenting the sheets a few days ago.

Holy shit.

She yanked her shirt over her head and he moved his hands all over the newly exposed skin. She rested one arm on the couch by his head as she ground her hips against him. His short huffs of breath came quickly as Graham's head fell back onto the couch.

The action allowed her a glimpse of her bite mark and she returned to trailing butterfly kisses around the bite. She moved her body against his in sync to his movements and he drifted his hands to the top button of her jeans.

But he started to chuckle as he did so. She leaned back a bit and he explained. "Your hair is tickling me."

She whipped her head back and forth, sending her hair all across his face and neck which caused him to chuckle even more.

She joined him in the laughter.

"All right. That's enough," he said with a hand around her bottom, he spun and fell so that she was now horizontal on the couch and he was over her. It was a very similar position to where they had been the previous night and then it became even more like the previous night.

He laid a hand on her cheek and his thumb brushed across her lips.

This time she reacted by kissing it as he lazily moved it back and forth.

He slowly lowered his head close to hers and his nose rubbed against her cheek and then her lips. He finally grazed her nose with his as his lips took the place of his rough thumb. He moved the hand that had been holding her cheek down to trace the side of her breast. Then along the side of her torso and over her stomach before going back to what he had previously been doing.

Unbuttoning.

She yanked at the hem of his shirt and jerked it over his head.

She marveled at his body once again and when he leaned back down to kiss her collarbone, he worked her out of her jeans.

He had to be used to doing it often, because in seconds he was pulling the pants off her ankles. He tumbled back down on top of her and began kissing all the exposed flesh.

Her hands rubbed his head as she subconsciously arched her body for more of his kisses.

"They're people," he whispered as he kissed the tattoo along her ribcage.

She just nodded, unable to form words.

He pushed aside her underwear and his slightly cool finger slowly rubbed her womanhood.

She shivered in pleasure and he hungrily brought his lips back to hers.

As his tongue traced her lower lip, he asked a simple question. "Are you sure?"

She opened her eyes and looked deep into his. She tried to lighten the mood created by his too serious question. "I somehow feel that should have been asked before we took off our clothes and you put your hand well…"

They both looked down the length of their bodies to see where he was pushing aside her bright pink, lace-trimmed panty.

"Right." He grinned one of the sexiest grins ever and began kissing her again.

Chapter 27

What a boy wants. . .

His fingers seemed to have a mind of their own as they played under her undergarments.

Her moans increased with every gentle glide of his fingers.

Her back arched and their breast-to-chest contact was filled with pulsating electricity. The same kind of electricity when they didn't touch in the Jane Austen Experience, only more intense.

Much more intense.

His mind was still reeling from the fact she'd kissed him in the kitchen. He had no clue why she had done it, but knew something must have triggered it.

But why? They had only been separated for the brief period of time that she left to get the food.

Her lips were sweet. His imagination had not prepared him for just how plump and red and bitable they really were.

She trailed her hands across his chest before she moved them to his belt buckle. She fumbled with it and soon her body dropped limply to the couch and she huffed a complaint.

"Why is this thing so difficult?" she whispered.

"Because it's Batman," he joked, mimicking the deep superhero voice.

They both laughed and he sat up a bit, took his hands away from her to unbuckle the belt.

Once it was open, she pulled the belt out of his belt loops and moved to the button of his pants. Her fingers tickled the hairs of his happy trail and his body reacted quickly to her touch.

As her fingers undid the zipper, they skimmed right above his boxer brief elastic. He was getting even more aroused, if that was even humanly possible.

Her touch was gentle. Her kisses soft.

It was way different than his previous encounters with the opposite sex, especially Caterina.

Most of the girls he had been with would claw and scream.

Lizzie would caress and whisper.

He worked his fingers at full speed against her center and soon her eyes closed.

Her mouth opened, forming a small 'o', and she latched onto his shoulders with her hands.

As her body shuddered and she fell limply to the couch, he knew just what had happened.

Her breathing was choppy and heavy. She dropped her hand from his shoulders to her breast.

He pulled his hand away from between her legs and went to rub it against his boxers only to realize that somehow his clothes had somehow come half-off while she had been writhing in ecstasy.

He smirked and looked into her now open eyes.

She looked embarrassed so he quickly put his other hand to her cheek. "What's wrong, Lizzie."

She shook her head. "Nothing. It's just…"

"You can tell me anything," he whispered and kissed her forehead to ease her upset.

"That has never happened to me before," she admitted. A furious blush worked across her cheeks and she squinted her eyes shut.

He leaned back, certain that his face betrayed his disbelief. "Really? Like ever?"

She nodded and covered her face with her hands.

He grabbed one of her hands to tenderly ease it away from her face.

"Don't," she said, but voluntarily moved her other hand away from her face.

"You never have to hide from me. Plus, you are rather cute when you blush," he said, smiled, and brought her hand to his lips for a kiss.

"How about we go upstairs? It will be a bit more comfortable than this couch."

"The poor boys who sit on this couch," she said, laughed, and sat up, adjusting her underwear as he pushed his jeans fully off.

"What they don't know won't kill them," he said with a wink.

He jumped up and put out a hand in invitation. She slipped her hand into his and he pulled hard and quick, making her stand and fumble against him.

He swept her off her feet yet again and headed for the stairs.

"Why do you insist on carrying me up these stairs? I'm very able to walk myself," she teased.

"Why ruin the romance of it?"

"Romance?" She laughed, but it had a hard edge to it.

He stopped at the top of the stairs, surprised by her reaction. It wasn't what he expected. He set her on her feet and she faced him.

"Yes. Romance," he repeated.

"I don't get it," she said, confused.

"No, *I* don't get it," he said, suddenly hurt and angry. As he continued, his voice rose in volume. "If this isn't romance, what is this? What the hell happened just now? Why did you start this if you didn't intend for it to go anywhere?"

"Start this? You started it in the kitchen! And what the hell was last night all about? You just broke up with your girlfriend and are probably frustrated. Sex releases endorphins--"

He cut her off. "I know what sex does. You apparently didn't until tonight. And once again we end up back at Caterina. Why? She has nothing to do with my life any more. And as for last night. . ."

He tried to think of something, some reason as to why he had almost kissed her, but nothing came to mind except one thing.

He was attracted to Lizzie.

He knew she probably didn't want to hear that, especially at that moment, so he made up the worst excuse ever. "I don't know why. It was a mistake. I guess I'm still on the rebound stage of my breakup I guess."

"From the break up that you said that has nothing to do with your life?" She was now almost shouting at him as well.

"You know nothing about my life or who or why I make the decisions I make," he yelled back.

"I think I do. You invited me to stay to help you get over your lustful ex-girlfriend. You play it off that you're some humble good guy, Mr. Goody Two Shoes, but behind closed doors you're just like every other man. Sex and lust power every decision. And even though Caterina was, and still is a psycho bitch, she gave you everything you wanted..." Lizzie said and continued.

"But nothing that you really need," she finished. She tossed his arm away and he stood there, eyes wide in shock and confusion.

"You truly think that of me? That all I wanted from you was your body?"

Her gaze darted all around, avoiding his gaze and then something clicked in his head.

"Caterina."

She finally looked at him, almost terrified. "Caterina. You saw her. Where?"

He thought about everything that had happened and suddenly figured it out. "You saw her at the market. She put all of this craziness into your mind, didn't she? You came back here determined to prove whether she was her right or wrong?"

He stepped even further away from Lizzie, disgusted with himself. He had never said to Lizzie that he cared for her and as the night progressed, everything they had done had only confirmed what Caterina had said to Lizzie.

"She is a proper mind fuck that girl," he said and fell against the wall behind him, drained.

"Another word I always wanted to hear. Proper," she said nervously.

He could tell she was trying to hide her embarrassment and that she was more and more frustrated with herself for buying into Caterina's head games.

"Lizzie, I'm so sorry." He reached out to comfort her, but she backed away from him as she covered her body with her arms, hiding little from his gaze.

"For what? I'm the asshole who believed what she said. I'm sorry this happened. Like you said, it was a mistake." She walked to her room when he finally spoke up.

"I don't think it was a mistake," he called out and she stopped dead.

He walked up behind her and said, "It was just the wrong timing."

He gently grasped her arm and urged her around to face him. Her eyes were wide and tears were pooling there. He leaned down and kissed her gently. Just as slowly, she returned the kiss and laid a hand on his chest. He pulled away and leaned his forehead on hers.

"Goodnight, Lizzie."

He walked into his room, shut the door and dreaded what he heard from beyond the closed door.

Lizzie's light sobs. Cursing, he resisted the urge to go back out and comfort her.

That could only lead to one thing.

One thing that neither of them was prepared for that night.

Chapter 28

Regrets

Lizzie had no desire to get out of bed or do anything else with her life the next morning.

Lying in bed, she deciding the best thing to do was take a shower to wash away the memories of the previous night.

As she showered, she scrubbed until all her skin was a bright red and she replayed everything he had said in her head. All the questions that had reared up.

What did he mean wrong timing? Did he really care? Did he actually want to be with her? Why did she have to open her mouth?

She felt stupid as she turned off the water and toweled herself dry.

As she walked back out into the room, she found a large breakfast spread on the desk, but no one was in the room. She took a few steps closer and heard a knock on the door.

She smiled at his thoughtfulness and said, "Come in."

The door clicked open and Graham popped his head in.

She held the towel closer to her body, although he had seen enough of her already.

"I...umm...wanted to apologize for last night. I should have thought before I acted and I'm sorry for making you upset and giving you the wrong impression of me," he said while he twiddled his thumbs and tried very hard not to be awkward.

It made him look even more awkward.

She smiled nervously and grabbed a piece of toast. "Graham, grow a pair. There's no need for you to apologize," she spit out before her mind could stop it. She covered her mouth and his eyes went a bit wide. "I am so sorry."

"No, it's cool. You just were saying what you feel." He looked at the room as if to try and find something to get him out of there. "I guess Steventon is off for today," he continued. "We can try again tomorrow. Have a good day," he said and grabbed the doorknob.

"Graham, I'm sorry. I'm just frustrated that I allowed Caterina to invade my mind and you apologizing for dumb assery is just the icing on the 'I fucked up' cake. So again, please don't apologize. I'm the one who made this awkward." She shrugged and took another small bite of toast.

He turned back to her and mischief glinted in his eyes. She could tell he was planning something. He took a few steps toward her and every step made her heart race faster. He rested a hand on her toweled hip and grabbed a bit forcefully.

"What are you doing?" She looked up at him anxiously.

"Growing some balls," he said and leaned his head down to hers. As his nose grazed hers, eyes fluttered shut, but his lips never met hers.

Instead, a rush of cold air hit her entire body and when she glanced down, she realized she was totally bare and Graham was waving the towel as he ran into his room and kicked the door shut behind him.

She couldn't control the laughter and somehow managed shout to his closed door, "Thanks for breakfast!"

"Thanks for the show!" he replied.

She laughed some more and threw some clothing on before Graham re-emerged from his room.

As she made her way out of the room to go down to the office to grab some books for her to read, she grabbed a strip of bacon. She found her clothing on the floor next to the couch and quickly picked it up to bring back upstairs with her. When she got back up to her room, she climbed onto the bed and started looking through the books she had selected from his office.

She smiled at *Catcher in the Rye*. It was her mom's least favorite book and Lizzie would beg her to read it because after every chapter her mom would complain about how whiney Holden was.

She decided to skip that book and grabbed a more modern novel that her mom had been pleasantly surprised by. *Perks of Being a Wallflower*. They had both enjoyed the book so much, that they had seen the movie three times in theaters.

She opened to the first page to begin her journey to western Pennsylvania with Charlie, Sam, and Patrick. About two hours into the book, she heard Graham huff in annoyance from his room.

"Lizzie, I'm bored!" he shouted out.

"You have friends. Go hang out with them. You're the one who decided we weren't going anywhere today," she hollered back.

"Everyone is busy. Plus it's both our fault for not going today. I don't know about you, but after last night I barely slept."

"I slept like a baby," she lied. She had actually only slept for about an hour. "Why don't you take a nap or read a book?"

"That's your thing," he said as he finally opened his door and made his way over to her room. He sat on the edge of the bed like a small child, pouting his lips for her attention.

"Well, Graham, I'm currently doing my thing and you're interrupting." She lifted the book back up to her face to continue reading.

He fell back onto the bed and moved his way up next to her. "How about you help make it my thing as well?" He shot her a pleading look. "Read to me."

"You can't be serious," she said in disbelief.

He met her gaze and she saw something there. Caring.

"You said you and your mother used to read your favorite books aloud and that you missed it when she stopped. So…" He shifted closer and leaned his head on her shoulder.

Her heart swelled and was sure to burst at how amazingly sweet it was that he remembered. She turned her attention back the book and began to read aloud.

As she read she gauged Graham's reactions. He'd laugh, sigh, and sometimes even sniffle at the sadder moments in the book. But close to the end, he whispered the last line in unison with her without even glancing at the page.

She looked over at him and he met her gaze. "Read this before, have you?"

"Several times. It's all about American subculture," he replied.

"You just snatched that from the quote on the back of the book." She flipped it over and pointed to the review.

"True. But I did read the book before. It was a very real book. Although everything that could go wrong in a child's life seemed to have happened to Charlie, his family, and friends."

"But they all learned from it and grew." She put the book down in her lap and checked the time. "Holy crap! We've been in here all day. It's almost six."

He said nothing as he wrapped an arm around her waist and pulled her closer to him. His warm breath washed across her neck, causing shivers to run down her spine. Images of the previous night flooded her mind.

"Graham," she said with a moan as she wiggled out of his hold. "Don't you think we should talk about what happened last night? Sure we both apologized, but we didn't discuss it."

"I would rather not. I would like to leave it in the past and move forward." He sat up and created some space between them.

"I don't think I can do that. Last night...last night meant something to me," she said boldly.

She couldn't face him, but she knew he was waiting to hear more. She wasn't ready to admit her feelings outright. It wasn't the time since he was still in the healing process from his break-up.

When he said nothing, she explained, "You made me feel something I have never felt before."

More visions of the night before crossed her mind and warmth built in her lower abdomen.

"The orgasm?" he asked.

She blushed and nodded. "I can't forget that happened and that it happened with you," she said and finally met his gaze.

He was watching her intently and she tried to look away, but he reached out quickly and cupped her cheek to hold her gaze. "I don't want you to forget. I just have to ask. Where is this conversation going?"

"Where are we going, Graham? What happened was not two acquaintances, or friends, or whatever we are, just fooling around." She was getting frustrated with the hundreds of thoughts racing through her mind and how she could not voice them all.

"Where do you want to go?" he asked.

Where did she want this to go?

She couldn't get last night out of her head. She had memorized every single touch. She also regretted that she had allowed Caterina's nastiness to ruin the whole night. Not to mention that he was still newly single and not even truly single because he and Caterina were solely taking a little time away from each other.

"I don't see us going far, if anywhere. We just met and you're on a break--"

He cut her off. "Oh, no. Caterina and I are done."

Her heart fluttered with that statement. "Well…" she said, hesitating, but then the reality of the situation came rushing back.

"In any case. Last night was amazing, for me at least, I will never forget it, but you are, well you, and once this hunt is over I plan to go back to America to be with my father. And you will be a pop star who is going to get even more famous after your tour."

He dropped his hand from her cheek. "Sure. That sounds like a very logical answer. I am me. Really, Lizzie? Is that really the answer?"

"What do you want me to tell you?" She raised her voice to match the escalating volume of his.

"The truth. How about we start with the whole truth and nothing but the truth. That's what your American law shows always say." He turned his entire body so he could face her directly.

"I like you!" she blurted out, frustrated with the situation. When it clicked that she had actually come out and said it, she realized she needed to cover her tracks. She glanced at him to see a small smirk forming on his face.

"We're friends and as a friend, I don't want this friendship ruined by what happened last night. And the thought of what could have happened."

"I like you, too," he replied, trying to cut off her awkward fumbling. "As a friend as well. And as for last night, let's not have it ruin our friendship. We did it and we both agree it was enjoyable, but you want to stay friends and I want to stay friends, so let's stay friends."

And with one word, repeated multiple times, her heart no longer fluttered, but crashed into the pit of her stomach. Friends.

She smiled, trying to mask the utter embarrassment deep inside. She was the one who said it first, so why was she so surprised that he agreed to it?

She looked down at her lap and he reached for the book and flipped through the pages.

"Do you want to know my favorite part?" he said and smiled.

She glanced up at him to urge him to continue.

"Do you really think that we pick people who are wrong because we think it's the best we can do?" he said and put the book down on the bed.

"Are we talking about anyone in particular?" she asked, already knowing the answer.

He rolled his eyes as he glanced at her.

She smiled and thought about his question. Finally she came up with a response. "I think that at one point she was the right person, but something changed. Whether it was the fame, the money, or most likely both, something other than your love consumed her heart and mind. It was a learning experience. You have grown from it and can now look toward the future to find the true real love you deserve."

"You're right, Lizzie. I mean, I learned so much from that relationship that I'm prepared for a new one. Well, after the European tour or maybe even during. A nice foreign girl with a fancy accent," he joked.

She let out a pathetic laugh, because even though she was thrilled that he realized he could move on, the moving on was not being directed at her.

Until she realized that he was tracing circles on her arm with the tips of his fingers. She had no clue how long he had been doing that since his touch had been so gentle. She closed her eyes and relished the moment. Soon after he began to hum and her body grew heavy as sleep called to her.

She fought it, not wanting to lose this moment.

Not wanting to miss even a heartbeat of her time with him.

Chapter 29

You've got a friend

Friends.

She wanted to be friends.

He must have been crazy to think she would want something more. Once all of this was said and done, she would be on a plane back to the States to move on with her life.

As he drew circles on her arm, her slight weight against him grew steadily heavier. He snuck a peek at her. Her eyes were closed and her mouth was slightly parted as she took steady breaths.

She was fast asleep.

He rolled off the bed and walked around to shut off the table lamp. A small smile lingered on her face and couldn't help smiling back at her. He leaned over, brushed her hair off her forehead, and gently kissed her warm skin.

He shut off the light and walked out of the room.

Friends.

Friends.

That word bothered him more than he anticipated. Why? And why did it disappoint him in the first place? Why? Why? Why? She was just an average girl.

Quit lying to yourself, mate, he thought. She's not just an average girl and you know why the word friend bothers you so much. You like her more than a friend. You're attracted to her, mind, body, and soul.

Shaking his head at the realization, he walked down to the kitchen to get a glass of water.

But as he walked down the entry hallway, a loud pounding sounded against the front door. He walked to the door and pulled back the curtain on the sidelight.

Although he couldn't make out a face because of the darkness, it was impossible to miss the mounds of curly hair.

Caterina.

Instantly angry, he unlocked the door and opened it just a crack. "What the hell do you want Caterina?" He wanted to scream, but he didn't want to wake up Lizzie and have her come down.

Caterina glanced at him oddly. He couldn't put a finger on it, but was surprised that there was no venom spewing from her lips or malice in her eyes.

"I came to talk," she whispered.

"We have nothing to discuss." He was about to slam the door when some rarely uttered words escaped her.

"I'm sorry."

He opened the door a bit more from the shock of hearing her apologize.

"Yeah, shocking. You could at least pretend to be less surprised," she said and rolled her eyes.

He cleared his throat. "I apologize, but it's not something I heard all that often from you. It's a little shocking. I'm glad to finally hear you say it, but it's going to take a lot more than that for me to forgive you for all the problems you've caused."

"But there is a chance you can forgive me?" she asked with a hopeful smile.

He let out a long-winded puff of air. "Of course there is, Caterina. We went through so much together. Things I don't think I can ever forget. But that doesn't mean I will ever be able to be your friend or anything more."

Her smile faded, but then quickly reappeared. "I guess I'll just have to work that much harder so we can be friends again." She took a step toward him and wrapped her arms around his waist.

He stood there stoically and said nothing. When she let go, her gaze drifted to a spot behind him.

He followed her gaze and found Lizzie standing there frozen, looking right at Caterina.

When he turned back to Caterina, he caught the evil smirk she sent Lizzie.

He laughed roughly and rubbed the back of his neck. "Wow, Caterina. You almost had me fooled. You'll stop at nothing to ruin everything I have that is not you or yours."

He was closing the door in her face when her venom returned. "You'll be begging for me soon enough."

He forced the door shut until he heard the click and then quickly locked the door.

He hurried to Lizzie's side and put his hands on her shoulders, but was still motionless.

"Lizzie?" he asked.

She met his gaze and her pupils were almost non-existent with upset.

He felt horrible and brushed her cheek with his hand, trying to soothe her.

It seemed to do the trick, so he moved close and wrapped his arms around her. "She is a scary person. Hell, I'm terrified of her," he said.

Those few words seemed to relax her and soon she gave him a tight bear hug. He kissed the top of her head and they released each other simultaneously.

"I was going to make a quick dinner. Want to join me?" he asked.

She nodded and they walked into the kitchen to cook, chatting and enjoying their time together. Driving away the unpleasant thoughts of Caterina with the easy camaraderie of the meal.

When the food was finished, the dishes rinsed and in the dishwasher, he walked her to her room.

"I'm sorry about Caterina. I hope she won't be back again."

Lizzie nodded, reached up and trailed her hand across his cheek. "I hope so, too, Graham."

Gulping at the rush of heat her simple touch created, he fought the urge to follow her into her room and instead said, "Steventon, tomorrow? Together?"

"That's what friends are for, right?" she said with a smile, but it didn't quite reach up into her eyes.

Forcing his own smile, he said, "Yes, right. That's what friends are for. In the morning then," he said and before anything else could happen, she had stepped into her room and closed the door.

Friends, Graham thought as he leaned against her door, wanting to kick himself for his stupidity.

It took all his willpower to walk away and to his room, but he did it.

He didn't deserve Lizzie yet. Maybe he never would.

Or maybe the next few days would prove otherwise, he thought with a real smile and headed for his own bed.

#

Knock! Knock! Knock!

Lizzie rolled over to see what time it was.

Seven a.m.

She groaned, climbed out of her nice warm bed, and walked to open the door.

"Graham, what do you want?" She rubbed her eyes, trying to adjust to the too bright day.

"We're heading to Steventon today, remember? Get dressed. And bring a raincoat. It's going to be misting most of the day."

"Welcome to England," she said with a roll of her eyes and closed her door to get dressed.

When she was finished, she walked downstairs and found Graham sitting on the couch with his very own backpack.

"Copying my awesome fashion sense?" She tapped her mother's bag which was slung over her shoulders.

"It holds a lot. I didn't know if there would be any places to stop on the way, so I stocked up on snacks, food, and drinks. Everything we could possibly need." He patted the bag, a proud look on his face.

"Sorry mine is just packed with books and notes," she said and laughed.

"Also very important," he argued.

"Thank you." She curtsied and looked toward the front door. "Shall we?"

He jumped up. "Let's."

#

Driving with him never seemed to get old. The scenery was always new and different and even with the fog rolling in and out, it fueled her amusement and excitement. The large glass and cement skyscrapers turned into quaint town homes and then to open acres dotted with small cottages and farms.

"So where in the church do you think this next clue will be?" Graham said, interrupting her thoughts.

"Not sure. A bible?" she joked. "The website with the history of the church stated that it had been relatively untouched over the years. I'm hopeful that wherever it was, it'll still be there today," she said.

He nodded and continued the drive, but something was still obviously gnawing at him. After only a few seconds, he finally said, "About last night..."

"What about last night?"

Lizzie had not been expecting Caterina when she had walked downstairs after waking from a too short nap. She had thought it was a figment of her imagination at first since she had fallen asleep pretty fast and woken up even faster when Graham left the room.

"Caterina was being her psycho self," he said.

"We had this discussion last night." She was confused about why he was bringing it up again, but he clearly had something on his mind. "I feel you need to say more than what you're saying exactly. Am I right?"

He nodded, but said nothing.

She grumbled beneath her breath and tuned to face the open road ahead of them. After long minutes when he had still said nothing else, she rolled her eyes and said, "Spit it out, Graham!"

"Why can't I stop thinking about her?" he blurted out like he had been holding it in until she had forced him to get it out.

That's when Lizzie realized she had now officially been friend-zoned. She sat up a bit and thought about his question. She tried to think of the most reasonable answer and as she thought through all that had happened in the last week, she knew.

"You said you were together for a long time. Most would assume that's years, and knowing you that's definitely true. Most people can't just forget and get over someone they've been with for so long in a matter of days. The fact that she likes to randomly pop in doesn't help you either. Give it a month. You will be on your tour with no time to think of her, or what she's doing, or who she's with. You'll be too busy being an idol to millions of girls," she said and smiled, trying to help him look on the bright side.

"Well, at that point, I'll be thinking about you," he shot out.

She whipped her head around so fast, she was sure she might have snapped her neck. She stared at him, heart racing, waiting for him to explain what he meant.

He rambled off a few questions. "Who's going to drive you all these places? Who's going to help you solve the rest of the clues?"

"The trains and my own two feet will take me where I need to go. I didn't need your help in the beginning and got around just fine. And as for helping, Kara can help, and once she leaves, I'll do the same as you."

He took a quick glance over at her, waiting for her to continue and she did. "I'll move on. Find another cute British boy to help out," she teased.

His jaw clenched and unclenched as he said, "So you plan to trust some random boy with this kind of secret?" He seemed genuinely upset by her statement.

"I trusted you. Some random boy who caught me sneaking into a closed location. You can't be the judge on who I trust. Only I can." She was a bit heated at the fact he was trying to make her feel bad about his leaving and her carrying on with her hunt.

"I didn't mean anything by it, Lizzie. Just be careful," he said, losing his anger and becoming more like a concerned friend with each passing second.

"I can take care of myself, Graham."

"I know you can," he said softly and she caught something mumbled under his breath that sounded like, "scares me."

They drove the rest of the way in silence so strong it was deafening.

The quiet provided too much time for her thoughts to run rampant around her head. Their kisses. His strong, but tender touch on her waist. His chest as she had cuddled with him unintentionally. Every touch and kiss and pleasure they had shared together invaded her mind until she had a headache.

She pinched the bridge of her nose to try and ease the pressure, but it didn't help.

"Headache?" he asked and she nodded.

"In the front pocket of my bag. There should be some of your American ibuprofen in there. It's amazing. I buy it in bulk whenever I am over there. I take like four after every concert."

"You should try some naproxen. That shit will have you screaming with the fans. Knocks out all pain instantly." She laughed as she rummaged through the front pocket. When she went to pull out the bottle, a small box fell out.

"Oops. Sorry," she said and went to pick it up.

"No. Lizzie. Don't," he tried to say but it was too late.

She wrapped her hand around what a small velvet jewelry box. She opened it up and sucked in a deep breath.

"Holy cow! That is one hell of a rock," she said.

He said nothing and she asked, "How long have you been carrying this puppy around?"

"About six months. I was always waiting for the right time," he said with a shrug.

She glanced over and the tension running through his entire body was obvious. She shut the box and put it back in the bag. She grabbed an ibuprofen, popped it in her mouth and then sat back in her seat, feeling bad at how upset he was.

She wanted to do something, anything, to try and help him feel better. So she did the only thing she could think of. She reached over and grabbed his hand as it rested on the stick shift. She placed it on her lap, knowing he would not need to change gears on an empty open road. She placed her other hand on top of it and gently rubbed her thumb across the top of his hand in a gesture meant to soothe.

Every so often, he squeezed her hand tight, and when he did, she gave a small squeeze back. She smiled as she glanced at him a little later and saw that he was more at ease.

After about half an hour, he blurted out, "We're here! This is the street, I think."

She glanced around and only saw a few houses and a lot of trees and shrubs. But then just ahead the street opened into this mind blowing view of the hills and the forest beyond. To their left was a small church, that just like the website stated, boasted amazing views of the countryside and looked like it had been plucked right from an Austen novel.

"That looks like where we should be going," she said and pointed to the church.

He pulled onto a small patch of grass-strewn gravel that she assumed was meant to be parking. He shut off the car, but not a single word was exchanged as they climbed out.

She grabbed her bag and walked to the front of the car. She stood there for a second and snapped a quick photo.

As she took a step toward the church doors, he took hold of her hand and weaved his fingers through hers. She looked down, not believing it was actually happening, but her heart was pounding so fast that it assured her it was really happening. She looked up at him with a sympathetic smile, which he echoed as they reached the old wooden doors.

She pushed on the door handle, but the door didn't budge. She tried it again, but it didn't move.

"Let me," he said. He let go of her hand, grabbed the handle and shoved against the door with his shoulder. It flew open and as he fell to the ground, he shouted, "Jesus Christ!"

Inside the church, a large number of people sat in the rows while a man and woman stood at the front with a priest between them.

"Bless these two," she added to Graham's very loud Lord's name in vain.

"Would you two care to take a seat so we can proceed?" the priest said and pointed to a few open spots on the pews.

She nodded, helped Graham to his feet and over to the pews. He rubbed his shoulder as they sat down.

The wedding continued. She got caught up in the happiness as the groom joyfully placed a wedding band on his love's finger and the bride reciprocated. They looked at each other with such love and admiration, clearly determined to make their marriage last.

She glanced at Graham who seemed genuinely uneasy. She nudged him and mouthed, "What's wrong?"

He shook his head and avoided her gaze, looking down at his shoes.

Lizzie thought back to the car ride and realized how the wedding could make him feel hurt, mad, and even possibly like a failure. She leaned over to whisper in his ear, "Don't let this get to you."

She patted his leg and turned her attention back to the wedding. Soon the happy couple were kissing and everyone was clapping and standing as the newlywed couple hurried out of the church. The rest of the bride and groom's party followed and then the rest of the guests.

She waited until everyone was out of the church before she approached the priest. She quickly apologized for their ruckus and he waved his hands to say an apology wasn't necessary.

"You two are not from around here. I know everyone who walks through those doors and I don't recognize your faces," he said and sat on one of the wooden benches near the altar.

"We drove up here from London. I'm a huge fan of Jane Austen and my friend over there is helping me visit some of the Jane Austen sites." She pointed to Graham who still sat stoically in the back of the church.

"Well this one is not visited often. A few odd travelers. You must be a very dedicated fan," he said.

"I actually came here on a scavenger hunt of sorts," she said, grabbed her bag and rummaged to find the note. When she pulled it out, she gently handed it to the elderly priest. If you couldn't trust a priest, who could you trust?

"This clue led me here, to this church. I'm hoping that we will be able to find the next clue here."

He grabbed his glasses off of his cloak and read the letter. She heard him mumble a few times and his lips moved as he read. With an amused face, he handed the letter back to her.

"This is very impressive. Very impressive. I've been here nearly forty years and can't think of anything to further this journey you wish to continue," he said, put his glasses back in their hanging position, and stood to leave.

"Please, Sir. My friend and I would just like to look around for twenty minutes or so. That's all we will need," she said.

He simply nodded and walked out the front doors which Graham had fallen through.

She breathed a sigh of relief and began looking around, flipping through all the bibles tucked into holders on the backs of the pews. Looking under every pew and kneeling pad.

When she went to look under one particular pew she noticed the black Vans, unmoved. Graham.

She sat up and exhaled a deep breath.

"This would go a lot faster if you helped," she teased, hoping to get him out of his mood.

He said nothing and just continued to stare past her and to the empty alter.

She understood that he was upset, but at the same time it bugged the hell out of her that he wasn't helping. She walked over to sit next to him. "Want to get your mind off all the crap you have buzzing around in there right now?" she asked.

He still didn't move, but she saw him blinking fast and his eyes were slightly red.

She grabbed his hand and softly said, "Look at me."

He shocked her by doing as she asked, slowly facing her. His gaze met hers, expectant. He wanted her help, but seemed too afraid to ask for it.

"We're sitting in a church right now, Graham. Everything you say, or think, or feel within the confines of this place is heard by a higher being, whether you believe it or not. So go up there, confess everything you feel you can't say to anyone else. I promise it will make you feel a whole hell of a lot better. If not, you can leave me here and drive off back to London," she said and smiled.

The stoic look on his face finally broke as he offered her a hesitant smile.

"I wouldn't leave you," he whispered and then looked over at the large cross at the front of the church. He rose, walked to the front pew and kneeled. Head bent, he raised his hands, palm to palm, up to his face. He was doing exactly what she had suggested.

Chapter 30

Divine intervention

Graham kneeled at the front of the church, hoping that the peace of the place would wash over as a whirlwind of thoughts pummeled his mind.

When Lizzie had opened the box in the car, he had nearly slapped it out of her hands. He had wanted to just die right then and there.

When she had grabbed his hand and placed it on her lap, he had felt even more disappointed in himself.

She was right though. The breakup had only just happened. It was only natural that he still thought about Caterina. Only he felt so weak when it came to all the shit about Caterina. And he hated it. He wanted to move on.

Feeling the comfort from the simple touch of Lizzie's hand made him realize he could see himself moving on with her.

That realization had hit him like a ton of bricks.

He knew he was attracted to her. Her kisses left lasting impressions. So did her intelligence, smile, laugh, personality. Everything about her left an impression.

Her supportive whisper telling him not to let the happy couple's wedding get to him had only solidified his total epiphany.

He wanted to be with Lizzie.

When she had sat down next to him and told him to share what he was thinking to the big man above, he knew he was going to confess everything. He needed to tell someone and if that was the only way he could, he would take it.

So that's why he was kneeling there on pew as he finally let everything out.

Hello, big guy. I guess I should call you by your name, God. So that girl back there told me to share everything I've been thinking and feeling.

I was feeling happy until last night and then this morning. That girl, her name is Lizzie, and well she found a ring I was planning to give to my now ex-girlfriend. I'm not upset Lizzie found it. I'm mad at the fact that I was planning to propose marriage to a girl who might just be borderline psychotic.

A few nights ago Lizzie and I almost, well, sinned.

Why am I trying to cover things up?

We almost had sex. And we would have if that psycho I mentioned before had not come up in conversation.

And I wanted to have sex with Lizzie. I still do, but she only thinks of me as a friend.

I told her I feel the same way. Maybe I should have been honest with myself and her.

Sometimes I think she sees me as more than a friend, but then she blindsides me with the friend card again.

I believe I can change her thoughts on that. Maybe with this hunt we're on. Which reminds me. If you could point us in the direction of the next clue, I would really appreciate that.

When he opened his eyes and looked up, he was feeling decidedly more content with himself. More focused.

That's when he caught a glimpse of something at the large wooden lectern where the minister had been standing during his sermon.

"Lizzie," he said softly and glanced back at her.

She realized that he was looking at something in particular.

"Lizzie," he repeated with more urgency.

"What?" she said and hurried over to him.

"I think I found the next clue."

He inclined his head in the direction of the lectern. On the very bottom, close to the floor and barely visible, two small letters were etched into the wood: J.A.

"Jane, you clever girl." Lizzie smiled and patted Graham's shoulder.

They walked over to the lectern, bent and confirmed that they were really seeing Jane's initials. After a quick look to make sure they were alone, they tried to lift the lectern to no avail. Then they pressed buttons and knobs to see if they opened hidden compartments, even twisting some of the moveable wood pieces to see if they could make something happen, but nothing did.

So much for that help buddy, Graham thought.

He stepped back, but his foot slipped out from under him and he kicked the edge of the lectern by accident. That's when the panel with Jane's initials finally shifted.

They looked at each other with wonderment in their eyes and then back at the panel.

Lizzie bent and yanked at the panel a bit harder. With a small squeak of wood against wood, a small hidden drawer came out.

An explosion of dust caused them to cough and they waved it out of their faces to avoid hacking up a lung. As the dust settled, Graham glanced in the drawer.

An envelope with a large number five scrolled onto aged parchment was covered in cobwebs.

He felt the smile grow on his face as he looked over to see tears forming in Lizzie's eyes.

Every clue seemed to be an emotional journey with her.

Maybe it was a way to thank her mom, or a way to remember her, but he knew that she would never be as happy as when she found a new clue.

He wrapped his arms around her and pulled her to him. He played with her hair as she just held onto him. He would have loved to stay like that for the rest of the day, but the world decided not to be fair.

"Sorry to interrupt, but I need to be locking up now. You're more than welcome to join the reception across the way," the priest called out from the front door.

Graham nodded. Lizzie moved away from Graham and quickly wiped away the tears.

When the priest walked toward one of the side aisles of the church, he quickly closed the drawer in the lectern as Lizzie placed the letter in her back pocket.

They strolled out of the church, trying not to look too conspicuous and as they stepped outside, the music from the nearby reception filled the air. "Want to join the party?" he asked.

She smiled and nodded. "Sounds good. Let me just go and throw all of this stuff in the car."

They made their way to the car and she grabbed the letter from her pocket and placed it in her backpack. She saw his bag in the seat and laughed. "I guess we didn't need all the food you packed."

"Better to be over prepared than under," he joked.

"I believe the saying is that it's better to be over dressed than under, but it works with your statement as well," she teased.

They locked the car and walked across the way to the small pub where the music and crowd noise was coming from. Inside, the bartender told them the party was out back and lead them through to the area.

When they were exited, Graham was surprised to see a large closed in tent with yards of Edison light bulbs hanging across the ceiling. Every table had a small bouquet of white and lilac flowers wrapped in burlap.

The bride and groom were busy taking photos with the bridal party and the other guests.

As they entered the tent area, all the woman, young and old, were whispering and looking at them as they passed by.

"I can see what Jane meant about the gossiping," he said.

She grabbed his hand excitedly and when he met her gaze, she said, "Jane said a dance is where you are able to converse one on one, no interruptions. Wanna dance?"

A smile played on her lips as she pulled him to the dance floor with all the other couples. The lips he had pictured biting and kissing. The lips that he had dreamed about kissing him back.

As she turned to stand right in front of him, he instantly put his hand at her waist. She daintily put her hand on his shoulder and they held their free hands away from their bodies. Slowly they swayed to the insistent beat of the smooth jazz band.

"How was your confession?" she asked.

"How do you mean?"

"I mean, did it help?"

"A bit. I was able to talk about some things I probably wouldn't have been able to with anyone else." He shrugged it off, but the fact of the matter was, he felt amazing being able to tell someone everything that was truly on his mind. Maybe that was why so many people believed and followed. Because they felt better having someone they could talk to without fear of judgment. He knew he would do it again one day.

"That's the point. My family had never been religious. But this one night when I was leaving the hospital after visiting hours were over and I was walking down the hall from my mom's room, I saw this sign that said 'Prayer Room'. I looked in and every religion was represented. There were family members of the sick, the injured, the incurable, all sitting there and praying. In harmony, just praying. I decided, for the first time ever, I would sit and pray. But I didn't pray for a cure. I knew it would never happen. I just prayed for enough time with my mother to finish all the books we had started. I prayed for her to feel no more pain and that I could be strong enough for the both of us," she said.

It was if she was confessing to him and Graham was flabbergasted. Lizzie had told him something so precious and so personal about something she would probably prefer to forget.

"Were you able to finish all the books?" he asked cautiously.

She met his gaze silently, her big doe-like eyes telling him what she was thinking and then she looked away and shook her head. He gripped her waist more tightly to pull her closer. Their bodies met and she laid her head on his shoulder.

"You're one of the strongest women I've ever met. A week after one of the most important people in your life left, you were on a plane to seek something they had left behind. *We* will finish the books you didn't get to finish. Together," he whispered and kissed the top of her head.

When he inhaled, he smelled the rain mist and her lavender shampoo.

She nodded and mumbled, "I'd like that."

The vibration of her voice and her nearness made him almost shiver with pleasure. He urged her away gently, cleared his throat, and stumbled as he asked if she wanted a drink. He didn't wait for an answer and walked to the bar. Grabbing two flutes of champagne, he chugged one, and snagged a second one to make his way back to Lizzie.

She was no longer standing on the dance floor, but sitting with a group of older woman who were talking amongst each other. He walked over and handed her the glass.

"What a gentlemen," one of the elderly women said. She was head-to-toe in enough costume jewelry to sink a whale, but she sat with the elegance of a queen. She had an air of confidence and pride that made him feel a bit intimidated.

"That he is," Lizzie responded.

"Now, young man. Lizzie here was just telling us what an amazing singer you are. Do give us a show? I'm sure the bride and groom would enjoy it thoroughly," she said, giving him the once over and a raised eyebrow.

"Oh, no. I really couldn't," he protested.

But she was quick to argue back. "Oh, pish posh! You must sing for us!"

Lizzie stood up next to him and tried to help him out. "He really can't. He's got to rest his voice for the big tour he has coming up." She wrapped an arm around his waist and then patted his chest with her other hand. "We're so sorry."

He smiled, repeated her apology and placed an arm around her shoulder. He urged her away and said, "Enjoy your evening, ladies."

He maneuvered them to an empty table and pulled a chair out for her. As they sat down, she tossed back the glass of champagne, slammed the glass onto the table and let out a deep breath.

"God! I needed that! Those women were so nosy! 'Where're you from?' 'Why are you here?' 'How long have you been together?'" she said in a mock British accent.

"You're accent is horrid, but very hilarious. And how did me being a singer come up?" he said with a laugh.

"They asked me what we do? I told them that I'm a recent college graduate and you're in a pop band. I told them how we met and I was almost tempted to tell them that we hooked up and give them all the details so they'd feel awkward and not ask any other questions, but I don't think they would have stopped," she said. She glanced around just as a waiter came by with more flutes of champagne. She grabbed two more and said, "Drink up there, Graham."

"I told you I'm not a big drinker," he said, taking slow sips of his second glass. He was not about to tell her that he had done the exact same thing with his first glass.

"Fine, more for me," she said with a chuckle and chugged another glass before reaching for a third glass.

He grabbed her hand as she went for the glass. "Pace yourself, Lizzie."

"It's a wedding, Graham! It's a celebration! Celebrate!" She jumped up and returned to the dance floor where a few more people had started to dance. Weaving her way through the crowd, she went over to the bride to congratulate her and they were soon dancing and singing like old friends.

Lizzie had that knack for befriending everyone she met. A simple smile and easy talk and it seemed as if they would do anything for her. He knew she would be okay once he left for the tour. The tour that was only two weeks away.

But would he be all right without her?

With that thought, he downed his second glass of champagne and walked over to the bar.

"Two shots of tequila, please."

Chapter 31

What happens at the reception, stays at the reception. . .

As she danced with random members of the bride and groom's family and friends, she could feel his gaze staring her down. They burned into her every time a new person would join her. When she finished dancing with one young man, she turned and located Graham.

He sat at the bar sipping on what seemed to be a rather strong drink. Every sip was met with his lips pulling back and a look of pain. She stopped dancing and made her way over to him.

"I thought you said you don't drink." He choked on the liquid as she walked up behind him and surprised him.

"I said I'm not a big drinker. It doesn't mean I don't drink," he explained and brought the shot glass back up to his lips.

Her own head felt like it was filled with the bubbles from the champagne. The feeling didn't faze her. It only made her feel more at ease. She placed her hands on her hips and said to the bartender, "A pint of Guinness, please."

"Haven't you had enough?" Graham asked with a raised eyebrow.

"Wow. You're acting like my dad. Don't worry, Dad. I will be fine," she said as the bartender handed her a pint glass of the dark brown, foaming, liquid.

She tossed a few pound coins onto counter of the bar.

Graham laughed. "We don't tip here."

"I know, but he deserves it. You're being super rule oriented." She waved away his annoyance.

"Maybe because I don't know who these people are and I don't know what they're capable of," he said softly.

"Capable of? Graham, these people are not paparazzi. They're normal everyday people. They're not out to ruin your reputation." She scoffed at how ridiculous he was being.

"No one is a normal every day person around me anymore." His gaze wandered around the tent and he nudged her to get her attention. "Look over there."

She turned around to find a table of younger women all gazing at Graham. The second Lizzie looked over, all of their heads turned away to hide their attention to the two of them.

"What about them?" She didn't like the way they were looking at them.

"See the one in the pink dress?" he asked.

She nodded as she spotted the young blonde with the deeply colored red lips and freckles that ran across her face. She seemed to be texting someone.

Graham said, "She's been snapping photos of us all night. Most likely sending them off to Twitter, Facebook, all those places where people share their lives. Now look over at the table you were sitting at before. The woman who was asking all the questions?"

Lizzie was still a little surprised over the first young woman, but she glanced over to the group of older women she had been talking to and nodded.

Graham continued. "She's now on her mobile. What do you think she's doing? Calling her grandkids? No. She's most likely on with a tabloid magazine to tell them where I am, who I'm with, and what we're doing. You have no idea how that every day normal you love so much can turn on you the second you have any semblance of fame."

She faced him and recognized just how upset he was. How angry he felt, but that he still had to contain the emotions so no one would snap a photo he didn't want to go viral.

She was impressed by how he was able to notice what people were doing. She inched closer, bumped his shoulder with hers, and looked down at their feet. The size difference was hilarious and it caused her to let out a little laugh, hoping to lighten his mood.

When she looked back up at him, worry and concern etched his features. She understood that if people caught her doing anything to him, or with him, it could be taken wrong.

"You have a talent for noticing people and you can read them and what they're doing. Maybe that's how you found me in that library, but I'm an ordinary girl who didn't take advantage of you, or change in anyway when I found out who you are. So don't assume everyone is out to get you," she said. She grabbed her beer off the bar and walked back to the dance floor.

She danced with the glass in her hand, not spilling a drop. Sip after sip the thick brew mixed with the bubbles in her head. The vibes of the music filtered through her whole body. Beyond the tent, the sky was darkening and turning amazing shades of lavender and ginger red.

She inhaled the fresh country air as someone slid a hand around her waist. She smiled and spun around.

To her surprise, it wasn't Graham but a young, handsome, blonde boy. He had a tall lean frame paired with jade green eyes and high cheek bones. Those jade eyes danced with mischief and fascinated her.

She laughed as they continued to dance. "Who are you?"

"Alexander. Most people call me Alex. And those most intimate with me call me A."

They never stopped dancing as she blinked rapidly and gazed at him from beneath her lashes. "So what does that mean I should call you?"

"Let's start with Alex and see where it goes from there," he said and played with the back bottom hem of her t-shirt.

She nodded. "Deal."

"And your name, pretty girl?" He smiled and a dimple dented his cheek.

Heat rose to her cheeks. "Lizzie. Everyone calls me Lizzie."

"It's a very easy name to remember, Lizzie. I saw you and your friend come into the church. My family wasn't too thrilled about the uninvited guests. But, you, well you were something special."

He eased his hand into her back jeans pocket and gently squeezed her butt.

Slightly shocked, she looked around and saw Graham.

His gaze was burning with anger as he watched Alex. His hands were fisted and his knuckles were sheet white. Was she witnessing jealousy on his part?

She felt bad about it, but she would take it if it meant maybe breaking out of the friend zone.

She looked back over at Alex and smiled. "Well aren't you quite the observer? I'm a people watcher myself."

"And what have you deduced about me?" he said and pulled her even closer. Gently squeezed her butt again.

"Confident and handsome and you know it. You have money, but don't necessarily know how to handle it and very into maintaining your physique," she said and he stilled.

She raised a brow and asked, "Did I get something wrong?"

He shook his head, as if to shake away a daze, and said, "No. You were perfectly spot on. On every single account. How on earth could you know all that?"

"I told you. I observe people." She wrapped her non-beer holding hand around his neck and got up on her tip toes to whisper in his ear. "Want me to show you how?"

Her lips brushed the soft skin by his ear and as she spoke, she shot a playful grin at Graham. When she pulled away, she met Alex's pleasant gaze.

He nodded and she reached around, snatched his hand from her pocket and pulled him out of the tent.

She kept on moving with him until they were far away from the crowd and the music. She faced him and peered all around to see if anyone else was near. She didn't divulge all her skills to everyone, but since Alex was helping her make the guy she really wanted jealous, she'd help him out.

"So, explain, dear Lizzie, how you came to know so much about me in such a very small amount of time." He took a step closer to her and shoved his hands in his pockets.

Her head was spinning as the alcohol took its toll, but she was still able to explain. "You wrapped your arms around a stranger, thinking I wouldn't say no. That speaks of confidence.

Your arm is strong and toned as is your general physique. That makes it obvious you try to stay in shape.

When I spun around and found a stranger beside me, you didn't step back so you assumed your looks were working.

As for the money, your suit is designer, but a few seasons old. It has some fraying, meaning you could afford it at some point. You're wearing it since you still need to keep up appearances, but obviously you can't afford a new designer suit. My guess is a gambling problem."

As she finished, her back hit something behind her. She put her hands up to feel the bark of a tree. Above her, the large branches and leaves of the tree covered them.

She had been so caught up in her explanation that she didn't realize that he had moved her toward the tree and a second later, he had her pinned against it.

He leaned forward and his breath fanned across her neck. A shiver ran up her spine and she hated they it actually felt good.

"If I bet you would enjoy what's about to happen, what would I win?" He brushed his lips along her collarbone.

She closed her eyes and tried to sober up fast, but it wasn't happening.

She took a deep breath, trying to gather herself, and replied, "Satisfaction for a job well done?"

Her fingers clawed into the tree bark as the world spun around her.

"How about a phone number?" he asked and nuzzled her neck.

"Fine. And if you fail..." she trailed off, gulping as her mouth went dry.

"I don't plan to," Alex said, his lips hovering over hers.

He leaned even closer and brought his lips over hers. They were thin, but moist. It wasn't *not* pleasurable, but she could only think of Graham as she kissed him back. The entire time, she pictured the brown eyed, buzzed cut, broadly grinning man she wanted to claim as hers. And as she kissed him, she could almost hear Graham's voice calling her name.

And then she realized Graham was actually calling her name.

"Lizzie!" His voice was getting louder and closer.

She moved away from Alex. "Graham?"

Alex shot straight up and glared at her. "The name is Alex."

Embarrassment and shame flooded through her and the world did another sickening spin. She shakily rubbed her forehead. "Oh my God. I'm so sorry. It's just that my friend--"

"Boy Band Wonder," Alex said and shoved his hands into his pockets again, suddenly losing all the confidence he'd had only second before.

She gave a hesitant laugh. "I call him that, too!"

He only replied with a weak smile and kicked at the dirt at the base of the tree. She felt bad that she had killed his mood and used him for all the wrong reasons. She put out her hand in apology and he seemed confused.

She rolled her eyes and with a playful smile said, "Give me your phone."

His face instantly lit up as he grabbed his phone from his pocket and passed it to her. She quickly put in her name and number and tossed the phone back.

"Friends, A. See you soon." She winked and ran to find Graham.

Graham was standing outside the tent, calling, and searching for her frantically.

She ran up to him to find out what he was so agitated. "Graham, what's wrong?"

"Where the hell did you go?" He grabbed her arm and pulled her away from the party. "Doesn't matter. We need to get out of here."

"What? Why?" She stumbled as she half-ran half-walked from the speed of his paces.

"Paparazzi. Do you think I over analyze now?" he almost shouted as he opened her car door and practically shoved her into the car. As she fell onto the seat, she peered out the window and found several people milling about the entrance to the church. They all had cameras around their necks and a few others had video cameras and microphones.

Luckily they had yet to spot them.

Graham raced to the driver's side, jumped in and quickly started the car.

Before any of the paparazzi could react, he sped off.

She buckled her seatbelt and held onto the handle of the side door as he took one turn and the car skidded a bit.

"Sorry," he said, shooting her an apologetic glance and slowing down a bit. He had been driving for about five minutes before he repeated his earlier rushed question.

"Where did you go? I was worried about you."

"You said before that it didn't matter what I did, but if you must know, I was just chatting with a new friend." She crossed her arms and tilted her chin defensively, but once again guilt slammed into her not to mention that she didn't like feeling like an eight year old instead of a twenty-one year old.

"So does chatting now mean making out in the woods with a total stranger? Hmm…must have missed the new Webster Dictionary definition," he said sarcastically.

Although his words annoyed her, she had to give him props for his sarcasm.

She glanced over at him and even in the dark it was obvious he was gripping the wheel so tightly that she thought he might snap it in half.

"Pull the car over," she ordered.

"Why?"

"Just pull the car over."

He harshly jerked the car to the side of the road and slammed on the brakes. She ripped off her seat belt, flung open the door, and climbed out, walking back in the direction from which they had come.

"What are you doing?" he yelled as he slammed his own car door and chased after her.

"I'm going back. I don't need you acting like I did something wrong. You're not my father. I have one of those already," she said as she continued to march away.

"So you think what you did was okay? You don't know who he is! Or what he could have done," he shouted.

He caught up to her and then stepped in front to block her way. She tried to step around him, but he continued to move in front of her.

"Ugh! Move, Graham!" she huffed out of exhaustion and annoyance. She couldn't fathom what more he had to say to her.

"No! You don't understand what could have happened!"

"What could have happened? Graham, I kissed a boy! Shocker! I do that! You didn't seem to have a problem when I was kissing you. Are you afraid to see it end up the same way it did with us?"

She was now shouting at the top of her lungs as well.

Luckily it was only farmland around them. They only things they would wake up with their scene were cows or sheep since Graham had driven them onto some side road where there was no signs of people or homes visible for miles.

"You were in public. You showed up with me and left with someone else. If the press finds that out, they're going to tear apart your character," he warned.

"I don't care what they think of me! I'm not a celebrity. They can call me whatever they want. They've already called me a home wrecker. A slut isn't much worse if you think about it."

Anger filled not only her every word, but every cell of her body as she continued. "And again, why do you care what anyone says about *my* character? It has not and will not affect you!"

He stood still as she looked up at him, not really able to see his face in the dark, but she could imagine it in her mind. She could feel every inch of him as he leaned closer.

"I care because I care about you, Lizzie," he said, the tones of his voice low and filled with caring, dampening her anger. "I care because over the past two weeks you have become my only semblance of reality. I don't want that to be ruined by some horny kid who found you attractive and won't remember who you are tomorrow morning," he said calmly, although a touch of distaste lingered in his voice.

Bing bing.

She jerked the phone from her pocket. It was an unknown number and the light from her phone illuminated where they stood. It also highlighted how close Graham was to her. The small space of the phone was the only distance between them.

She unlocked the phone and scoffed, "I don't think he will forget me."

She lifted the phone up to Graham's face so she could see Alex's text.

"Lizzie, I really enjoyed our brief encounter. Dinner tomorrow?" Graham read out loud.

She pulled the phone back and responded with a simple "Let me get back to you."

"As you were saying, Graham?"

He just sighed, sounding exhausted. "Just get back in the car. I just want to get home and get some sleep."

"I will get into the car on one condition," she said and waited for him to give her the go ahead to continue. He said nothing, however, and she decided to continue with her bargain. "You stop telling me what I can and cannot do. You're my friend and not my father. Besides, I can handle myself. I'm a big girl."

He huffed deeply and the heat of his breath hit her face and neck, but the smell of it alarmed her.

"Graham! How much have you had to drink?"

"Enough."

"Jesus, Graham! You could have gotten us killed! You bitch at me for being irresponsible? We're not going anywhere. Get in the car."

She yanked his arm and opened the back door of the car. "Get in."

She almost shoved him into the car.

He just mumbled and she slammed the door shut and climbed into the passenger seat. She took the keys out of the ignition.

"What are you doing?" he asked.

"I can't drive stick, plus I had some alcohol also."

"Right, well then…" He reached to the floor of the back seat and grabbed a big duffle bag. She heard the zipper and then something large and fluffy landed in her lap.

"What's this?"

"It's called a blanket. You use them to sleep with," his said, sarcasm dripping from his voice.

Again she had to acknowledge that his sarcasm had improved since she had met him. She liked that he was finally sticking up for himself and not being whipped the way he had been with Caterina. It said to her that on some level, he trusted her not to hurt him back.

She smiled. "All right, jackass. But why do you have a blanket in the back seat of your car?"

"To be prepared for anything and everything. You think I only over prepared with the food I packed? You're mistaken my friend. I'm prepared for the freakin' end of the world," he said proudly.

He moved around in the back seat and she heard a rustle. As her eyes adjusted to the dark, she realized he had curled up with a blanket to sleep.

"You are something else, Graham," was all she could think to say.

"I will take that as a compliment. Now sleep. We have to get home to open the next clue," he sad and yawned.

"Goodnight, Graham," she whispered as she snuggled up with her blanket, wishing that she was snuggling up with him instead.

Chapter 32

The morning after

Graham stirred and the shock of the cold had him instantly awake.

He groaned from a crick in his back and remembered what had happened the night before and why he was sleeping in the backseat of his car. He replayed the scene in his head, even while he tried to get back to sleep.

Memories assaulted him of that boy with his hands around Lizzie's waist and the way Lizzie had looked at Graham while whispering in that other boy's ear. When she had run out of the tent, he had followed for only a few feet when he saw her pinned up against a tree kissing that stupid boy.

Graham had played out all the ways he could have stopped her from being with that boy, but he had pulled back because he had no claim to her.

Idiot, the little voice in his head said. All he needed to do was to stop being so protective and tell her how he really felt.

And the cold of the car was now tempting him into thinking about the best way to stay warm.

He sat up and found Lizzie balled up in her blanket and shivering in the front seat.

"Lizzie," he said, his voice groggy. He poked her to wake her up.

"Leave me alone, Graham," she said, her eyes closed and her voice trembling with the cold.

"No, I won't. If you shiver all night, you'll probably get sick. We can't have that. You need to continue your journey."

"What do you suggest then?" she asked as she tucked the blanket tighter.

"Body heat," he said frankly.

She whipped around and was beyond still as she gazed at him. Her eyes were wide with concern.

He rolled his eyes and with a laugh, he jerked her blanket off and into the back seat with him.

"Hey," she shouted, coming to her knees and spinning so she could fully see him.

"Now you have no choice but to come back here," he said and smirked.

"I could technically die of hypothermia, but I would rather not so..."

She climbed into the back and slipped in front of him. He instantly warmed with her against him. But whether it was actually her body warmth or the warmth at being so close to her, he didn't know. Either way, he was warming up quickly.

He grabbed both of their blankets and covered them up.

As the minutes passed silently, her shivering became less and less harsh.

"I am going to fall off this seat if I fall asleep," she laughed.

He slid his hand across her stomach and he lifted her shirt with his pinky a bit, grazing her silky smooth skin. It was familiar already to his touch and he pulled her tighter to his chest.

"Don't worry. I've got you," he whispered in her ear.

She gave one final shudder, but not from the cold.

He moved his hand up and down against the flatness of her belly and the pace of her breathing matched that rhythm, growing faster.

He smirked and thought, "Take that, Alex."

#

The glare of the first rays of the sun woke him early in the morning.

When he opened his eyes and inhaled, he smelled a familiar fruity scent and smiled. Lizzie was still sound asleep in his arms. His grin broadened and he wanted to linger, but knew he should start the drive home.

He lifted his around from around Lizzie, who instantly protested and began to squirm.

He stopped all movement and looked at her. She had a small frown on her face which made his heart beat faster with the thought she might miss him even in her sleep. His smile broadened and he forced himself to gently ease away from her and over to the driver's seat.

When he was finally settled, he looked for the keys and found them sitting in one of the cup holders. He grabbed them, started the car and began the journey back to London. As he drove, he occasionally glanced in the back seat through his rear view mirror to make sure Lizzie was still sleeping.

The silent drive only gave him too much time to think about all that had happened in the past few days.

Lizzie had kissed another guy and was not remotely sorry for it. Trying to make her realize that they shouldn't be together seemed to be useless as well. Although friends were friends forever.

But the way she looked at him was not always as 'just friends.'

The way she reacted to his touch was anything but friendly. And he enjoyed the way she reacted, because he felt the same way when she touched him.

Stop being such a wimp and tell her how you feel, the little voice in his head said to silence his wayward thoughts.

"Graham?"

He looked in the mirror to find Lizzie sitting up in the back and pushing her brown hair off her face.

"Morning, sunshine," he said with a cheery smile.

She glanced out the window as she stretched. "We're already back in London? How long was I asleep for?"

"For the whole trip, but we should be home soon so you can finish your beauty rest in an actual bed." He laughed as he stopped at a red light.

"No, way. We have the next clue to worry about and I think I may have a date tonight." She rubbed her eyes and stretched again, reaching up as far as she could and exposing her stomach. He loved seeing her exposed creamy skin.

"I do think you agreed to that, but there is always rescheduling," he said, attempting to convince her to beg off with any date with the boy from last night.

"Nope. I need to start finding a new partner in crime for when you leave. This date could help."

She sat up and neatly folded the blankets. Well, as neatly as Lizzie could do anything.

When she was done, she climbed into the passenger seat and a few minutes later, he parked in front of his home.

"Who knows? We might finish before you need a new partner," he said as he got out of the car and walked around to help her out of the front seat.

"I'm kind of like Dr. Who. I'll always need an attractive partner until I find the one to spend the rest of my life with," she joked.

"You are such a true little nerd. It's kind of adorable," he said, letting his thoughts just fly out of his mouth without restraint. He was excited to see they had an effect on her. Her cheeks turned that shade of red he liked so much and a half-smile crept onto her lips.

"Thanks, Graham." She leaned back into the car and grabbed her gear and his.

He took his pack from her and together they walked to his house and through the front door. When they walked in, they found the boys sitting in the living room.

"Crap," Graham whispered.

"Graham!" Emmet shouted. "Forgot what day it is, did you?"

"No, Emmet. I didn't."

Lie.

"We just got held up last night and are running a little late," he explained.

"Which reminds us," Jude said walked over. "Hands up. Both of them."

Graham glanced at Lizzie who seemed just as baffled by the order, but they both obeyed and slowly lifted their hands, holding them out for Jude's inspection.

"Thank, God. Running off and getting married to the next pretty girl who gives you an ounce of attention would have not been a good way to get over Caterina," Jude said and exhaled with relief.

Graham peered at his friends and before he could say anything Lizzie asked, "How did you know where we were?"

"The press," Graham answered for his friends.

"Since you're back now, care to join us for our breakfast?" Emmet asked.

"I really need a shower. Enjoy your boys' breakfast," Lizzie said, excusing herself.

He caught her friendly wave to Christian and Nick as she made her way up the stairs.

"Mate," Emmet said and wrapped an arm around Graham's shoulder. He had a Cheshire cat grin on his face and was shaking his head.

Graham sat beside Nick, and Emmet took a spot on the other side of the couch.

"What are we going to do with you?" Emmet asked.

"What do you mean?" Graham said.

"You just broke up with Caterina. Like only about a week ago and you've already moved onto the next girl," Emmet said with another shake of his head.

"Calm down, Emmet," Graham said and held up his hands for silence before Emmet would regret saying anything else.

"Lizzie and I are just friends. I've been helping her through some tough times and she has been doing the same for me. Nothing is going on between us."

"Don't lie, Graham," Nick said with a harsh laugh. "It's unbecoming."

Christian tossed one of the trashy tabloid magazines down on the table. In the corner was a photo of Lizzie and Graham dancing at the wedding. The caption read, "Newly single, but already taken?"

Graham shot to his feet and angrily faced them. "You can't tell me you actually believe this garbage? Just last week they said that Emmet was engaged to a monkey and Nick's girlfriend was a ghost! Just because they have a photo of Lizzie and me doesn't mean that anything is going on. We're friends and I would appreciate it if you would all accept that. Now if all you came here to do was accuse me of having a rebound girlfriend, then you can kindly show yourselves the door."

"Calm down, Mate! Emmet was just being a little jealous boyfriend-type," Jude teased and walked over to get Graham to sit back down on the couch. "Now sit down, have some fruit and toast. We actually came to discuss the travel plans for the next six months of our lives. We don't need to pack doubles of things, right?"

Nick bent down and grabbed a bowl of fruit from the coffee table. He handed it to Graham and although he was still steaming over their inquisition, he sat down.

They were his mates and were only concerned about him. As they quickly began to discuss the packing process and who was going to bring what, his upset slowly fled in the face of his friends' good-natured teasing about his not needing hair care products any more. He got caught up in the excitement of planning for the European tour since he and the boys would never have been able to afford those kinds of trips if it hadn't been for their newfound fame.

But as excited as he got, it was tempered by the fact that Lizzie wouldn't be going with them.

Chapter 33

Just friends?

Not going downstairs as the boys berated Graham with questions about their relationship was one of the hardest things she had ever done.

It was really none of their concern what their status was and the fact they had made her out to be an easy rebound for Graham truly bugged her.

She held back and walked into the bathroom to turn on the shower and let the room fill with steam. When the glass of the shower and mirrors fogged, the steam warmed the small space. She climbed into the shower, but quickly slipped down to sit and let the water pummel her body.

As she sat there in a comforting fetal position, her mind wandered over all the questions she had.

"What do you want, Lizzie?" she asked herself. "To be Graham's rebound? Or Alex's first choice? What will you do when Graham leaves because he will leave? Will you pine over a boy who told you he just wants to be your friend?"

She reminded herself that she hadn't come on this trip to meet the love of her life, only Alex was kind, good-looking and not a half-bad kisser. But he's not Graham.

"Shut up," she whispered to herself. To the mind that seemed to have made itself up as it said, "You want Graham."

There was a knock on her bathroom door.

"Yes?" she quickly replied.

"Lizzie? It's Nick. I just wanted to say that we're off. See you soon," he said and then lowered his voice. "If you need Kara's help for you know what, just give her a call."

"Oh…yeah…Thanks, Nick," she called out from behind the shower curtain.

"Good luck on your date tonight. I'm sure you will knock his socks off…but nothing more, mind you. It is only the first date," Nick said and laughed.

She smiled and shook her head. "Get out of here Nick!"

She could hear him laughing all the way out of her room. She stood up and finally showered. When she finished, she toweled herself off and walked out of the steam engulfed room. The cooler air washed over her, causing her to shiver.

She wrapped the towel around herself tighter and looked into her suitcase to figure out what she would wear that night. She grabbed her phone to text Alex, see if the date was one and ask what she should wear. As she awaited his response, a very light knock came at the door.

She wasn't sure she actually heard a knock until someone knocked a bit harder.

"Yes?" she asked.

Graham opened the door and stuck his head through the crack.

"Hey, Graham," she said and smiled.

He walked into the room. "Hey."

He walked over and sat next to her on the edge of the bed. "So your date tonight…" he trailed off, twiddled his thumbs and he bounced his legs nervously, causing the whole bed to shake.

"What about it?" she asked calmly, even though her heart was starting to racing as she thought about what Graham was going to say. Earlier in the car, she had been able to tell that he was trying to convince her not to go.

"Where are you going?" he asked.

"Don't know. I just texted him to confirm and find out. I need to plan what to wear," she said.

He smiled nervously. "Are you sure you should do this? You only met this kid yesterday," he said, the spark of jealousy obvious in his voice.

"Yeah, I'm sure. He's just a boy, Graham. Shocking as it sounds, I've been on dates before. And I'll probably go on many more after this one. Can we change the topic now, before I start to regret what I say."

"Why don't you just be honest with me?" he asked.

"Like how you're being honest with me?" she spat out. She stood up and paced in front of him. "Graham, I've told you everything. I'm telling you the truth now. What more do you want from me?"

"Do you want to go on this date?" he asked, his voice was slightly raised.

When she stopped pacing to look at him, she could read him, but only for a second. His pulse was racing and he swallowed hard to wet his lips.

He wanted her to say "No."

And with that she replied, "Yes."

It wasn't a lie, although she knew she was going for all the wrong reasons. Maybe. As she'd thought in the shower, Alex might be a good partner once Graham left and she planned to make it clear to him she just wanted to be friends. Although she kept on hoping that maybe Graham would admit he had feelings for her like she had for him, but he didn't.

There was a light bing and Graham jerked away to her phone which buzzed by his leg.

Alex's name popped up and Graham rolled his eyes.

He stood and walk to the door where he paused for a moment, one grabbing the frame of the door. "Good luck tonight. I hope he turns out to be the guy to replace me when I'm gone."

It took every ounce of will power not to stop him and tell him no one could take his place. She somehow managed to nod and look at the text as he closed the door.

`Whatever you feel comfortable in. I m a simple man 2 please. ;)`

She laughed and rummaged through her suitcase to pull out a mix of comfortable things while shooting for something with a dressy air about it.

"Perfect," she said as she picked a few items from those now strewn over the surface of the bed.

#

As she finished getting ready, she searched for her wallet. Remembering it was in her backpack, she grabbed it, but as she pulled it out, the newest clue fell out as well.

"Oh crap!" she exclaimed.

She ran to her door and hollered, "Graham!"

Within seconds he was flying through up the stairs and down the hall. "What? What? Is everything--"

He stopped dead and just stared at her.

She looked down at herself also, thinking that maybe she had a horrible stain on her outfit or that maybe what she had chosen was awful. She ran over to one of the full length mirrors in the room "What? Is there something in my teeth?"

"No. Not at all. You look amazing. Alex is a lucky guy. I hope he realizes that," he said solemnly as he walked up behind her.

He shook his head, almost like he was trying to forget what he had seen. "Why did you call me in here? Is everything alright?" he asked, a concerned look on his face again.

His words were still echoing in her head.

Alex is a lucky guy.

She knew better than to continue that conversation. "Yeah, everything is fine. But we forgot about this."

She raised the envelope and he dashed over to her, grabbing it out of her hand.

"Oh, man. How could we forget? Let's open it."

She looked at her watch and then back up at him. "Yeah, sure. I've got about half an hour before Alex picks me up."

They went over to her bed and he grabbed her hand.

The current that ran through that simple connection was enough to power a small city, but she said nothing as he put the letter in her hand and said, "I believe it's your turn to read this one."

She felt the grin form from ear to ear on her own face as she peeled back the wax seal and opened the letter to reveal the elegant handwriting. She took a large breath and began to read the clue out loud.

"I love and cherish the idea of love. It is the food to nourish my inspiration. Plays are some of the most alluring ways in which to express one's true feelings, while hiding one's true self. You can mask your truths in others vows and professions of love, vengeance, hate, or happiness. But love can hinder your regard for what is acceptable in society. Rules are put in place for such reasons. However, some rules are meant to be broken and you are bound to be set free. I should know from some of my own misguided judgments, love can make you do such silly things. Best of Luck, Jane Austen."

When Lizzie finished, she closed the letter and with a small huff, fell back onto her bed.

"Great." She sat back up on her elbows and looked at Graham's back. "Now all I'll be thinking about all night is that damn letter."

He shrugged and said in a whisper, "Isn't that all you should be thinking about?"

She sat up straight. "Really, Graham? You want to start this argument right now?"

"It's not an argument. I'm telling you that it should be your main focus. Shouldn't it? Not letting some bloke try to get into your knickers."

She jumped to her feet and jammed her hands on her hips. "Well, excuse me! I don't remember you telling me to stay focused on the clues when you had your hand in them."

"That was different," he said and shot up as well.

"Why? Because it was you? What makes you so special? And why do you assume I'm trying to get him in my pants? Or that I want him there for that matter? If that's truly what you think of me, then you don't even know me, Graham," she said, hurt by his attitude. Her heart was no longer racing. She wasn't even sure it was still beating. Maybe it was cracking. Breaking and crumbling.

"You know that's not true. Lizzie." He stepped toward her, but her heart hurt too much and she moved away. When she looked into his eyes, she saw how much that simple act pained him. And so with hurt determination he took another step forward. This time she didn't move.

He reached out to caress her arm with his hand, slowly stroking up and down. He grasped her hand and gently lifted it to his lips.

Her heart exploded into a million tiny pieces.

He looked up and said, "I'm sorry. I think, no, I *know* you're extremely intelligent, beautiful, charismatic, sarcastic, genuine, funny…" he trailed off and stood up straight, but continued to hold her hand.

"The list can go on and on. I just want you to be safe, and smart, and think about this. You met him last night. You know nothing about him and you're about to go alone to some unknown place with him."

She had no clue what game he was playing, but his touch caused her pulse to race and her body to overheat. She gently eased her hand out of his and placed both of them behind her back.

Graham moved closer and her whole body reacted. She knew she needed to get him to either admit he had feelings for her or she had to get out of the room so she could meet Alex.

Or maybe you could just tell him you like him and see what he says?

"It's a date. It's a thing two people do to get to know each other. If something goes wrong, I know the phone number for the police. I know your number and the boys' and if all else fails, my father taught me how to defend myself. I would therefore appreciate it if you stop treating me like I'm five."

He smirked. "Prove it."

"Prove what?" she asked.

"Prove you can defend yourself."

He grabbed her arm and pulled her against him forcefully. It didn't hurt and his grip was nothing like her father's.

She smiled up at him innocently and gently stroked his strong hand. She then grabbed his thumb and pushed it back. He yelped in pain, distracting him, and she wrapped a leg around to push against the back of his knee.

It gave beneath the pressure and he fell to his knee as she pulled his arm up over his head and then behind him.

His breath was labored and he whimpered with pain as she continued to apply pressure to his arm. Leaning down, she put her lips to his ear once again and whispered, "Trust me now?"

He didn't speak. He just nodded his head violently and she let go. He fell to the ground on all fours.

"Now will you let me go on this date without any more questions?"

She grabbed her clutch, tucked it under arm, and placed her other hand on her hip. She watched him crawl onto his butt.

"Yep, I will," he said, his face slightly red.

"Thank you," she said with a decidedly too giddy girly voice.

She walked out of the room and down the stairs to wait for Alex to call and let her know that he had arrived.

Chapter 33

The big date

Graham thought that seeing her dressed in that electric blue high-low skirt with the loose fitting white V-neck, ready to go on a date with another man, was painful. But being tossed to the ground and writhing about in the most unmanly way possible topped it.

She left the room and while he tried to regain some dignity, his doorbell rang.

Damn, he came to the door like a real gentleman would.

Graham forced himself to stand and at least make it to the stairway to hear what they were saying.

"Wow, Lizzie. You look amazing. It's very you," Alex said.

Graham scoffed.

"What is he gay? 'So you'? What's that even mean? Twat," he thought.

"Thank you. You look very handsome as well. This looks new. Win big?" Lizzie said and giggled. That sent all the hairs on Graham's body to stand on end. She had only ever giggled like that with him. Or at least, since he had begun to spend so much time with her. Now this Alex boy was getting the same flirtatious sound.

Alex joined in her laughter. "I seem to be extremely readable. Are you ready?"

Graham heard no answer, only the slight squeak of the front door as it opened and then shut. Graham weakly walked back to his room, grabbed his phone, and quickly dialed Nick.

Nick said, "Hey, Mate. What's--"

Graham cut him off. "Let's go out, Nick. Anywhere. I don't care."

"Want me to call the boys?" Nick asked in a serious tone, obviously sensing Graham's mood.

"I said I don't care. Just be here in an hour." He hung up the phone and walked to his closet, humming.

When he realized what he was humming he laughed and sung the lyric from their first big hit. "Don't let another minute go by."

#

Alex was a very attractive young man. He was also well spoken, sarcastic, genuine, flirtatious, and a comical guy.

After they pulled away from Graham's, he wove his car in and out of traffic with ease while they talked about their lives.

She left it at the most recent history, but he didn't seem to mind.

When he finally parked the car, she was disturbed to see rundown old buildings, closed and boarded up shops, and scary people walking the streets.

Graham was right. I am going to get murdered.

Alex got out and ran around to open her door.

"No need to be chivalrous," she kidded, trying to hide how nervous she was.

"Call it good breeding," he replied and offered his hand to help her climb out. She placed her hand in his and slipped out of the car.

"Where are we?" She didn't mean to show how terrified she was, but she could hear it in her own voice.

He shook his head of slightly spiked blonde hair and laughed. "It looks, well, extremely dodgy, but I promise you're not going to be murdered in a back alley and chopped to bits."

It was almost like he had read her mind.

His smile was now even wider than before. "I started to watch people last night. I guess you made an impact on me in a single day and I think I did pretty well just now."

"Extremely," she said.

They laughed as he locked his car and he put an arm around her waist. Together they walked toward one of the buildings. As they slowly approached, she heard yelling, cheering, boos, and glasses shattering.

A big burly black man, dressed in all black, stood at the large steel door of the building.

"Robbie! Good to see you this fine night," Alex said and greeted the man with a bro hug.

"Always good to see you, Alex. You brought a date?" He looked Lizzie up and down.

His stare made her a bit uncomfortable, but Alex pulled her close and smiled. "I did. Good matches tonight?"

"Every night has good matches," Robbie said and jerked open the steel door.

Lizzie's nose was assaulted by the odor of beer, and B.O. Her eyes watered, but she was able to control her reaction to the smell.

Alex led her into the very loud building and over to the bar.

"What can I get you?" he asked.

"A pint of whatever you suggest."

He shrugged and said to the bartender, "Two pints of whatever is on tap."

The bartender quickly brought them over. Alex paid and she raised her glass. To be heard over the noise of the crowd, they screamed "Cheers" and chugged the beers back.

A second later, they both made the same horrified face.

"Oh, God!" he said and spit out the beer.

"It's like piss water," she said and swallowed. She laughed and wiped some of the foam away from her upper lip.

Alex reached over and with his thumb, wiped off a bit more foam that she must have missed. It didn't give her the same rush as Graham's touch, but it did cause a small shiver.

"So shall we watch the festivities?" he asked, moving his hand away and shoving it into his pocket.

"What exactly are these festivities?" she asked.

"The best underground matches you will ever see."

"Matches?"

"Boxing," he said as he pulled her through the crowd.

They bumped into several people who greeted Alex with either guarded smiles or looks of dislike. When they broke through the worst of the crowd, they stood in front of a boxing ring where two men were currently beating the living crap out of each other.

As she watched the two men fight, she glanced at Alex who moved his arms jab for jab to those in the ring.

"Is this what you lose your money on?" she blurted out. She covered her mouth at her rude question. "I'm so sorry."

He laughed and grabbed her hand off her mouth. "Don't be sorry. I'm an easy guy to read. Yes. This is where I lose a substantial amount of money. I also win on occasion, shockingly enough."

"Yes, of course you do," she agreed, although she could still feel the heat of embarrassment on her face.

"Lizzie, calm down. It's really okay. But if you must know, tonight I placed no bets." He titled his chin up with pride.

"Really?" she said, impressed. "Most people with that kind addiction can't be in an area where gambling is happening and not place a bet," she said and immediately regretted her words again.

What the hell is wrong with me? Am I trying to ruin this date?

Yes you are! her inner voice shouted back. Because you would rather be out with Graham, you stupid girl, it said.

"What if I said I placed another kind of bet?" He wrapped an arm around her waist and pulled her close.

She shot up her hand between them to maintain a bit of space. When she looked up, he had a charming smile on his face.

She took a sip of the crappy beer and smirked. "Another bet? On me? What happens if you lose this one?"

"I go home alone," he said and winked.

She couldn't control how hard she was blushing. He was able to do that.

She shot him a half-glance and with a small smile said, "Keep playing your cards right and that won't happen, Alex."

She moved her hand down his chest and his body reacted instantly. It made her smile more broadly. It also made her feel good about herself that he was responding to her.

He moved the hand on her waist, grazing her rear as he went to grab her hand. Apparently his touch affected her as well since goose bumps erupted across her arms.

They shifted to another part of the ring to get a better view of the fights.

As they watched, they chatted, cheered, and booed like the rest of the crowd.

Soon it was the final match, and she was actually sad to see it end.

She had been having an amazing time with Alex and could see him being a great new companion. He made her laugh and he stayed by her side. He was sweet.

She liked him.

When the crowds funneled out and she realized the end of the night was approaching, she didn't stop herself from asking, "Want to come back to mine?"

"It's not really yours is it? Isn't it Graham's" he said seriously.

She was legitimately annoyed at him for that statement. "Wow. You are right. Sorry I even asked. You can just drop me off then."

They exited with the crowd into a parking lot and she rushed to find Alex's car, embarrassed.

"Lizzie, wait. I didn't mean it like that. Lizzie!" he shouted as he chased after her.

She realized that she didn't remember what his car looked like.

A hand grab her arm and she spun around, frightened until she realized it was Alex. Relief filled her and he relaxed as well.

"My car is over here," he said and pulled her in the direction of his car.

She followed him and whispered an awkward thank you when he opened her door and she climbed in. He shut the door and walked to the driver's side.

They were silent as he drove her back to Graham's.

It only reminded her more of what Alex had said.

It wasn't her home. It would never be her home no matter how comfortable she felt there.

Chapter 34

Worst night ever

Graham had just finished dressing when the raucous knocks came at his front door.

He rushed down the stairs and ripped open the door. His four best mates had dressed in their best for a night out. The smile broadened on his face to match the excitement on his friend's faces.

Emmet launched himself at Graham, wrapping his arms around his neck, and pulling him into the group. Then they were all jumping around, lightly punching him, and laughing. It felt good to be with his brothers again.

As they stepped out of his house, Graham saw that Nick's SUV was parked at the curb. Nick unlocked it and they all piled into the car, laughing and punching each other. Playful as they had been before Caterina had come into his life.

When the SUV pulled up in front of the bar, a small crowd of paparazzi were hanging out. They got out of the car and Nick tossed the keys to the valet, cameras flashing in their faces as they all waved and ran into the building.

"This is going to be epic," Jude said excitedly as they walked down a darkened corridor toward the sounds of a crowd and music.

With every step they took the walls vibrated harder and harder from the music blasting down the hall. When they entered the club, it was a totally different world from the regular London life outside. The walls were covered in LED light panels that looked like dripping gold. Chandeliers all around reflected the light, causing rainbow formations on the dance floor and on the bodies of the hundred or so dancers there.

Graham instantly thought of how Jane Austen would describe such a scene, and that was immediately followed by thoughts of how Lizzie would read the people.

"...Graham?" He only heard the tail end of a question.

He looked around. "Sorry?"

Nick laughed. "Spaced out again, did ya?"

"Sorry, yeah. Must have," Graham admitted.

"I said 'Who wants shots?'" Nick repeated.

"Oh, yes, definitely," Graham replied.

They sauntered into the VIP section and a very attractive waitress in a tight black dress and sky-high heels came over. Her hair was a dirty blonde, her eyes brown, and she was the kind of mindless distraction that Graham had used at one time.

"Two bottles of your best vodka and five pints of lager," he quickly ordered.

She smiled sexily and sashayed away, but she didn't interest him.

"Wow, Graham! What has gotten into you?" Emmet said in shock.

"The question is, 'Who has he *not* got *into*,'" Christian joked.

The heat of anger rushed through his body, but Nick's arm went around his neck and pulled him over playfully.

"We can get anyone we want. The fact that Graham doesn't get his rocks off with every girl that looks at him just makes him a nicer person," Nick said in his defense.

Graham slapped Nick's leg and shoved him off just as playfully, but thought his mates should know the truth.

"Thanks, Nick, but Christian is right. I lied this morning. I like Lizzie. I don't feel it's just a rebound from Caterina. But tonight she's on a date with some bloke she met at the wedding last night and I feel...I feel..."

"Jealous," Emmet finished his sentence for him just as the attractive waitress came back with two large bottles of Vodka and the five pints.

"Thanks, Babe." Graham went to hand her his card, but she waved it away.

"First round is on the house for our very special guests." She winked at him and went to walk away, but her grabbed her hand to pull her back to the group.

"Why don't you stay a while?" he said and nudged her toward the empty seat next to him.

Four pairs of eyes latched onto him as Nick's defense of his not getting off on any available girl was being challenged.

"I'm working right now, but if you're still here when my shift ends, I'll come back." She hopped up onto those sky-high heels again and hurried away to attend to some other VIP guests.

"Okay, so what the hell is she supposed to be?" Nick asked, pointing at the empty space the waitress had previously occupied.

"Maybe I do need something to take my mind off things." Graham grabbed one of the vodka bottles.

"Who is this new Graham and where has he been hiding?" Christian asked, jumping with excitement as Graham cracked open the bottle and started to pour shots.

"Behind a crazy ex-girlfriend and then a gorgeous American who won't give him the time of day," Nick explained.

Graham peered at his friend and was actually able to read his emotions. Nick was alternating between concerned, worried, and genuinely upset.

Christian passed around the shots and they all clanked the glasses together before pouring the liquid down their throats. It burned, just as it always did, but tonight it invigorated Graham.

"Another?" he asked.

Nick's eyes went wide and his friend stared at him. Christian laughed and poured another round, and everyone followed the same routine. Cheers, clink, and drink.

Shot after shot, Graham tossed them back and by his tenth shot he wasn't feeling anything. No pain, no fear, no love, no anything. He searched for the sexy waitress, but all he could see were doubles of the boys.

They were all laughing and having a good time, but when he looked over at Nick, his buzz faded.

"What the hell is up with you? Loosen up, Nick!" Graham said, his words slurred.

"Whatchu mean?" Nick asked with a bit of worry in his eyes.

Graham pouted. "You're killing my happy mood."

"I just don't get why you're doing this to yourself? You like this Lizzie girl, right? Then just tell her. Don't be jealous when some dude made the move you couldn't't," Nick said, obviously annoyed.

Graham could tell by the timbre of his voice, his rocking back and forth on the couch, and his simple wording, even in the state he was in. But given the state he was in, he was not in the mood to be rational. He jumped up and shoved Nick, who put his arms up in defense.

"Who the hell are you to tell me how to react? Who the fuck are you?" he said, his anger loosened by drink.

"Shit, mate," Emmet said and tried to stop him, but Graham pushed him back onto the seat.

"Stay out of this, Emmet. This is between me and St. Nick," Graham said.

Nick looked up from his seat. "I'm your friend. One who'll tell you when you're being a bloody moron. And right now you're being a bloody fucking moron," he said with disgust.

"Fuck you, Mate," Graham said and shoved him again. This time Nick surged to his feet.

"Push me one more time and see what happens," Nick threatened.

Graham wanted the challenge so he would feel something. With that mindset, he jabbed Nick's shoulder in challenge.

A second later, Nick's fist smashed into his face.

Pain coursed through his jaw as he stumbled back, but stayed upright. He tasted iron and knew his lip was bleeding. He licked his lip and the small cut stung.

The heat of tears filled his eyes, but that didn't stop him from rushing forward and tackling Nick down to the couch.

They wrestled each other and threw punch after punch as the rest of the boys tried to break them up. As Emmet and Jude pulled him away, Nick yelled, "You are so fucked in the head and no one else will tell you! You like this girl! Just fuckin' tell her! She feels the same way! You're just too stupid to realize it!"

Graham stopped fighting. Questions raced through his head as he stood there, breathing heavily and staring at Nick.

Nick obviously wasn't done with Graham. Over the loud music he yelled, "You miss everything she does when you're not looking. For someone who's so good at reading everyone, you'd think she'd tell you that you're jealous of her date. She was hoping you would stop her, only you didn't! So now you're being a massive prick when you should be home snogging your new girl."

Nick's face was bright red as he finished and drew a deep breath. The flesh around his right eye was already swelling and turning black and blue.

Nausea hit him almost as fast and hard as Nick's fist.

He fell back into the couch, disgusted with himself.

How could Nick have seen and known all of that? How could he have missed all of that?

"I need to get home," he said and stood. He immediately stumbled, but caught himself.

"Now is probably not the best time to be telling her how you feel," Jude warned.

"Making sense? Jude? Shocking!" Christian kidded.

"Now's not the time, Christian," Nick said and pulled his arm out of Christian's grasp.

He walked over to Graham and offered his hand for a truce.

Graham grabbed Nick's hand with both of his and drew Nick in for a hug.

They slapped each other's backs in true brotherly form, the earlier anger totally gone. When they let go, Nick smiled and said, "Let me take you home. I'm sure the rest of the boys haven't finished their night, but I'm done."

Graham glanced at the other boys who all seemed to be in agreement. With their arms over each other's shoulders, Graham and Nick walked out of the VIP section. As they were leaving, the waitress he had flirted with earlier walked past.

She pouted. "Leaving so soon?"

"He's had a few too many and has a busy day tomorrow," Nick said, covering for him.

"Sorry to hear that." She pulled out a small piece of paper from her pocket and handed it to Graham. "Just in case your plans fall through."

Graham grabbed the paper, thanked her, and left the club with Nick.

#

When they pulled up in front of Graham's, Lizzie quickly opened her own door before Alex even had the chance to get out of the car.

"Lizzie," he whispered, but she raced out of the car.

At Graham's door, she frantically searched for the house keys as Alex got out of his car and followed her up the stairs.

"Lizzie, I am really sorry," he apologized.

"No, it's cool. You're right. It is technically Graham's house."

She wasn't in a mood where she wanted to deal with apologies, and emotions, and blah blah blah.

Alex's cupped her chin with his fingers and gently urged her face up to meet his gaze.

She was surprised to see he had a defeated smile on his face.

"I almost had a royal flush, pressed my luck and ended up with a three of clubs to lose the bet," he said.

She couldn't control her surprise that he had remembered her earlier reference to his placing a bet. "Well with that analogy you might not be a loser just yet."

She finally pulled her keys out of her purse. "Want a night cap?"

His eyes widened with shock that she was giving him a second chance.

She was still battling with herself as to whether she actually liked him – as in like like – or if she just wanted to see Graham's face if he saw Alex in his house.

She decided it was a little bit of both.

He smiled, nodded, and she unlocked the door. They walked in, and but there was no Graham. He must have gone out.

"I am just going to change out of this," she said and gestured to the couch. "Make yourself at home."

"Well in that case," he said, grabbed her arm and kissed her hard. She shot her hands up in shock, but she was pleasantly surprised that his kiss was not half bad.

She dropped her bag and keys on the floor and wrapped her arms around his neck.

He was very forceful with his kisses, and bit her lip so he had access to her mouth with his tongue. He tasted a bit of the bad beer and cherries.

They moved down the hall and she suddenly felt the wall behind her as his hands roamed over her body. He moved them to her bum and grabbed her firmly.

She let out a light squeal, jumped up, and wrapped her legs around his waist.

He moved her off the wall and searched for somewhere to go.

She pulled her lips off of his to explain. "I've never done anything like this. Believe me, I'm not this kind of girl."

"Did I insinuate you were?" he asked and kissed her neck.

"No. It's just. This is a first for me," she said with an embarrassed laugh.

"Do you mean you're a…" He paused and backed off a bit.

When she realized what he was asking, she jumped off him and placed her palm on her forehead. "Oh my God. No! No! I just meant the whole sleeping with someone on the first date thing."

He let out a relieved breath, but still took a few steps away from her.

When she examined his face, she realized it was no longer filled with lust, but stricken with sadness.

"Alex?" she asked, concerned with the sudden mood change.

"I feel like such an ass," he said.

She was sure the confusion she felt was evident on her face, but he had already made his way over to the couch in the living room and plopped down. Dejection filled every inch of his body as she sat next to him.

When he looked over at her, his jade green eyes gave away everything that he was thinking. He was one of the easiest books to read.

"Who set you up to do this?"

"How. . ." He was speechless as she slouched down on the couch and raised her eyebrows in annoyed anger.

He expelled a rough breath. "Right. Can I first say that I was desperate for the cash? And I was very down on my luck?"

"I get it, Alex. Just tell me who?" Lizzie said, pushing him along.

"Caterina. Graham's--"

She cut him off by putting her hand up to beg him not to say anything more. "I know who she is."

"Lizzie, I'm so sorry."

"Seriously, Alex. Don't waste your breath, but let me ask you something. Why did she want you to do this?" She was feeling anger, pain, annoyance, and embarrassment.

"She wanted me to sleep with you to ruin Graham's good opinion of you. She also asked me to find some old letters you wrote or someone wrote to you," he explained.

"That little bitch. She is freakin' relentless." She rolled her eyes and tears threatened, but she bit her lip and held them back. She turned to look at him again. "How much is she paying you?"

"Lizzie."

"How much is she paying you?" she said, seething with anger.

"About a thousand pounds," he answered quickly.

He seemed to be afraid of what she might do. His pupils were so small, they were barely even visible. He leaned away from her and bounced his knees at an alarming rate.

But she was just as upset at the sum of money Caterina was willing to throw at this handsome stranger to try and ruin her and also Graham's life.

She thought about why Caterina was trying to use Lizzie and faced Alex fully. He flinched at her quick movement.

She patted his shoulder and then let her hand rest there, trying to soothe him. "Don't be afraid of me, Alex. I'm not that mad at you. I know you need the money. I don't fault you for trying to get by, but I do have one more question for you. If you answer correctly, I have a counter offer for you."

He nodded rapidly. "Yes, anything. She is actually a bit terrifying."

"Trust me, I know," Lizzie said playfully and smiled before she continued. "Why did she want you to ruin Graham's image of me?"

"If I was a psycho ex, the way he looks at you would set me off, too." He sat back, a little more relaxed, his legs bouncing less and less every second. As he regained his normal composure, Lizzie's was coming undone.

The tears of anger were turning into tears of self-consciousness. Alex's hand rested on her leg and she watched as he just left it there. He made no moves up or down. It was just a friendly gesture.

"Have you never seen it?" he asked, but she was too afraid to meet his gaze, so she continued to stare at his slightly calloused hand resting on her thigh.

He continued. "You really haven't? Oh wow…for a girl who could read me from cover to cover, you seem to be blind when it comes to Graham."

At that she finally looked up at him to catch his comforting smile. He shook his head and said, "Lizzie. When I danced with you at that wedding his gaze was glued on us. I felt like he was trying to Vader me."

"Vader?" she asked.

"You know? Strangle me with his mind?" he explained and then tried to reenact being choked by nothing but air.

"Oh," was all she could manage to reply. Her mind was wondering how she could have missed that. She guessed that he was also jealous of the fact she would be replacing him once he left. But as she thought about him, her mind recreated the electricity that ran through her body whenever he touched her. She remembered that it felt like no one else was there when they danced. Finally, she thought about how she felt when she kissed him.

Graham didn't push away in disgust or disinterest. He pulled her to him like he was a flame in need of oxygen. Like if he didn't have her, he would dwindle and soon be snuffed out.

"You really like him, too, don't you?" Alex asked and broke into her thoughts.

"What?"

"I've been talking for the past few minutes about the most random things. I believe the last thing I talked about was a gorilla running amuck in the streets of London. And you sat there, saying nothing."

"I'm sorry," she apologized.

"Don't. I owe you way more apologies than I could ever give."

When she finally felt fully out of the daze, she remembered she wanted to give him a counteroffer to Caterina's.

"Well, I'll forgive you if you choose to accept my counteroffer. If not, I'll announce to the entire world, or at least your gambling buddies, that you have a severely small package and try to compensate by winning big at the boxing rink." She was joking in a way, but at the same time, she was deathly serious.

"Can I already accept? Not even knowing the terms and conditions?" he said and smiled nervously.

"Sure, but I'm going to tell you the counteroffer. Caterina is paying you a thousand pounds to spy on something very important to me."

"The letters?" he asked.

She nodded, "She can't have them and I hope she'll never get her hands on them. I'll offer you two thousand pounds to not give her any of that information."

"Deal," he blurted out.

"I'm not finished." She knew the pot needed to be even sweeter to keep him on her side. "As for the whole Graham thing…"

"You want us to pretend to be together so he will get jealous and fight for you," Alex said, reading her mind.

"Yep. But I know who you need a price so I will offer you another five hundred pounds."

"So you want him to have a bad image of you?" Alex asked, confused.

"Not really. I want him to realize he cannot act like I'm his when he hasn't even said anything of the sort. I'm not his to claim," she said.

Silence followed, but that was soon broken by Alex clapping. "I'm all in. How do you think we should start?"

A devious smile crept onto her face. "Do you want to spend the night?"

He replied with a cheeky grin and offered her his hand. She grabbed it and he pulled her to her feet and up the stairs.

"Which is your room?" he asked.

She pointed to her door, but he quickly walked into Graham's room instead.

"What are you doing?" she asked, a little unnerved. She had never spent much time in Graham's room.

All the superhero memorabilia was not a surprise to her. But the stacks of books and paperwork were. She walked over to see his itineraries for his European and U.S. tour. He had made lists of all the sights he wanted to see in the countries where he was going. The pile of books by his bedside nearly matched her own. On the top of the pile was one of her mother's favorites: *Peter Pan*.

She couldn't contain the smile that blossomed on her face. That was until she heard the words, "Take off your clothes."

She spun, eyes wide, and her jaw dropped open. "Excuse me?"

"You want him to be jealous? Looking like we fooled around in his room will do just that," Alex messed around the sheets, and threw his jacket on the ground. He quickly unbuttoned his shirt and Lizzie saw that besides a handsome face, he had a chiseled body.

He looked over at her. "What are you waiting for?"

She kicked off her shoes and tossed her white top on the ground. She felt too exposed in front of Alex. Being shirtless felt uncomfortable, unnatural, and wrong.

He seemed to understand her awkwardness and handed her his button-up shirt. "Put this on."

She whispered her thanks and she slipped her arms into the sleeves, but he stopped her.

She could tell he was nervous asking what he was about to ask.

"You need to lose the bra. Put it under his pillow. It will be a not so nice surprise for when he comes home or when he wakes up." Alex's smirk was downright devious, but playful.

Although she felt awkward, he made her laugh and feel bit better. "Have you done this before?"

"Not on purpose," he said. He laughed, tossed his pants on the ground, and stood in nothing but his boxer briefs.

Knock. Knock. Knock.

Someone was at the front door.

Her heart was about to beat out of her chest.

"Showtime," Alex said and pointed at her. "Bra," he reminded, motioned to the bed, and then ran across the hall into her room.

The knocking came again, louder.

"Coming," she called out and unhooked her bra. She raced to Graham's bed, tossed it under the pillows, and ran down the stairs.

Chapter 35

The worst night ever continues

Graham was feeling sicker with every second that passed as Nick drove him home. He started taking deep breaths, but they only helped a little bit. Luckily, it wasn't long before Nick stopped the car in front of his house.

Nick climbed out and then helped a stumbling Graham up his stairs.

"Where are your keys?" Nick asked.

Graham rummaged around his pockets, but was having no luck in finding his keys.

He shrugged and Nick rolled his eyes and walked to the door. He knocked hard and they waited a minute, but heard nothing. He pounded on the door harder and heard a low, "Coming!"

Graham couldn't help but smile at the sound of Lizzie's voice. She was home earlier than him.

Date must have ended badly, he thought happily.

But when she opened the door, nausea reappeared. Her hair was tussled and she wore nothing but an oversized blue button up. He leaned over the side of the stairs and spewed all the food and alcohol he had consumed earlier.

"Graham!" both Nick and Lizzie shouted in concern, obviously upset about not just his drunkenness, but his swollen eye and bloody lip.

"Graham, are you okay?" she asked.

He couldn't look at her again. If he did, more than just vomit would come out of his mouth.

"Maybe you should put some clothes on, Lizzie," Nick suggested.

She cleared her throat and moved away from his hunched over body. "Oh…right."

Nick leaned against the banister beside Graham and rubbed his back, repeating the word, "Sorry," over and over again.

Lizzie walked over to rub his back, but Nick's arm stopped her from even touching him. She looked heartbroken, but turned her attention to Graham anyway.

"Graham. Are you okay?"

"Go put some clothes on," Nick repeated and glared at her.

His look made her feel totally trashy. "Right."

She stepped back into the house and ran up to her room.

Alex was lying on the bed, reading one of her many books. He glanced up as she walked in, then ran over and wrapped her in a big hug.

"What happened?" he asked, a soothing cooing sound in his voice.

His strong friendly hug caused her to be even more frustrated with herself.

"He threw up when he saw me," she mumbled into Alex's rock hard chest.

He let go of her and led her to sit down next to him on the bed. "What?"

"I think he was beyond trashed. But it wasn't just him. Nick was there. They both looked beaten to hell like they'd been in a fight or something. When Graham looked at me he just. . ."

She motioned with her hands to show how his vomiting had occurred.

"You realize that's a positive, right?" he said and rubbed her back.

She shook her head to deny it, but he nodded and pressed her. "Yes. He was so distraught at the fact you went out with someone else that he got himself piss drunk, most likely fought his best friend, and then threw up at the sight of you half naked in another man's shirt. He's jealous as shit that I got to be with his gorgeous girl."

"He's right," someone said from the doorway.

Alex looked back behind her and she slowly turned to find Nick leaning on the door frame.

"Nick," she said.

"No words necessary. You must be the boy ruining Graham's life." Nick put his hand out to shake Alex's.

"I also go by Alex," he said and shook Nick's hand.

"Nice to meet you, Alex," Nick replied as they released each other's hands.

"So please explain what he was just talking about?" Nick asked.

"We were just--" she said, but Alex cut her off.

"She's using me to get what she actually wants which is your best mate."

"Alex!" she hissed and back slapped his rock hard abs.

"What? He seems to be on our side," Alex said and reacted to the light blow.

"I don't say that I agree with the method, but I do see validity in it," Nick replied.

"Nick, please don't kill me," Lizzie begged.

"I just don't get why you won't tell him you fancy him. This isn't a Jane Austen novel. Women are allowed to show their feelings. And he's just as ridiculous for not telling you how he feels. This whole thing is ridiculous. I think you and Graham need to be honest with each other. It was nice to meet you Alex," Nick said, not waiting for anyone to argue with him as he hurried out of the room and then out of the house.

"He has a point, Lizzie. Why don't you just tell him? Granted I lose out on all the money you offered, but I would be aiding a friend which seems to outweigh the money right now," Alex said and walked over to stand beside Lizzie.

"I guess...I don't know...I guess I always wanted that storybook romance," she said and shrugged tiredly, deciding that it was long past time for the day to end. "I need to get some sleep," she said.

Alex nodded and said, "There's a reason they're called stories and fairytales rather than facts and truth."

Alex walked to the bed, grabbed a pillow and then tossed it onto a loveseat at the far side of the room.

"Thank you, Alex," she said as she climbed into bed and shut off the light.

"Good night, Lizzie."

Chapter 36

The worst morning after the worst night ever

His head pounded and nausea threatened again. His lips cracked and the one was swollen and tender. His parched mouth felt as dry as a dessert.

Graham was hung over and there was nothing he could do about it.

As he sat up in bed, his hand swiped something under his pillow.

When he grabbed it and brought it out into the light, nausea turned to full on sickness.

He ran to the bathroom, fell to his knees and shoved his face into the porcelain throne.

He heard a noise from his bedroom and flushed the toilet, rinsed out his mouth, and walked into the bedroom.

Lizzie had made his bed and was now putting a breakfast tray at the end of the bed.

Images of her last night in only Alex's button up shirt came flooding back and he felt sick again. Now, however, she was in a pair of sweats and a shirt from what he assumed to be her former university in the States. His stomach settled a bit.

She smiled kindly and was about to speak when her gaze went to what he still held in his hands. They instantly bulged with a mix of shock and upset. He followed her gaze to his hand, where was clutching her bra within an inch of its life. He again flashed back to the night before and threw the bra like it had a flesh-eating bacteria crawling over it.

She ran over to grab it and shoved it under her arm as she began to pick up some of the other clothing she and Alex had apparently tossed off in his room.

"I was hoping to explain and apologize, Graham," she said.

"What's to explain? You shagged some guy in my bed." His callous demeanor was matched by the tone in his voice.

She looked up at him, even more upset and hurt. She bit her lower lip to mask how upset those words had made her. She turned away from him and continued with what she was saying. "I was hoping I could talk to you about what happened, but I see now is not the right time. I made you some breakfast. There's some ibuprofen there as well. I was going to start looking into the clue today when I get back."

She was walking out the door when he asked, "Get back from where?"

"Alex--"

"Hey babe," said Alex from out in the hall.

Speak of the devil.

A second later Alex walked in, wearing the button down from last night and boxer briefs.

"Oh, great. You found them." He grabbed his pants from Lizzie's hand and quickly put them on. He shot a glance at the breakfast on Graham's bed. "Mate, I was gonna ask if you wanted to join us, but I see you are already set."

Alex grabbed Lizzie's hand. "See ya, Mate."

"Cheers," Graham said and met Lizzie's gaze directly, silently pleading with her not to leave.

But she did and he realized he should have just come right out and asked her not to go.

He smacked his forehead, but it him right back with a fresh bout of nausea, and then his eye throbbed with pain. He looked at his floor length mirror and finally saw his face.

"Holy shit."

What the hell had he done last night?

He went downstairs to the kitchen, but Lizzie and Alex were gone. He walked to his freezer where a note was tacked to the front of it with a magnet.

Made you an ice pack. It's in the freezer. It should stop the swelling. Lizzie

He opened the freezer, pulled out the ice pack and placed it on the side of his face. It stung at first, but then the cold started to numb the ache.

He wasn't really hungry, so he decided to get to work on the next clue.

He went into Lizzie's room to look for Jane's note, saw Lizzie's mess, and rolled his eyes.

He rummaged through the piles of stuff to find her backpack, tossing aside piles of clothing, books, shoes, and bags until he found the tan leather bag beneath a pile of clothing.

He smiled as he reached for the bag and when he pulled it from the pile, the contents of the bag spilled out.

"Shit," he whispered and started to pick up all the papers and her notebook. He had seen her writing in it once, but never again. He knew he shouldn't pry, but he was curious about what she had been writing.

Although he knew he shouldn't, temptation won out. He untied the leather strap and opened the notebook to a random page.

Day 4

This Graham boy...Graham, Graham, Graham. He is ridiculous. He is also brilliant, but I shouldn't have to need his help. Or that girlfriend of his. I don't know how he deals with her. Oh well. I told them I don't need them anymore. Although I sort of wish he would still continue telling me all of his Jane Austen knowledge. Bizarre for a pop star to actually be intelligent as well. Not very common. But I have to say he is a shot of life.

He smiled at that and skipped ahead a few pages.

Day 9

Waking up to a half-naked Graham was not how I expected to wake up, but it was very pleasant. I have grown accustomed to him. His mannerisms and such have caught me off guard. He is such a great guy and I wish Caterina could have seen that. The weird thing is, I am relived she is out of the picture, for now, at least. I can tell how much he still cares about her, but tries to hide himself in the work. I hope in the future he can move on. I mean after her threatening me I don't know how he has never seen that side of her.

The next clue is so close though, mom. I can taste it. I wish that this was a phone call and I would be hearing you tell me to make a move on Graham, or some helpful hint to solve the next clue, but it is not possible and it never can be.

I think about you all the time. What you would say about Graham? London? Dad? My new friends?

He chose to stop reading at that point. He had already invaded her privacy way too much. He went to shut the book when he caught sight of the last page.

List of words a Brit should say...

He read down the list and laughed. She had crossed off a few words. He remembered that some of them had been said by him and the others she had probably heard on the streets.

At the bottom of the list was a sentence that seemed to have been added more recently. It was in a different pen color and looked as if she had taken her time writing it and doodling all around it.

I love you.

His mouth went dry and this time it wasn't due to his hangover. Who did she want to say that? Alex? She'd just met the bloke!

He slammed the book shut, grabbed Jane's letter, and walked out of Lizzie's room.

He hurried to his office, stopping at the kitchen to toss his ice pack in the sink, and sat at his desk. He opened the letter to read it once again. As he did so, he rubbed his fingers on his upper lip and began to think about what the clue could mean.

After he was done, he set the letter aside and typed some words and phrases into the web browser as he started his research.

Time passed while he tried phrase after phrase. He finally heard the front door open followed by loud laughter from two different people. The one laugh gave his body goose bumps while the other made his blood boil.

He bit back his temper and hid behind his closed office door until he heard them make their way up the stairs.

Then came a loud shriek and screaming.

"What the hell? GRAHAM!"

Angry stomps sounded on the stairs and a moment later, Lizzie ripped open his office door.

"Haven't you heard of knocking?" Graham asked.

She stormed toward him and he jumped up before she tackled him in his chair.

"What the hell Graham? Why are you going through my stuff? Did Caterina teach you some of her tricks?" she yelled.

Damn. That was low.

"I was just looking for the clue. I wanted to get started on finding the next location. I'm surprised that you even noticed I was in there. Your mess is, well, a mess."

"I have a place for everything and nothing was in its place, including this." She lifted notebook and his eyes went wide with surprise that she had been able to discover his snooping.

"Did you read this?" she asked.

He shook his head and lied because he didn't want her to be any more upset than she already was. "No. It fell out when I was getting the clue."

She peered at him intently and he could tell she was trying to read him. Luckily she couldn't. She let out an exhausted breath and said, "Stay out of my room."

"It's mine, technically," he blurted out.

"Right. Well for only one more week, right?"

"One and a half," he corrected her.

"Great."

She walked out of the room and he exhaled a breath he didn't even realize he had been holding in.

As he returned to his desk and sat back down in front of his computer, he heard more footsteps coming his way. After a quick knock, Alex stuck his blond head and obnoxiously chiseled face into the office.

"Hey, Mate. You gotta second?" Alex asked.

Graham said nothing, but nodded for Alex to enter. As he walked in and sat on the couch, Graham could tell that whatever this conversation was about to be, he was not going to be a fan of it. Plus, it was taking all his will power not to punch this boy in the face.

"So Lizzie is a great girl, huh?" Alex asked.

Graham clenched his fists on the keyboard and replied, "She is."

"Why did you never make a move on that?" Alex asked.

"That is really none of your concern," Graham warned.

"Sorry, Mate. It's just that, well, I see the way you look at her. I also know you read her diary thing." Alex was now leaning forward on his thighs.

Graham gave him a questioning look and Alex continued. "You left it untied. When I snuck a peek in it, I remember tying it back up." Alex grinned broadly.

"What?" Graham asked angrily.

"I saw it last night. She was writing in it before she went to sleep. When I woke up she wasn't in the room, so I took a glance. So I know what actually happened between you two. And I'm just saying that she is with me now. I don't appreciate you making a move and I thought I should make my sentiments known."

Alex stood and walked back to the door of Graham's office. He stopped there and faced Graham. "Don't hurt her any more than you already have. Let her be happy with someone willing to give her the attention she deserves."

Graham was speechless. Floored. Any other word to reflect the fact that he had no clue what to say.

Alex didn't wait for him, walked out of the room, and then out of the house.

I am so screwed, Graham thought.

Chapter 37

Time is slipping away

How could he go through my stuff? Lizzie thought hours later. *Who does he think he is? And then treating me like an annoyance stuck in his house. I am not a rodent. I didn't have to stay here. Well I sort of did, but I didn't... Damn it, Graham!*

She had asked Alex to leave so she could work on the next clue, but instead of going back down to help Graham do research, she decided to pack. In a week and a half, like Graham had reminded her, she would be gone and so would he. The time would pass way too quickly.

She neatly folded all of her clothing neatly and slowly packed her bags, reluctant about leaving him and worried about where she would go.

She grabbed her phone, searched for a number, and dialed a friend she had not spoken to in some time.

Fanny answered in her melodic voice. "Austen House."

"Fanny?" Lizzie asked, although she already knew the answer.

"Lizzie? Oh dear! How are you? I see you and Graham in the papers. Congratulations are in order. I knew you two would end up together," Fanny gushed.

"No, Fanny. We're not together." She knew that to keep up her ruse with Alex, she had to tell several people about him. "I met someone else. But listen that's--"

Fanny cut off and then stabbed a knife into Lizzie's heart. "Someone else? Oh, Lizzie. How could you? Graham is such a perfect young gentleman and he seemed to be so taken with you."

"Fanny, please," Lizzie begged as her eyes burn with hot tears. "I just.. .I was just. . .Is my room still available?"

There was a dead silence on the other end of the phone and Lizzie looked to see if she was still connected.

"Fanny?"

"Oh, yes. Sorry, dear. Yes. Your room is available. I didn't let anyone have it while you were gone. I was hoping you would call and say you no longer need it, but I see that's not the case."

The guilt that Fanny was making Lizzie feel was unfathomable. Her heart began to ache and she looked down at the first suitcase she had finished packing.

"I'll be there the end of this week. I have missed you, Fanny," Lizzie said, trying to sound like her heart wasn't being ripped out of her chest, But the cracking of her voice betrayed the sentiment.

"I have missed you, too, Lizzie. Do tell me Graham will still be coming around?"

"Only for a short while. He goes on tour in a little over a week," Lizzie explained.

"Great. I hope the new boy is as nice as Graham," Fanny said, but it still sounded as if she was reprimanding her for her choice.

"Of course, Fanny. You would very much approve of him," Lizzie said and laughed at how much Fanny sounded like her mom.

"See you at the end of the week," Fanny said and Lizzie heard the click of the phone on the other end.

She continued to fold as neatly as she could. Slowly and methodically, trying to let some of the anger and hurt she was feeling from Graham fade away. As she thought of him, his voice echoed in her head.

Wait! That's not just in my head, she realized.

"Lizzie!" he shouted from the bottom of the stairs. The voice of her heart's betrayer.

"Lizzie," he shouted again.

"Yeah," she hollered back.

"You might want to come down here," he said, his voice blossoming with hope.

She put down her folded shirt and rushed to his office where Graham was bouncing on the balls of his feet by the printer.

"What's up, Graham?"

He smiled. "I think I found the location of the next clue."

That perked her up as she walked over and grabbed the papers he was printing.

"Thomas Lefroy," she said out loud.

"The only man Jane supposedly every truly loved. They were torn apart by his uncle. He also bought the original first edition copy of *Pride and Prejudice* and said it was 'for an old friend'," Graham explained.

"Wow! You figured this all out while I was gone?" She was impressed and yet upset that he had been able to do it out all on his own.

He nodded like a proud toddler and handed her another piece of paper. When she read it, her eyes went wide. "What's this?"

"Our plane reservation. We leave tonight," he said with a huge smile.

"To Ireland?" she said, her voice squeaky with shock.

He nodded enthusiastically, his grin broad and unrestrained.

She let out a large exhale of air and shook her head. "Graham, I--"

"Don't say anything. Just go and pack."

"Already done. I am moving back to The Austen House at the end of the week," she blurted out. She had been hoping to tell him at a better, more relaxed time, like when she was leaving, but it didn't look like that would be possible.

"Oh," was all he replied.

She gave a final nod and left the room. When she got back to her room she shut the door and braced herself for the pain. Her body shivered and her heart raced. Everything in her told her to break down and cry, but she kept it together to pack a small overnight bag for her next journey.

#

She called Alex to let him know where she would be going and with whom and he let out a small laugh.

"That's going to be interesting. Need a ride to the airport?" he asked and deciding that she needed the buffer from Graham for just a little longer, she accepted his offer.

Alex came by less than an hour later and she climbed into the front seat while Graham sat in the back. Every so often she looked in the rear view mirror to see Graham's stoic face staring out the window.

Alex grabbed her hand, wove his fingers through hers, and dropped a quick kiss on her knuckles.

She knew what he was doing and she knew she should just tell Graham the truth, but for some reason her mind ran away screaming whenever she had the chance.

When Alex pulled up to the terminal, he put his hazard lights on and climbed out to unload their bags from the trunk. Graham and she climbed out of the car and grabbed their bags. At the curb, Graham gave Alex a small nod and headed toward the entrance of the terminal.

Lizzie took her bag and Alex pulled her to him and whispered, "I know you want to tell him. Maybe this trip will give you the motivation you need, but since you haven't told him, and I am still in this for the money, let's make an impression."

He pushed a strand of hair out of her face, cupped her cheek, and gently, but forcibly, placed a kiss on her lips. She tried to lean away from the kiss, but he drew her toward him again.

"We're going to miss our flight, Lizzie," Graham hollered from the entrance.

Alex stepped back. "Sorry, Mate. I just can't keep my hands off her."

As Lizzie rushed away to catch up to Graham, a large smack to her rear echoed through the air. She turned to glare at Alex who gave her a small wink.

"Take care of her for me, Graham," Alex shouted and hopped back into his car.

Lizzie awkwardly walked up to Graham who looked ready to punch a wall. He said nothing and they walked in to check their bags and made their way to sit and wait for the plane to pull up on the runway.

There was no one else in sight by the gate and she was slightly confused. "Where are the rest of the people?"

"Private jets don't have other people, Lizzie," Graham replied.

"Private? Jet?" she repeated.

He said nothing, grabbed his backpack, stood up, and walked to the door leading to the runway.

By the door, she looked out the window. A small private jet sat on the tarmac. Lights illuminated the lavish interior of the plane. It was more than she had ever expected to be exposed to in her entire life.

"Are you coming?" he asked and opened the door to the jet bridge. They walked to the end and to a staircase that led down to the ground. She followed him and they walked in silence to where the jet was parked.

Portable stairs led to the open door of the jet and Graham climbed up the stairs.

She took baby steps along the stairs, more and more anxious with every step. When she entered the plane, it was like something out of a movie. Wood paneled walls, leather sofas and chairs, marble dining tables, and a small bar, stocked with drinks.

Graham plopped down on one of the couches and she sat across from him in one of the chairs.

"This is so fancy," she joked.

"Perks of having a good amount of disposable income," he said, but with laughter in his voice and continued. "So I found out where Thomas Lefroy was last known to live and work. He was a very big judge in Dublin. Lord Chief Justice, in fact."

"Jesus. Who is the one who is supposed to be solving these clues? You're very impressive Graham," she said, grabbed her journal and began to write about the latest happenings.

"Are you writing in that journal again?" Graham asked and sat up to try and read over her shoulder.

"Yeah, but nothing you need to concern yourself with or sneak into my room to read." She slammed it shut so he couldn't see anything.

"Oh, come on." He tried to lean over and grab it, but she moved it out of his reach.

She jumped up and he tried to grab it from her. They ran around and as she tried to avoid him, she tripped and fell onto the couch. He jumped onto the couch next to her and playfully battled her for the journal.

As innocent as the play had begun, her body soon reacted to his body rubbing against hers. When he trapped her against the back of the couch, it was obvious she wasn't the only one affected.

She had to tell him how she felt and so she stopped moving and dropped the notebook. She gazed at Graham who was looking into her eyes as he rested beside her.

"Graham, I really wanted to talk to you about last night," she almost whispered.

He moved off of her. "I'd prefer not to discuss it."

"You need to understand that nothing happened between me and Alex," she blurted out.

He looked over at her with a mix of shock and relief that she hadn't expected, but enjoyed.

She went on with her explanation. "Alex had this stupid plan to make you jealous and I went along with it because…" She hesitated, but knew she just needed to tell him. Get it out there like she normally would anything else on her mind.

So why did this seem so impossible?

"Because?" he said, urging her on although she couldn't read why it was so important to him.

"Before I tell you why, can you answer a question for me?" She said, trying to change the subject since she had cold feet.

"Depends on the question," he replied.

"Why did you and Nick get into what looks to be a brutal fight?" She reached over to skim a finger along the cut on his lip and then up and across the black and blue patch by his eye.

He flinched from her touch, confirming that his injuries were still painful.

"If you must know, it was just a stupid argument," he said, but that didn't really answer the question.

"It couldn't have been that stupid for you to come to blows," she argued.

"True," he said and rubbed his hair. It was no longer the buzzed head he'd had when she first met him. It had grown a bit. "Why do you want to know so badly?" he asked.

"Why do you want to avoid the question so badly?" she shot back.

"The same reason you don't want to tell me why you were pretending to sleep with Alex," he quickly retorted.

She let out a small huff, knowing he had a point, like he usually did. "I did it because I thought…I thought it would make you…" She just couldn't finish the sentence. She tried with all her might to just tell him. It could do no harm at this point since he was leaving in a week and their time together would end.

"You thought what?" he asked and inched closer. His leg rubbed against hers as they sat on the couch. Goosebumps popped up all over her body, warmth and electricity pumping through her from that simple touch, just like it had the first time.

She looked over at him. His hazel brown gaze stared directly into hers. He leaned closer and closer and she took one large inhale and closed her eyes.

He is about to kiss me! This is happening! He must feel the same way!

She waited for his kiss, but instead the jet door slammed shut and the pilot came over the loudspeakers to instruct them to buckle up for takeoff.

She opened her eyes to find that Graham had been just about to cup her cheek. But now he clenched his fist, moved away from her to one of the chairs, and buckled in.

Disappointment surged through her, but she didn't let it stop her from taking the seat beside him. She buckled herself in as well and settled back for takeoff.

Chapter 38

An Irish adventure

After take-off, they didn't dare bring up what had almost happened. In fact, Lizzie couldn't really think of anything else to say for the moment and so they soon both fell asleep.

She was awakened by the pilot warning them that they should prepare for landing.

She opened her eyes to find Graham's head lying on her shoulder. She smiled at how peaceful he looked, even with the black and blue eye and split lip. She wanted to reach up and touch him again, but resisted. Instead, she let him sleep through the landing and as they taxied to the terminal. When they had stopped, she lifted her shoulder to shrug him awake.

His head bobbled off her shoulder and then he jerked upright.

"Hmm. What?" he asked.

"We've landed. They're opening the door," she said in a whisper.

"Oh. Perfect. Emmet should be--"

"Hello, beautiful people!" Emmet came pounding through the open plane door, his Irish accent more pronounced than it usually was.

Graham rose from his chair and smiled. "Hello, Mate."

"Hello ter Graham. Lizzie, it's great to see you again. Welcome to lovely Ireland," he said and grabbed Lizzie's arm to lead her out of the jet. On the top of the stairs, he said, "Breathe in that fresh Irish air and admire the scenery."

She smiled and looked around, but everything around them was pitch black.

"Well, tomorrow mornin' admire the scenery," Emmet joked as they walked down the stairs.

She laughed and looked back to find Graham exiting the jet and following them.

Together they all went through the virtually empty terminal and out to the curb where Emmet's car was parked. Emmet opened her door and helped her into the car. Graham again climbed into the back seat.

"I'll drop you off at the hotel and pick you up in an hour or so to take you out for a few pints," Emmet said.

"Umm...Emmet. I'm exhausted. I just want to go to bed." Graham added a yawn to sell his point. "How about we save those pints for tomorrow night? It might be a cause for celebration anyway."

Lizzie glanced at Emmet who looked genuinely disappointed they weren't going to go out. She patted his shoulder to comfort him. He looked at her with puppy dog eyes and she shook her head to tell him his tactics were not going to work. He harrumphed and slouched in his seat.

"Fine. I guess we'll go out tomorrow," Emmet said in a sad whimper.

About an hour later they arrived at the hotel and Emmet dropped them off, promising to see them the next day.

Lizzie waited with the bags while Graham went ahead to check them in. After the bellhop took their bags, she headed in to the front desk where Graham was in a very heated discussion with the man behind the counter.

He looked over as she approached and just nodded at the man and walked back to her.

"What's up?" she asked.

"They booked the rooms incorrectly. So instead of two rooms we now have only one. With only one bed and they're out of rollaways," he said and rubbed his head with frustration.

"That's ok," she said with a shrug.

"We can share the bed. We shared a backseat of a car and a bed has a lot more room than that," she joked and tipped the bellhop. She grabbed her bag from and started toward the elevators.

Graham likewise grabbed his bag and chased after her. "Are you sure? Alex won't have a problem with this?" he asked.

"What he doesn't know won't kill him. Plus, we aren't dating. We only went on one date, Graham," she rationalized. She hoped it might lead to a way to breaking the ice so she could tell him how she really felt about him.

"But he drove us to the airport?" he pressed. "And well, he seems to believe you two are together."

She didn't know how to answer the question so she simply shrugged as the elevator doors opened and they stepped on. He pressed the button for their floor and the doors closed.

He stood in front of her and stared.

"Please tell me what is really going on between you and Alex," he demanded.

"What on Earth do you mean?" she asked nervously.

"Don't lie to me, Lizzie. I saw your journal. The list of words you want to hear Brits say," he admitted.

"Why? How?" She sputtered, but then realized how mad that made her since he had previously claimed that hadn't read it. "You liar. Well now I know how truthful you really are!"

She had written that entry after they had left the wedding. She had been so enamored by the thought of love and having such a love that a person could not live without, that she had scribbled the words down on her list. She had never really expected anyone to say it. She had just liked the thought of it.

"I'm sorry, truly. I was just trying to find out more about the young woman I was letting stay in my house! But answer my question. Do you love Alex?"

She couldn't control her laughter. "You can't be serious! I just told you that I went on one date with the guy and had a decent time. Do you think that I'm some crazy girl who would think she's instantly in love with him? You don't know me all that well I guess."

The elevator stopped and opened on their floor.

She pushed him out of the way, but she could feel him following, his gaze digging into the back of her head. She stopped dead in her tracks, realizing she had no clue where she was going. She turned to find him swiping the keycard at a nearby door.

"Seriously, Graham!" she complained as she barely made it into the room before the door closed. "What is your problem? Why are you so freaking obsessed with Alex and me? You're still hung up on Caterina and you don't see me questioning you about her, do you?"

"I have been over her since she trashed my home. In fact, I haven't thought about her since we went to that wedding and you found that ring! I haven't thought about anyone but you!" he shouted. And when he finished the sentence his face went from pure anger to total surprise at what he had just said.

"What?" was all she could manage to ask.

"Nothing," he said, grabbing his bag to unpack.

"No. That was not 'nothing', Graham. You said you've been thinking about me? What do you mean by that?" she pressed and walked around the bed and over to where he stood.

"Don't look into it, Lizzie," he warned.

"I just wanted to make you jealous," she admitted, finally finished the sentence she had been trying to say on the plane.

"What?" He stopped unpacking, shook his head and faced her, confusion on his features.

"I did what I did with Alex to make you jealous. I don't know why I did it. I should have just been honest with you and tell you that I didn't really like him, but you seemed so annoyed with him that it made me wonder why. I'm not proud of it and I'm sorry I did it, but I wanted to use him until you told me why you detested the idea of me being with him."

She couldn't believe that everything was pouring out of her like a waterfall. She had just had to break open the dam to let the water run through.

"That's fucked, Lizzie. Really and extremely," he said in a tone of a voice she had never heard from him before. It was a mix of hurt, revulsion, and humor.

"I just thought it would be a meaningless kind of thing to get you to admit that you cared about me. I need to know and to be fair, you read my journal and lied about!"

Her heart beat faster than it had ever done as adrenaline, fear, and love pushed through her.

"You could have just asked, Lizzie," he whispered so lightly she almost didn't make out the words.

"You could've also. And I believe I just did and you still haven't said it," she replied. She jammed her hands on her hips and stepped away from him.

"What do you want me to say? That seeing you with another guy made me angry as hell and I still can't fully figure out why? Or that I wanted to deck that little pompous ass every time he looked at you?" He tossed his clothes down on the bed and stormed away from the bed and over to the large window with the view of Dublin. He leaned a hand on the window ledge and just stood there, looking down over the city.

"Graham…" was all she could say as she walked over and gently touched his back.

He flinched for a millisecond and then relaxed into her tender touch. She wrapped her arms around his waist and fit herself into his side perfectly. She looked up. He was watching her every move and then wrapped his free arm to wrap it around her.

He moved away from the window and wrapped his other arm around her. He squeezed her tightly and she responded by hugging him just as tightly. The way he made her feel in that moment was unlike anything she had ever felt before. She never wanted to leave his arms or be away from him. But in a week he was leaving her, most likely forever.

She let go of him and walked back to her side of the bed where her small suitcase lay. She grabbed a pair of sweats and a t-shirt and went to the bathroom. She didn't look at Graham or say anything else. Inside, she took her time changing to give Graham time to likewise change.

When she walked out, Graham was already fast asleep on the one side of the bed. She cautiously slipped beneath the covers on the other side, shut off the lights, and closed her own eyes.

Gradually she fell asleep, but just as she was about to nod off, Graham muttered under his breath, "I'm a fucking idiot."

Chapter 39

A long night and the morning after

As Graham lay in bed, faking sleep, it occurred to him that he hadn't expecting any of what had happened in the last few hours.

He had almost kissed her on the plane. He had confronted her, only to end up admitting that he read her journal.

And surprise, she had admitted that she was trying to make him jealous using Alex.

How could he not have seen that? That she cared about him too!

How could she not see how much *he* cared about her? And why hadn't he told her before now?

When she climbed into bed next to him, he had dared not to move or speak or anything else that would lead to even more embarrassment for both of them.

He was still playing out the events of the day in his brain when he felt and heard her steady breathing.

He whispered the one thought that had been going through his brain all day. "I'm a fucking idiot."

Admitting it seemed to release the tension from his body and Graham finally felt sleep drift over him, but it seemed like only minutes had passed when the bright light of morning shocked him awake.

Shafts of sunlight streamed onto the bed through the hotel windows. He could have sworn he had shut the blinds before he fell asleep. He opened his eyes and past his blurry vision, he realized Lizzie must have opened the shades.

He sat up, stretched, and his eyes finally adjusted to the light.

Lizzie was sitting at a modest desk in the living area of the room, looking over some notes.

He climbed out of bed and walked over to sit in a chair next to her. She jumped a bit, most likely from not realizing she had woken him up.

"Morning," he half smiled, his morning voice croaky.

"Morning," she replied with a similar half smile and tried to avoid looking at his bare chest and the boxers he wore.

He glanced at all of the papers scattered around the desk and picking up a few, he asked, "What is all this for?"

"I was just looking over some of the notes. Something is bothering me about this clue. Didn't it seem too easy? Finding the next location? I mean how did you figure it out?" she asked, seemingly not able to believe the fact he had solved it all on his own.

"It was simple. Jane stated in the clue that love can hinder a person's regard for what is socially acceptable. In the few letters that have been recovered from her sister and brother, she talked about how she would hang out with this Lefroy guy in social situations that might not be considered normal. It seemed like the perfect fit," he explained and shrugged.

She squinted her eyes for a second as she thought about all the facts. He could tell she was questioning all the points that he had listed and it frustrated him. Almost as much as he had been frustrated with her in the beginning. But he had followed along with her anyway. He needed to convince her to do the same thing.

"Remember the third clue? You tried so hard to convince me that you were right, and even though I was beyond skeptical, I listened. Can you do that, this once, for me?" he asked, grabbing her hand.

Her gaze quickly darted to their joined hands. His hand seemed to have a mind of its own as his thumb rubbed the soft skin along the top of her hand.

He let go of her and rose to grab some clothes.

"You're right, Graham. I will trust you." She smiled and turned in her seat to look over at him.

"Thank you, Lizzie," he said and with a pile the clothes in his hands, he walked into the bathroom to start his morning.

When he walked out, freshly showered and dressed, Lizzie was lying on the bed, a book in hand as she waited for him. As she saw him, she rolled her eyes and teased, "Jeez, you take longer than most girls I know!"

She jumped off the bed and went to use the bathroom. He grabbed the book she had been reading. *Peter Pan*.

When she walked out a short time later, he was still sitting there, reading the book.

"It was my mom's favorite and least favorite at the same time," she said.

"How so?" he asked and put the book back down on the bed.

"She loved the concept of Never Never Land and being able to have all these crazy adventures, but she hated the idea that when you grow up you can no longer be a child. Her logic was that you can always be a child at heart. Although before she passed away she said she never got the adventure we had always read about. That's why she gave me that first letter. I just don't understand why she didn't go on the adventure herself," Lizzie said and grabbed her bag.

"Where exactly are we going today?" she asked.

"We are going to find that first edition of *Pride and Prejudice*," he said, walked to the door and pulled it open for her to exit.

"Do you know where it is?" she asked as they made their way to the elevator.

"I found the old address of dear old Mr. Lefroy. We're very lucky that the home is still there."

"So you plan to knock on the door and what? Just hope the owners let you in?" she asked as they walked through the hotel lobby and out to the curb.

"It worked last time. And last time it was your idea," he gave her a clever smile as they climbed into a cab and it whisked them away to the estate.

As they pulled up in front of it, he thought that the house looked like something out of a movie. Large iron gates, stone walls and immense green pastures surrounded the home, if you could call it that. It was more like a small castle.

He was enraptured when he saw the statues lining the driveway and let out a small chuckle, not because of the statues themselves, but because of the crazy lavishness of the property.

A guard greeted them at the gated entrance.

Graham flashed his smile and said, "Hi, I am Graham Harris. I'm here to see head of this fine estate."

"Do you have an appointment?" the guard asked.

"Umm…no, but--"

"No appointment, no admittance," the guard said and started to walk away from the car.

"But sir, I am sure they would love to meet me," Graham called out to keep the guard close. He didn't want to use his celebrity in *the* most cocky way possible, but he needed for them to be able to get inside the estate.

"And I'm sure they would also like to meet the Queen of England, but no appointment, no admittance," the guard reiterated, walked to his guard house and slammed his door shut.

"You would turn away the Queen of England?" Lizzie shouted at the closed door.

She looked all around and climbed out of the cab.

"What are you doing?" Graham asked, hopping out as well.

"He isn't going to let us in," she said and began walking away down the road around the walls of the estate.

"Yeah, so we go and make an appointment with the family and try again tomorrow," he said as he almost ran beside her to keep up with her.

"We don't have that kind of time, Graham." She was still walking along the edges of the stone walls, searching as if to find an alternative and then she stopped.

He looked at her and then followed her gaze to see a small, vine entangled, iron gate. A gate that looked very similar to the gate where they had not been able to gain access.

A mischievous smile crept onto her face.

"You can't be serious, Lizzie. That's breaking and entering!" he muttered.

She stepped up to the gate, pulled on the handle gently and without even trying, it opened with ease.

"It looks like someone has been sneaking in and out from here." She pointed to a small piece of tape holding the lock in the open position.

"Must have teenagers," he assumed.

"Hopefully teenage girls." She smirked and wedged her way through the vines and held them back for him.

"I feel like I should be doing that for you," he joked.

"Chivalry is as dead as Jane Austen, my friend." She smiled as he ducked and wove his way through the vines as well. When he exited onto the estate grounds on the other side, a rush of adrenaline coursed through his body. The blood rushed through him so fast, he could actually feel it pumping through his veins. He was soon on the tips of his toes, bouncing up and down gently to try and burn off some of the rush.

She chuckled and he asked, "What?"

"You seem more excited than most people who break and enter," she said as she crept around the vines along the edge of the stone walls, looking for a way to reach the large estate house without being discovered.

"It's not something I've done before. Me and my old mate Andy would always joke about it, but never actually go through with it," he said.

"Well, congratulations! Your childhood fantasy has come true. Now come on. We have a clue to find," she said and looked all around again.

"Are you ready to run?" she asked.

"Run? What?" he asked, but she bolted toward the estate house without answering.

"Lizzie," he tried to reprimand, but chased after her. When he caught up to her, she was hiding around the corner from the front door. She was breathing heavily and his eyes went to her rapidly rising chest.

He shook his head. "What the hell, Lizzie?"

"We couldn't just stroll up and let the guard see us!" she said softly, her breath labored from the rush to their hiding spot by the front door.

"True, but now what?" He searched all around to see how they were going to find a way to the front door without being seen.

"We can't go to the front door because the guard will see us. So we need to sneak around and find their back door," she said.

"You think this place has a back door?" he asked.

That's when Lizzie stood straight up, eyes bulging as she looked behind him. "Oh, right. Trying make me think someone is right behind me."

He turned to find a young girl standing there, staring at them, her hands on her slender hips.

"I know there's a back door," she said. "The question is why are you two trying to get in?"

Chapter 40

New friends in old places

"Hi," Lizzie said and took a step toward the girl, but she quickly moved away.

"Right. Sorry. We didn't make an appointment to meet with your parents, I assume. We were trying to find a way in to meet them."

"Meet my parents?" The young girl tossed her head back and laughed. "Good luck. I can't even see them without an appointment. They're very important and busy people," she scoffed and crossed her arms, striking a defensive pose.

"Is that why you sneak out? To get their attention?" Lizzie asked.

"Lizzie," Graham warned and laid a gentle hand on her arm.

The girl watched their interaction and then her eyes opened wide. "Wait! Now I know who you are! I knew you looked familiar!" she said.

"I'm Graham Harris," Graham said and held out his hand, but the young woman pushed past him and walked over to Lizzie.

"You're the girl who is going on that Jane Austen quest thing I see all over Tumblr!" She grabbed Lizzie's hands and shook them excitedly.

"Excuse me?" Lizzie was confused as to how the young girl knew anything about the trip.

"Yeah, you're her! Oh, man! This is so cool! I can't believe you're here! I mean, I knew Graham was helping you, but wow! This is amazing!"

"How do you know about Jane and the hunt?" Lizzie asked and tried to calm the girl who looked ready to jump out of her skin.

"I guess when you were staying in the Austen House, some girl was able to sneak into your room and snap a few photos of your notes. I guess she thought you were plotting to steal Graham and wanted to prove you were a lad nabbing bag of scum. But she came across the letter you found," the young girl explained.

"What? How could they have gotten in? How did I not know about any of this?" Lizzie said and paced along the short-cropped grass.

"You guys can come in and I'll show you." The girl tossed her hair to the side and led them to the front door.

"Yes, please. We'd appreciate that greatly," Graham replied for Lizzie, who was currently speechless.

"Follow me," she said, grabbed Lizzie's hand, and pulled her to the front door.

"What's your name by the way?" Graham asked.

"My name's Erika, but most call me Air," she said with a smile.

"That's a beautiful name. Air," Graham said, oozing charm.

"Of course it ism Graham. By the way, what the hell happened to your face?" Air said and rolled her eyes.

Lizzie grinned and Graham's mouth dropped.

They walked to the front door and Air grabbed her keys and unlocked the front door. When they entered, the loud clacking of high heels sped toward the front door.

"Erika Lindsay! Where the hell have you been?" the woman asked as she entered the grand foyer and took in the sight of her daughter with two strangers.

"Who are these people?" she spat and shot daggers at them with her gaze.

Lizzie had no doubt this woman was Air's mother. They had very similar facial features and skin color. Unlike Air's easygoing nature, this woman's every look and tone was demeaning and unfriendly.

Lizzie braced herself, stepped forward, and offered her hand. "Hello. I'm Lizzie Price and this is Graham Harris. We're newfound friends of your daughter."

Her mother glared at her hand and then up her arm until she met Lizzie's gaze for only a second before looking back at Air. She didn't shake Lizzie's hand or offer her own in greeting.

"You are in serious trouble, Erika! What do you think you're doing, sneaking out in the middle of the night? You should never leave this property without our permission."

"Which means never," Air said and grabbed Lizzie's arm. "If you'll excuse us, I have to show my friend here how famous she is." She pulled Lizzie along a small corridor and up some stairs, Graham following behind them.

Air pushed through a large and into an immense room blazing with late morning light from all the large windows along one wall. The remaining walls were filled with artwork. More artwork decorated the ceiling and all around the room, there was hand carved wood and marble.

"This is your bedroom?" Lizzie said in shock.

"Yeah. You grow bored of it after a while. No wall space for posters or repainting. Everything is 'historic'."

Air rolled her eyes again and moved rapidly to a small desk where she flicked a finger across her laptop touchpad. Her computer screen jumped back to life and she hopped onto the large desk chair. She typed rapidly and Tumblr soon popped up on the screen. She scrolled through the entries and then motioned to it.

"Here you go." She pushed herself away from the desk so Lizzie could get a proper look at the computer and Graham stood beside her to likewise look at the screen.

There were photos of Lizzie walking out of The Austen House and Graham's. Snapshots of the first letter and her notes. Lists of the places she'd been and even a photo of her walking through the airport terminal with Graham. Item after item plastered the boards. She even had her own hashtags and had apparently developed something of a cult following.

Graham leaned his body weight on the desk and looked over her shoulder. His exhale swept past her. The minty freshness of his toothpaste still lingered on his breath.

"Wow. You have become your own celebrity," he said with a heavy breath as he tried to contain his amusement.

"Look! They even have pictures of us at that wedding and they've added all these cheesy love quotes and photo filters. This is, hilarious," she said, joining in his laughter. "These girls are crazy!"

"Hey! I happen to be one of those girls," Air said and walked back to her computer. She closed the tabs and faced Lizzie and Graham. "So what are you two doing here?"

"We're sure you know of the history of your home. It seems like it's been keep intact," Lizzie said gaze at the room, still in wonderment.

Air nodded and Lizzie continued. "One of the original owners was the only man believed to have been loved by Jane Austen. Since you know the journey I am on, you should know why I'm here. Why *we're* here. We believe the next clue is here somewhere."

"Me? What? How? I think I would know if I had it!" She seemed shocked at the idea.

"The original owner bought the first publishing of *Pride and Prejudice* after Jane passed away. We think she hid the note in the first edition because she spoke of how he promised to purchase it from her," Graham said, providing the reasoning for why the clue had to be on the estate.

"But he never purchased the book. He purchased one of the first rejection letters from the publishing house. It was indeed for *Pride and Prejudice*, but under its original name: *First Impressions,*" Air explained.

Lizzie had no clue what to say. Graham might have been wrong with his research. She met his gaze and could see his confidence faltering.

"Do you have that letter? Maybe it could help us in some way," Lizzie said.

"Sure. I'll go get it." Air walked out of the room and Lizzie quickly jumped out of the seat to stand beside Graham.

"I was wrong," he said.

"Graham, don't worry--"

"I asked you to believe me. Trust me. I was so sure and I was wrong," he said. His gaze met hers and it hit her like a ton of bricks. She was able to read him fully and without any filters for the very first time.

He thought he had failed not only himself, but also her. He was very upset and his breathing was getting more and more rapid. He ripped his gaze from hers to find something else to concentrate on.

She grabbed onto his strong arms and gently urged him to look at her. "Listen to me, Graham. Everything is going to be okay. This is not a set back or a failure. This is simply another cool Jane Austen location we got to visit and where we learned and gathered insight."

Her words did little to calm him down. She reached up and cupped his cheek. Ran her thumb along his lip.

"Ow, that's still sore," he said, but she couldn't stop from tenderly swiping her thumb across again before trailing her hand up the side of his face to brush it along the bruises there.

"Eh-hem," someone said and cleared her throat.

Lizzie jumped away from Graham to find Air standing there with a picture frame in her hand.

Lizzie walked over to Air and Graham followed, but neither of them said anything as Air gave them a look that said she'd caught them red handed. But in that look there was also understanding. It was a funny mix, but Lizzie avoided a reply to the look. Instead, she simply turned the frame toward her so she could see what was behind the glass.

The rejection letter was yellowed and even brown in spots. Almost illegible in areas as the ink had faded, but she could make out certain words.

Graham stood beside her and tried to read it as well. "It's barely comprehensible!" he exclaimed.

"Thanks, Captain Obvious," Air replied. "The previous owners didn't really understand the value or importance of the letter and didn't maintain it all that well. But I can tell you, Jane Austen wrote *nothing* in that letter. She played you guys."

Graham was clearly annoyed with Air as he looked at her with displeasure.

Lizzie generously thanked Air for the help and Air asked them to take a photo before they left so she could post it on her blog.

Graham graciously declined because he didn't want people seeing his face all busted and bruised because it would only raise questions he didn't want to have to answer.

Air didn't seem to mind his request. She snapped a shot of Lizzie for the blog and one of the three of them that she promised to keep private.

The young woman walked them to the front of the house where Air's mother was still standing by the door. Lizzie wondered if the uptight woman was worried that they would take anything from the house or try and kidnap her daughter.

Lizzie didn't think twice about walking over to the woman and giving her a piece of her mind. "I know you don't know I am. You don't care, but I thought I should tell you something. Your daughter is extremely intelligent, fun, and full of life. You should make some time for her. My mom always did and we had one of the best relationships a mother and daughter could have. We were best friends. When she passed, I didn't regret anything, except the fact we no longer had any time to spend together. All Air wants is for you to take the time to care."

The woman's face reflected her surprise at Lizzie's comments, but also showed how insulted she was. Lizzie concluded her comments with, "You have a lovely house."

A house and not a home unless the woman changed her ways.

She grabbed Graham's hand and they hurried out the door and to the front gate. The guard shot them a questioning look, but opened the small pedestrian gate so they could leave.

Graham called for a cab and the trip back to the hotel was as silent as the trip to the house.

She couldn't stand it. After last night, she had been hoping he would bring up what had happened but he hadn't. It frustrated her, but she could have easily said something as well. Now they had to deal with the clue and how it was possible that Graham had been wrong. The letter they had seen that afternoon hadn't provided any ideas about the location of the next clue.

When they pulled up to the hotel, Graham climbed out and held the door open for her. The doorman pulled open the hotel door and they walked through the lobby and to the elevator.

As she had done the night before, she moved to stand in front of him. Looking up at him, she finally said, "Are we going to talk about what happened last night?"

"I think we both said what needed to be said." He seemed unwilling to discuss it any more.

"No, I don't think we did. You almost kissed me and I almost let you. You told me you've been thinking about me and I'm still not sure what that means, but I think it means something. I *need* to know what all that means." She again poured her heart out with all that she wanted to say.

He finally met her gaze. "It means that everything that Caterina tried so hard to stop from happening, finally happened."

"If you're going to be cryptic and mention that evil woman the rest of the elevator ride I would rather--"

He crushed his lips onto hers, stopping her entire train of thought.

She hadn't felt those lips on hers since the night they had almost slept together. She hadn't realized just how much she missed his kiss. The soft strength of his lips pressed against hers and she reacted with the same strength in her kiss.

He moved his hands to her hips to hold her close and she raised her hands to his head and caressed the short strands of his hair.

He probed her lips with his tongue, asking for entrance she willingly granted and soon they were dancing their tongues against each other. Then she tasted something funny. Like iron.

She drew away to see that the cut on his lip had reopened from the force of their kiss.

"Oh, God. I am so sorry," she said and dug a tissue from her purse.

A smile crept across his lips and his face was bright and happy.

"You cannot seriously be apologizing for something I have been wishing for since the last time." He brought his hand to her cheek while she dabbed his lip with the tissue. Her heart was racing and her hand trembled as she tried to control herself.

"No, you idiot," she teased. "I'm apologizing for making your lip bleed again!"

He grabbed her hand and smiled. "It's ok. It was worth it."

Chapter 41

Her kiss

He had no clue where the courage to just reach out and kiss her had come from, but he was relieved when she didn't smack him, but instead grazed her soft hands across his hair. Just like when she had done that playfully the first week they met, it sent shivers all over his body.

He had not realized just how much he had missed her kisses until he was able to have another one.

It just made him want more.

He went to lean in for another kiss, but she backed away. "No. Not until that lip heals."

"But that means I do get more?" he said and grinned.

She laughed and blushed and he took that as a 'Yes.'

The elevator door opened and they were walking toward their room when a blonde set of locks caught his attention.

"Emmet?"

"Ah. Me mates have finally returned. I came around 10 and they said you had already left for the day. Glad that you're back. To the pub?" He didn't want for an answer and grabbed Lizzie's arm to guide her back to the elevator.

"Emmet! We just got back and might I also point out it is only two in the afternoon?" he said.

"And I will point out this is Ireland. There is no wrong time to head to the pub," Emmet replied.

The elevator door dinged open and they all climbed in.

Graham looked over at Lizzie who was staring right back at him, cheeks full of color. He slid his hand over hers and weaved his fingers through hers. With a gentle squeeze something changed in him. He had been happy before, but holding her hand now was pure euphoria. It meant something so much more than it ever had before.

His heart raced, pumping endorphins through his entire body. Electricity coursed through the simple touch of their hands.

When the elevator door opened into the lobby, they were bombarded by a crowd of photographers. Flashes went off in their faces as they photographers shot picture after picture.

"Guess they found out where you guys went after taking the private jet from London last night," Emmet said and then looked down to see their hands. "Or they found out what you guys are doing together? Does this mean—"

He could not control his happiness and finish his sentence. He wrapped his arms around each of their necks pulled them to him in an awkward hug.

"We haven't really discussed anything. Nothing is really set," he tried to explain, but Emmet clearly didn't want to hear any of it.

"Whatever, Mate. I'm telling the boys." Emmet ripped his phone out of his pocket and texted the boys which caused Graham's phone to vibrate.

"Oh come on, Man. You sent it to the group chat? Now both our phones are going to off like crazy!"

He hit the volume control on his phone and grabbed Lizzie's hand. "I guess they were going to find out sooner or later."

"But we still haven't figured it out ourselves," she said and laughed, but he knew she was serious about finding out. He also knew she had a point. They had not discussed a single thing. All they had done was kiss. They had done a lot more before only to get into an argument. Eventually they had figured out where they stood. Kind of. This time they'd had no time to discuss what had happened.

"Come on, Mate. You've been in love with the girl since you met her. We all know what's gonna happen," Emmet said and then raised his head from his phone, apparently realizing what he'd just said.

Graham shot a look at Lizzie who stared at Emmet like he had grown a second head.

He had no clue what to say because his mind had blanked on him as well, basically telling him to not make a big deal of it right now.

"Come on. My thirst for Guinness is growing!" Emmet said, finally cutting the silence.

They pushed past the last of the paparazzi only to find a throng of young girls outside the doors of the hotel. They swarmed toward them, but the bellhops held them back until they were in Emmet's car. They carefully pulled away, but as Graham looked, some of the girls were running after them to try and follow the car to their next destination.

"Well just for you Lizzie, I pulled a few strings and got us a personal tour of the Guinness factory. Not a truly uncommon thing, *but* I was able to close the whole place down so we won't be bothered. Graham didn't seem to think of that when you went to that place in Bath," Emmet joked.

Lizzie let out a small laugh and looked at him. He gave her a little annoyed smile, but didn't really mind it at all.

They chatted for the rest of the ride about different things to see and do in Ireland since they were already there, but in the back of his mind, the fact he had been wrong about the clue was eating away at him.

Lizzie had questioned his research, and she had been right to do so because he had not even been sort of close to right. He actually just wanted to just go back to the hotel and figure out how he had made such a mistake.

What did I miss? I missed something. Something Lizzie probably wouldn't have if I'd let her have time to look at the clue instead of dragging her to Ireland.

That's when he Lizzie laid her hand on his knee and gave a reassuring squeeze. When he met her frost blue gaze, he pictured himself relaxed with the only girl he really wanted.

Lizzie.

She gave a halfhearted smile as she leaned in and whispered, "Stop letting this little setback upset you so much. When we get back to the hotel, we can look over everything and see what we might have overlooked."

He knew she was trying to calm him down, keep his senses at ease, but it only made him angrier with himself. She didn't make it sound like he was a moron, but he felt that stupid and her comforting wasn't helping. So he said nothing and looked ahead as Emmet drove to their final destination.

Walking around the Guinness brewery was nothing but a blur because he wasn't paying much mind to what was going on. He was still too involved with Jane's next clue and trying to figure out what it actually meant. When they reached the pub, he quickly walked over to grab one of the pints sitting on the bar for tour patrons.

Emmet followed just behind him and had Lizzie in fits of laughter.

They walked over to grab a few pints as well and Graham was quiet as they sat down together at one of the tables in the pub.

Luckily, they ignored his cranky behavior and he sat there by himself, trying to figure out what to do next about the clue.

#

Lizzie didn't understand why Graham was taking Jane's misdirect so hard, but it seemed to be eating him alive. She had been slowly peeling back the layers that made it difficult to read him.

When they were in the car, she could tell he was nit picking his misread of the clue and was not letting it go. But when she tried to calm him down, she only seemed to make him more frustrated.

Walking around the large factory was a cool little touristy thing she would have to tell her father about. She had not been keeping her promise of calling once a week and it made her feel horrible.

She made a promise to herself to call him that night as she sat beside Emmet, nursing a pint of stout and chatting with him.

"So, Lizzie, we have discussed most of the basics. Graham told us to not ask what you're really doing here, but Nick seems to know. Plus our fans seem to know also. Actually, don't tell Graham, but we all kind of know what you are up to," Emmet joked.

"What?" she choked out.

"Well, after all the digging around, we figured out your whole little Jane Austen hunt thing. You should look at all those blogs they have set up about you. Some of them are trying to help you. But besides all that, we all know you're here to repair our little Graham's heart." He pouted his lips and gave her the biggest puppy dog eyes he could manage.

"You are crazy, Emmet." She jokingly pushed his shoulder.

"What happened between you two? Is it something I can even ask about?"

"It seems you already know a lot more than I want you to, so why not give you a bit more to go on. Yes, before my mother passed she gave me a clue that led me to England to find something Jane Austen had left for someone to find. At the first location, Graham caught me sneaking in and, well, he chose to tag along after that."

"You didn't argue though, did you?" Emmet clearly assumed Lizzie would fawn over Graham like most fans did, but she wasn't anything like those fans.

"I did a lot in the beginning, but we sort of got used to it after one or two days. Graham is some sort of Jane Austen genius. Even with Caterina tagging along, I started to enjoy not being alone. She didn't last that long though, did she?" Lizzie joked.

Emmet chuckled and she continued. "And then I had a run in with her after she trashed Graham's place. What she said truly got to me so I tried to prove her wrong. Graham and I..." she trailed off, not wanting to really go into detail.

"No!" he exclaimed.

"No, we didn't quite get to it, but we managed to get into a fight," she said. Remembering the night still brought shivers to her body.

"We mutually decided to not discuss the night and just move along with finishing this hunt before he had to leave for your European and U.S. tour. Congrats on that by the way."

Emmet nodded his thank you.

"Well then what has changed?" Emmet asked and risked a glance at Graham who sat nearby, slowly sipping his stout.

"Not sure. He just kind of kissed me in the elevator before we got off and then you showed up. So like I said, we never really discussed it."

She didn't know why that fact bothered her so much. It wasn't Graham's fault that Emmet had showed up and decided to take them out.

"My apologies for ruining what could have been a very fun time," Emmet said with a wink. "But in all seriousness, you are good for him. You're bringing back the Graham us boys have missed. His rebelliousness had caused some tension."

"I could see," she said pointed to her eye as if it was Graham's.

"Yeah, well, if it makes you feel any better that was because of you," Emmet admitted.

Lizzie shot back in shock and stared at him. "About me?"

"Yeah. Graham was trying to talk up some waitress and Nick said the only reason he was doing it was because you were on a date with some other bloke. Graham was not a fan of that and well, you have seen the result."

Emmet likewise glanced at Graham.

"So he really was jealous," she concluded and her heart seemed to swell. "I guess I could read him more than I thought I could."

"Well you obviously can't read him *that* well because he has been infatuated with you since he met you. He was embarrassed about telling us because he knew we would joke with him and after his last relationship, the joking would not have been taken as funny. On his end, I mean. After we all met you and got to know you, we could tell you were good for him. Amazing, actually. We got our little Graham back. I'm personally thanking you and hoping to see you around more often."

She felt guilty. She had not thought about what would happen after she found the last clue. After everything that had happened, she wasn't sure she could just pack up and leave. She'd already done that to her father, but when she left home, she had planned to return. In this case, she had never planned to come back. She didn't have a reason to originally, but now she had so many reasons. Emmet, Nick, Kara, Fanny, and most of all, Graham. They had become her family away from her family.

As Emmet excused himself and walked over Graham, she looked out the windows and thought about what she planned to do once everything was said and done. As she looked out on the view of Dublin, she realized she couldn't just leave. She couldn't go back to her normal life, her crap job, and her boring unadventurous life.

With that realization, she smiled.

I am not going anywhere. This is where I belong.

Chapter 42

Friends and more

Graham glanced over at Emmet and Lizzie, who seemed to be having a lot of fun together. But then he realized that Emmet was flirting with Lizzie and something inside of him made him want to drag his mate away from her.

That's when Emmet met his angry gaze and excused himself from his conversation with Lizzie. He wrapped his arm around Graham's shoulders, pulled him away from the table, and tried to soothe over the situation.

"Before you choose whether to punch me in the face or not, let's remember one punch from me will have you on the ground in five seconds flat," Emmet teased and he had to admit, his friend had an extremely valid point. He was still sore from his fight with Nick, but on top of that, Emmet was a little bigger and brawnier than he was.

Graham relaxed a little with his friend's good humor and Emmet breathed a sigh of relief.

"Thank God that worked. Now would you care to explain to me what the hell your problem is right now because you've got to realize I'm not really flirting with Lizzie, right?"

"Right, I know. You're like with all the girls," he teased back and shook his head. "I messed up on the clue, Emmet. I made a mistake and I just can't let it go. I just can't. I know Lizzie is disappointed and won't say anything because she's a genuinely nice person," he explained.

"Listen to me, Graham. That girl is not disappointed in you by any stretch of the imagination. When you were in your own little world this entire trip, we got to know each other. Everything she said led back to you." Emmet glanced back over at Lizzie who was sitting at the table, admiring the views of Dublin through the pub windows.

Graham noticed how relaxed she was. Not a single ounce tension was visible in her body language.

Emmet returned his attention to Graham "That girl has not said one single negative thing about you. That girl is not disappointed with you. She's in love with you."

#

Lizzie wanted to tell Graham the good news about how she planned to stay in England, but when she turned to watch him as he talked to Emmet, he looked terrified as he stared at her.

She could only make out one feeling from him and it was fear. What had Emmet said to him? she wondered.

She decided to ignore the look and continued to drink her Guinness. When the one pint was done, she got up and got another. As she sat back down at the table, Graham and Emmet came over to talk to her.

"Lizzie, what do you think of my country," Emmet questioned.

"It's amazing. I could get used to it," she said, admiring the view of Dublin. A place she unfortunately would not be in much longer. She sighed and took another sip.

"You like Guinness," Emmet pointed out.

"Yeah. I always have. So it's awesome to get some for free," she kidded. She looked over at Graham and asked, "What about you, Graham. Do you like it?"

"Not too much," he replied, but didn't say anything else.

She nodded and sensed he was not in the mood to talk and so she resigned to talking to Emmet the rest of the afternoon.

When the car pulled up to the hotel, Lizzie quickly gave her goodbyes to Emmet and climbed out of the car. The paparazzi had not left their positions in front of the hotel and they were soon bombarding her with their cameras, rude statements, and inappropriate questions. She put her hand up to block the flashes from the cameras. A second later, Graham took hold of her hand and wove his fingers with hers. He gently pulled her toward the door as she closed against the bright flashes.

When she was finally able to open her eyes in the hotel lobby since hotel security had blocked the paparazzi from following them, Graham was standing in front of her. She searched his face to try and read what he was feeling, but she couldn't. Again it frustrated her.

"Are you ok?" he asked gently. She nodded quickly and he peered at the concierge. "I need to book our flight out for tomorrow morning. I'll meet you in the room in a couple minutes. All right?"

She again just nodded and headed toward the elevator, but Graham pulled her back with a strong hand on her arm.

"I forgot something." He finally smiled, lowered his head, and gently pressed a sweet kiss on her lips. A smile erupted on her lips and throughout her whole body.

Maybe I *can* tell him I am staying, she thought.

He let go of her and when they separated, his smile was heartwarming.

Her blood heated and she felt the blush all over her body.

She took a step back, turned to the elevators and hurried to their room

Inside, she sat and waited anxiously for Graham. She bounced her up and down and then shot to her feet and tried to work off her nervousness by pacing, but pacing only made her feel even more antsy.

Click.

Her gaze shot to the door. It opened slowly and Graham walked in. He had no emotion on his face, but when he looked up and saw her, he smiled wildly.

"Everything is set. We leave tomorrow morning at nine a.m. meaning we have to be out of here by seven." He made his was over to her and again leaned his head down to hers.

"So what to do until then..." He trailed off as he cupped her neck with his hands and inched them up to rub her cheeks with his thumbs.

His touch was intoxicating. Her gaze glazed over and she couldn't see clearly. All her inhibitions had all been lost with the single touch of his hands on her body. She leaned her body into him, but she knew she had to talk to him first. They both needed to discuss what was happening.

She pulled away and smiled nervously. "We need to talk. Graham. Plus I told you no more kissing until that lip of yours is healed."

He laughed and exaggerated his fall onto the bed. "What do you want to talk about?"

"How about what we're doing? What is this?" she said motioned between them. "What are we? Friends? Friends with Benefits? More than that?"

"What do you think Lizzie?" he asked with total seriousness. It made her unsure how to answer.

"I don't know. You leave in a week. And I leave you in a few days," she said, trying to both answer question while finding a solution to their dilemma.

"I leave in a week, but I'll be home in a few months. The question is 'What are you going to do?' Do you finish this whole journey and leave? Go back to the States?" he asked, provided yet more questions instead of answers.

"I was thinking I might stay a little while. I don't really have anything to go back in the States except my father. I could always pay for him to come and spend time with me here. Maybe even think about moving him here," she explained.

"Move your father here? Lizzie, that doesn't sound like staying a little while. That sounds like staying here for quite some time." He shifted closer to her. "Is that what you really meant? You want to stay here?"

She said nothing, but simply stared at him and that seemed to be answer enough for him because he brought his lips down onto hers again.

She could feel the smile in his kiss and the happiness that crept into the kiss sent joy up her spine.

"I would really like to meet your father one of these days," he said with a great big laugh against her lips.

She pushed him jokingly. "In all seriousness, what do you think we should do?"

She sat there with a smile on her face that slowly faded as she awaited his answer. But soon logic set in and she came up with a solution she thought could be good for both of them.

"Since you leave in a week, it just seems silly to try and dive into a relationship. I think we should enjoy this right now and when you come home from the tour, we can figure out what to do. I mean, who knows how many more clues there are! I could be here forever!" she teased.

He nodded. "You're too logical sometimes, Lizzie, but logic usually makes the most sense. However, even with your logic you did tell me to enjoy this right now, so tomorrow night I am taking you out on a proper date."

He hopped off the bed and grabbed his laptop.

"What are you doing?" she asked.

"Planning a date fit for you, my dear Lizzie," he joked.

"Well then, while you do that I'm taking a shower and then passing out. Seven a.m. is not a time I usually like to hear and I most definitely don't like to wake up at that hour."

Without waiting for his answer, she headed to the bathroom.

Chapter 43

Hope for the future

She had thought about moving? Is it weird that I cannot stop smiling at that fact? he thought.

As his mind replayed the look on her face over and over again, a smile blossomed across his face again. She hadn't even needed to say a thing for him to realize she really meant it. And the more he thought about it, the more Emmet's statement settled in his head and refused to let go.

She is in love with you.

He played that statement over and over and remembered her face. It made so much sense that he couldn't think of any other explanation for her wanting to stay in England.

She was in love with him.

Instead of terrifying him like it had when Emmet first made the accusation, it comforted him and caused him to say words he had only thought about with one other person.

"I love her, too."

He covered his mouth with his hands, but realized she couldn't hear him while she was in the shower. But he couldn't let that slip before the time was right.

And now was not the right time.

She walked out of the bathroom, steam pouring out with her. She was only in a towel.

His mouth dropped open and turned dry. He had forgotten how amazing she looked with barely anything on.

"Sorry. I forgot to grab my clothes before I walked in," she apologized.

He snapped out of it to reply with a flirty retort, "Nothing I haven't seen before."

She rolled her eyes and went back into the bathroom . She returned throwing a shirt over her half-naked torso. He saw her tattoo again and realized he had never figured it out.

She climbed into the bed and grabbed the book she had been reading that morning.

He no longer wanted to work on setting up the perfect date. Especially not with the girl of his dreams lying in bed across from where he was seated.

He wanted to be curled up next to that girl.

He closed his laptop, quickly undressed, and climbed into bed beside her.

She smiled as he wrapped his arm around her waist to pull her closer and rested his head on her stomach.

She raised one of her hands to rub his head close to the base of his neck, making him shiver with pleasure.

He loved having her hands on his head. Her touch there was gentle and playful.

He let out a small moan, but tried to cover it by saying, "Read to me."

"Again?" she laughed.

"Yes, please," he begged.

"Well since you said please…" and with that she began to read him. *Peter Pan*. That's when it occurred to him.

Her tattoo.

"You have that quote on you and those people are Peter, Wendy, and her brothers." He sat up, proud of his deduction.

She smiled. "Good job. I can't believe you remembered."

"Yes, plus I just saw it again. It refreshed my mind." He moved his hand to shift across her tank top, right above the spot where he knew the tattoo was etched on her skin. Her eyes closed at his touch and it caused him to try his luck. He trailed his hand down a little lower and moved her tank top away to skim across her skin.

The electricity coursing through that touch was enough to power a small city.

He grabbed at her side to turn her to face him, but she ended up with his face smacking into the middle of her chest.

They both laughed. "I probably should have moved up before I did that."

"Yeah, but I'm sure you don't mind where you are now," she joked.

He moved away from her and laughed. "You're right. I didn't mind. But if we want this to work, and I mean really work, we should take our time. Build up to it, ya know," he reasoned.

"A boy who doesn't want sex right in the beginning of the relationship? I find this to be very intriguing." She moved her body down the bed so that she was now face-to-face with him.

"I had that kind of relationship before and it went to shit very quickly. I want us to be for the long haul," Graham explained and grabbed one of her hands. He kissed every finger tenderly and gazed into her eyes.

She said nothing and just smiled at him. She closed her book, put it on the bedside table, and then moved back toward him. She brought her hand to his cheek and scooted even closer to him.

His breathing got faster with her every move. As she closed her eyes, she leaned in to kiss him.

It was a gentle kiss. One he had never felt before. It was careful, timid, and shy.

He wrapped his arm more tightly around her waist and moved her closer. He kissed her back just as timidly and she reacted with a small moan.

He was trying to control his reactions to her every touch and kiss, her every reaction, but it was proving to be almost impossible. He knew he had to stop this before he could no longer control himself.

He pulled his lips away and said, "Good night, Lizzie."

She smiled, turned away from him, and shut off her light. He turned to cuddle her to his chest and she softly said, "Goodnight, Graham."

Surprisingly, it wasn't all that hard to fall asleep beside her, maybe because he was now more certain that there would be more nights like this in the future.

When he woke up the next morning, something was poking his shoulder.

He looked around groggily and found Lizzie standing over him, jabbing him awake.

"Graham? Graham?"

"Yeah, sorry. I'm awake, I think," he said and popped up.

"Sorry to wake you, but we need to get to the airport." She almost cooed as she rubbed his cheek.

He kissed her palm and climbed out of bed. "All right. If I have to."

She laughed and together they grabbed all their things and quickly packed their bags.

They held hands all the way to the airport and on the plane they snuggled up with each other.

When they climbed off the plane, they were once again holding hands and smiling for the whole trip back to his home.

It was so normal and comfortable. He had thought about what it would be like so often, that he was surprised at how much more amazing her hand felt in his. It was like an energy force that could power him through the day and if he let go, he'd lose all of his liveliness.

When they got home, she went to get a drink and he walked up to his room, but he reached it, he looked over to Lizzie's room. It was bare. There was no longer her clutter on the floor and on the desk.

He put down his bags and walked into her room.

Her bags were neatly stacked next to the bed. Another book sat on her bedside table.

When he turned to leave, she was walking in with a glass of water to her lips. She choked on the water, surprised by his presence in the room.

He apologized and she quickly told him there was no need.

"It's going to be weird leaving here in a few days."

She looked around the room and placed her small suitcase to sit next to the rest.

"Yeah, but you can always come back. You have a key," he reminded her.

"I would never intrude that way. This is your place. But I would like an invite every now and again. Whenever you come back from the tour," she said and put the glass down on the bedside table.

"You read an awful lot," he joked and motioned toward the book.

"A book a day keeps the idiots away," she joked. "My mom always said that. And then my dad would say something about being one idiot that just couldn't stay away."

"They seemed to be in love," he said.

"They were. I hope to think they still are even if they're apart," she said and looked up to the ceiling.

He knew she was looking toward heaven and took a step closer to her.

"I have a feeling they do." He kissed her neck and then backed away. "I should get going and plan our lovely date for tonight."

He walked back to his room and gently shut the door.

Seeing everything gone from her room had made his house feel empty. More than he had expected. He didn't want her to leave. He just wanted her to stay in his room. Her room.

Our room? he thought. They weren't even a couple and he already wanted her to move in? he wondered. Well, she had already been living there for some time. But he knew he wanted more than her living across the hallway.

He unpacked and realized he still needed to finish packing for the tour, but he also needed to plan the dream date. He'd choose that over packing any day.

When he had finally sorted out what to do, he walked over to Lizzie's room and told her to dress comfortably because there would be some walking involved during their date.

As the night approached he dressed in his best casual wear and approached her room once again.

He knocked on the door and she apprehensively opened the door.

When he took in her entire outfit, he was floored by her wearing something even as simple as a pair of jeans, a flannel, and some vans. Her waves of dark hair fell down her back and she wore the barest amount of makeup to accent her eyes.

"You look amazing," he said, smiled, and grabbed her hand.

"So do you," she responded as he playfully dragged her out of her room and down the stairs.

They walked out of the house and he opened her door for her to climb in.

As he was driving to their first destination, he couldn't help but look over at Lizzie's hands. She wouldn't stop rubbing them against each other. He took his hand off the gear shift and laid his hand over hers to stop her nerves. He brought it to his lips and kissed her shaking hand.

"You need to calm yourself, Lizzie. I'm the same guy I've always been."

"I know, but it's our first real date. I always get nervous. Even with Alex, who I didn't like as a date." She laughed.

"Oh, that guy. Man I still hate him. Even though I know he was only trying to help you make me jealous. Which, by the way, touché. It worked," he joked.

"That was actually not his intention when we first met. Caterina paid him to make you hate me and also to steal the clues so she could solve the mystery all by herself. She thought that would have you come running back to her," Lizzie explained.

"She what? Please explain this in way more detail."

"There's really not much more to say. She paid Alex a very large sum of money to spy on us, ruin your interest in me, and solve the clue. I worked things out with Alex luckily," she said and laughed, obviously trying to ease his upset.

"Damn that Caterina," he hissed.

"Hey, Graham. It's ok. I'm over it, over her, and you should be, too." She raised their joined hands and kissed his gently. "Now about this date you have planned…"

"Right." Her kiss soothed him and he changed the subject. "We're almost there."

He slowed the car and parked. They both exited onto the quiet residential area.

She looked around, confusion spreading across her face. There were no restaurants or small coffee shops. The area was simply filled with homes.

"Where are we?" she asked.

"We're standing across from Kensington Gardens. It's one of the largest parks in London," he explained. "It's also home of Kensington Palace where Diana used to live and where William and Kate currently reside."

"Ok…" She still was confused.

He walked around the car, took hold of her hand, and led her up the block as he looked for the correct address. "It's also where a famous author by the name of J.M. Barrie met the boys who were his inspiration for one of your mother's, and your, favorite novels."

She halted in the middle of the sidewalk. "Graham? What are you up to?"

"I am just giving you a quick history lesson before our first location." He tugged at her hand and she walked alongside him.

"First?" she asked.

"Full of questions aren't you? Picture it as a different kind of scavenger hunt. One in which I know all the locations."

He found the plaque he was looking for and stopped. "Here is where that favorite book was written." He showed her the house and she covered her mouth and took a step towards the plaque to read the historical information.

He yanked out his phone. "I am sure you would love to snap a photo to send to your father."

She spun around in delight and her eyes were getting red and tear-filled, but she smiled one of the happiest smiles he had seen and quickly snapped the photo.

She joined him by the curb and admired the quaint house.

"Wow. Just wow. This is already better than any other date I have been on," she said, laughter coloring her voice.

"Well then I guess I should stop now," he teased, but wrapped an arm around her shoulders to lead her away from the house. "I'm going to need to stay on top of my game."

They strolled into Kensington and walked around the gardens. She enjoyed all of the lovely flowers and fountains, and then they were nearing the next stop on their journey.

"With a decided theme in mind, it is only fair to bring us to the next *Peter Pan* date spot."

They turned a small corner and stopped.

"Graham," she said, awe in her voice. She hesitantly strode to the large Peter Pan statue that stood in front of them.

"This is just amazing." She touched the rocks Peter stood on and circled the statue, admiring it.

"Well you're doing this whole hunt for your mother. She asked you to do it to get some adventure in your life. Your mother loved Peter Pan's adventures so I thought you should enjoy some more adventures of your own. That's not to say Jane did not give you a chance for an adventure of lifetime, but wow! I have said adventure a lot, haven't I?" he said and laughed nervously.

"It's ok." She walked over to him and got on tiptoes to kiss him. "This is the most amazing thing anyone has ever done for me. Ever. Thank you, Graham. I will never forget this." She smiled and kissed him once more.

He relished her kisses and never wanted them to end, but he did have one more very important spot to take her. He grabbed her hand, pulled away from the kiss, and hurried back to the car with her almost chasing him.

"Now to our last stop where we can be like Wendy and Peter for a little while." He drove around the garden, up past Buckingham Palace, past Big Ben, and into a parking structure.

He hurried her out of the structure and her eyes went wide as she realized their next destination. The glow of the London Eye was visible in her gleaming blue gaze.

"Now, since we cannot fly, and I could not find a fairy to sprinkle some pixie dust on us on such short notice, I chose the next best option to help up fly off to Never Never Land...The London Eye."

They walked onto the line and he handed the man the tickets. The man guided them off to the side and waited for an empty pill-like glass tube to come round. It paused and they entered with one attendant following them.

The man held a bottle of champagne and two glasses. He poured the champagne and then placed the tray in front of Graham and Lizzie. They picked up the glasses and Lizzie stood by the glass, gazing out onto the sights of London. He took a quick sip and walked over to her.

"What do you think?" He gestured to the brightly lit Big Ben clock.

"'Second star to the right and straight on 'til morning,'" she said, smiled, and offered her glass for a toast. "I say it at every location, but this is amazing, Graham. And you planned this in a single day? How can you be so romantic so quickly?"

"I have wonderful inspiration," he said and they both laughed. "So cheesy. I'm so sorry."

"It was very cute. Totally memorable."

"Memorable enough to go in the journal?" he asked jokingly.

"You've read what I've written including the boring day-to-day events on my trip. You think I would skip such a night like tonight?"

"I never apologized for that. I really am sorry. It just kind of happened and I regret it. I never meant to use it against you or to be a total jackass about it." He laid his hand over hers that rested on the balance pole that wrapped around the entire glass pill they were in.

"I've obviously forgiven you." She leaned sideways and raised her head to accept his light kiss. But her lips were lethally addictive. He could never have just one.

He traced her bottom lip with his tongue and then gently nipped at her lips.

"Graham," she moaned and took a step back. "We should probably keep the PDA to a minimum in here." She inclined her head in the direction of the attendant standing in the corner.

"No worries, ma'am. I've seen some pretty weird things. Snogging is one of the least offensive," he joked. It caused both of them to laugh.

Graham held her hand and they just watched the view as they went around on the immense Ferris wheel. When they climbed out, they walked happily, hand-in-hand, to his car. But as they drove to his home, an odd sensation of heart break took hold inside him.

He knew the reason why when she said, "I cannot believe this has to end in a week."

Chapter 44

The end is almost here

She didn't know why she said it, but it was just on her mind. She wished she could take it back, but it was too late to do so. Instead, she just sat in the car in silence.

"I am going to miss you, Lizzie," Graham said quietly.

She looked over to watch his movements. His jaw was clenched, his chest was rising and falling at an alarming rate, and his hands held the wheel with intense strength.

He was stressed, obviously upset, and it was her fault.

When he pulled up to the house she looked at his front door nervously. Anxiously.

They hurried out of the car and he bolted toward the door. She ran after him and before he could open the door, she jumped in front of it. He let out a light chuckle, but she could tell there was a lot more behind that chuckle.

She wrapped an arm around his neck and ran her hand through his short-cropped hair. His gaze bore into hers and she grinned nervously before slowly moving her face toward his. She grazed his nose with hers and she could smell his champagne breath as he exhaled.

She pressed her lips to his, knowing she could never resist her kiss. Not anymore. She had held back for so long that being able to actually feel his lips on hers again was like a dream.

He moved her back against the door, but never letting his lips leave hers.

She heard the jingle of his keys trying to find the lock and then the loud clunk of the lock. When the door opened, they hurriedly stumbled into the house. He wrapped his arms around her waist, pulled her to his chest, and the door slammed behind them. He must have kicked it closed since his hands had never left her body.

He broke from the kiss and trailed his lips down her neck as he unbuttoned her flannel shirt. She let out a small moan and grabbed at his soft cotton t-shirt. It was more like clawing, she needed to feel him against her again so badly.

She pulled his shirt over his head and her flannel fell with it to the floor.

He slipped his hand under her thighs and she jumped up to wrap her legs around his waist. Joined like that, he carried her up the stairs and to his room.

"Lizzie," he almost groaned, pulled his lips away from her collarbone, and she searched his face, worried she had done something wrong.

"Yes?" she said and offered him a smile.

"I told you that I want to take this slow. I don't want to mess this up." He rubbed his thumb up and down her thigh.

"I understand, Graham," she said and kissed him again. "Slow it is."

She released her legs from around him, but instead of her feet touching the ground, she landed on his bed and realized why he had said anything at all.

"Oh."

"Yeah, oh," he said with a laugh.

"Graham, I didn't intend to…"

She couldn't lie to him. She wanted to be with him, intimately, and so she plowed on. "I didn't intend for this, but I can't lie and tell you I don't want it. I know you want to take things slow, but what if you leave and you don't come back?"

"I *am* coming back, Lizzie. I want it, too. God, more than you could even imagine." He cradled her jaw again, gently urging her to look at him. "But I don't want to rush it. You said it in the car, this ends in a week. You leave in less. I can't imagine what I would do if we destroyed what we could have in the future by rushing things."

She shied away from him and got off the bed. Toeing off her shoes and pants, she climbed into his bed and said, "Then let's not rush. Let's just go share some more time together."

He had watched all of her movements with a smile on his face. He went to the opposite side of the bed, undressed until he was only in his boxers, and then climbed into bed next to her.

She lay on her side to look at him, admiring the contours of his chest, the bits of hair that trailed all the way down to below his boxer briefs. The muscles of his chest shifted as he let out a sweet smelling breath that fanned over her face.

She placed her hand on his chest and he took a large very deep inhale.

She slid closer to him and his hands encircled her waist. She laid her head on his chest and her lips were tickled by his chest hairs.

"Just so you know, Graham," she whispered against his skin. Goosebumps rose up on his flesh.

"I don't plan on going anywhere anytime soon."

"Glad to hear that," he said and for long hours they just talked and held one another until they fell into slumber, together.

#

Graham loved waking up with the feel of her body intertwined with his.

Her legs were in between his and he had his arms wrapped tightly around her waist. The feel of her sent his hormones raging.

He needed a cool shower and fast.

As he was trying to move out from between her legs, she inhaled and stretched. Her stretch only had her body pressing ever closer to his.

He swallowed hard and his whole body heated.

She opened her eyes and smiled at him in a warm and affectionate way, and he knew he had to move before he lost all control.

He wiggled away quickly and fell off the bed with a loud 'Oof.'

"Oh, God," she said, obviously concerned.

A second later, the sheets were rustling and her feet hit the ground beside him. She bent down next to him.

"Are you ok?"

"Yeah, yeah. I just wanted to get a shower and not wake you," he said and pushed some of her long black waves of hair away from her cheek.

She sat beside him, legs pretzeled against her, and pulled her knees to her lips, her gaze focused on him intently.

Too intently.

He jumped to his feet and raced to the bathroom. He turned on the water and climbed into the jets of cold water that shocked his body into alertness and non-arousal. When he felt more in control, he changed the water to a warmer temperature. The heated water cascaded down his body and as he showered, he tried to think of how he could tell Lizzie he was in love with her. He played out the scenarios of how she would react.

Would she reject him? he wondered.

No, you idiot, he reminded himself. Emmet had told him that she felt the same. And for fuck's sake, would a girl who doesn't feel the same way feel scared that you wouldn't come back and tell you that she wasn't going anywhere? No, because she's in love with you as well.

So man up before you leave and tell her how you feel, he urged himself and prepared himself to face Lizzie.

#

Days passed and every night Lizzie climbed into his bed and cuddled up next to him.

During the day, they would each do their own things. At noon they would try and have a small outing to show Lizzie a few more sights before he was gone and then they would get home and go their own way again, mostly to pack.

They left their doors open and shouted out to each about different things.

They even tried to figure out the location for the clue that had mistakenly taken them to Ireland.

During all that time, Graham had not been able to man up the courage to tell her how he felt.

The night before she was set to move back to the Austen House, Lizzie climbed into the bed and snuggled up to him. He had only had her in his life for a little over a week and he was thinking about how stir crazy and home sick he was going to feel when she left the next morning.

"So tomorrow after breakfast I figured we'd drive over to the Austen House and I'd unpack my stuff. Then you can come back here and finish your packing because you leave in three days! Aren't you excited!" she said, beaming and trailing her hands along his chest.

"Yes and no," he said truthfully.

She gave him a questioning look so he continued. "Should we talk about what's going to happen? I leave and then what?"

"I keep looking for the clues until I solve them all. You go on and do your fabulous European tour and then when you come back. . ." She snuggled as close as she possibly could and said, "I will be waiting for you. I mean should I buy flowers and chocolates? That's what a boyfriend does for his girl when she comes back from a trip, right? And since you're the 'girlfriend' in that scenario should I get you like some video games and energy drinks?"

Hearing her say those words made his heart go ablaze and he smiled.

"What?" she asked.

"So do you consider we've got the whole boyfriend/girlfriend thing going on?" he asked, unable to contain the joy bubbling inside him. He felt like such a young child with all the excitement he was feeling.

"I guess. I mean we never really talked about it and we just kind of dove into this unnamed situation…" She trailed off not only in her sentence but her fingers stilled their action against his chest.

"The date didn't prove how much I wanted to be with you? Saying how much I want to take it slow so we can make this work didn't prove it either?" he pressed.

"It's not that. You just never asked."

He grabbed her hand and brought it to his lips. "How stupid am I? Of course. Lizzie Price, will you be my girlfriend?"

They both laughed and she nodded. He laughed again and kissed her soft plump lips.

"So, Girlfriend. What are we going to do once I leave?" he asked trying to get back on topic.

"We are going to deal with the distance. We are going to talk when we can and when it is possible, we will see each other."

She wrapped her leg around his waist and before he had time to react, she spun so that she was straddling him. "And now since I am officially the girlfriend of famed pop star Graham Harris, I would like to do one thing."

"Name it," he said and put one hand on either side of her waist.

"I want to be with you." She leaned down and kissed his cheeks, his forehead, and then his lips. She braced her hands on his chest as she kissed down from his lips to his neck and to where her hands were touching his chest.

Fire ignited across his body as she continued to kiss every inch of bare skin she could reach. He roamed his hands up and down the sides of her torso and closed his eyes.

Her hands went to the elastic of his briefs and the tingling sensation he always felt with her touch burst to life.

He reached for her hands which caused her to look up at him. "I just want to make sure that this is really what you want."

She nodded. "I want to be with you at least once before you leave."

With that he spun around to have her lying on the bed beneath him as they laughed into the ecstasy of the night.

Chapter 45

A night to remember

The next morning, lying next to a naked Lizzie, all Graham could think about was the night they had just shared.

The blanket barely covered her body and he just wanted to take her again and again.

She stretched awake and her eyes fluttered open. She smiled and nestled up to him.

"Last night…" she said, but couldn't finish.

"Was…" Graham tried to help her continue.

"Amazing," she said groggily, wrapped her arm around his torso, and kissed around his chest.

"Beyond," he added and rolled over to kiss her. "I am going to get up and make you some breakfast and then we will get you back to the Austen House and unpack."

He popped out of bed and threw on some pants.

"I'll be down in a few minutes. I'm gonna hop in the shower." She sat up and wrapped the sheets around her. He felt like he was in a movie, and although it was a cheesy romance movie, he thought of everything else that brought him to that moment and chose to think of it more as a thriller with some romance in it.

After they finished breakfast and loaded up the car, he drove a route he had not done in ages. It felt like months ago when really it had only been weeks. Pulling up to that small awning made him breathe a sigh of relief and distress. Relief because he knew she was going to be in a safe place with a woman who probably cared for Lizzie almost as much as he did. Distress because he had to leave her there.

He pulled up and Fanny rushed out the door with the wildest smile on her face. She ran down the stairs. "Graham! Oh, Graham! I didn't think I would be seeing you!" She crushed him in the tightest hug since he went to see his own mother.

"And why would you think that?" he asked, trying to get some more air into his lungs.

She let go of him and shrugged. "Lizzie said she had met someone else. I assumed you were out of the picture."

That's when Lizzie let out the loudest laugh. Both Graham and Fanny stared at her.

"Sorry, Fanny, but you were practically begging me to bring him here. You wanted us to be together and were so disappointed when I told you we weren't. But to make you feel happier, the 'other' guy didn't work out and Graham and I sort of did."

Fanny clapped her hands over her mouth in joy and ran over to Lizzie. She wrapped her arms around the girl and it looked just as tight as the bear hug she had given him.

"Then why are you not staying with him?" Fanny finally asked.

"He leaves in a few days," Lizzie explained.

"Such a shame the house will be empty for such a long time. Lizzie and I could stop by and check on it, if you like," Fanny said and shot him a suspicious look.

Graham shrugged as he unloaded the trunk. "Sure. Lizzie has a key."

Fanny nodded and walked up the stairs to hold the door so they could carry in all of the suitcases. Inside, they immediately dragged them up the stairs and to Lizzie's room on the third floor.

Nothing in that room had changed. It looked just like it had the first day he had begged her to let him help.

"Wow, Fanny. You really kept this place exactly the same," Lizzie said.

Fanny laid a hand at her collar and tapped her chest. "I didn't have the heart to change a thing."

Graham felt his own chest constrict with love pains and sadness. He wrapped his arms around both Lizzie and Fanny, and pulled them toward him for a big hug. "I am going to miss my girls!"

"Oh, Graham!" Fanny slapped his chest playfully and left the embrace. She walked out of the room and hollered, "So glad to have you back, Lizzie dear."

"I am glad to be back, Fanny," Lizzie shouted as tossed her bag on the bed, unzipped it and began unpacking.

#

Night came before he realized the whole day had passed. He kissed Lizzie goodbye, not really wanting to leave her there, but knowing he had to go home and get some things done. And now in three days he would be gone.

When he got to his house, four very familiar cars lined the street and he knew what he was about to walk into. Inside the four boys, his brothers, were sitting on the couch, all speaking in hushed tones.

"Boys whispering in my own house, about me, seems ironic." They all turned to look at him and jumped out of their spots on the couches.

"Graham," Nick said as Graham approached.

When he reached the table he noticed that they had taken all of his books and papers from his office and scattered them around the coffee table, the floor, and their own laptops.

"What are you boys doing?" Graham was happy, scared, and excited at the same time.

"We were hoping you would be here to help, but we heard you moved Lizzie back to the Austen House," Nick said walking over to his pile of papers.

"Yeah, I just left there, but that didn't answer my question. What you guys are doing?" Graham reiterated.

"Right. Well, the boys figured out what you and Lizzie have been up to, and I'm not very good at keeping things like that from them. Plus, Kara has practically become a Jane Austen nut since you guys left the house a couple of weeks ago," Nick said and smiled.

"Help? How?" Graham had so many questions, but those two were the only words his mouth seemed able to form at the moment.

"I knew why you were coming to Ireland. Our fans follow your every move. They figured it out before we did! And when you guys came back to the hotel, although you seemed to be happy at the time, your mood changed so drastically when you started talking about the mistake you made. I assumed it had to do with the scavenger thing, because there was no way you were upset about being with the girl you're in love with," Emmet said and chuckled as he looked through the papers on his makeshift desk on the coffee table.

"So you all chose to come to my house, use my research, and what? Find the next clue?" Graham walked over to see all of their computers opened to different Jane Austen sites, videos, and biographies.

"Seven heads are better than two, Graham. You let Nick and Kara help and they proved to be helpful in a big way. Now it's our turn to help out as well," Jude offered together with a smile.

The brotherly love in the room was impossible to miss and Graham nodded.

Jude's smile was wide as he looked back at his computer screen to do more digging.

"You guys are seriously the best four brothers I could have ever asked for," Graham said and walked over to sit in between Christian and Emmet.

#

Lizzie didn't sleep.

She had lain in bed the whole night contemplating what she was going to do without Graham. She remembered the times when she did not even want him helping her, trying to push him away as much as she could.

She smiled at how different things were now. She could never imagine how it would be without Graham, Kara, and the boys. Fanny had become like a second mother and the rest of her new little gang was like her family away from home. She realized she felt more at home in London than she could have ever felt in her small town in the U.S.

Graham was one of the largest reasons for feeling that way. She was fascinated with him. She had never felt that way about another person before. She had loved her parents, her friends, and the rest of her family, but this love was the kind of love Jane Austen wrote about, and dreamed about for herself.

Graham was her Darcy, her Edward Ferrars, her Edmund Bertram. The hero to her heroine. She was unconditionally in love with Graham Harris. And with that realization, she knew she would not be succumbing to sleep that night.

The sun rose and lit up the room only she was already awake.

She forgot how much she loved the light pouring into the small room. It was like she watching liquid gold pouring into the room and it drenched her in its richness.

She sat up and out of habit, like she had never left, she walked over to the door.

A light knock came and she flung the door open.

Fanny was taken by surprise by the large burst of air that whooshed past her, but she smiled nonetheless.

"I brought you some tea and biscuits. Graham called and said that he and the boys should be here in a few minutes. He suggested that you should get dressed and ready to leave." Fanny said the last part with worrisome resignation.

It was then that Lizzie found it hard to swallow or even breathe at a normal steady rate. The boys were leaving. They'd be gone for more than a quarter of the year.

She nodded to acknowledge Fanny's request and then walked over to grab a cup of tea to steady herself.

She didn't want this day to come. It had come so fast that she'd no time to prepare herself.

She wanted to look her best for the last time Graham would be seeing her for quite some time. But she also wanted him to remember her the way she'd been when he had first met her.

She selected jeans, a pair of low cut boots, a t-shirt, and a fitted hoodie and quickly dressed.

She had just finished when the phone rang and Fanny advised that the boys were on their way up to her room.

She had barely hung up when there were dozens of knocks on the door.

She flung the door open to find not only the boys, but also the fan girls in the hotel, who were still stalking the boys, surrounding them.

The boys rushed in and she slammed the door before any of the girls could claw or push their way in as well.

"Jesus! I forgot about that little detail," Nick said, smoothing his clothes back into place.

"Yeah, how do you suppose we can get out of here?" she asked.

"The same way we entered. They're not gonna leave and we can't get out the window," Graham said and walked over to Lizzie. "Hi," he said, smiled warmly and bent down to kiss her.

"Hi," she said as part of the kiss. They kissed over and over, never wanting to leave the kiss. She almost forgot there were four other members of Graham's band in the room. Almost, she thought as they broke apart and found the boys standing there, smiling and jostling each other playfully.

"Before we leave, we have something we want to share with you," Emmet said and took a step forward. He dropped his backpack, unzipped the large portion, and pulled out a large folder. He handed it to her and she looked at the folder to see it had all of their signatures and a note saying 'Best of Luck.'

"What is this?" She opened the folder and found mounds of research and handwritten notes. "You guys did all this?"

"I told you we knew what was going on. We camped out at Graham's the past few days and just did a bunch of research. We found some possible hints for that clue you guys have been looking at. Hopefully one of them might actually be a decent lead. We didn't have enough time to dig too far, but—"

She didn't let Emmet finish as she embraced him, giving him the strongest hug she could muster.

"You are all such amazing people. I have no clue what I did to deserve your friendship, but I am so glad I have had the luck of having it."

She walked around to every single young man and gave them large hugs, thanking each one individually. She put the folder on her bed and grabbed a lightweight coat.

"We should probably head out. We don't want you missing your flight."

"Lizzie, it is a private jet. It leaves when we show up," Jude said and laughed.

"Right. Celebrity. Forgot," she joked and walked to the door. "Ready?"

They all nodded and crowded around her as she cracked open the door and the boys rushed down the hall and stairs. She was the last one out the door and stopped to make sure it was locked so that none of the girls could sneak in again.

She knew they were probably extremely crafty and might find some other way in, but she hoped it would not be possible this time around.

They clawed, complimented, insulted, and were just being all around fanatics as the Graham and his mates fought their way to the curb. When the group was finally outside the hotel, they were bombarded by the paparazzi.

"Not a single break?" she muttered under her breath.

"Start getting used to it. You are a part of us now," Graham said as he grabbed her hand and pulled her into the van with him.

As soon as the rest of the group was in the vehicle, the driver quickly took off. She was surprised at how much room the van had considering the boys were leaving for months there weren't that many bags in sight.

"Packing light?" she joked.

"No. We just had another van filled with all our gear already sent to the airport," Jude explained.

When they pulled up to the airport's security entrance and the guard saw who it was, the van was waved onto the runway, and they drove to where the private jet sat on the tarmac. She would never really get used to this kind of VIP treatment.

When the van was finally parked, everyone filed out and Graham offered his hand to help her step out last.

His hand was clammy, but strong, hinting at how much he didn't want to let go of her.

She also felt the need to hold onto his hand as long as she possibly could.

At the foot of the stairs, all the boys gave their goodbyes to Lizzie and Graham kept his hand on her back as one by one they gave her large and enthusiastic bear hugs.

They dashed up the stairs and onto the plane, laughing and pushing each other good-naturedly. She laughed at how excited they were to embark on such an awesome trip.

Graham stepped in front of her, obscuring her view of the jet.

"I am going to miss you more than you could ever know, Lizzie," he said and reached for both her hands. He pulled them to his heart and she could feel the fast beat and how warm his body was beneath her fingers.

"I'm going to miss you, too, Graham. But we have texts, video chats, emails, social media, blah blah blah," she said, trying her best to lighten the mood. He grinned and somehow that boyish smile made her feel better, even it was only for one small second

She took a step forward and trapped their hands between their chests. "We will still be together once you come back."

"You can't promise that," he said, shaking his head and it broke her heart.

"I didn't just promise it, I am saying it with any doubt or reservation." She squeezed his hand a little tighter, offering reassurance.

"Come on, Man. We need to hit the runway or we'll lose our spot!" Christian shouted out from the open door of the jet.

Both Graham and Lizzie glared at Christian who seemed to realize that rushing them was not going to work. He nodded and ducked back into the plane.

"Well, I guess this is goodbye. At least for now." She forced a smile and met his gaze.

He started to chuckle and it hurt her feelings. How could he be laughing at her right now? she thought and stepped back, annoyed.

He noticed her upset and quickly shook his head. "No. No. It's not you. I was just…" He started to chuckle again, but regained his composure quickly and continued. "I was just hoping you would say something like that."

"Why?" She crossed her arms getting more frustrated.

"So I could say this." He was back again to serious Graham and he cupped her cheeks in his hands and said, "Don't say goodbye because I'm not going away and I don't want you to forget me."

He planted a firm kiss on her lips, but her mind wasn't even focused on the kiss.

He had obviously read *Peter Pan* just hoping he could share something from it with her. She had never felt so loved by another human being as much as she felt loved in that moment.

When her mind finally registered that the man she loved was kissing her, she quickly wrapped her arms around his neck to relish the kiss for just a little bit longer before she knew he had to leave. When he pulled away, he laid his forehead against hers and they looked into each other's eyes.

"I will call you when we land." He gave her one last kiss and finally took several steps away. He grabbed the knapsack he had put on the ground, turned to board the plane, and skipped up the stairs.

He stopped at the door and cheekily blew her a kiss. She caught it and said to herself, "I love you."

He waved and climbed into the plane.

The driver came back to her side, escorted back to the car, but she didn't climb in. Instead, she stood there as the jet moved off the tarmac, catching a glimpse of Graham as he peered out the window, searching for her as she was for him.

She stood there as the jet taxied toward the runway and it wasn't until she watched it take off and fly away that she got into the car to head back to the Austen House.

Chapter 46

Leaving on a jet plane

Graham wasn't sure he had read her lips correctly, but every time he replayed the scene in his head, he would swear that the last words she said to him as he boarded the plane were "I love you."

He shook his head to drive that thought away as he sat on the plane. The rest of the boys were listening to music, chatting, or playing games on their phones.

Graham sat there with a pile that was similar to the one his mates had given Lizzie. He needed to figure out the clue out, not only to make up for getting it incorrect the first time, but also because that would give him an excuse to see her again and tell her that he loved her too.

As the plane flew through the sky, a couple of hours passed as they headed to their farthest European location. His eyelids were growing heavy since he hadn't slept much last night and soon the words meshed together as he lost his concentration.

"Need help there, Graham old pal?"

Christian stood beside him and then shifted to sit across from him.

Graham rubbed his eyes, leaned his arms on the table and then rubbed his whole head in frustration.

"What's on your mind?" Christian laid two fingers to his lips, mocking a psychotherapist.

"I think Lizzie might have said she loves me," Graham blurted out.

"Think?" Christian asked.

"I was climbing onto the plane and well, I saw her mouth something. I am not sure I was meant to hear it, read it, or what, but I swear the last two words were 'love you'," he explained.

Christian grabbed the stacks of papers in front of Graham, scanned through them, and laughed. "So you really haven't stopped thinking about it," he said handed one of the pieces of paper to him.

"I love you, too," was written all over the sheet.

Christian put the rest of the papers down on the table and looked at Graham with such a readable face.

Graham responded with his own personal Lizzieism. "You realize that I can read you almost as easily as you can get a girl's phone number. You're about to ask me if I really do love her and if I've told her. No, I haven't. I didn't know if it was the right time. I also haven't figured out the possible location of the clue and I am still stumped as to where it could be. I was so sure of my first answer that I convinced her as well, but I was wrong."

He glanced at Christian who was about to protest, but Graham read him again.

"I know, I know. It was a misdirection. Jane wanted us to think that Ireland held the answer to the clue, but I hate that I fell for it. Lizzie wouldn't have. In fact she questioned it when I insisted I was right."

"You need to stop beating yourself up over this. You got something wrong. It didn't end the world or ruin your chances of being with Lizzie. If I do say so, it brought you together. So look at the positives of a bad situation, Graham," Christian said and rummaged through the papers again. He picked up one particular piece and continued. "Look through the clue. I would have guessed the same location and I barely even know who Jane Austen is!"

"That doesn't make me feel better, Christian," Graham joked.

"Well at least you were able to get her to agree to let you help her out in the first place. Now, close this folder. We're going to land soon."

Christian pushed the papers back across the table and stood up to go and clean his little area of the plane.

When they climbed off the jet, the chaos began.

Screaming, crying, yelling, and fainting were all they witnessed on their short walk to the vans. As they pulled away, the girls pounded on the glass. It was no different than any other city in which they had performed back at home.

When they got to the hotel, Graham climbed out of the car and before he could even take a few steps, fans swarmed forward and grappled for a touch of him.

Guards immediately surrounded them, yelling and pushing away the crowd of girls so they could make it into the hotel.

He tried to be kind and sign what he could, and laughed when one girl shoved a Jane Austen novel in front of his face.

He laughed and took the time to autograph the book before he walked into the hotel. Minutes later, he was finally able to shut the door of his room. Unfortunately, he only had a few minutes of privacy to call Lizzie and to tell her he had landed and made it to the hotel safe and sound.

Someone answered, "Hello, Graham." It was a voice he had hoped never to hear again.

"Caterina," he said and looked around the room, wishing that someone else had heard him.

"I heard what your little girlfriend did to ruin my plans with Alex and I was not very happy with that. I'm sure you can take care of his intensive care bill at the hospital. My friends got a bit carried away with their scare tactics," she said with a sickly sweet voice that didn't mask the evil there.

Although he had wanted to punch Alex himself, he would never inflict that kind of pain on him.

He knocked on the conjoining door and prayed that one of the boys would open. Sure enough, Nick opened. He put his finger to his lips to ask him to stay quiet and turned on the speaker

"What did you do to Lizzie, Caterina?"

"Oh, nothing, Dear. Not yet at least. I want the next clue. I want to know where it is—"

"We don't know where it is damn it, Caterina!" Lizzie shouted in the background.

"Shut your trampy little mouth," Caterina said and it was followed by a loud slap.

Graham wanted to climb back onto the plane and head back, but he knew there was no way he would make it in time to do anything to help.

Nick covered his mouth, trying to contain his anger.

Graham tried to stay as calm as he could. He could hear Lizzie in the background, but she wasn't crying, she was laughing.

"You honestly think he is going to do anything to help you? You do realize he dumped your ass? Flat out. You tried to get him back by getting me out of the picture. How did that work out? Oh yeah, Alex chose me. Maybe you should stop trying to throw men at me. You're simply giving me too many options."

He knew that Lizzie was trying push his ex over the edge so that she might make a mistake of some kind, but at this point he didn't know what Caterina was capable of. She had cracked and he had never imagined that he would be in a situation like this.

"Lizzie, please don't provoke her," Graham begged over the phone.

"She can't hear you begging, Graham," Caterina cooed. "I will give you, and this precious little angel of yours, twenty four hours to figure out the location of the next clue. If it is not found…let's just say Alex will have some company in the hospital."

The line went dead.

Graham stared at Nick, who just stood against the door, still unsure if what they'd just heard had actually happened. Graham knew what he needed to do and took a deep breath.

"Get all the boys. We have work to do. We have all night to figure this out. I'm sure Lizzie will be working around the clock as well."

Nick nodded and Graham walked over to his bag to grab all the paper work the boys had made for him and Lizzie.

His friends soon flooded in with one of the suitcases and tossed it on his bed.

Confused, he stared at all of them until Christian unzipped the bag and tossed open suitcase. Inside, stacked neatly and color coordinated, were books, papers, and notepads covered with scribbles and notes.

"We weren't about to leave you high and dry, Graham boy. We knew you would still be trying to figure it out on tour. Sitting on the plane simply proved it," Christian explained and pulled out his personal notebook and a small stack of books. The rest of his mates followed, dragging out their own notes and papers.

Taking up every available space in the room, from the bed to the couch and desk chair, they sprawled information all around them and began to shout out different answers or locations they thought possible.

Sadly, for each suggestion shouted out, someone would provide a rationale for why it couldn't be the right answer.

Graham was reviewing his own notes when his phone rang. It was Lizzie's number and he quickly answered, "Damn it, Caterina. Give us some time."

"It's Lizzie," she said. Her gorgeous sultry voice came through the earpiece and calmed his nerves despite the situation they were in.

"Lizzie. Thank God you're okay. Did Caterina leave you?" he asked, concerned.

"No. She's sitting next to me." Lizzie seemed irrationally calm, but he knew that she was putting on her strong brave face. He could see, or rather hear, through that façade. She was terrified.

"I wanted to call because I think I finally figured out a piece of the clue," Lizzie said.

He shot a look at the boys and snapped his fingers to get their attention.

They all looked up at him and he waved for them to come and sit around him. He put the phone on speaker and asked Lizzie to continue.

"I was re-reading the clue. She was talking about her own love life and was trying to throw us off, but what she wanted us to focus on was the part about plays. How they can make a person 'act' in love, but actually bring people together to see the light about someone else. Sound familiar? It should," she said and he could hear the smile creeping on her face.

The boys scrambled through their notes and Jude tapped one of his books.

They all looked at him as he held up the book. *Mansfield Park.*

"*Mansfield Park?*" Graham asked.

"Yep," she said with the kind of confidence she always had when it seemed as if they had found the next clue. "In the book, Fanny and her family put on a play in the story after all the drama of Mary trying to falsely flirt with Edmund, who Fanny loves. The play causes even more problems and drama within the whole house. Like in the clue when Jane talks about love making you do 'silly things'."

"So you think the location of the next clue is in this *Mansfield Park* place?" Christian asked.

Everyone, including Lizzie, laughed.

"What?" Christian said in protest.

"*Mansfield Park* is not a real place, Christian. Jane used real locations to create these manors. But I think Lizzie means that the clue is in the play that they tried to put on," Emmet explained.

As they had before, all the boys once again searched through their papers.

Graham shook his head, remembering what he had read about the play in his papers and said, "*Lovers' Vows.*"

"Right again, Graham," Lizzie said and let out a small giggle, but her joy was soon cut short by another person grabbing the phone.

"All right, so it's in that stupid play," Caterina said.

"Not exactly. It's either in a copy Jane owned herself or it might not even be the play. It could be the story in the play or the author of the play. It could be anything. We still need time, Caterina," Graham said, frustrated.

"You still have about seventeen hours," Caterina said nothing else and then the line disconnected.

Graham was about to toss the phone across the room when Emmet reached up and ripped it out of his hand. "Do that and we lose more than just the phone."

Emmet stared at Graham, but knowing that Emmet was right, he put the phone down.

Christian and Jude started to read *Mansfield Park* while Nick dug through the history of the play and its relation to Jane Austen.

Emmet's job seemed to be keeping Graham focused.

"Graham, we're going to solve this. We will keep Lizzie safe. When we figure this out we'll send for her to come here with us," Emmet said, rubbing Graham's back to try and reassure him.

Graham laughed harshly and glanced up at the ceiling. "Lizzie would never allow that. She needs to stay and finish this craziness. She wouldn't leave until the last clue was solved. For her mother."

"Then we'll send one of our bodyguards to follow her around. He'll protect her. I know how you feel about her, Graham. You want to do anything to keep her safe, but you don't want to over step your boundaries."

"When did you become this therapist, Emmet?"

"When I realized how much you two are meant to be together." Emmet patted Graham's back and hopped off the bed to grab his book. "Now let's make sure nothing happens to Lizzie."

#

The sun was just rising and before they knew it, their manager Paul was knocking on Graham's door telling him to get up to go to rehearsals.

When Graham didn't answer right away, Paul unlocked the door and peered inside to see what was happening.

As Graham sat up, he realized that Christian and Jude had fallen asleep on their papers. Nick and Emmet were slumped over piles of books and notes.

Graham glanced at Paul who looked royally pissed.

"Have you boys been up all night? Come on! The night before your first big concert! For what?" Paul shouted. He grabbed the book that was on Christian's lap. "*Mansfield Park*? What do you boys need to know about Jane Austen?"

"Just something to help out a friend," Graham explained.

"That Lizzie girl, right?" Paul said as he walked around, shaking the boys awake.

Graham nodded.

"Well, Graham, I hope you help her soon because you can't be doing this during the tour. You need rest and you need to focus. Now get showered, dressed, and down to the van. We leave in half an hour."

Paul marched out the door and his friends just looked around at each other, exhausted.

"Did we figure anything out?" Graham asked, ignoring the fact they had to be down stairs in half an hour. All the boys shook their heads and Graham glanced at the time.

"And now we have fourteen hours left."

"I think I found something!" Nick, who had started reading through his notes again, shot up from his seat on the floor and walked over to Graham on the couch. The rest of the boys followed suit.

"It was rumored that the author of the play, Elizabeth Inchbald, and Jane had become friends after Jane had asked to use the play in her story. They had sent letters to each other until Jane's death. She kept those letters in her journal together with all of her plays. Her journals eventually made their way to the Folger Shakespeare Library."

"Great, so it's in a library," Graham said, rubbed his forehead, and grabbed his phone.

"Wait, Graham," Nick said and stopped him. "We can get it."

"What do you mean?" Graham asked while everyone stood there, wide eyed and staring at Nick.

"It's here in the States. Only about a six hour drive from where we sit right now." He turned his computer so all of them could see the photo of the large, modern, stone building.

"That looks like a freaking fortress," Emmet said and grabbed the computer, looking for more information about the location. "It says you can't take out any of the books. They have to all stay inside at all times. Plus, you need to call to make an appointment to take out a specific book and provide credentials for each person that will be present while reading the books."

"Book a flight for Lizzie, Nick. She is coming back to the States tonight," Graham said.

"I will deal with Caterina," he finished.

He grabbed his phone and figured out just the kind of diversion he needed. He dialed Caterina.

"Graham. Please tell me you found what I need. Your dear Lizzie seems daft at the moment," Caterina spat out even before he could say a word.

"I have what you want," he said through gritted teeth.

"Oh really? I am impressed, Graham. Maybe you really are the Boy Wonder everyone thinks you are," she mocked.

"I want something in return," he said as a devious smirked played on his face.

"Negotiating, Graham? You really think that's a smart idea?" she warned.

"I will give you the location of the next clue, and when I do, you leave Lizzie, Alex, and any of my friends, alone. Never contact them, me or Lizzie. If you do, I will get the biggest and most embarrassing restraining order against you. You won't even be allowed on the same continent as me, or any of the people I love. Do you understand?"

"Love, Graham? Do you love this girl? Wow, too bad I was the only one who got to hear it. You have yourself a deal, Mister. Now give me the answer."

"It's in the London Library. The play *Lovers' Vows* will have the next clue. Last time it was in a book, you had to tear the binding to find the clue. So if it's not in the pages of the book with the play, you'll have to find where it's hidden in the binding."

"You're sure of this, Graham?" Caterina asked, seemingly buying the lie.

"One hundred and ten percent sure," he said, trying to keep the timbre of his voice steady so as to not give away the fact that he was lying out his ass.

"Great. Well then, Lizzie. I guess I'll have to bid you *adieu* and hope to never see you again. Good luck trying to finish your little hunt. I'm sure your mom won't be too disappointed. Oh wait…"

Caterina barked out a sinister laugh and Graham could hear what sounded like the phone dropping, but the call didn't end. A door slammed shut and then there were some scrabbling noises and another voice answered the phone.

A voice he had been dying to hear. "Graham? You still there?"

"I'm here, Lizzie. I'm always here for you." He took deep calm breaths knowing she was safe.

"I need to get to that next clue before she does, Graham. How did you guys figure out the location? I looked up everything about that play and found nothing," Lizzie said.

"Nick found it. But listen. We're buying you plane tickets. You're coming home and meeting us here," he said and smiled.

"What do you mean?"

"We can't be sure if Caterina can be trusted to keep her word in the next few days."

He looked around to see if the boys had booked her flight and Emmet gave him a thumbs up. "Pack some stuff up, for about a week or so. Get yourself to Heathrow airport in the next two hours. Find the Virgin Atlantic desk and pick up your tickets. We should see you in about eight to ten hours."

"But the clue, Graham," she said, arguing with him.

"We will get the clue, Lizzie. Trust me. I would never let you down," he said and with a broad smile, continued. "It feels like more than only a few hours since we've been apart. I'm glad I get you back so soon."

She laughed freely and without restraint. "You are such a cheese ball, Graham. But I've missed you, too."

"Then pack your bags so you can get here to me!"

"I guess I will see you soon. Bye, Graham," she said and he could hear her smile.

"What did I tell you about saying goodbye," he joked.

"Right, well then what should I say instead?" she asked.

"I'll have to think about it," he responded. "See you soon."

He hung up the phone and got the boys ready to get to the concert venue for rehearsals.

As they climbed into the van, Graham texted Lizzie to wish her a safe flight, and soon he and the boys were standing on stage, doing their sound check. Things were almost back to normal.

As soon as Lizzie arrived, everything would be normal.

#

"Man, it still always amazes me how many people are at these shows. What a rush," Graham yelled over the screams still coming from the stadium.

His mates jostled him as they were rushed along through the halls of the stadium and down to the service bays where their tour bus was parked. As the girls gathered around the parking area saw them, they began yelling and shouting to them and pushed against the barriers keeping them away from the roadway.

They boarded the bus and as they drove out of the service bay, girls yelled and hit the windows, and some even tried to run and keep up with the bus. Others hopped into cars to tail them, but soon fell back as a security guard blocked the roadway behind the bus.

When the bus finally pulled up to the hotel, there were more swarms of girls waiting outside for them.

"These girls man," Christian said with a smirk and looked out into the sea of girls.

Graham loved his fans and always took the time to thank them for all their support, but at that moment he couldn't wait to see if Lizzie had arrived.

He rushed through the crowd, pausing for far less photos and autographs than usual. Inside, he bolted through the lobby and onto the elevator.

When the doors opened on his floor, he ran even harder and faster to his room.

He swiped his key, heard the beep to unlock, and pushed the door open like it had been holding him hostage from the one thing he wanted most.

When he saw Lizzie lying on the bed, sound asleep, he realized that door really was the barrier that kept him from his one want.

Lizzie.

He gently shut the door to not disturb her, but it was no use.

She must have heard the door and jumped off the bed. She tried to get rid of the bed head from her nap and wiped away the little bit of drool that had escaped her lips while she slept.

She had never looked lovelier to him.

He smiled and walked over. It had been only hours and yet those hours felt like years. He had never felt like that with any other girl and he was sure he would never feel it again.

He wrapped his arms around her and pulled her as close as he possibly could. He buried his face in her hair. The hair that always smelled of flowers. He inhaled, making sure he would never forget her scent. When she wrapped her arms around his neck, she quickly rubbed her hands through his hair.

She let out that giggle that made his heart beat even faster.

"You're so sweaty," she said and laughed hard, causing them to separate.

"That's what happens when you run around on stage."

He met her gaze and he could tell that she was just as excited to see him. He leaned in and kissed her chastely, afraid that if he took it any farther, he wouldn't be able to stop.

"I need to grab a shower, but when I get out, I need to tell you everything that has happened in the last twenty four hours."

"I witnessed it, Graham. It doesn't need to be rehashed," she said, suddenly very uncomfortable.

He knew that even with the brave exterior she was putting up, she was still a bit terrified of Caterina.

He drew Lizzie back against his chest.

"She is never coming near you, or us, or even Alex ever again. You understand? I made a fool proof plan for that," he said. He kissed her nose and walked into the bathroom to take the quickest shower of his life.

When he finished, he walked out to his room where all the boys surrounded Lizzie. "Wow, guys. You sure know how to always make yourself at home," he said.

"Remember who solved the clue Graham?" Nick reminded him.

"That was you?" Lizzie smiled at Nick. Graham could tell she was impressed as Nick nodded.

"How in the world did you find the location of the clue? I searched high and low through all the hints, but couldn't," Lizzie said.

"Being computer savvy helps me semi hack into sites," Nick said.

"You hacked the site?" Graham and Lizzie said simultaneously.

"I said semi. It was pretty easy once I figured out that I needed to be a student at a university to let me search on the site. I simply selected a university and created a fake email from that school. I asked for permission and pow! Instant access to see if they had the books needed," Nick explained.

Now even Graham was impressed with Nick.

"But you live in London. Couldn't you just say you were interested in the history of the city?"

"Oh right...you haven't told her yet have you?" Jude asked.

"Told me what?" Lizzie looked over at Graham, waiting for an explanation.

"I thought I would send our little Caterina on a little bogus journey." He smiled, proud of himself.

"Keep going?"

"The clue is not in the London Library. It is here in the States. That's why we got you the plane ticket so fast. So she wouldn't realize that we sent her to a false location and then try and come back to hurt you," Graham said.

"But when she finds out—"

He cut her off. "Already thought of that. I told her to rip the binding. London is covered in all those CCTV cameras, so a security guard in the library will see what she's doing and well, you get the idea. Ruining public works, historical public works. I may have also called and told them there is a crazy woman ripping up very rare books."

Lizzie smiled and let out a small chuckle and soon the rest of the boys were laughing hysterically. Lizzie walked away from the group and over to Graham, who was still standing in just a towel. She whispered in his ear, "Don't bother putting clothes on."

She patted his chest and turned to face his friends. "Although I do enjoy the fact you have all come to see me, jet lag and pure terror have me worn out."

Christian held up his hands to stop her from saying any more. "We get it. You want some alone time with your man. But just remember that Nick is next door so try to keep it down in here."

They all walked out the door.

"'My man.' I liked the sound of that," she said and rubbed her hands all over his bare chest as she repeated 'my man' over and over again in between kissing his neck, torso, and then finally his lips.

When her lips finally touched his, the fire was already ablaze throughout his body.

"Lord have I missed these lips." He kissed her and found the place for his hands on her skin. She let out a small moan. "And I have missed those moans."

She moved her hands to his towel and gently pulled it away from his body.

They quickly fell onto the bed and took their time exploring each other's bodies, almost methodically.

And quietly so as to not disturb Nick.

Chapter 47

A sweet morning and sweet justice

Lizzie woke up to a loud knock on the door after the most restful night sleep she had gotten in the last few days. Graham was still fast asleep in bed and she didn't want to wake him. She wrapped the sheets around her naked body and walked out of the bedroom and out to the suite. She closed the door to the bedroom and moved over to the door to look into the peep hole.

Emmet's blinding smile filled her vision.

"What do you want, Emmet?" she whispered through the door.

"Let me in! You gotta see this," he said and knocked again.

She ripped open the door. Emmet stood there, fully dressed, with a laptop in hand. He didn't even acknowledge she was naked as he ran over to the coffee table and sat on the couch. He waved her over and she shuffled over to make sure the sheets did not fall off her body.

"This better be the most important news you share in your entire life," Lizzie sat next to him and looked at the computer.

"Oh you are going to love it," he clicked the play button on a video and soon a news video from one of the gossip channels played on the laptop.

"Caterina Jones, ex-girlfriend of Graham Harris, was arrested this morning after she was caught ripping apart a historic novel in the London Library. It's suspected that she is also tied to damage to a rare book in the Oxford University library where she was filming a music video. Jones claimed she was looking for a letter left by Jane Austen and attempted to put blame on Harris. Harris is currently on tour in the States with Greetings From Victoria. His possible new love interest, Lizzie Price, is now also in the States. How could Harris be looking for something in London if he's on tour? Do you think Jones has finally lost it? Do you think her break up with Harris caused a mental breakdown? Let us know on our Face--"

Lizzie shut the laptop before she could hear anymore.

"Hey," Emmet complained. "No need to slam. You should be happy. You're free," he said.

She couldn't control the overwhelming feeling of how right he truly was. She didn't have to fear that Caterina was going to show up back at the Austen House or hurt Alex again or come after Graham.

Caterina was probably going to a looney bin once they realized how unhinged she was.

Lizzie couldn't control the relieved laughter that built up in her system. She let out a loud chuckle and heard Graham call out from the bedroom.

"I will leave you to tell him the good news." Emmet grabbed his laptop and snuck out before Graham came out of the bedroom.

"Who was that?" Graham grumbled as he walked out, wiping the sleep from his eyes. He looked at Lizzie who stood in the middle of the room.

"It was Emmet. He had to show me something. I think you might like to see it as well." She grabbed Graham's laptop off the table, typed in the link for the online gossip site, and replayed the video for Graham.

His face went hard, but she was able to get small clues as to what he was feeling as his emotions went from shock, to sadness, to amusement.

"So what's going to happen to her?" Graham asked.

"I don't know. If they don't think she's crazy and send her away, I assume she'll probably get off with community service. I don't really know what your whole crime and punishment laws are."

She shrugged and rubbed his back. She could tell he was upset. "Are you ok?"

"I will be. It's just tough to see her going crazy. She was the first person who understood this crazy thing that happened to me. The luck it took to get me here. It's sad to see this happen."

"She did it to herself. She became obsessed with the fact you could make *her* famous. You needed someone who would be there to support and keep you going. All she did was break you down. By the end, she made you believe you needed her to be what you are. You don't. You got here, by yourself, with your talent. Those boys are who supported you through your growth and change. And they're not going anywhere."

She pepped talk like she was a coach trying to get her team riled up. "And I am not going anywhere."

He stopped moving and she was worried she had said something wrong. But he moved closer, wrapped his arms around her waist and pulled her as close as he could.

"I could not have been luckier catching you that day. Can you only imagine how different this scenario would be?" he said and laughed.

"We would not be in this scenario," she said and laughed along with him. There was yet another knock on the door.

Graham threw on his sweats and went to open the door. The boys all flooded in and were smiling and high-fiving each other on a job well done for getting Caterina out of the picture.

When they saw Lizzie sitting on the bed with the sheet wrapped around her, they patted Graham on the back.

She rolled her eyes, grabbed a bunch of clothes, and headed to the bedroom so she could change.

When she walked back into the room, Graham had also dressed and had her backpack slung over his shoulder. All the boys were standing beside him.

"Ready?" Graham asked.

"For?" she replied.

"To get the next clue. It's a long trip, but with the boys coming along I'm sure we'll be able to kill the time," Graham said.

"Don't you have like a tour to go on?" she asked.

"Today we're on our way to the next stop which also happens to be about an hour from where the clue is. The boys set up a meeting for us to go and look at the book tomorrow before we get shipped off to the next tour location," Graham explained as their friends walked out of the room ahead of them. "It's going to be a piece of cake."

Graham waited as she tucked some loose things into her suitcase and then grabbed it. They followed the boys out of the room and down to the massive tour bus. Security guards helped them advance through the crowds and onto the bus.

Inside, LEDs were lit up in multiple colors. Large flat screen TVs were at various spots along with every video game console you could imagine. For resting, there were small bunks, a kitchen and lots of spaces to just hang out.

The tour bus was the place where the boys were going to have to spend a great deal of time for several months so it made sense to have everything possible to keep them occupied.

Graham tossed Lizzie's bag onto his bunk, grabbed her hand, and walked over to a wall where he pressed a button. The wall opened to reveal stairs and he led her up the narrow staircase.

"I guess you can't carry me up these puppies," she joked.

When they reached the space at the top of the stairs, she was mesmerized by the three hundred sixty degree view through the tinted windows. Graham led her over to one of the couches and they sat down to just enjoy the company of each other.

#

"We're here!" Jude exclaimed as he ran up the stairs and grabbed everyone's attention.

They climbed out of the secret second floor and made their way to the front door of the bus as it pulled up in front of their next hotel. Girls were already lining the areas around the front entrance. Luckily, their bodyguards had already set up barriers so that they could make it into the hotel without being terribly mobbed.

"It's show time, boys," Nick said and jumped up and down, getting his body pumped for all the grabbing, signing, crying, and everything else that came with the territory of just getting to the lobby of the hotel.

As the bodyguards came to the door of the bus, the girls got more frantic, knowing that the band would soon be emerging from the bus.

When the doors opened, the screams nearly pierced Lizzie's ears. She had never heard them that loud before.

"Jesus," she said under her breath. Graham chuckled next to her as they walked down and were tussled about with each step and he quickly signed everything he could reach.

He smile glowed with every girl's hand that he shook and photo that he signed. He may not have been comfortable with the craziness that had been thrust upon him, but he loved that he was there and wanted the girls to feel the same way.

As they finally got into the hotel the sounds from outside were dimmed by what Lizzie figured were soundproof doors and windows. They barely had time to drop their things in their hotel room before they were quickly led to a small van and were on their way to the concert venue.

Lizzie enjoyed every minute of her time with Graham, watching as he sang, joke around with the boys, and genuinely enjoyed himself.

It warmed her heart to see him so happy and to know she was part of the reason why.

After the concert, they ran back into the van and sped off to the hotel.

As he had been the other night, Graham was drenched with sweat from his exertions on the concert stage. He showered and climbed into bed where he snuggled up on her stomach and again asked her to read to him. When she started to losing steam, she closed the book and turned to shut off the light.

She wiggled down to be face-to-face with Graham, loving to look at him as he lay beside her.

"Are you excited for tomorrow?" Graham asked mid-yawn.

She nodded and ran her hands up and down his torso. "I'm excited to have these few more days with you."

"Yeah. We barely even had time to miss each other," he said and pulled her closer. "I need to take in all these opportunities to have you this close to me. I know you may be gone again after tomorrow night." He encircled her and brought her as close he could.

She loved being wrapped in his arms. She loved his breath on her neck. She loved everything he did to her, with her, for her.

She was just plain in love with the guy, but still too afraid to tell him.

As they nodded off, a whisper leaked from Graham's lips. ". . .ov you, too…"

She laughed at his sleep-talking and allowed herself to slip into peaceful slumber in his arms.

Graham woke up the next morning itching to get a move on and find the next clue.

He gently rubbed and kissed Lizzie's back as she stirred awake and faced him. They both smiled and without saying a word, hopped up, and threw on simple, incognito clothing.

They crept out of the hotel room and tip-toed down the hall to the elevator.

When the elevator doors opened, they were shocked to see all the boys standing there with food either shoved in their mouth or stacked on take-out containers.

Lizzie and he started laughing hysterically at the guilty looks on the faces of his band mates.

"Some of this stuff is for you," Emmet tried to explain.

"We thought you would need energy for today," he said, swallowed the food that was in his mouth, and handed them one of the two plates he held.

Graham grabbed it and offered it up to Lizzie. She snagged a strip of bacon and crunched it in her mouth.

"All right, you boys are never, and I mean never, up this early. What's going on?" he asked.

"We're coming with you," Christian answered. "We know we can't go in with you two, but we want to be there when you actually get the clue!"

"And we want to help get you the answer that much quicker," Nick added.

"Thanks you guys," Lizzie gushed.

Graham peered at all his friends' faces and could tell they were up to something. But Lizzie was quickly hugging all of them with her bright smile, so he held back from trying to figure out what it was.

They all got back onto the elevator and Lizzie slid her hand into his. She rose on tiptoe and whispered against his ear, "What do you think they're up to?"

He laughed on the inside and smiled from ear to ear. He should have known she would see it and he kissed her forehead.

The slight bump of the elevator announced that they had made it to the lobby.

They managed to rush through the lobby and out to the small van without too much of a scene.

Nick slipped into the front passenger seat and told the driver the location. He turned to look at Graham and Lizzie. "Ok, since you can't take the book out of the building you *need* photos. The clue is going to be in there somewhere and we need to be sure we have everything we can use."

"Now who has become the dad in this band?" Graham joked.

"I became the dad when you became a love struck boy again," Nick teased and all the boys ooh'd and ah'd.

The heat of a blush flooded through Graham's face. He hadn't blushed in years and he was shocked it was happening at that moment.

"Boys he's blushing! That never happens," Emmet joked and play punched him in the arm. "Lizzie, you need to take in this moment. The last time I think we saw him blush was after our first real TV interview when the woman told us we were cute chaps who had a huge future ahead of us. We think he thought she was a hottie. She was but, well, just take this moment in."

Lizzie leaned forward a little bit to see his face and he tried to hide it by covering his face, but she grabbed his hands and tenderly urged them away.

"Stop it. You look adorable when you blush," she gushed which caused even more heat across his face.

"Aww. Now you two stop all the lovely dovey crap until we are out of sight," Emmet warned and nudged Graham's shoulder.

Graham shook his head and put up with his friends' goodhearted teasing as they drove to the library. Especially as Lizzie held his hand and tucked herself into his side.

In no time, they arrived at their location.

"We. Are. Here," Nick shouted and interrupted all of the chatter from the back of the van. "Now go, you two. We only have about three hours before we need to be at the venue for tonight's show."

"Umm…go?" Graham said and just stared at Nick.

Nick's eyes went wide and he nodded to the door of the van.

Graham scooted off the bench seat and toward the side door of the van. Lizzie followed him and they left the van. On the sidewalk, Lizzie and he stared at the large gray stone fortress that stood in front of them.

After a quick peek at her, he took a deep breath and they walked together into the building.

In the lobby, they handed all their credentials to the security guard and once they were cleared, they found a librarian who was only too pleased to see such young people take an interest in such peculiar small works.

She sat them down at a lone table in the corner of a large reading room. Only two other people were sitting in the entire place. She walked away and when she came back she handed them each a pair of gloves and masks.

Once they had covered their mouths and put the gloves on, she placed the book in front of them.

It was actually two small leather bound volumes. The journals almost looked like the one Lizzie had been carrying around. The woman then left them to do their work.

He glanced at Lizzie, asked if she was ready, and with her quick nod, they both opened the books.

Hand written notes, letters, and drawings covered every page. Many were new play ideas. Some were ramblings about how society was treating Elizabeth. She seemed to be going against the grain of what the rest of the world was doing. She spoke her mind and didn't seem to care who disagreed.

Graham instantly knew why Jane had loved her work.

As he combed over his book, Lizzie pulled out her very own journal and wrote something down.

"What do you have there?" he said and leaned over to see what she was reading.

"Elizabeth is talking about a letter Jane wrote. She says that Jane is not very well and the letter seemed to be rambling. If Elizabeth didn't know about the hunt, she might not have realized that the letter was the next clue. She might have thought that whatever Jane was writing made no sense. I think she's describing our next clue," Lizzie concluded.

"What date was that?" he asked.

"June 23, 1817. That's less than a month before Jane Austen passed," Lizzie whispered. She gently turned the page and stopped short.

"What?" Graham asked examining her carefully. He wasn't sure she was even breathing.

He grew so worried that he shifted the book away from her and began to read.

As he did so, he froze as well.

"This was possibly the last letter she ever wrote," Lizzie said, still not moving a bone in her body.

Graham stared back down at the journal sitting in front of him.

"This letter contains the final clue. That means the last location has your 'handsome reward and the Universal Truth'." He had no clue what else to say.

"I need to write this down before our time is up." She scribbled as fast as she could, copying down what was in the journal. But then she stopped short and glanced at him again.

"This sounds familiar. The words I mean. Like I've read this before."

"How could you have read it before?" he asked, confused.

"I don't know, but I have. I usually remember these kinds of things. There is something about these words that is familiar," she said and then continued to write as she pondered what it was.

He looked to see the librarian returning. "Write faster, he urged."

She looked up as well before ducking he head back down and writing as fast as she could scribble legible words.

When she finished, she closed her notebook and then closed the journal.

Graham followed suit and the woman approached and told them their time was up.

He took off his mask and gloves and Lizzie did as well.

They thanked the woman for her generosity and help.

She offered her appreciation for their interest and then escorted them to the door of the library. At the security checkpoint they opened their bags so the guard could confirm that they hadn't taken anything and then they went outside to the fresh air.

He inhaled deeply, feeling as if they had made some progress and Lizzie did the same.

Looking toward the curb, he realized his band mates were all standing on the sidewalk, hanging out beside the van. He was surprised that no fans had spotted them, but he assumed that research libraries were not the kind of spot that teens frequented.

He slipped his hand into Lizzie's and they returned to the van where everyone piled back in. As soon as they sat, the boys shot question after question at them.

"Guys, calm down. Lizzie needs time to think," Graham said and tried to shush all the questions by raising his hand to urge for quiet.

"Well, we want to think with her!" Christian complained. "Read the clue. Read the clue," he chanted and soon his other band mates joined in.

Graham shook his head and glanced at Lizzie. With a roll of her eyes, she took out her leather notebook, turned to the notes she had taken, and started to read.

"My Dear Friend Elizabeth,

I have been feeling weaker and weaker by the day. I wish to continue, for there is so much more I have yet to accomplish, but the comfort of my bed seems to be the only satisfactory location for my pathetically feeble body. This might be the last letter I write until I get better, and with that I need to confide in you this little bit of knowledge. This letter must always stay on your person until someone comes to call for it. Please, dear friend, I need this one last gift of your friendship.

I shall keep this as simple, but intimate as I may be able. This sweet view, sweet to the eye as well as the mind. It exudes all that is without being oppressive. The English culture, English comfort seen under a sun bright. It warms my skin, like none other and brings me all the happiness of sitting at my window and inspires the mind.

Best of Luck, Jane," Lizzie finished reading.

She closed her book and just stared at the leather bound journal. She was rubbing the front like it was new, and unknown, and yet with love and familiarity.

"So this is her final clue? You did it?" Emmet asked.

"Once I find where this leads, yes, I will be done," Lizzie said. She smiled, but he could tell something was worrying her.

"What's wrong, Lizzie?" he asked, pulling her a bit closer.

"I just don't want this to end. I didn't expect it to end so soon. I'm just sad to see this crazy ride is almost over," she said and sighed.

"It just means we'll have to find another crazy ride to hop on," Graham offered, trying to keep her spirits high. "So I am to assume the next clue is most likely back in the UK?"

She nodded in agreement with his statement.

Graham knew that she needed to, and maybe, even secretly, wanted to do this last part alone. For her mother and for herself.

As the van pulled into the hotel parking lot, the number of fans had dwindled, possibly because they needed to head to the concert soon, much like they had to.

"I'm going to stay back this time, guys," Lizzie said as they went up to their rooms. "I want to get everything packed up so I can hop on a plane tomorrow morning."

They all gave her solid, loving hugs, and went to their own rooms.

Graham opened the door to his room and she walked in ahead of him. She immediately went to sit at the desk where his computer was set up.

She typed swiftly and a moment later, with a triumphant grin, she slammed her hand on the desk.

"I knew it!" she said and jumped up.

He ran over to see what had been looking at.

"What?" he asked.

"I knew I'd heard that quote," she said and continued. "Granted Jane's recitation wasn't word for word, but they were from her own book. *Emma.* Her last full work. After she died they published her first two written novels, but *Emma* was the last full story she wrote and was able to publish. She was talking about her love of the English countryside," Lizzie said and gave him a wide happy smile.

"So you've already solved the clue? You know the location?" he asked, stunned.

"She said she would keep it simple..." Lizzie said, paused to think about it and then forged ahead. "But she lived in two or three places that inspired her, so I need to narrow it down from there," she explained.

"If she was writing it as her final goodbye, it would be safe to assume that it was the last place she ever lived. I mean that would be my guess." He shoved his hands in his pockets and stepped back from the desk. "Granted, I was way wrong the last time, so maybe I wouldn't take my advice, even if I was me," he said and chortled.

She smiled and nodded, agreeing with his thought process. "No. You're probably right. But since you leave for the show in a few, my time will be focused on you. Plus you need to get your mindset into tour mode, not creepy Jane Austen genius."

She wrapped her arms around his neck and he bent his head to nuzzle it into her neck.

Her vibration of pleasure registered all over his body.

She had such a whirlwind effect on his mind and his body that he was never able to control how much he wanted to take her.

As he kissed his way down her neck and to her collarbone, her moans got more and more mind dizzying.

Her last breathy exclamation was half-moan and half-plea. "You need to get ready. My boyfriend cannot disappoint his fans."

He pulled back and looked into her eyes. "You don't really want me to back to England with you, do you?"

"Wow. I'm impressed. You are getting better at the whole reading people thing," she teased and kissed him chastely.

"You've taught me well." He kissed her again and then finally forced himself away from her temptation.

"Fine, fine. I'll leave, unwillingly and not truly wanting to leave, so I can pay the bills."

They both laughed as he made his way to the door, but he couldn't help but turn back and kiss her one more time before he left.

Chapter 48

Setting something free

Graham ran out of the elevator and raced to his room to tell Lizzie all about the concert.

When he flung open the door he didn't see her anywhere in the room.

He walked to the bathroom door and knocked, but no one answered.

He opened the bedroom door, but she wasn't there either. Her bag wasn't there either and his heart started to pound in his chest with fear.

He returned to the living area of the suite and searched all around before spying the piece of paper sitting on his laptop.

He sat down heavily, knowing what it was going to say and dreading it.

He braced himself with a deep inhale, lifted the piece of paper and read the letter.

Graham,

My mother always told me to never underestimate the power of a well-meaning and well-written letter. Jane Austen had several of her male leads write letters expressing themselves fully to the ones they cared for desperately. And even in other works, letters convey sentiments that are too hard to say sometimes.

The reason I've left without saying goodbye is because you told me not to say the word. As well, I do not think I could actually leave if I had to see you as I walked away. Mr. Darcy said it best. 'You have bewitched me body and soul'.

I guess what I'm trying to say is that I have never been able to show or tell my emotions to someone I care for. I use other people's words to express how I feel. But I think this is my chance for once in my life to say what I feel.

When I first met you, I thought you were an annoyance, a common pain in my ass. You would not take 'No' for an answer no matter how many times I had given it to you. And after not wanting to be around you for all that time, I found I didn't like it when you were gone. You grew on me and I soon found that I was wrong about you. Something else my mom said was that I may have gotten my first impressions wrong, but I would always find the true person behind my initial suspicions. It was why she loved the fact she had named me Lizzie. Like from Pride and Prejudice.

Then you called me out on my journal. The words 'I love you' scribbled in my little notebook. The list of things I wanted to hear a British person say. When I wrote it I never really wanted to hear it or expected to hear it. I still do not expect to, but I think it was something that I wanted to say to a British person. It was something I wanted to say to you, but have been too terrified to say.

I thank Jane for giving me the courage to even admit it. And I thank you for opening my heart to something I never could imagine possible at this time in my life. I will be seeing you once you return and hopefully we can go from there.

Best of Luck (on your tour),
Lizzie

#

That night, Lizzie was already on the plane back to London. She had called her father to tell him what had been going on the past few weeks, especially since she had been M.I.A throughout most of the time. He understood and said he had been following her in the tabloids.

She couldn't believe she was now her own mini-celebrity and shook her head at the weirdness of fame.

When the plane landed, she hopped into a black cab and asked the cabbie to take her to the Austen House.

She walked in and Fanny came out of her small living room.

Lizzie waved, tired physically and emotionally, and was about to head up the stairs when Fanny offered her a cup of tea. Lizzie couldn't say "No" after all that Fanny had done for her. With a smile, she walked back down the few stairs and to the living room. She sat on the couch as Fanny brought out her dainty tea set.

"What is on your mind, Child," Fanny asked as she poured tea into the cups and then sat across from Lizzie.

"I just got back from being with Graham. I didn't even say goodbye. I wrote him a letter. I'm such a coward," Lizzie said, grabbed the cup, and brought the steaming hot tea to her lips.

"You are not a coward. You knew you couldn't leave him if he was standing right in front of you."

Fanny sat a little further up in her seat and continued. "I saw the way you looked at him the very first day when you tried to kick him out of here. I also saw his face when you told him to leave. The reason I set my mind to having you work with him was because I knew you two were meant for each other. You both did not see it, but I did. I did."

Lizzie sat across with the cup still held halfway to her lips, considering what Fanny had said. When Fanny spoke again, Lizzie broke out her trance-like state and put down the cup of tea.

"Dear, Lizzie. Dear, dear Lizzie. What am I going to do with you?" Fanny laughed and leaned back in her chair.

"Once you find out let me know." Lizzie slapped her legs and stood up. "I need to get some sleep, Fanny. I will see you tomorrow."

Lizzie grabbed her bag and walked to her own bedroom. Word had spread of her return and all along the way girls stopped her to sign books or clothing. Whatever they had on them and Lizzie graciously did so, knowing that was what Graham would do.

Finally falling onto her bed, she didn't even realize she had fallen asleep until the gentle knock came at the door.

Fanny, Lizzie thought.

She groaned, but got out of bed to let Fanny in to drop off the morning tea service. But instead of just dropping off the tea, Fanny started to clean up the clutter of Lizzie's room. Her actions reminded Lizzie of her mother as the older woman picked up clothing and moved around papers and books. The way she moved about from one pile to the next was eerily similar, but it made Lizzie feel even more at home.

"You remind me a lot of my mom, Fanny. I don't think I ever told you that, but you do," Lizzie said and smiled as she grabbed the piping hot cup of tea.

Fanny smiled warmly and continued her chores.

Lizzie put the cup down and walked over to Fanny, grabbing her fragile hands.

Fanny turned with warmth glowing from her heart.

"You really do not need to do this, Fanny. I am quite all right with the mess for now. It helps me think," she said and continued to hold Fanny's hands in her own.

With a small nod and a bright smile, Fanny walked away and gently closed the door.

Lizzie gathered all her papers and her computer. She booted it up and tried typing in the Austen family residences.

As she looked through the clue she had copied again, Graham's point about it having to be Jane's last home seemed more and more probable.

Jane had quoted her own book, the very last novel published prior to her death. She had to be describing the very sight she was seeing at that very moment. With that idea in her mind, Lizzie searched for the last known residence of Jane Austen and quickly found it.

The Chawton House where a museum had been set up. The museum was rumored to have outstanding views of Chawton, a collection of Jane Austen memorabilia, and even some of Jane Austen's personal items. It was open daily and you could pay extra to have a tour guide walk you through and share what would a day there with Jane would have been like.

Lizzie could not control the happiness running through her body.

She grabbed her phone and texted Graham, saying that she thought she had found the last location. But she knew that she still needed to find the actual place within the house which Jane had been describing in the clue.

She quickly tossed up her hair, hopped in and out of the shower, and grabbed all of her things to rush out the door and catch the next train to Chawton.

Girls once again flooded the hallway and slowed her down by taking photos with her and signing things, but she managed to speed them along and got to where Fanny was sitting at the front desk. She offered Fanny a bright smile and walked over to give the woman a hug.

Fanny let out a little bit of a surprised squeak at the strength of her hug, but hugged Lizzie right back.

"I will be back later tonight, Fanny. Hopefully with the spoils of my journey!" Lizzie exclaimed and walked out the door and to the tube station.

The paparazzi luckily didn't follow her down into the tunnels, which was a relief.

She had to transfer to get to Chawton, but as she sat on the last leg of the trip, her heart raced and her palms were sweaty. Her stomach had butterflies at the squeak of the breaks as they arrived at her final destination.

She jumped out of her seat, scaring a few of the other passengers with abrupt motion and the quickness of her steps. Bolting off the train, she hurried to locate a map of the area and find the way to Jane's house.

As she perused the map, she realized the house wasn't a long walk from the train station and walked briskly to the house. Along the way, she was captivated by the old homes, the classic English countryside, and the many local shops that dotted the streets. Her breath was soon taken away when she turned a corner and saw the large brick building that boasted the sign announcing the museum.

She had made it.

She walked into the brick structure and a mixture of wood, flowers, and a slight perfume quickly tantalized her nostrils. A young girl fully dressed in 1800s garb walked up to Lizzie with a bright smile on her face. She greeted Lizzie.

"Can I help you with anything?" she asked.

Lizzie, still in awe of standing in another Jane Austen home, looked at the young woman for a bit longer than she anticipated. The woman raised her eyebrows with puzzlement and Lizzie realized how uncomfortable she had made the guide.

"I'm sorry. I'm just here to look around, but I did I read that you offer tours," she said.

The young woman nodded. "I'd be the person to give you the tour."

"How much would it cost to have a private tour?"

"Nothing extra," the guide said and Lizzie paid for the tour.

The young woman walked her around the house, sharing details about the daily chores, the various rooms, and even living quarters for the animals. But nothing struck her as a place the final clue, or whatever it was, could be hidden.

As she walked around, she tapped walls without the guide noticing. Jumped on the balls of her feet to listen for any loose floorboards, but nothing gave her any indication that she might have found a secret hiding place.

"This was Jane and Cassandra's bedroom," the young guide said as they entered one room.

Lizzie peered into the room as the girl described and that's when she knew the clue was going to be found in that area. She didn't know why the feeling was so strong, but something was telling her this was the place.

Two beds sat across the room from each other. A full length mirror was on one side of the room while a large armoire sat on the other wall. In the middle of the room was a large window.

Lizzie stepped up to the window and put her hand to her heart. The words Jane had described echoed through her. There was a sweet view of the English countryside where the hills rounded the world into something so precious nothing could ever spoil their beauty.

Lizzie put her hands on the small ledge of the window to try and see as much of the view as she could. A small creak snared her attention.

She glanced down. The ledge wigged with the pressure of her hands. She turned to the tour guide. "Did you hear that?"

"This house creaks something awful with almost every movement you make," the young woman replied.

"But this is wiggling as it squeaks," Lizzie said repeated her motion over and over again to recreate the noise.

"I'm sorry, but you have me a bit confused," the guide responded.

She walked over to Lizzie and watched as Lizzie repeated the motion of putting pressure on the ledge so that it wiggled. She peered at the tour guide. Her forehead was all scrunched and she seemed a bit mystified.

"I don't think I ever noticed that before," she said.

"It might have been that you just weren't looking for it. However, I was," Lizzie said and then leaned all her weight on the ledge. With that the whole thing broke off and sent dust flying everywhere.

Tiny pieces of wood broke off in every direction.

Lizzie glanced at the guide and found that her features were filled with fear, shock, and curiosity. "Don't worry. I'll pay for the damage and you can simply say that I lagged behind the tour group and you didn't even see me do this."

Lizzie waved the last bit of lingering dust away and stared down at the hole where the small window ledge had once been.

There was an inches wide gap between the window and wall. Rolling up her sleeve, she gently eased her hand down the space. The guide let out a squeak of protest, but Lizzie calmed her by trying to talk to her.

"Did Jane write in this room?"

The girl shook her head. "No. It wasn't common for the young ladies to sit in their rooms all day. Most of the time she wrote down in the living room."

She stopped and put her head down, as if remembering something.

"Wait," she said.

Lizzie paused and glanced at the girl.

"It's said that Jane lived her last few months in here. She was too weak to make it downstairs to write. Her father brought her writing desk up and she sat by this window so she could continue her writing."

"Bingo," Lizzie said and smiled.

She tried to push her hand ever deeper into the gap searching for something. Anything. She had just about given up hope when she felt something. Several somethings actually.

They felt like sacks and she grabbed one and pulled it from the crevice gently. It was in fact a small burlap sack.

The guide looked at it in shock.

Lizzie put her hand back into the gap to grab the others. Two more small burlap sacks.

She felt around one final time, but those were the last of them.

"What are those?" the guide said and gingerly grabbed one. "How did you even know they were there?"

"I don't know what they are and I had no clue they were there. But I knew I was sent here to find something. These are the spoils of my travels. The end of my adventure," Lizzie said and picked up one of the bags.

She carefully untied the ribbon that held the burlap bag closed. The ribbon fell to the ground and she eased away the burlap. The contents from inside bloomed open.

Dozens of envelopes spilled from the sack.

Lizzie seemed very confused and opened the other two sacks just as gently to find that they, too, were filled with a dozen or so envelopes.

But as she shuffled through all the envelopes and the letters they contained, she noticed one had some unexpected words on it.

Lizzie reached for it. The words 'The End' were written calligraphy-style on the face of it. Her knees were trembling so badly that she had to sit on the floor or risk falling down.

The tour guide grabbed up all of her layers of dress and sat down next to Lizzie to admire what she had found.

Lizzie smiled at the young girl and carefully opened the envelope which contained the final letter.

Dearest Person or Persons,

Congratulations on finding me. I knew the right person would be able to hunt, track, and unearth my several witty, and I dare give myself applause, ingenious clues. This is my favorite place to sit. How the warmth of the sun beams into the room at a certain hour in the day rejuvenates a weakening heart like mine. I feel as though you may be confused as to why letters are my final gift to you and rightfully so. Most dream of finding untold riches, the love of a lifetime, or simply a better something than what they already have.

You, my dear winner, are not like those who walk the normal path. If you were, you would not have read my books or even continued our little game. These letters are my *universal truths and* my *handsome reward for you to do with as you please. These are the letters to my truest confidants. I tried to keep my life as secret as possible. I fear in the coming years celebrity will be a new form of torture, even if I am not there to see it.*

I do not know who will find these letters and I do not know when they will be found, but I do have the faith that someone, someday, will find them. To you I wish only the kindest, gentlest, love and admiration.

Best of Luck and Goodbye,

Jane

"Holy Hell," the young woman said, causing Lizzie to shoot a look at her out-of-character response.

The guide had a few of the letters in her hands and bounced them up and down with excitement and surprise. "These are from Jane Austen. *The* Jane Austen. These were thought to have been destroyed. These unlock a whole new side of Jane Austen we never even knew!" the girl exclaimed and reached for more of the letters, but Lizzie stopped her.

"You need to understand that she didn't want these found by just anyone for a reason," Lizzie said as she tried to fill the bags with the letters and tie them back up.

"You cannot tell a soul about these or about what you saw here today. For Jane," she said and met the guide's gaze. She could see that her mind was racing with doubt and her face had a small nervous tick near the edge of her lip, confirming the young woman's unease.

But before Lizzie could try to convince her further, she handed over the few letters she had in her possession to Lizzie, nodded, and repeated, "For Jane."

Lizzie grabbed the letters and stuffed them into her knapsack along with the rest in the burlap bags. She stood up, slung her knapsack over her shoulder, and walked to the door. But before leaving, she turned and noticed the guide's downtrodden face. She walked back to the young woman, reached into her bag and grabbed one of the letters.

"This never happened and you do not have this letter," she said and handed the girl the yellowing piece of parchment.

The girl held it to her heart and gave Lizzie a quick and grateful hug.

"Thank you. For Jane," the guide said, repeating the promise.

Lizzie walked out of the room and away from the building.

She didn't realize she had streams of tears falling down her face until a breeze from outside chilled the salty wetness on her cheeks.

She swiped them away and took a deep inhale to calm herself. With none of the rush she'd had to arrive, she ambled back to the train station, pausing to enjoy this place that had been the last one where Jane had lived and which she had loved.

As she stepped onto the train back to London, she glanced back at the town and said, "Goodbye, Jane. And thank you for a wonderful adventure."

#

She walked into the Austen House to greet Fanny, but couldn't find the words. Instead, she ran to her with open arms and hugged her with all the love and happiness she was feeling.

Fanny wrapped her arms around Lizzie squeezing just as lovingly.

"You are one of the most chipper people I have seen. What happened to make you so happy?" Fanny asked.

"Can we talk privately?" Lizzie said as she glanced around all the girls lingering around in the hotel.

"Of course," Fanny said. She walked Lizzie into the living room, closed the door behind them and they sat in the same chairs where they had so often to share some tea or news.

"Do you know why I came to London? Why I paid for such a lengthy stay?" Lizzie asked.

"I thought you just needed to get away. I had hoped it was nothing criminal, which I found to be the most ludicrous idea immediately after getting to know you. Then I found out you had some interest in Jane, but I don't think I really knew what you were trying to find," Fanny said, her narrowed gaze confirming to Lizzie that she was frustrated that she still did not know the answer.

Lizzie felt safe enough with the older woman to finally share her entire secret. "My mother died and left me a letter. A letter from Jane Austen telling me to find a universal truth and a handsome reward. Jane said that to do that, I would have to solve the clues she left for me. Graham caught me looking for the first clue. He begged to tag along, but you know most that. I've been on this journey for the last month and now I can tell you why I am so happy."

Lizzie smiled, opened her bag, and dumped the sacks on the coffee table. "I found the truth and the reward. In each of these bags there are over a dozen letters written by Jane to her sister and her brother. Historians do not believe these letters exist because Jane had asked her sister to destroy all her letters."

Fanny grabbed one of the bundles reverently. "These are really..."

She untied the bag and the letters fell out all around her. Her eyes welled up with tears. "Oh, my."

"I want you to hold onto them. At least for right now, until I figure out what I plan on doing with my life now that this part of my adventure is over."

Lizzie stood up, walked over to Fanny, and gave her another big hug.

"Oh, Lizzie! I forgot to tell you I left you a little something in your room. A little gift if you would like to call it," Fanny called out as Lizzie exited the living room.

She went her room, unlocked the door, walked in and stopped dead in her tracks, "Graham?"

Chapter 49

Unexpected meetings

"Graham?" she repeated and Graham stood up and faced her. She looked totally off guard and totally surprised.

"Hey, Lizzie," he said lamely. He had thought about what to say to her the entire flight back and the second he saw her, all thoughts flew out of his mind.

Her gaze traveled all up and down his body as if making sure he was really standing in her room.

"What are you doing here?" she said and rushed to stand in front of him. She put her hands on his chest, again as if to confirm he was really there. Her touch caused all his thoughts to come flooding back and he pulled her letter out of his pocket and held it up to her.

"Did you honestly expect me not to say or do anything about this?" he asked.

"That was not why I did it. I expected you to say something about it. I just didn't expect you to come back across the Atlantic Ocean to do so," she said with a laugh and shake of her head.

"You said you love me in this letter." He stepped closer to her and she nodded. He figured that her lack of words was because she was afraid to speak. Or maybe she didn't understand where this conversation was going and was afraid of saying the words out load.

"I'm assuming those feelings haven't changed?" he said and dipped his head so she couldn't avoid his gaze.

She rolled her eyes. "How fickle do you think I am, Graham? I only wrote that letter a day ago!"

"So the feelings are still real?" Graham asked, needing to hear her say it.

But she said nothing and instead wrapped her arms around his neck. Kissed him with her full luscious lips until he was nearly breathless.

He encircled her waist with his arms and pulled her even closer.

She brought her hands to his hair and rubbed them all over, knowing how much he loved that. It caused goose bumps to erupt throughout his entire body.

"I love you, you idiot," she said and kissed him again.

"I love you, too," he replied, kissing her one more time before pushing her away so he could ask her another question.

"Did you figure out where the clue led?"

"I did," she admitted and grabbed his hands. "Follow me."

She pulled him out of the room and they snuck down the stairs as quietly as they could to Fanny's living room. When Lizzie walked him in, he realized that Fanny sat at the table, reading a letter. On the table sat a large stack of letters.

Lizzie let go of his hand and sat down next to Fanny. He followed her and glanced down at the pile. He realized the letters seemed quite old.

"Welcome to the treasure chest, Graham," Lizzie said. She smiled and spread her arms out to gesture to all the letters.

"What is this?" he asked, reaching for one of the pieces of parchment.

"This was what the final clue led me to." She grabbed a letter and explained. "These are all of Jane's letters that were supposedly burned and trashed. But Jane had them saved and shoved into the window ledge where she sat writing during her last few months."

He grabbed the letter and read the final goodbye from Jane.

He plopped down into a chair, in shock. Once he finished the one letter, he glanced at all the others. "Have you read them all?"

"I just got home. I had no time," Lizzie said and that's when they both heard a light whimper escape from Fanny.

Lizzie put an arm around Fanny, asking why she was so upset.

"Lizzie, I'm not upset. I'm happy. Thrilled. You called this place home," she said and wiped a tear away as it rolled down her plump cheek.

"Of course it is, Fanny," Lizzie said, also choking up.

"Oh, man! Are you both about to get really sentimental on me?" he said and moved away before he got all caught up in it.

"You get back here," Lizzie said and pulled him into the group hug.

#

They next morning he lay in bed with Lizzie sleeping soundly next to him. He hated that he had to get going. He moved away from her gently, but it caused her to stir and wake up.

"Sorry. I was just going to get a shower and head out," Graham said and smiled.

"You were gonna leave without saying goodbye?" she teased with a pout and sat up in the bed. Her hair was everywhere and he laughed at how attractive she was, even with her hair all over in spikes and tangles.

"I was going to wake you right before I had to leave." He sat back down next to her on the bed.

"It's ok, Graham. I'll see you in a few months when you come back for good." She placed her hand on his cheek.

He leaned forward and kissed her sweetly. She inched her body up and tried pulling him back into bed. He smiled, but shifted away.

"Sneaky, Lizzie," he joked.

"I tried," she admitted. She let go and climbed out of bed, and started grabbing at the clothes that were strewn all over.

It reminded him of the first time he had met her. He had admired the curves of her body even when he was simply trying to get her out of the library.

"I am going to miss you more than I missed you before," he confessed.

"Puleez, Graham. I was only out of your sight for maybe twenty four hours," she joked, obviously trying to ease their upcoming separation. She threw on a shirt and spun to face him. "Come on. Get out of the bed! We need to get you to the airport!"

He reluctantly climbed out of the bed, showered, and quickly dressed for his trip back. They walked out of the Austen House, but not before he gave a final peck on the cheek to Fanny. At the curb, they got into the black SUV that had carted them around to so many places. Everything seemed to remind him of the different parts of their incredible journey together. The vehicle they sat in reminded him of their sleepover in his car after the wedding that had almost caused him to give up on trying to impress Lizzie.

Their intertwined fingers brought him back to when they were not allowed to touch while they had danced for the tour group in Bath. Her smile reminded him of every other smile he saw on her angelic face when she found a new clue or location. When she looked at him with her questioning ice blue gaze, he could tell she was trying to figure out what he was thinking.

Before she even asked, he replied, "I'm thinking back to all the time we have spent together and oddly, I feel that even in that short amount of time, we've actually gotten to know each other quite well."

"You were basically begging to be with me from day two," she joked.

"No way! You secretly wanted my help!" he replied, a teasing smile on his face.

She shook her head and moved closer to whisper in his ear, "You're right, but you dig begging."

She kissed the small patch of stubble where his jawbone and ear met and then laid her head on his shoulder.

"You're right," he admitted.

The car pulled up to the airport terminal and not to the area for the private jets.

"No private jet this time?" she asked.

"When it's just me or one of the other boys, management doesn't really splurge. Also they have no clue I left last night because the boys have been covering for me," he said and laughed.

"You can get into serious trouble, Graham!"

"I didn't really care. I wanted to see you and tell you that I love you. And that I have probably since we first met." He cupped her cheek and leaned in to kiss her.

"You are so stupid sometimes, Graham," she whispered when his lips were barely an inch from hers.

"But I would not have the boy I love any other way," she said as she met his lips for the kiss.

As he covered her lips with his, it was the kind of heart beating faster, hands gripping harder, show stopping kisses he always enjoyed with her.

When he reluctantly pulled away, he thought of what he had wanted to say to her once she finally admitted that she loved him. "You know that Jane said that a man of good fortune must be in want of a wife."

She stepped back and looked at him quizzically, and he continued. "I'm not into that big of a commitment right now, but I wouldn't mind having someone to come home to every night as long as it's you."

"I think that's a commitment I can commit to," she said and pecked him on the lips. But then she gently pushed him away. "Now go before your manager really starts to question the boys."

"I love you," he said and kissed her one more time.

"I love you more," she replied, a broad smile on her lips.

He walked into the airport and turned to see her standing, watching him walk away.

She waved hesitantly and it was obvious she was trying to keep it together for his sake. She climbed back into the car and it occurred to him that he had a lot to thank Jane for.

Following Jane brought him the best ride of his life and to the best girl he could imagine.

"Thanks, Ms. Austen."

Chapter 50

Adventure is just around the corner. . .

"Today is the big day, Lizzie," Fanny said as she walked around dusting all the house fixtures, fluffing pillows, and everything else a mother would do if her son was coming home.

"That it is," Lizzie called out from the small office in the back of the hotel that had become hers months earlier. She finished cleaning it and poked her head out to find Fanny running all around.

She walked over and laughed. "Fanny, please calm down. Graham won't be here for another six hours. We have time, so let's get the tea to all our guests."

In the three months since Graham had left and she had finished following Jane, she had decided that she would stay to help Fanny with the new overload of guests that had swarmed to the hotel after Graham's first visit. After a month of helping, Fanny had asked for Lizzie to become a business partner and help the Austen House grow.

"He is only going to be here the holiday week. Everything needs to go perfectly," Fanny said and smiled nervously.

"Then you're going to need an extra pair of hands," said a most familiar voice.

Lizzie's shot around to find her father standing in the doorway of the Austen House.

"Dad?" She put the tea tray down and ran over to wrap her arms around him. He squeezed as tightly as she did, each of them making sure that other was really there.

"Dad what are you doing here?" she asked with a heavy exhale as she tried to control her emotions.

"I thought it was time to meet the boy who took my daughter half way across the world," he said, put his bag down by the door, and walked around the entryway.

"So these are the clues?" he said and walked over to the wall of framed letters.

"Those are the ones. Mom would have loved this whole trip. Jane wrote her final letter and shared her riches." She grabbed her dad's hand and pulled him into the back room where all the other letters had been either framed and hung on the wall or were they were still piled on her desk, waiting to be read and digested.

Her father's eyes went wide, his mouth dropped, and tears welled up. His breathing was suddenly abnormal and his hand squeezed hers tightly.

"All of these..." His voice trailed off and he grabbed one of the letters from the desk and began reading. "These are all from Jane Austen?"

"Yep, all two hundred or so," she explained. "There were three small bags in a window sill at her last house. In each bag there were a dozen or so envelopes and in each envelope there were a half a dozen or so letters."

She followed her father as he slowly strolled around the room, his gaze traveling over all the letters on the walls.

"Your mother would be so proud of you, Lizzie. Not that she wasn't proud of you before, but this. . .this is just such a miraculous journey. I know I have to thank her for leaving this for you. It's such an amazing parting gift."

Tears fell freely down his face.

"Parting gift?" she questioned. "You make it sound like she was just a guest who left."

"We all are just guests on this Earth," he said and walked over to her.

"Wow, Dad." Tears rolled down her cheeks and she sniffled and said, "Mom never gave you enough imagination credit."

"Lizzie you have a visitor," Fanny advised from the lobby.

Lizzie glanced at the clock on the wall. "It can't be Graham. He's not due for another few hours."

She walked out of her office with her dad and went to the front lobby. She stopped dead when he turned and his jade green eyes gazed into hers.

"Alex," she said on an exhale, flustered by his visit.

"Lizzie," he smiled, walked over to her, and wrapped his strong lean arms around her.

"What are you doing here?" she asked, still unable to believe that he was there.

"I just got out of rehab," he said and released her. He shoved his hands in his pockets.

"Rehab? They beat you up so bad you need rehabilitation." She rubbed his arm, her heart breaking that she might have been the cause of his pain.

"No. Well, yes they beat me pretty badly, but that wasn't your fault. I was referring to the rehab for my addiction." He smiled his charming smile and added, "I couldn't have done it without your words giving me the strength to do it."

"That's great Alex. It really is," she said and patted his shoulder.

"I came back, not only to visit, but to pay back a debt."

"You are not in debt to me." She shook her head, confused.

"Yes, I am. The money you gave me helped me pay off many of my debts and that helped me get clean and out of a bad time. Too bad that right after I got the living shit kicked out of me. But luckily your dear Graham paid my bills and I was able to use what was left of my money to help myself stay gamble free," he explained.

"Graham paid all your bills?" she asked.

"Yeah. He told me not to tell anyone, but I thought you had the right know. But that actually was not the reason I came." He pushed off onto the balls of his feet in an awkward silence, but then explained.

"You asked me not to steal or tell Caterina about the new letters and I kept my word." His voice trailed off, but then he came back with a simple, but shocking sentence, "To an extent."

"What do you mean, Alex?" she said past gritted teeth.

Fanny interrupted them. "Mr. Price. How about we grab you a cup of tea in the kitchen?"

"Oh, no. I'm not a huge tea fan and this looks like it is about to get really, *really*, good." He crossed his arms and leaned against the staircase.

Fanny obviously didn't like that answer and despite his protests, pulled him out of the room and to the kitchen.

Once they were out of sight, Lizzie turned back to Alex and stared him down. "You better explain as fast as you can before *I* put you in the hospital."

"I didn't steal anything from you. But given the circumstances and the fact you never stated anything about Graham, I stole something of his."

"You *what!*" she shouted.

"At the time I thought I could sell it for more money to gamble, but I didn't realize what I had stolen."

Alex pulled small leather book from his back pocket and handed it to Lizzie. Graham's name was stamped into the leather of the front cover. "I am really sorry for doing it, but things still worked out didn't they," he said. "While I was in the hospital, I saw on the telly that you two are now together. Our brief scheme paid off."

"Yeah, although it was a stupid idea. I don't think anyone should go through, or do, what we did to someone they care about. Just telling them the truth is the smartest decision."

"Agreed," Alex said and nodded. "I should get going. Things to do, people to see, you know. It was great seeing you again. Tell Graham I'm sorry and..."

He gave her one final hug. "Take care of yourself, Lizzie."

"You, too, Alex." She rubbed his back and with a light pat they parted ways.

As the door jingled open and closed, Lizzie's dad and Fanny returned from the kitchen area.

"Who was that boy?" her father asked with a raised eyebrow.

"An old friend," she said with a reminiscent smile and thumbed the embossing with Graham's name on the leather cover.

"So he stole your boyfriend's journal, but he's still a friend?" he asked.

"It's a very complicated story that doesn't bare repeating. But he returned it, instead of stealing it forever." She smiled and brought the journal to her chest.

"Well, are you going to read it?" her father asked.

"He read mine so it only seems fair," she joked, even knowing none of them knew what she was talking about. She opened to a random page.

For a girl who can infuriate me, she can also cause such sexual frustration. We kissed. In fact, we almost shagged and then she tells me she did it because of Caterina. Caterina really does know how to kill a mood. As for Lizzie, I don't know how I should feel about her. I used to bug her, to make her mad, just for the joy of frustrating her. Now I try to better our friendship in hopes something else comes of it...

She skipped ahead a few pages and continued reading.

I think I love her and now she met someone else. For fuck's sake I should have just told her I wanted to be more than her friend. I thought we both had an unsaid attraction to each other. Apparently that was only me.

She frowned at how stupid she had behaved, but she didn't mind because she was okay with the road they had traveled and would not want it to have been any different.

She looked up to see her father and Fanny watching and then small smirk erupted on her father's face.

"What?" She rolled her eyes, laughing.

"You really do love this boy, huh?" He walked over to her and rubbed her arms.

"I do," she confessed. Tears filled her eyes, but she did not dare let them fall.

She took a deep breath to compose herself. "More than I ever thought imaginable."

"That's great," she heard from behind her and spun around to see the love of her life, Graham, standing at the front door.

"Because he feels exactly the same."

Her mouth hung open as he walked over to her and placed his hand on her cheek.

"You're early," was all that she could think to say.

"Yeah, well I left a little early to come see my girlfriend." He leaned in and kissed her.

Her father cleared his throat and she pulled herself away from Graham's lips and glanced at her father.

Graham did the same, a bright blush on his face.

She began the introductions and Graham tensed up, but she grabbed his hand to help him calm down.

As her father shook Graham's hand and smiled, she knew it was all going to be just fine.

#

As the day dwindled away and night came, her father retired to his room and Fanny excused herself. That left Graham and Lizzie alone, snuggled up under a blanket on the couch, and staring at the roaring fire.

She leaned forward and reached beneath the mountain of books on the coffee table to pull out his leather journal. "I forgot to give this to you."

"You had it? I was wondering where this had run off to. I assumed I had just forgotten to pack it." He laughed and flipped through the pages.

"Actually, Alex stopped by this morning to return it. Part of his rehabilitation is making amends," she explained, smiled and grabbed the blanket to bring up to her chest.

"I think I'll have to thank him. Although he did steal it, didn't he?" He tossed it back onto the table and surrounded her with his arms.

"You paid his medical bills. Isn't that enough?" She gazed into his coffee brown eyes and he seemed surprised that she knew. "You didn't need to do that for him."

"Caterina did that to him. After everything I thought it was only right." He kissed her forehead and then the tip of her nose and finally her lips.

"I love you Graham," she whispered.

"I love you, too, Lizzie. Which is why after this tour is over, I'm going to sell my house and move in here and help with the business." He cupped her cheek and saw the excitement in her eyes.

"Graham. I--"

"In my off time, of course," he said with a smile. "I'll be a private investor."

She grabbed him hard and hugged him tightly. It was obvious she didn't want to let go and he understood. He had only six more days with her before he left.

They needed to make every second, every touch, count.

"But there is one condition," he said.

"Anything," she replied, not caring at all what the condition was.

"When I left those months ago, I didn't really get to see any of those letters that Jane had left to us. I would like to read a few," he said.

She moved away from him, stood up and offered her hand in invitation.

He graciously took her hand and stood. She led him down the hall and turned into a back room.

When she flipped on the light, his eyes lit up as he gazed around at all the walls.

"There are so many letters," he said.

"Each envelope had more than one letter. There were usually six or seven. She had an amazing life that no one will even know about. A full life, but at times sad. The one man she loved was never to speak to her again, and the man who proposed never understood that she could not marry without love. She was like her characters. Only she didn't get the happily ever after," Lizzie said.

He picked up one of the letters and let out a half-hearted laugh.

She turned to him and instead of explaining the laugh, he read out loud. "I may not have found the love my characters dearly strived for and obtained. but I do not feel I have lost a single ounce of my hope for all those who read my stories. They are tools to teach by, to learn by, and to dream by. I could not have asked for anything more, my dear Cassandra, because if I did I would be foolish."

She walked over to look at the letter and then up at Graham.

He smiled and leaned down to kiss her once more.

"She did help me. Her books were very much like tools to learn by," Lizzie said and kissed him again.

The heat between them ignited as it always did. He pulled her as closely as he could and ran his hands all over her and she did the same, grabbing at him as if she never wanted to let him go.

She finally drew away, breathless from their kiss, and looked up at him. "I have to thank Jane for bringing you to me. If it weren't for that silly clue in the library, I would still be the lonely weird girl always sneaking in and out of places."

"I thank Jane every day for bringing me to you. Maybe this was her whole plan all along. The universal truth is love and truly a handsome reward," he said, pleased with himself.

She shoved him jokingly, but then went back to hugging and kissing him again.

Theirs wasn't the perfect kind of fairy tale, but it was more than they both could ever have imagined. But Jane would have never had a romance that was just like a typical fairy tale.

Real life love and romance was hard to come by, but when someone found it, they knew they had to nurture it to keep it alive.

As Graham met Lizzie's gaze, he knew that together they would nurture and grow their love with every breath they took.

The End

Made in the USA
Lexington, KY
23 June 2014